DREAM CITY DREAMING

A NOVEL

CINDY ANGELL KEELING

ISBN: 979-8-9874890-0-0 (Hardcover)
ISBN: 979-8-9874890-1-7 (Paperback)
ISBN: 979-8-9874890-2-4 (eBook)

Library of Congress Control Number: 2022923358

Cover design: Lynn Andreozzi
Cover art (public domain): *Two young women making a ride on their bikes on a summer day*, Paul Gustav Fischer (c. 1895) (woman on bike); The World's Columbian Exposition of 1893, Chicago: A view of the Administration [Building] . . . seen from the Wooded Island, John Ross Key (1894) (background art)
Author photograph: MK Photography
Interior formatting by Formatted Books

Printed in the United States of America

First printing edition 2023

Published by Petite Parasol Press

Villa Park, IL

cindyangellkeeling.com

For Dennis

CHAPTER ONE

May 2, 1893—The St. Louis Daily
NOTES FROM THE FAIR:

Grand Opening of the World's Columbian Exposition

I am not a woman who gapes. But there I stood with 100,000 other open-mouthed spectators, speech deserting us as we took in the spectacle of the White City. Classical buildings surrounded us like white mountains bedecked with lights. And, oh! The fountains, the Venice-like waterways, the electricity.

Has heaven girded this spot of earth with a reflection of itself? Gilded this utopian vision for all the world to see? For they are here, the people of the world. Gaze in any direction to be rewarded with a rich representation of humanity. Words cannot convey the wonder of this magnificent place. I entreat you, dear reader, to journey to Chicago and see it for yourself. It will be an experience of a lifetime.

—Zenobia A. Thom,
Special Correspondent

———◦———

JUNE 27, 1893. LOUISIANA, MISSOURI

In a modest home overlooking the Mississippi river, slanting rays of sunlight illuminated cake crumbs on three plates. "Happy birthday, sweetheart," Juna Lewis told her son Henry for the third time. "Would you like another slice?"

Henry shook his head, causing dark-blonde curls to dance across his forehead. She'd need to give him a haircut soon. "A fourth piece would do me in, but thanks, Mama. It was *stupendous.*"

She exchanged a quick smile with her father-in-law, Seymour Lewis. "That may be overstating things a bit, but I'm glad you're making use of your new thesaurus."

"You and Grandpa give the best gifts," Henry said, and pulled out his new pocket watch. "Eight-oh-three," he announced, and closed the lid with a tiny *snap.*

Seymour gestured with his pipe, causing vanilla-scented smoke to billow gently around him. It added a spicy layer to the lingering smells of potatoes and roast beef. "You'll find it useful for keeping track of where you need to be," he said. Amusement belied his normally gruff voice.

Henry aimed a wry grin across the table. "Like getting to meals on time?"

"I won't retire the dinner bell just yet," Juna said with a laugh as she began stacking the dinner plates. Henry tended to get caught up in his own interests and let the hours get away from him.

"Before you clear the table, I have some news," Seymour said in a more serious tone. "I've heard from our Mr. Peterson."

She settled back in her chair. "Good news, I hope." Seymour set down his pipe and pulled a folded paper from his pocket. Thinning, grey eyebrows drew together as he shook it open. A niggle of dread tightened Juna's stomach. Peterson was their sales agent in Chicago. Was it bad news about their Chicago business accounts? With the current financial crisis, they could be ruined if those accounts fell through.

"Peterson says that—" Seymour paused for a long moment; his expression grim. Apparently coming to a decision, he turned the paper so that she and Henry could read it for themselves:

GREAT NEWS! LEWIS VINEGAR HAS WON A BRONZE MEDAL AT THE COLUMBIAN EXPOSITION.

"That's wonderful," Juna cried as she clapped her hands together. "You had us going there, you old rascal."

Henry playfully swatted his grandfather's arm. "When did you find out?"

Once Seymour stopped laughing, he set the paper down and pulled a handkerchief out of his pocket. "I've been sitting on that telegram for three days," he said as he wiped his eyes. "Thought it would make a good birthday gift for the future president of Lewis Vinegar."

Juna beamed at her son, noticing that his face had reddened a bit. "Imagine that," she said. "Lewis Vinegar is now award-winning." She turned back to Seymour in excitement. "We should have a new label designed."

"Good idea, my dear." Seymour rubbed the stump of his left wrist. "I'm of a mind to give Peterson the honor, since displaying the vinegar was his idea. In the meantime, he's contacted me with a proposition. He's offered to act as Henry's mentor and tour guide. After giving it some thought, I've decided to send you both to Chicago."

Juna sat up in alarm at the same time Henry cried, "To the Exposition?"

Seymour's eyes crinkled. "Now that you're in long pants, I reckon you *should* go."

"*Smooth!*"

"I'm not sure he's strong enough yet," Juna said over Henry's whoop of excitement. "It's only been a couple months since he was—"

"He's plenty recovered. Aren't you, son?" Seymour said, clapping Henry on the shoulder.

"Yessir," Henry said. "I ran up the hill from town yesterday." Juna refrained from pointing out that he'd been collapsed on the front porch while catching his breath—but had to admit that, while he was thinner than she liked, his color was good, and his energy was improving.

"Henry will benefit from seeing new technologies and the latest in manufacturing," Seymour continued. "And Peterson will be there to advise you on what to see and do, Juna. No doubt there will be plenty of things to interest you."

"Well, of course. But Henry and I have never met the man," she said, grasping at excuses.

"You know I hold him in high esteem," Seymour said. "After all he's done for our business, we owe him the chance, don't you think?"

"Yes, I agree we do," she said slowly, then brightened as a solution came to mind. "Henry will be even stronger in a few weeks. We could go in August, before school resumes."

"I'm *fine*, Mama," Henry insisted.

Seymour regarded her for a moment as he puffed his pipe back to life. "I understand your worries, Juna, but I've already made the arrangements. You leave in one week and will stay for three."

"One week! That's barely enough time to prepare," she said. "Where will we stay?"

"I contacted your sister, who happily took charge of arranging your accommodations."

Juna stared at him, incredulous. "Before I even agreed to go?"

Seymour's expression softened. "I only meant to surprise you. She's delighted you're coming." He reached out and tapped her arm gently with his left forearm. "I've tried my best to make it easy for you."

She breathed in and out, trying to frame a response. The truth was, she relied on Seymour's take-charge style. He was as protective of her as she was of Henry. While he'd clearly put his foot down about the situation, he'd also gone to great lengths to make sure they would be taken care of in Chicago. Her father-in-law was more stubborn than a mule on Friday, but his heart was in the right place when it came to his family.

Henry seemed to be holding his breath as he waited for her to come to terms with the situation. He'd been longing to attend the fair for months. Would it be right to deny him this experience? "All right," she said, raising her hands in surrender. "I'll go along with it. Just promise me you won't overtax yourself."

Henry dashed around the table and gave her an enthusiastic hug. "Thanks, Mama! Don't you want to come too, Grandpa?"

Seymour shook his head. "I'm too old to go gallivanting around. I'll stay here and mind the factory. It'll be your turn soon enough."

"All right, then. I'm going to tell my friends the good news."

"Be back by nine-thirty," Juna called as he hurtled toward the kitchen door. She turned back to see Seymour regarding her with a thoughtful expression.

"Don't coddle the boy, Juna. He's fine. Walking around the fair will be just the thing to get his strength back."

He was right, of course, but still. She stood up and began clearing the table. "It's a tall order, but I'll try my best."

Later, after they said goodnight, Juna stood with her head pressed to the cool glass of her bedroom window. Peaceful noises of crickets and peepers drifted in on the warm summer air, and the river reflected the moonlight in long patterns that changed with the current. She felt like a baby bird about to be pushed out of the nest. When her husband died six years before, her grief anchored her to this house. She'd allowed Craig's parents to take charge of her life and help care for Henry. When her mother-in-law passed away the following year, Juna found renewed purpose in looking after Seymour and Henry.

She'd been happy with this new version of her life, of course, but lately she'd felt a restlessness circling her; a sense of wanting to be *more*. What *more* might entail was as indistinct as the river at the bottom of the bluff. Tracing her finger on the smooth pane, she wondered if it even mattered. As a woman who relied on her father-in-law's—and eventually her son's—generosity, any ambitions she might have were secondary. Weren't they? *No,* she decided, her dreams—whatever they might be—were important, too. Would this journey to the world's fair provide the answer? The question shimmered inside her like a secret jewel.

She reached for a gilded frame on the bedside table. A handsome man with kind eyes smiled out from the photograph. "Craig, my darling," she whispered. "Be with me."

———◦———

One week later, they stood on the train platform a short distance from the river. Other passengers boarded the train as handlers took charge of loading trunks and other luggage. Juna could hear noises from the nearby docks as men loaded and unloaded boats with tobacco and other cargo, including barrels of their apple cider vinegar. She looked back toward their thriving, picturesque town and could just see the corner of the red brick building that housed Lewis Vinegar.

The conductor called, "All aboard!"

"Get going, you two," Seymour said, his voice a bit gruffer than normal. He hugged Henry, then her, goodbye. "You'll be fine. Peterson will do right by you."

She kissed his smoothly shaven cheek. "I'm counting on it."

Inside the train, they settled into a row of comfortable chairs. Henry claimed the seat closest to the window. He rifled through his satchel and pulled out a guidebook to the fair, which Juna noticed was already dog-eared. With a short blast of the whistle, the train gave a small jerk forward and began its journey northward. Their travels would include two train changes and an overnight ride.

She opened her handbag and retrieved a newspaper clipping—a piece written by her sister on the opening day of the world's fair. *Would* this be 'an experience of a lifetime?' she wondered. A thrill shivered over her each time she read those exuberant words.

Chapter Two

Dear Mrs. Lewis,

I was pleased to hear from your father-in-law that you and Henry have agreed to allow me to be a mentor and tour guide for the next three weeks. The fair is a wondrous endeavor and not to be missed. I relish the idea of mentoring Henry and showing him the many exhibits and opportunities that abound here.

In order to make your entrance to Chicago as pleasant as possible, I have arranged for a cab to meet you at Central Station. Proceeding from there, I beg you to indulge me in a surprise that should delight you both. The driver will know what to do. After he has delivered you to the proper place, he will take your baggage to the house where you'll be staying. I have arranged everything with your sister.

Once you arrive at the fair, make your way to the rotunda of the Agriculture Building and I will meet you there.

Your servant,
Archibald Peterson

"I wonder what Peterson's surprise is?" Despite a wakeful night, Henry was alert with excitement as he turned one way and the other, making their traveling trunks bump against his legs. Central Station was a busy place with echoey marble floors. Arching windows provided ample morning light and views of Lake Michigan. Long wooden benches held weary couples and wiggly children. Men in well-tailored suits read newspapers.

"No idea, but our instructions seem clear enough," Mother said as she tucked away Peterson's letter. "The driver may already be here. I wonder if he'll have a sign with our name on it?" Her eyebrows pulled together as she looked around the place. "I wonder where we should meet him?"

Henry nodded toward the main entrance. "There's bound to be an area where the cabs pull up. Let's go out that way." They exited the station and looked out from under a substantial stone archway to a line of one- and two-horse cabbies. Beyond the service road, a large field swept northward. Impressive granite and limestone buildings of the business district stretched west, fronted by a busy avenue where delivery wagons and other conveyances rumbled past.

"My goodness," Mother murmured. "It's so . . ."

"Yes'm," Henry breathed. "It sure is."

The driver of a two-horse cab jumped down from his perch and approached them. He was a stout man with a long, drooping mustache. Watery grey eyes protruded slightly from under hooded eyelids, reminding Henry of crocodile eyes. Despite a dour countenance, the man touched the brim of his bowler in a polite gesture. "Are you Mrs. Lewis and Henry? I was instructed to look for a young man and his mother."

Mother smiled in relief. "We are, indeed."

The man's gaze slid past Mother to rest on Henry for a few uncomfortable seconds. "My name's Kramer. A Mr. Peterson hired me." After loading their trunks, he handed Mother an envelope with their names neatly inscribed on the front.

"How curious." Mother opened the envelope and pulled out two tickets. "What in the world?"

Henry leaned down to inspect them. "*Smooth,*" he said, drawing out the word. "It's for the whaleback, *Christopher Columbus.* I've read all about it."

"Is this Mr. Peterson's surprise?" Mother asked.

Kramer pointed toward a distant dock where a long, white ship waited for passengers. "I presume so." He opened the door to the cab. "I will drop you at the dock, then deliver your luggage to the home of a Mrs. Wilson."

Mother raised her eyebrows at Henry. "It seems our Mr. Peterson wants to impress us."

"It's working so far," he said, and climbed in after her.

One hour later, they stood at the edge of the upper deck as the whaleback sped toward the Exposition. Seagulls circled overhead. A brisk wind rippled Juna's skirt and pushed at her broad-brimmed hat. Behind them, men and women strolled along a wide promenade, and parents tried to keep up with their scampering children. Passengers who preferred a less windy ride sat inside the grand saloon, where a brass band played a lively march.

A passenger train made its way north along the shoreline. Juna thought someone waved but couldn't be sure. As she gazed at the endless city beyond, worrisome questions poked their way into her excitement. Would it be hard to navigate this enormous place? Would they be safe on its streets? Taking a deep breath, she reasoned with herself. One simply needed to be sensible, like Zenobia, who'd been here since May reporting on the fair. It seemed she came and went with no issue. And, of course, they'd have Mr. Peterson to advise them. "Did you ever expect to see such a sight?" she asked.

"Well, I'd *hoped* to see it," Henry said, giving her a lop-sided grin.

A woman standing beside them pointed south and said, "Be prepared for a stunning vision once we pass yonder outcrop." Henry leaned over the handrail as if pure eagerness would make the ship go faster. Juna bounced along with the music, exhilaration swirling within her.

As they rounded the outcrop, the level of excitement was palatable among the passengers. The band played with increased vigor, as if to say, *Here it comes.* Seconds later, they joined in a great cheer at the first view of the fairgrounds, where alabaster palaces rose up in gleaming contrast to the cloudless sky. Domes and towers punctuated this vision like architectural exclamation points. "Astonishing," Juna said, as similar sentiments in at least three languages burst out around them.

"It's *stupendous*," Henry said, beaming down at her.

She tucked her hand into his elbow. "Zenobia wasn't kidding, was she? If I didn't know better, I'd think we were someplace in the Far East." She pointed toward a long, massive building situated along the lakeshore. Its arching glass roof was equally massive. "That has to be the Manufactures Building."

"It is," Henry said. "Those people on the promenade look like bugs next to it."

"They do, indeed," she said. "I daresay we'll feel as insignificant as bugs next to all the Great Buildings."

"I just wish I didn't have to meet with Peterson."

She looked up at him in surprise. "What's wrong, dear?"

He jiggled the air in his cheeks. "I know Grandpa wants me to be mentored, but do I really have to go around the fair with some old coot?"

"What makes you think he's an old coot?"

Henry shrugged. "I just reckon he's old."

"If he is, just think of all the wisdom he'll have to impart. And remember," she added, ignoring Henry's eye roll, "'the old coot' is exactly why we are here. Besides, won't it be exciting to see our vinegar proudly displayed at the fair?"

"Yes'm," he said with more enthusiasm.

After the boat docked at a wide pier that jutted far into the lake, Juna paid a dime for her and Henry to ride a continuously moving sidewalk that took riders to and from the fairgrounds. They sat on a covered bench, while others chose to stand or walk. The Peristyle was the dominant feature at the end of the pier, stretching north to south in front of them. A wide colonnade topped with sculpture, its large columns and arching gateway offered tantalizing glimpses of the fairgrounds beyond. "Remarkable," she said, nearly dumbstruck by the scope of their surroundings.

"It sure is," Henry said, looking back and forth as if he couldn't take it in fast enough. They entered through a building at the south end called the Casino, which featured restaurants and comfort facilities. After refreshing themselves and neatening windblown hair, they headed back outside. Other fairgoers moved past them. Some walked purposefully, others looked awed and undecided about which direction to go first. Women opened umbrellas and parasols to protect their skin from the July sun.

They hurried to the middle of the Peristyle, which provided a glorious view of the Court of Honor. Five enormous exhibition buildings surrounded a vast lagoon dotted with gondolas and small boats. Henry gave a low whistle. "It's bigger than I expected."

In a prominent spot at the other end of the Grand Basin, a stunning golden dome surmounted four square pavilions. "That's the Administration Building where we'll meet Zenobia later," Juna said, admiring how the gilding reflected the sunlight. "Illustrations don't do it justice, that's for sure. Goodness, it'll take at least twenty minutes to walk there."

Henry gave her a mischievous look. "Bet I could make it in ten."

"You might, at a dead run," she said, eyeing him. "You may have the advantage of being a boy in trousers, but I wore my best walking shoes. Let's call it fifteen minutes." She grinned when he snorted at her joke. In truth, her walking shoes were ancient. She hadn't had time to buy a new pair and break them in before their trip. When Seymour Lewis made a decision, even angels dare not take time to tune their harps. Therefore, *old and outdated* trumped *new and fashionable.*

Henry pointed toward the Great Building on the south side of the basin, which featured a goddess on its central dome. "There's Agriculture. See the *Diana?*" The metal goddess held a bow and arrow and perched impossibly on one foot.

Juna watched in awe as the sculpture turned gently in the breeze like a giant weathervane. Suddenly overcome, she pressed her fingertips to a tiny gold apple that hung at her neck. "Isn't this the most wonderful place you've ever seen? Your father would have loved it here—" Her voice caught on an unexpected swell of sadness. Henry reached for her hand, and she leaned into his side, missing her husband. How she wished Craig was here to experience this moment with them. They stood in silence, taking in the beauty of the place amid the chattering crowds, gentle splashing of water, and the vibration of many feet walking along the Peristyle.

At length, she took a bracing breath and gave Henry's hand a squeeze. "This will be a grand adventure. Let's find Mr. Peterson, shall we?"

They set off across the expansive grounds, with limestone crunching pleasantly under their feet. As they rounded the southeast corner of the basin, the distant sound of an orchestra provided accompaniment. Flags mounted on each building waved and snapped in the wind. An electric launch glided past, and Henry jogged over to get a closer look. "We have to ride one," he said when Juna joined him. "Can we do it today?"

"That would be fun," she said, leaning against the balustrade, "but let's see what your aunt has planned for us first." They watched the boat circle a colossal golden statue that rose high above the water in the east end of the basin. A yellow- and white-striped awning shaded the boat's passengers from the sun, including a tour guide at the front of the boat. Juna was too far away to hear more than the rise and fall of his voice as he gestured animatedly toward the statue: a female figure with arms upraised, holding a staff in one hand and a ball with an eagle in the other.

The view across the basin to the north was completely filled with the mammoth Manufactures Building. It would take days to explore that building alone. Juna drooped a little at the thought. Three weeks would hardly be enough time to see everything the fair offered, but she was determined to do her best.

They entered the Agricultural Building a few minutes later. A hum of noise and the pleasing smell of grains emanated from the cavernous main hall. Juna looked around the rotunda. Perhaps it was Henry's influence, but she pictured Mr. Peterson with grey hair and a potbelly. The only man who seemed to be waiting was a much younger man on the other side of the room, leaning against the wall as he frowned at his pocket watch.

"Do you suppose that's him?" she asked Henry in an undertone.

"Maybe," Henry said, looking pensive.

The man looked up as they approached and smiled as he straightened to his full height. "You must be Mrs. Lewis and young Henry," he said in a big voice that echoed in the rotunda. "Welcome to the Columbian Exposition. Archibald Peterson, at your service."

As he shook hands with Henry, Juna could see that her son was making a quick reassessment. Peterson was much younger than he'd predicted— only a few years older than she was, perhaps forty. His mustache and short beard ended in curved, waxy points, and he stood several inches taller than Henry, with broad shoulders. She noted that his suit, shoes, and hat were of good quality. It pleased her that this handsome, well-dressed man represented Lewis Vinegar.

"What did you think of the whaleback?" Peterson asked.

"Fast," Henry said with a grin.

"Elegant and impressive," Juna said. "Thank you for arranging it and the driver."

"I wanted your first view of the fair to be memorable," Peterson said, looking pleased. "I'm glad you waited until after the Fourth to arrive. The big day was certainly patriotic, but included rain, immense crowds, and unintelligible speeches. The Commission outdid itself with the fireworks, however." When Henry made a sound of disappointment, he turned and added, "Don't worry, son, even the regular shows are spectacular."

Henry perked up again. "Sounds good."

After inquiring about their travels from Missouri, Peterson got down to business. Addressing Henry, he said, "You come highly recommended by your grandfather. We'll have a full session tomorrow, but I thought we'd visit the Missouri Pavilion today. You'll be wanting to visit your vinegar, after all."

"Yes, sir," Henry said. "Most definitely."

Juna was relieved to see that Henry's eagerness had reappeared. "We're absolutely thrilled about our medal," she said.

Peterson led them down a wide central aisle past pavilions and exhibits—some fancy, some small and rustic—from the United States and other countries, such as Great Britain and France. There were grains of every description presented in attractive containers, displayed as art, or stacked in neat piles. New York's pavilion was devoted to a large display of potatoes. "The finest you'll ever see," Peterson said, keeping up his long-legged pace.

There were examples of nearly every kind of fruit and vegetable and their by-products: canned meats, oils, baking soda, and more.

Juna stared, astonished, at a twenty-two-thousand-pound cheese from Canada. They made their way past handsome pavilions that featured displays of chocolate, bee-keeping practices, and wine-making. The atmosphere bustled with countless conversations and products being demonstrated. Well-dressed men and women rubbed elbows with the more down-to-earth sort of folk she was accustomed to seeing back home.

It was an international experience. Over there, a man wearing a turban was in earnest conversation with a cigarette manufacturer. Nearby, women jockeyed for position to view the process of silk making. She peered into a cafe, where a woman wearing a feathered hat sipped a hot chocolate. Across the hall, two girls in identical dresses stood wide-eyed, giggling at the spectacle of it all. And there, a weary couple with a baby rested on a row of chairs. This symphony of accents and languages flowed over and through her. Juna breathed it all in. And this was just one building!

As she strolled along, she became aware of a curious sensation. Flowing like a current beneath her more prominent feelings of awe was something else—a sense of being unmoored. For the moment, she had no expectations of her. No house to clean or meals to cook. No laundry or shopping list waiting. No immediate obligation to her father-in-law. She had a good life in Missouri, of course. But, oh! Now that she was here in this splendid place, unencumbered by regular duties for a time, it was easy to believe that anything was possible. She looked at Henry and they shared a happy grin.

They reached the impressive Missouri pavilion, which held, among other things, specimens of grasses, wheat, rye, oats, barley, tobacco, and corn. A life-size statue of a horse decorated with grains instantly enamored Henry. "The coat looks real, doesn't it?" he exclaimed.

"It certainly does," she said, enjoying his bright-eyed enthusiasm.

Peterson led them to the vinegar display. What a thrill it was to see their own product prominently featured with several other Missouri brands, all good ones. "Would you look at that, Henry?" Juna said, pointing to the half-gallon glass jug of Lewis Vinegar. It featured a handsome label with a stylized apple and LEWIS VINEGAR emblazoned on it. A modern effect, she thought. She touched a finger to the small notice that declared it a medal winner. "I wish your grandfather could see it."

"Me, too," Henry said, and leaned in for a closer look. "I like the bottle and label."

"We have Mr. Peterson to thank for that," she said, giving Henry a meaningful look. It had been the man's idea to bottle it for the Chicago market. Back home, they shipped their vinegar to stores in barrels.

Henry turned to Peterson. "It looks good. Thank you."

Peterson gave a gracious nod. "Lewis Vinegar is a superior product. It was simply a matter of bottling it up and finding an artist to design the label. I've made several promising contacts here that I'll be discussing with you."

"What sort of contacts?" Juna asked, eager to hear more.

Peterson smiled. "I won't bore you with the specifics. I've already sent a letter to Seymour, and will introduce young Henry as we come upon them." He turned back to Henry to continue their conversation.

"I do have an interest," Juna murmured, feeling slightly deflated as she stepped away to look at a shelf of canned peaches. Peterson's response irked her, but in her experience, that's just how it was with men. Any effort to ingratiate herself into the family business was met with an indulgent smile and a smooth dismissal. They might as well pat her on the head.

She heard Peterson say, "We'll explore this building first, then move to the other ones."

"Yessir."

Henry sounded a little subdued. She imagined he was as overwhelmed by the place as she was. And they'd had a long trip, after all. Turning around, she said, "We look forward to seeing more of this building, Mr. Peterson, but my sister is expecting us."

"Of course," he said. "May I escort you? I'd like to meet Miss Thom in person, and will be happy to point out items of note along the way."

"We're lucky to have you as a tour guide," Juna said. "Please lead on." Out of the corner of her eye, she noticed Henry jiggling the air in his cheeks.

Chapter Three

Col-um-bian Expo-si-tion. Henry silently rolled the words around his mouth while gazing into the rotunda of the Administration Building. There were lots of statues and art. A crowd of people were staring up into the big dome, but he couldn't see much from where he stood just inside the entrance. He could scarcely believe his luck. After months of reading, dreaming, and begging, he was finally, *finally*, here. Fierce emotion pricked at his eyes. When he'd taken ill after Christmas, he was afraid he wouldn't live to see the world's fair. Then he was worried that he wouldn't be recovered enough to attend. Then it became a matter of trying to convince Mother that he was strong enough to go. She was dead set against it until the miracle happened on his fourteenth birthday and Grandpa put his foot down. He was as overjoyed as the rest of them that their vinegar had won a medal. It was just that he hadn't counted on Peterson being part of the bargain.

He wanted to explore the fair in peace. He wanted to go at his own pace and see the exhibits that *he* wanted to see. Exhibits that had nothing to do with business or vinegar. He rubbed his chest at the twinge of guilt that happened whenever his secret dreams slammed into his sense of duty and love for Mother and Grandpa. He blew out a breath, determined to make the best of it.

"The Administration Building is a favorite thoroughfare for folks arriving by train," Peterson said, gesturing in the general direction of the Terminal Building at the edge of the fairgrounds. "See those elevators and stairs over there? They lead to offices used by administrators and journalists like your aunt." His mentor had pointed out the various buildings on their walk over, which Henry conceded was interesting information, but even Mother was looking glassy-eyed as she stretched up to look for Zennie.

A flash of color caught Henry's attention. He touched Mother's arm and nodded toward a man and woman exotically attired in bright silks. "Do you reckon they're from India?" he asked, thrilled at the prospect of seeing people from other cultures.

"I imagine so. What a beautiful garment the woman is wearing. Perhaps we'll find out the name of it when we visit the—"

"Juna! Henry! There you are," a familiar voice called as Zenobia swooped down on them. His mother and aunt collided in a hug and happy exclamations. They were a study in contrasts: his aunt—Mother's younger half-sister—was taller, dark-haired, and quite beautiful. Mother was fairer, softer, and pretty in a non-fussy way. Her blue dress looked plain next to his aunt's dark yellow suit that sported puffed-up sleeves wider than her head. Her matching hat had a long, black feather.

"Henry, you've grown four inches since Christmas," she said, engulfing him in a cloud of fabric and perfume. She held him at arm's length and gave him the once-over, then pulled him back for a kiss on the cheek. "You look good, sweetheart."

"I'm nearly as tall as Grandpa," he said, straightening his cap. "And, you."

Her merry laugh echoed around them. "Another six months will remedy that. How was your boat ride?" she asked, clearly in on the surprise.

"Wonderful," Mother said. "It was an impressive approach."

"Yeah. That whaleback was fast," Henry said.

Zenobia nodded. "It's the best way to arrive the first time." She turned to Peterson, who'd been waiting quietly off to the side. "You must be the famous Mr. Peterson," she said, extending her hand. "I have you to thank for my sister and nephew being here. Consider me a friend and ally."

"I am at your service," Peterson said, shaking her hand and beaming at her. "I will take my leave, now," he told them. "Henry, I'll meet you tomorrow afternoon back at Agriculture. One o'clock, sharp."

"Yes, sir," Henry said, trying to appear enthusiastic.

"Enjoy yourselves," Peterson said, touching his brim to Mother and Zennie before striding away.

"He seems a capable man," Zennie said.

Mother glanced at Peterson's retreating form. "He does move through the world with confidence and knowledge."

Henry's opinion ran closer to *loud* and *know-it-all*, but he simply nodded in agreement. He reckoned his mentor was all right, even if he'd take some getting used to.

"What would you like to do next?" Zenobia asked, rubbing her hands together. "We can leave if you're tired. Mrs. Wilson's house is just a few blocks from the north entrance."

Henry shot a pleading look at Mother, who said, "We're open to your advisement, but Henry may burst out of his skin if we don't ride one of those electric boats."

"That is a fine idea and a good way to get your bearings," Zenobia said, grinning at his whoop of excitement. "Though, I recommend taking things slow as to not get overwhelmed. I've been here two months and still haven't seen everything."

"'Taking it slow' sounds like a sensible idea," Mother said, glancing at Henry.

Before his health became the favored topic of conversation, he quickly asked, "Why is everyone looking into the dome?"

"An excellent question," Zenobia said. "Let's begin our tour there."

They moved to the center of the room, where Henry craned his head back to stare at an epic-sized mural featuring Greek-like figures. The scene covered the top third of the dome high above them, where daylight flowed in from a wide oculus. "There's a Pegasus, and is that Apollo?"

"Behold *The Glorification of the Arts and Sciences*," Zenobia said. "Remarkable, isn't it?"

"It certainly is," Mother said. "It's so . . . expansive."

Henry's attention was now riveted on a section that featured voluptuous nude women. He figured they were angels or muses, as they were pulling back a curtain to reveal the scene beneath them. He cleared his throat and focused on something else. "There's a chap giving up his shield and sword. Do you suppose he's embraced art instead?"

Zenobia *mm-hmmed*. "That's a good observation. Do you see the man kneeling at Apollo's feet? One explanation I've heard bandied about is that Apollo is crowning the Arts."

"It's beautifully rendered," Mother said. "But how in heaven's name did the painters get way up there?"

"Scaffolding."

"Ridiculously high scaffolding from the looks of it."

"Would you believe the painter of that mural, Dodge, is a young man in his mid-twenties?"

"Why, no."

"His equally young friend, MacMonnies, designed the wondrous fountain out front."

They continued chatting about the mural, but Henry paid little attention as he stepped this way and that to look at it from different angles. It seemed to tell a story of the transformation of a warring society into a more peaceful one. He heard a girl say to her companion, "Look at that giant naked backside, Judy. Do you reckon it belongs to a Greek warrior?"

Henry snickered to himself as his eyes fell on a prominent figure wearing a breechcloth. It didn't cover much. He couldn't hear the other girl's response, but there was a great deal of laughter between them as they moved away.

A few minutes later, Henry, his mother, and aunt left the building. Outside, they passed a large statue of Columbus and stopped to admire the fountain that featured a sculpture of a boat manned by allegorical figures. Zenobia explained their meaning: "It's guided by Father Time. Fame is at the prow, and those maidens with the oars represent the arts and industry."

"Impressive," Mother said. Henry agreed. He especially liked the sea horses and half-clothed mermaids that surrounded the boat.

As they walked to the nearest dock, Zenobia told Mother about a gala event she covered for the newspaper. "Oh, Juney," she said. "You should have seen the costumes. Mrs. Potter Palmer looked like royalty in a pink creation by Worth of Paris, and Mrs. Henry Field was an absolute picture in peach-colored silk…"

Mother swooned over descriptions of the dresses, which Henry found amusing. Since when was his mother interested in Chicago society and ball gowns? Having no interest in either, his thoughts wandered. It was good to see her happy and her attention on something else besides *him.* She'd had a rough winter and spring worrying over his health. The fact that she was already enamored with the Exposition was encouraging. *Take care of your mother,* Grandpa admonished him the night before they left, adding the usual refrain: *You'll be the man there.* He'd then held a match to the pipe clenched in his teeth and mutter-puffed into a lecture about the dangers of the city and the value of being alert and responsible. At fourteen, Henry didn't feel much like a man, but he took his role as his mother's protector seriously.

They reached the dock and boarded the crowded boat. Zenobia sat between Henry and Mother on a bench near the front. The boat's driver, a cheery Irishman, drove smoothly and occasionally remarked on a building or other sight as they made a loop of the Grand Basin. Henry enjoyed the breeze on his face as they moved along, passing other launches and several gondolas propelled by men in red jackets.

"Those are *bona fide* gondoliers from Venice," Zenobia said, and whispered something to Mother that made her laugh. After circling the basin, the boat headed up the north canal and entered a wide lagoon with a long island in the middle. Henry could see gardens among the trees and people strolling along paths.

"How beautiful," Mother said. "Those flower gardens are lovely."

"The Wooded Island is a nice place to rest one's brain after visiting the exhibits," Zenobia said, and pointed to a temple-like building on the north end. "That's a Japanese exhibit called Phoenix Hall," she said. "The Japanese have fine exhibits in most of the major buildings."

Henry, fascinated by anything exotic, strained to catch a glimpse of an actual Japanese person, but was disappointed to only see tourists wandering around the sleek structure. "May we visit it today?" he asked.

Mother deferred to Zennie. "Will there be time?"

"Perhaps, but tomorrow is another day. I promise you there will always be something interesting to see."

They continued past the stately Government Building and the Spanish-style Fisheries Building, and passed under a bridge into the north pond. Dotted around the grounds were attractive exhibition, state, and foreign buildings. The Palace of Fine Arts reflected prettily at the top of the pond, where ducks swam. Broad stairs, flanked by two lions, led to a columned entrance. "That would make an excellent photograph," Henry said. Though he did not own a camera, he had a keen interest in photography, and liked to view his surroundings with a 'photographic eye.'

"Indeed," Zenobia said. "Most of the state buildings are on the grounds north of the Art Palace. The Missouri Building has a fine location there."

"When will I meet with Mrs. Fletcher?" Mother asked. She would be helping at the state building for a few hours each week. Apparently, Zenobia knew someone who knew someone.

"Tomorrow morning, about eleven o'clock," Zenobia said. "We'll make a quick stop there, find a place for lunch, then you can escort Henry to the Agriculture Building for his meeting with Mr. Peterson." She bumped against him and said, "If you aren't completely exhausted, perhaps we can visit the Midway afterward." Henry gave a loud whoop. The Midway Plaisance was reportedly the most exotic and fun place at the Exposition.

"Look there," she said, pointing west. "Can you see the Ferris Wheel?"

Henry drew in a breath at his first glimpse of the impossible-looking ride in the far distance. Cars as big as trolleys were slowly rising. Up, up, up. "Have you ridden it?" he asked. "Can you see across the lake?"

"I have, and it's thrilling. You can see quite far on a clear day."

He heard a happy squeal behind them and turned to see a young girl of about five excitedly bouncing on her seat as she spotted the Ferris Wheel. "Look! Look!" she cried, as her mass of blonde curls bounced along with her. "I want to ride it." Her parents promised her a ride 'very soon.' Henry caught the girl's eye and winked at her, causing her to smile and press her face into her father's side.

They circled back under the bridge and rounded the top of the island. The Illinois Building sat in a prominent spot just north of the lagoon. It sported a dome markedly taller than the rest of the major buildings. "It's ostentatious," Zenobia said, "but since Illinois is the host, they're entitled to show off a bit."

"Is that the Woman's Building?" Mother asked as they came even with a modestly sized building that featured terraces and loggias. Statuary rimmed the roof, and large pots of flowers decorated the balustrades.

"Yes, it is," Zenobia said in a ringing voice. "Every American should be proud of this shining example of accomplishments by and for women. The array of exhibits will amaze you."

"I look forward to visiting it," Mother said.

While low on the list of places he wanted to visit, Henry decided to keep an open mind after hearing his aunt's heart-felt endorsement. When they disembarked in front of the Horticultural Building, Henry heard the little girl's mother say, "Hazel, sweetheart, would you like to visit the Children's Building? It isn't far."

Blonde curls bounced as the girl cried, "Yes, Mama." The family set off with Hazel jumping and swinging between her parents.

"Come," Zenobia said. "I have a surprise for you."

"This is heavenly." Juna did a slow turn, taking in the giant glass dome that filtered greenish sunlight into the rotunda of the Horticultural Building. Hundreds of plants were illuminated. Palm trees, ferns, and bamboo covered a "mountain" in the center of the room. Greenery and blooms from all over the world perfumed the warm, humid air. "Heavenly *and* magnificent," she amended.

Wings extended north and south from the main room to end pavilions. "There are good cafes here," Zenobia said, "but first, follow me." She led them around the base of the mountain, where she handed a young woman three tickets. They crossed a small stream on wide stepping-stones and entered a cave with crystal formations artfully lit with colored lights.

It was Henry's turn to spin. "*Smooth,*" he said.

"How in the world did they do this?" Juna asked, enjoying her son's enthusiasm.

Zenobia shook her head. "I've no idea, but it's a replica of a cave in South Dakota."

Juna pulled off her glove and touched an edge of a formation. "It's like a secret place among the hustle and bustle. If you can't find me on a busy day, look here."

Their peaceful experience ended when a group of school children rushed into the cave. Zenobia checked her watch pin and spoke over the gleeful exclamations. "If we eat now, we'll miss the worst of the supper rush."

They exited the cave and followed her past lush plantings of pansies, orchids, and ferns, as well as horticultural exhibits from other countries. Juna breathed deeply of the sweet air that was underscored with the subtle tinge of lumber and paint. "I look forward to exploring every inch of this building." They passed a lovely garden with small evergreens and boulders placed *just so*. "How charming," she said. "It even has a stream with a dear little bridge."

They enjoyed ham sandwiches in an upstairs cafe that commanded a good view of Wooded Island and the fairgrounds beyond. The buildings glistened golden-white in the late afternoon sun. Afterwards, they made their way back downstairs, saving the exhibits for another day—though Juna did pause a few times to admire several ornamental shrubs, and Henry darted into another room to look at some potted orange trees. As they reen-tered the rotunda, a man's voice rang out.

"Why, Miss Thom, how nice to see you."

Zenobia whirled around. "Uncle John! What a lovely surprise."

Juna turned to see a short, middle-aged man in work clothes and dusty boots. Bright eyes of indistinct color were set above a clean-shaven face, although his sideburns and hair needed a trim. The effect was that of a rumpled favorite uncle. "This must be your sister and nephew," he said, smiling at them.

"Yes, indeed." Zenobia made introductions and proceeded to gush. "Mr. Thorpe is the head floriculturist at the fair, responsible for the miraculous displays you see everywhere. If it weren't for him, this place would be boring as a desert."

He winked at them. "My reputation has been inflated, I assure you," he said, looking pleased all the same. "What are your plans for fun at the Exposition, young man?"

Henry aimed a self-conscious smile at Thorpe, who was several inches shorter than him. "I want to rent a Kodak and take pictures."

"Well! Aren't you a lucky Jim. There's no better place for photography. I've heard it said among our professionals that early morning and evening are prime time for correct light. The Wooded Island is particularly beautiful in the early morning with the dew on the roses." Mr. Thorpe's gaze became dreamy for a few moments before he turned his attention to Juna. "And how about you, Madam? Are you a shutter-bug, as well?"

She laughed and shook her head. "More of a plant- and fruit-bug."

"Ah, a compatriot," he said. "You'll find spectacular displays of fruit here, especially in the California exhibits." He glanced around and beckoned them. "I want to show you something exquisite," he said in a hushed voice. "It's just over here."

They crowded into a grotto behind a large tropical plant, where ferns were thick on the side of the mountain. "I have little secrets tucked here and there," he said in a mysterious voice. "Can you see it?"

She scanned the area and spotted the orchid at the same time as her sister. It was the purist white and featured six star-points that radiated out from the center. "Oh, how beautiful. Do you see it, Henry?"

Mr. Thorpe traced the air around it. "*Angraecum campyloplectron* is a beautiful jewel. I keep it hidden from all but the most inquisitive visitors."

After waving off their effusive gratitude, he saw them to the main entrance. "I'm away to a meeting with the powers that be," he said, looking resigned and pulling at the hem of his jacket. "I prefer the dulcet tones of a tricolored pansy to the ramblings of learned men with bright ideas." He winked at Zenobia. "Kindly keep my little diatribe to yourself," he said, and set off in the direction of the Court of Honor. After a few paces, he turned abruptly. "By the way, Henry, you'll find the photography office just behind this building."

"Thank you, sir," Henry said, and received a quick salute before Mr. Thorpe dashed away. They found themselves grinning at each other.

"What a dear man," Juna said.

"Most everyone loves him," Zenobia agreed. "Some of the uppity-ups give him trouble. He rails against extra fees for special exhibits like the cave, but they pay him no heed. He's very supportive of the Woman's Building. I've seen him personally deliver vases of flowers to Mrs. Palmer's luncheons."

"Who's that?" Henry asked.

"Mrs. Palmer is the president of the Board of Lady Managers, the governing body of the Woman's Building. She is a lovely and capable woman." Zenobia gave them an appraising look. "You've had a long day. Shall we go to Mrs. Wilson's, or would you like to stick around for the light show?"

"Light show!" Henry said. "Please, let's stay."

He looked so desperate, Juna didn't have the heart to say no. Tiredness aside, she didn't want to miss it, either. "How can I refuse?" she said, and was rewarded with an enthusiastic hug.

"The light show, it is," Zenobia said. "Let's wander back toward the grand plaza. I have the perfect spot in mind, but we'll need to claim it early."

They took their time walking back to the grand plaza. Henry looked longingly in all directions. There was so much to see, and he couldn't wait to explore it. Zennie led them to a bench on the north side of the basin, with a good view of the fountains. "We're lucky," she said. "These fill up fast."

Mother sat down with a sigh. "Thank goodness. My feet are begging for mercy."

Henry wandered around, promising to stay within Mother's sight. He watched electric launches and gondolas and all sorts of people coming and going. As the evening wore on and it got darker, the Court of Honor took on another appearance entirely. Each of the major buildings was outlined in strings of light, including the dome of the Administration Building and the edge of the basin. Even the Peristyle was lit from the inside, creating a softly glowing path between the Casino and Music Hall. The whole place took on a pleasing, magical quality. A murmur of anticipation rolled through the gathered crowd, which sent him hurrying back to the bench. "Now, for your true welcome," Zenobia said.

An orchestra in the bandstand began to play, and the fountains leapt skyward in a rainbow of colors. Brilliant light burst out from arc lamps positioned on the roofs of the Great Buildings. Wide beams swept the grounds, the water, the buildings, and the people, giving each a millisecond of electric recognition. "Incredible," Henry said, barely able to breathe. *"Stupendous."*

As the light show continued, people shouted their enthusiasm. Cries of "Well done!" and "Bravo!" were mixed with the same sentiment in other languages. And that was when Henry noticed a group of Japanese standing a few yards away. In the instant he looked over, a beam of light swept across his bench, and a second later across the Japanese, revealing colorful robes and elaborately styled hair. In the next moment they returned to being silhouettes, but not before he'd seen the girl. She stood with her hand on the balustrade, and had given a startled smile when the light flashed over her pretty face.

He found it hard to concentrate on the show after that. There was just enough ambient light to gently illuminate her profile. She seemed delighted with the show, and pointed and exclaimed with the other members of her party. As the light beam swung toward the fountains and the great golden dome, a miracle occurred. For one breath-catching moment, she met Henry's eyes. Afterward, his mind told him he'd been imagining a special connection, but his heart told him otherwise.

The orchestra played a dramatic melody as the show came to a close. "Woo! Woo!" he yelled, joining the vigorous applause.

"How marvelous," Mother said, wiping her eyes. "Marvelous."

"I'm so glad you're here," Zenobia said, embracing them both. It was that kind of moment.

"What a day," Mother said. "We've been going like sixty."

Zenobia laughed. "Welcome to my life."

"How do you manage?"

"I try to follow my own advice and pace myself, take transport when necessary, and each night I fall into bed and sleep like there's no tomorrow."

Mother gave him a weary smile. "Sleeping sounds like a grand idea, doesn't it, Henry?"

"Sure does," he said. Fatigue pulled at him despite the thrum of excitement in his bones, but he wasn't about to admit it. "Where to now, Aunt Zennie?"

"We'll take the intramural railway to the north part of the grounds," Zenobia said. "From there, it's a short walk to Mrs. Wilson's."

As they headed toward the nearest platform, Henry looked around for the girl, but she and her family had already blended in with the dark, bobbing masses. He released a breath of disappointment. He supposed that was that.

Being on the elevated train gave them a good view of the grounds. They passed behind some of the main buildings and caught quick glimpses of the Wooded Island, which had tiny lights strung all around. Plenty of people were walking along promenades, lit by evenly spaced lamp posts. As the train paused at the platform near the entrance to the Midway, he took in the sight of the crowds coming and going on the broad avenue that stretched westward toward the distant Ferris Wheel. He couldn't wait to visit!

They disembarked at the northernmost platform and joined other fair-goers who were heading for the exit. All around them, people discussed their big day at the fair. Outside the gates were souvenir booths, food vendors, and people coming and going. The street was busy with carriages picking up and dropping off, and cabbies lined up, waiting for the weary. The sharp *clang-clang-clang* of a cable car rang out in warning somewhere to the south of them.

"It's just four blocks west and two blocks north to Mrs. Wilsons," Zenobia said. "Close, but far enough away that noise from the fair isn't bothersome."

Mother looked around nervously and clutched her handbag to her stomach. "Is it safe to walk here at night?" Henry noticed some shady-looking characters hanging about and was instantly on alert.

"Safe enough," Zenobia said, "but I don't recommend walking alone. On occasions I need to stay late, I ask one of my male colleagues to escort me or I take a cab."

They moved along the sidewalk, squeezed together by the crowd. "I look forward to meeting Mrs. Wilson," Mother said. Henry noticed she was limping slightly and realized she must be exhausted, as she hadn't inquired after his health since before the light show. He lifted her handbag off her shoulder and slung it over his satchel. She gave him a quick smile and hooked her arm around his before adding, "What a generous woman to open her house to complete strangers."

"I vouched for you," Zenobia teased. "Though you'll have to wait 'til tomorrow to meet her. She's elderly and retires early." They turned north into a quieter, darker neighborhood where they passed a variety of homes—some with one or two windows glowing, others were dark silhouettes. A few minutes later, Zenobia said, "Here we are," and led them to a tall, narrow brick home with lamps glowing in the front windows on the main floor.

"How welcoming," Mother said. Inside, they entered a wide hallway that led past a parlor on one side and a staircase on the other. The house smelled of good food and beeswax. Like home.

Zenobia spoke softly. "Mrs. Wilson's bedroom is the first door past the parlor. The water closet is opposite, and the dining room and kitchen are beyond. Our bedrooms are on the second floor. Her housekeeper lives on the third floor, but I told her not to wait up for us."

By the time he fell into bed, Henry was so tired he ached all over—a fact he kept to himself when telling his mother goodnight. The open window let in the cooler night air, along with a blend of the usual night sounds of crickets and tree frogs, an occasional rumble from a train, dogs barking, and faint indecipherable sounds from the Midway. He'd hoped for a view of the fair, but he'd ended up in a tiny bedroom on the north-facing side of the house. Mother and Zennie's rooms both had views of the Ferris Wheel some six or seven blocks away. Lucky them!

He relaxed into his pillow and revisited the day. Images of buildings, boats, sweeping arcs of light, and the pretty girl drifted though his brain. The Exposition was even better than he could have imagined and he was certain of one thing: He, Henry Franklin Lewis, was going to make the most of it. Before he returned home to carry out his expected duties in their pungent factory, he was determined to *live*. He'd nearly died last winter and missed all of this. Now that he was here, how could he let any opportunity pass him by?

Despite being dog tired, he could hardly wait for tomorrow.

Chapter Four

July 6, 1893—The St. Louis Daily
NOTES FROM THE FAIR:

The Midway Plaisance

If the Fair proper is a lady's gown, the Midway Plaisance is an outrageous hat with feathers and ribbons. Every sort of visitor is seen here, from "bloods" to sporting types, to "ma and pa," to the most cultivated socialite. What levels the ground is the kaleidoscope of chaos.

I met a woman outside the Streets of Vienna who was completely confounded. "Everywhere I look," said she, "there is something, someplace, or someone enticing me to 'come and look.' It's as if I'm being split into a hundred pieces—each piece with a mind of its own."

I nodded my sympathy. "To conquer the Fair, you must look around and pick one direction at a time. Forget about trying to see everything or you'll be pulling your hair out by the day's end."

The woman was relieved. "Oh! Thank you for the suggestion. That's exactly what I'm going to do." She marched away with determination in her step for about twenty yards. Then the poor, befuddled woman began to zig here and to zag there. I nearly went after her, but she zigged right into the Javanese Village and disappeared from view.

I relaxed my vigil. I was sure the charming Javanese, with their quiet, unhurried ways, would calm her right down. I imagined her sipping a cup of tea and listening to the pleasant splash of a bamboo fountain. She needed a few serene moments to regain focus and stamina.

—Zenobia A. Thom,
Special Correspondent

Juna awoke to the smell of sausages and the sensation of a warm, purring cat draped over her left leg. She reached down to gently scratch its head and was rewarded with a wet nose pressed against her palm. "And who are you?" she asked. The small grey kitty gazed at her with yellow eyes, half-closed in pleasure. It must have wandered in during the night. She'd left the door ajar in case Henry needed her.

She stretched and looked at the clock, surprised that it was already past eight. It felt rude to sleep in so late, but judging by the quietness of the house, she wasn't the only one. Back home, she would have been up at dawn, fixing breakfast for Seymour and Henry and starting her daily chores—perhaps kneading bread dough or washing clothes. By this time of the morning, she might be resting for a few minutes upstairs beside her bedroom window. It was her favorite place to watch the Mississippi as it flowed past the base of the bluff, its color changing with the light and sky. It was a peaceful respite during her normally productive day.

Lying here like a princess on holiday was a new sensation entirely. While lazing in bed was enjoyable, a wave of guilt pressed against her for not being 'up and at 'em.' What if Mrs. Wilson needed her help with something? Was she expected to cook for herself and Henry? She certainly didn't want to increase the housekeeper's work unnecessarily. As if in league with her slothful side, kitty stood up, stretched, and made herself comfortable on Juna's stomach, purring like a tiny dynamo. Juna closed her eyes, enjoying the sweetness of the moment.

Footsteps in the hall preceded a soft knock on her door. Zenobia peeked in. "Good morning," she said, and stepped into the room. "I see you've met Lovey."

"An appropriate name," Juna said as the cat jumped off and rubbed against her sister's legs. "You're dressed and I'm a lie-abed. What will Mrs. Wilson think of my bad manners?"

"She'll think nothing of it, as she's gone to visit friends for the day. Hattie left a nice breakfast for us. I'll roust Henry. We'll leave at ten-thirty for the Missouri Building."

"Oh, my goodness." Juna scrambled out of bed and twitched the covers up. "I'd completely forgotten about that."

"Relax. We have plenty of time," Zenobia said as she left the room. A moment later, she rapped on Henry's door. "Rise and shine, Henry Lewis. Sausage and eggs await." This was followed by an unintelligible mumble from inside the room.

Two hours later, they were back in the north part of the fairgrounds, walking down a broad avenue past a variety of uniquely designed state buildings. "This part feels like a town, doesn't it?" Juna said, fanning herself. It was a warm day. "Such interesting architecture." They'd just passed the Minnesota headquarters, which was an Italian renaissance design with a roof covered in Spanish tile.

"Each building has distinguishing features," Zenobia said. "Most are built with materials native to the state or territory. Some states, such as New York, have outdone themselves in the elegance department. They host wonderful concerts and dinner parties. Other headquarters are more rustic, but just as enticing." She pointed at a Southern-style structure that had low columns supporting a second-story balcony. "That's Louisiana's."

"The state, not the town," Henry said, making them laugh. It was a reversal of their usual explanation about their hometown of Louisiana, Missouri.

Zenobia continued her tour. "In addition to displays featuring their chief exports, there is a good Creole restaurant and a special exhibit of schools dedicated to teaching Negro children." As a teacher herself, Zenobia clearly approved.

"That sounds like a fine exhibit," Juna said. As she gazed around, a ripple of overwhelm passed through her. Heavens, there was so much to see! Volunteering at the Missouri Building had sounded like a good idea back home, but now she wasn't so sure. Had she agreed too readily? It was her nature to help out, but was she cutting herself short? Of course, one couldn't walk constantly, and there was a limit to how much information one's brain could absorb.

"Here's Missouri," Henry said as they approached a stately two-story building. Square towers angled out from a central dome. "I hope they have something to drink."

"You'll find comforts of every kind here," Zenobia said. "We'll have time to refresh ourselves before meeting Mrs. Fletcher." Inside, the rotunda featured a mosaic floor, post office and telegraph office. Fountains on either side provided a lovely effect. Juna pretended not to see Henry hold his hand under the spray of water. Hallways led off at angles to a library, offices, a men's parlor, and other rooms.

Zenobia indicated a flight of stairs that swept up to the second floor. "Mrs. Fletcher is most likely in the auditorium. She'll be with us shortly, no doubt. We'll wait in the woman's parlor—you too, Henry—and have a lemonade."

A pleasant older woman named Mrs. Cable brought them refreshments in the well-appointed parlor, including a slice of pound cake that was tasty, if a bit dry. Delighted to learn that Juna would be volunteering, she said, "We take pride in offering visitors an elegant destination. The ladies, especially, love to relax and put up their tired feet. You just missed a large group, but we'll get another wave soon. You can be sure."

"It's beautiful," Juna said, taking in the plush chairs, ornate wall coverings, draperies, and other tasteful decorations. She was unexpectedly giddy. This would be an enjoyable place to spend a few hours each week. As long as she was taking a break from the exhibits, why *not* be useful and promote her home state?

An efficient-looking woman in her early fifties entered the parlor and hurried over to welcome them. "Mrs. Lewis, I presume?" After they made introductions, she said, "I appreciate your willingness to volunteer. Miss Thom speaks highly of your family, and it's nice to have another Missouri daughter to greet our guests." She smiled at Mrs. Cable. "Annie here will show you what to do. She manages the parlor splendidly. When would you like to begin?"

Juna glanced at her son and sister. "How about tomorrow morning? Zennie, can you deliver Henry to his meeting with Mr. Peterson, if need be?"

"Of course."

"Thank you," she said, and twitched a finger toward Henry when he murmured, "I'm sure I could find my own way."

Mrs. Fletcher clapped her hands together. "Wonderful. Now, if you'll excuse me, I need to ready the auditorium for an afternoon lecture."

"What sort of lecture?" Juna asked.

"Missouri fruit production. It's a weekly series over the next month. Four different lecturers."

"How interesting," Juna said. "Our father was an apple farmer."

Mrs. Fletcher raised her eyebrows. "Was he?"

Zenobia gave Juna a sly look. "Do you know that my sister is named after the Junaluska apple? Our father saw it listed in a fruit catalogue and thought it sounded pretty."

"Alas, Father didn't read the description," Juna said. "It described the apple as 'ugly.'"

Right on cue, the women emitted a shocked, *"No."*

Juna shrugged. "Reportedly, it tasted good."

"If I didn't know better, I'd think you sisters had rehearsed that," Mrs. Fletcher said, laughing along with Mrs. Cable. "You're going to be a fine addition here, Mrs. Lewis. A sense of humor comes in handy when serving the tired and foot-sore public."

"I hope I'm up to the task," Juna mused after they left the building.

Zenobia linked arms with her. "Juney, all they need is your pretty smile and a piece of cake, and they'll be back in good spirits. Your gentle manner will be a blessing to them."

Juna took a moment to look around at other women walking along the avenue. Some walked quickly, others trudged along. Two women were being pushed in rolling chairs by young men in light blue uniforms. Would she be a blessing to tired visitors? It was a nice thought. "I hope so," she said.

Henry snorted. *"Incontrovertible.* Now, can we please walk faster? I'm starving."

———◇———

They found Peterson waiting in the rotunda. "I'm sorry we're late," Juna said as they rushed up. "I'm afraid we tarried over lunch."

"There's nothing to apologize for, madam. Time seems to stretch and evolve at the fair, some days more than others." He checked his watch and snapped it shut. "I want to show Henry the model farm buildings and some of the new machinery today. May we escort you to a cafe or canning exhibit first?"

Now that the moment had come to release her son into Peterson's care, Juna felt a flash of anxiety. Despite Seymour's trust of the man, he was still a stranger to them. What if he was careless? What if he allowed Henry to become lost—or worse—in this big place? Besides that, Peterson was a big man who filled a room with his boisterous presence. Her quiet Henry would be worn out by the end of their sessions. She took a breath and forced herself to get a grip on her imagination. "You two go on. I'll wander around the exhibits."

"Very good," Peterson said. "I will return him promptly at four o'clock."

"You'll be staying in this building?" The question was out of her mouth before she could stop it.

Peterson seemed to sense her reservations and gave her a patient smile. "We won't be far away," he said, and pointed in two directions. "Mostly over there, and over there."

"All right," she said. "I will meet you here at four o'clock." As they started off, she called, "Henry, do you have your watch? And your notebook?" He held up a hand in reply as he walked away.

Juna trailed them into the main hall, chewing her lip and watching until the pair melded with the crowds. Then she turned and headed in another direction, determined to enjoy herself.

CHAPTER FIVE

The best part of touring the Agriculture Building with Peterson was his penchant for eating frequently. 'Must keep up our strength,' he'd say, carefully wiping crumbs off his mustache and beard. Henry didn't mind that part; he liked sampling things. The worst part was Peterson's tendency to hold forth on practically everything. They'd viewed farm implements, toured a model farm, attended a class on using pesticides, observed a fruit tree grafting demonstration, and inspected the latest in cider presses and pruning tools—all with his mentor's added commentary. "But I already know this stuff," Henry told him. "We have all kinds of tools. And besides, we buy our cider from the mill."

His complaints fell on deaf ears. "It never hurts to see the latest and best," Peterson said. "Your grandfather wants you educated, and by gum, you're gonna be educated. You'll thank me someday when you're running the factory."

Henry pretended to agree. Fact was, the thought of running the factory filled him with dread. Peterson had introduced him to several men connected with apple farming or related businesses, but they all blurred together. Some had advertising cards that he tucked into his satchel as proof for Grandpa. He longed to visit the anthropology displays, Indian villages, and Aztec ruins. He'd rather be a photographer or an explorer than run a vinegar factory, but stepping into his late father's shoes was expected. He couldn't let his family down.

He studied one of the many *bas-reliefs* that decorated the interior of the building: a woman holding sheaves of wheat. Sunlight slanted in from a skylight, illuminating her pale, half-naked breasts. It would make a nice photograph, if only he had a camera. He could hang it on his bedroom wall and scandalize Grandpa, just for fun.

Peterson's voice intruded into his fantasy. "Pay attention, son. You'll have plenty of time to observe sculpted bosoms. God knows there's enough of them around here." He slapped Henry's back like it was a big joke between them. Henry felt his face go hot and pretended to study a soil sample from Georgia. He heard the snap of Peterson's watch. "It's time to make our way to the entrance. We dare not keep your good mother waiting."

"No, sir," Henry said, controlling his glee at his imminent release. Peterson was nice enough, but *dang,* the man was an endless fount of knowledge. Henry knew he should be more grateful, but if he heard one more detail—of any kind—his head would surely explode.

Back in the rotunda, they found Mother sitting on a bench watching for them. "There you are," she said, jumping up with a smile. She touched his arm. "Did you learn a lot?"

"Yes'm," he said. *"Lots."*

"I sufficiently stuffed his brain for the day," Peterson said, clapping him on the shoulder. "Did you enjoy yourself, Mrs. Lewis?"

Mother's eyes were bright as she answered. "Oh, yes. There's so much to take in. I particularly liked the Liberty Bell made of grains at the Pennsylvania exhibit. Did you see it? It was artfully done."

His mentor beamed at Mother. "We did, indeed."

"Yeah, it was neat," Henry said. "It even had a crack."

Mother's lips twitched a little as she retrieved her handbag from the bench. "Thank you, Mr. Peterson. We're to meet Zenobia and head to the Midway."

"Marvelous," Peterson said. "There are many interesting concessions, and you'll want to ride the Ferris Wheel, of course." Henry stifled a groan and steeled himself for a list of recommendations. Instead, his mentor offered a handshake. "We'll meet here one last time tomorrow, Henry. The following day is all yours."

Henry was immediately re-energized by a rush of anticipation. "Yes, sir!" he said, and shook Peterson's hand with enthusiasm.

———◇———

Finally. He was *finally* at the Midway. Exhibits, food tents, and souvenir booths lined the wide street. With so many things vying for his attention, Henry hardly knew where to look. Sprinkled among the crowds of visitors were natives of other countries: men wearing tunics and turbans, some plain and others more richly attired; women in colorful, draped garments and veils, walking in groups or with male escorts. A stout, brown-skinned man wearing a grass skirt. Africans, Egyptians, Europeans. Chinese men in pointed hats, one with a braid that practically swept the ground. Henry twisted one way and the other, taking it all in. Even the air smelled exotic.

Zenobia led them past the Libbey Glass Company; an Irish Castle; the Hagenbeck Animal Show; and the entrances to the Javanese and South Sea Settlements, where barkers enticed paying customers inside. "It's another world here, isn't it?"

Strains of tinkly, odd-sounding music drifted out from theaters, and popular songs blasted from unseen phonographs. "Look at that," Henry said every minute or so, usually about the time Mother made an exclamation of her own. Far ahead, the great Ferris Wheel got impossibly bigger and higher.

Zenobia promised to take them to her favorite food counter. "Smell that?" she said. "Kabobs are my new delight."

Henry's mouth watered at the delicious fragrance of meat grilling in unusual spices. "Is that the place?" he asked, pointing to a brightly painted hut.

"Yes," she said. "There are chairs where we can eat and watch the world go by."

"No tables?" Mother asked.

"Only if you pay for the privilege. You'll find your money slips away quickly here with all the entrance fees for exhibits, restaurants, and gardens with shady tables. Not to mention all the intriguing souvenirs." She laughed.

"I've become philosophical about it in the weeks I've explored this corner of the world. It's still cheaper than taking a steamer to India or the Nile."

This was why Henry loved his aunt so much. She was adventurous and took things in stride. They stepped up to the counter where signs showed the fare and prices. A man with a thick, black mustache and merry eyes took their order. His wife, who wore a robe-like dress and head covering, smiled at them as she waited to fill the plates.

The man said, "Madam, the tall son needs two orders."

"One will do," Mother said, sounding panicked. She turned to Zennie for help, missing the man wink at Henry. They managed to find chairs partially shaded by a fence, glad to rest their feet. Henry bit into a fragrant flat bread folded around the most delicious meat he'd ever tasted. A yogurt sauce dripped down his chin. He groaned in pleasure. Mother and Zennie ate their own with equal gusto.

"Heavenly," Mother said.

Zennie wiped her mouth with a napkin. "I knew you'd love it."

"Can we buy the spices on the Midway?"

"Of course."

After washing their food down with orange cider, they continued past entrances to the German Village, the Turkish Village, and the Moorish Palace before arriving at the line for the Ferris Wheel. Henry stared up at the cars hanging above them. "It does turn slowly," he said, figuring Mother might need some reassurance.

"It's thrilling, isn't it?" she said, surprising him. "I can only imagine the view."

Zenobia tilted her head back and shaded her eyes. "It's spectacular. The first time I rode it, I decided if I never lived another day, I'd die happy."

The line moved reasonably fast, and they were permitted to board once their car slowed and stopped, even with the platform. Swivel chairs were available, and one could look out in any direction, but Henry made a bee-line for the front of the car. He wanted the best view of the fairgrounds and the lake. Mother and Zennie joined him, both holding lightly to the railing as the wheel resumed its progress, moving the car back and up. It was a slow process of moving and stopping, moving and stopping, as they rode the wheel toward its apex.

The view directly in front of them was the mammoth axle on which the wheel turned. Thick spokes were attached to the giant rims. They could see through to the other cars now heading back down. "What strikes me most is how sturdy it is," Mother said. "And such a smooth ride."

Henry agreed, glad for the many thousands of tons of steel that was holding them up. The Midway fell away, revealing a bird's-eye view into the nearby concessions with the tops of rustic huts and theaters inside the fences. The people below were reduced to umbrellas and hats above splotches of moving color. As they neared the top, everyone—except a young girl who shrieked—marveled at the view as they looked down the length of the Midway to tops of domes and the major buildings. Beyond it, boats navigated the blue water.

Mother looked a little teary. Henry was reasonably sure it was from excitement. "Pretty neat, huh?" he said, embarrassed that his voice sounded froggy.

She gave his hand a quick squeeze. "Did you ever think you'd be up so high?"

Zenobia smiled at him from where she stood on the other side of Mother. "It's been a revelation for every man, woman, and child who has stepped on this wonder of engineering."

They soaked in the view as long as they could before they began their slow, inevitable descent. A feeling of regret was quickly replaced with happiness when Henry remembered they'd be going around a second time. "*Smooth,*" he whispered. He'd always loved being high up, climbing to the tops of trees or looking out of tall buildings—tall for Louisiana, anyway. The vinegar factory was only three stories, but he liked to look out of the window at the river and imagine he was the captain of a steamboat chugging along the Mississippi.

He crossed to the back of the car and saw something that made his heart beat faster. In a concession further down the Midway, a hot air balloon was tethered to the ground. Passengers rode toward the sky in a large basket. It rose higher than the Ferris Wheel and was still going up. "Extraordinary," he murmured. *"Prodigious."*

Any hope of riding it that day was dashed by Zenobia needing to get back for a meeting, and Mother wanting to spread out the fun. "We'll come back another day," she promised. "I want to return to Mrs. Wilson's and get to bed early tonight."

Henry suspected she was frightened of going up in the balloon, but he didn't dare point it out. And he'd seen her studying him when she didn't think he was looking, no doubt worried that he was tiring out, which he wasn't. Well, not much, anyway. He considered pleading his case. Instead, he gave her a wistful smile and said, "May I have an ice cream as a consolation?"

It worked.

When they arrived back at Mrs. Wilson's home, they found their hostess sitting at the piano in the parlor playing a lively piece that, to Juna's ear, sounded like Mozart. A short, plump woman with auburn hair—presumably her housekeeper—stood to one side, turning pages. Juna touched Henry's arm and stood in the hallway, unsure what to do. The housekeeper noticed them and leaned down to whisper to her employer.

Mrs. Wilson played one last chord and swiveled around to face them. "There you are," she said in a voice roughened by age, but strong, none-theless. She was older than Seymour by at least ten years—seventy-five, or so—an aged beauty with thinning white hair coiled into a bun at the top of her head. She reached for her cane and held onto her housekeeper's arm as she stood up. "Thank you, Hattie," she said, and waved for Juna and Henry to enter the parlor. "Come in, come in."

Juna rushed forward with Henry on her heels. They introduced them-selves to the older woman, who smelled faintly of roses. "We're happy to meet you," Juna said. "You're very kind to give us lodging."

Mrs. Wilson smiled. "We adore Zenobia. How could we resist meeting her dear sister and nephew?"

"I fear we're making extra work for you both."

Hattie hooted at this, and Mrs. Wilson gave her a fond look. "If I'm not mistaken, Hattie is relieved to have more than her one old lady to look after."

"Oh, I—I see," Juna said. "Though we're happy to help with chores. We'll tidy our rooms and I'll see to our laundry." Beside her, Henry nodded in agreement.

"Very well," Mrs. Wilson said. "That is most considerate of you. We will provide breakfast each morning, and supper for nights you are at home. Hattie is an exceptional cook."

"That sounds wonderful," Juna said. Tomorrow she'd slip the housekeeper money to help pay for food. Henry was growing fast and had the appetite to prove it.

"I'll see to supper now," Hattie said, and hurried out of the parlor. "I'll serve at half past the hour," she called on her way down the hall.

Juna smiled to herself, relieved to be in a relaxed household.

Chapter Six

Juna spent the next morning with Annie Cable, who showed her where the various supplies were kept in the Missouri Building. Meeting rooms and private apartments for staff or visiting dignitaries were upstairs along with a good-sized auditorium and a kitchen. Downstairs in the elegant parlor, women stopped by to put up their feet, sit and chat, or meet up with friends from their home state. They all seemed to appreciate the cake and lemonade that were offered, especially the children. Annie recognized several visitors from her hometown of Hannibal, Missouri—thirty miles upriver from Louisiana—and made a point of introducing them to her.

"Why, I've been using Lewis Vinegar for years," one lady said. "Best thing for constipation," she added in a low voice.

Later that morning as Juna was straightening pillows, a middle-aged woman wearing a dark red dress and straw hat strode into the parlor. She lifted a hand in greeting and spoke in a cheerful, confident voice. "Good morning, Mrs. Cable."

Annie stood to greet her. "How nice to see you, Mrs. Rhodehaver. More catalogues?"

The woman pulled a stack of pamphlets from her satchel and placed them on a small table near the door. "This is the last batch before the session begins next Tuesday. We're almost fully enrolled but do have a few spots left. Three more state buildings and I'm done. Tally ho!" The woman charged out with a smile and a wave.

Juna looked at Annie in amazement. "Who was that?"

"Mrs. Ruthella Rhodehaver, enthusiastic graduate and self-appointed ambassador for the Columbia School of Oratory," Annie said. "She has the money and time to help them out by giving tours of the Exposition, delivering catalogues, and generally talking up the place."

"A real fireball," Juna said. As she went about her duties, her thoughts returned again and again to Mrs. Rhodehaver. How would it feel to march through life with her kind of single-minded purpose? Could she, too, develop a skill that could help her family, such as promoting their vinegar to potential customers? She didn't know if Seymour would go for it, but surely it was worth a try. And if she was honest with herself, she knew there was a deeper reason: she envied Zenobia and her natural outspokenness. While she loved her sister with all her heart, there were moments of self-comparison—and she always came up lacking. It was her own fault for diminishing herself, but there it was.

At the end of her shift, she drifted over to the table with the pamphlets and pretended to neaten the already-neat stack. Her heart beat faster as she glanced behind her. Annie was across the room chatting with a visitor. Before she could change her mind, she slipped a catalogue into her handbag and hurried out.

She left the state building and strolled along the dusty avenue toward the California Building where she was to meet Henry for lunch. The fair was such a lively place. People walking in groups or alone; going here, hurrying there. She passed families with young children in tow; old men walking slowly but looking delighted just the same; couples arguing over where to go for lunch—the Cafe de la Marine or a simple lunch counter? Grandmothers resting on benches. Smartly dressed college boys swaggering along with their jackets slung over their shoulders. She smiled at a woman in bright silks walking with her husband, who wore a light-colored tunic and trousers. When the woman smiled back, Juna felt a thrill of connection. She'd met foreigners before, of course—she lived on a water route, after all— but they were often from Europe.

She wondered how Henry was getting along today. He'd have so many opportunities here, so much to see and learn. He was fortunate to have his mentor's guidance. They all were. The year after Craig died, Peterson showed up at the factory and introduced himself to Seymour. She and Henry were in St. Louis visiting Zenobia. By the time they got home, Seymour had entered into a business arrangement with the man, who went on to make significant sales to businesses in Chicago.

It was a good move for Lewis Vinegar. Profits were holding steady, even as the financial panic affected local customers and businesses. With so many banks failing, many businesses had shuttered or were barely hanging on. Thanks to Archibald Peterson, she and Henry could spend three weeks here in Chicago. They would be frugal, of course. Seymour Lewis might be solidly prosperous, but he was not rich, by any means.

A half-hour later, she and Henry were eating sandwiches on the roof garden of the mission-style California Building. Spiky potted palms and flowering shrubs framed the vista of the fairground. They were just north of the Woman's Building and the entrance to the Midway. "What a majestic view," she said. "Zenobia made a good recommendation."

Henry nodded. "Mm-hm." He seemed happy enough, looking out at the Wooded Island and beyond. He took a gulp of fresh-squeezed orange juice and raised his eyebrows. "This is delicious. Better'n apple juice."

"Tell me about your morning," she said. "What did you see?"

"Well," he said, "after poking around Agriculture some more, Peterson took me to see the replicas of the *Nina, Pinta,* and *Santa Maria.* They're docked by the lake. Did you know they were sailed over from Spain?" After that, they stopped to watch a rescue demonstration in the Grand Basin. "A man fell out of a boat and the rescue crew saved him. 'Course," Henry added in a wry tone, "Peterson is an expert on boat safety. He lectured me all the way up here." Before she could respond, Henry leaned forward. "Mama, I was wondering. Could I please rent a camera tomorrow and go around by myself?"

She caught her lip between her teeth, considering his request. "I don't know, sweetheart. It's such a big place."

"I'll stay in the main part of the grounds, I promise. I know my way around. Peterson had me study the map in great detail. I see loads of boys my age roving around. Mr. P thinks it would be okay. We talked about it. He says it's safe enough." He fixed her with such a desperately eager look that she felt herself weakening. She took a slow breath, grasping for words.

Henry rushed on. "He suggested I have a plan. Here it is: I could escort you to the Missouri Building, then go rent a camera. Then I could meet you and Zennie at a set time in the afternoon. Please, Mama? I'm fourteen, not eight."

She had to admit his plan sounded reasonable. "Will you have lunch on your own, then?"

He grinned. "Yes, if you give me some spending money." He knew Seymour had set up an account for them in one of the banks at the fair.

She quirked a smile at him. "It seems you've thought this through." It hadn't escaped her notice that Henry was referring to Peterson as an ally now that it suited his agenda. Fourteen-years-old, indeed. "I will think on it," she said, unwilling to make a snap decision.

After lunch, they took time to wander around the exhibits in the California Building. They gawked at a one-hundred-foot-high palm tree in the middle of the rotunda; a train carved from a four-hundred-year-old redwood tree; and a fountain spewing red wine. "I wonder if people bring their own cups?" Juna said. "Do you suppose they get protests from the Temperance League?"

Henry smirked. "Ask Peterson, he's sure to know." As they perused a wide array of fruits and fruit products, he said, "It sure smells good in here. Can we buy some?"

"It's too tempting to pass up," Juna said. They got in line at the fruit counter and purchased five oranges—two for them and three for Mrs. Wilson, Hattie, and Zenobia. They found a bench in the outside garden and savored the juicy sweetness of their oranges. "You know I trust you," she said. "I just can't help being a mother hen. Promise me you'll be on your toes and mindful of your belongings. And keep track of the time, all right?"

"I promise. Thanks, Mama!" Henry said, giving her an exuberant hug and a sticky kiss on the cheek.

———◦———

That evening, Juna added a good splash of vinegar to a basin of hot water and stirred it with her fingers. "This is perfect. Thank you."

"We're old hands at fair feet," Hattie cheerfully assured her. "Any number of visitors have stayed here since the Exposition opened. We keep a kettle of water at the ready, though I never thought of adding vinegar to it." She draped a towel over the arm of the chair. "Just leave the basin on the washstand and I'll collect it in the morning." She closed the door behind her.

Juna pulled off her slippers and submerged her feet into the water. "Ahhh." She wished she'd brought some dried herbs. Lavender would be soothing. Sage, too. Or thyme. She resolved to inquire about an apothecary tomorrow. "Ahhh," she repeated, and wiggled her toes. If it was possible to count her steps during the past three days, she was sure it would number in the millions. Henry was already asleep in his tiny bedroom across the hall, most likely dreaming about cameras.

Remembering the catalogue for the Columbia School of Oratory, she pulled it out of her bag. It was a long sheet printed on both sides and folded accordion style. She angled it toward the lamp. Mary Blood and Ida Morey Riley were the principal and secretary of the school. Lessons would be given in Physical Culture, Voice Culture, Phonics, Reading, and Elocution, with special guests lecturing on a variety of subjects within those topics. She felt a thrill at reading these fancy words. "Elocution," she said, emphasizing the syllables. "Phonics. Culture."

She realized with a start that the session began in two days. According to the catalogue, the class lasted three weeks, Tuesday through Sunday, from nine o'clock a.m. until twelve-thirty p.m. The classes were aimed at visitors to the fair, as the catalogue pointed out that sight-seeing could be done in the afternoon and evening. They even sponsored tours of the fairgrounds by members of the faculty and 'other cultivated persons.'

This worried her a little. Would they perceive her as a country bumpkin? She thought of the lively and confident Mrs. Rhodehaver. Was she representative of the students? To be sure, Juna was well-educated. Her stepmother had seen to that. She'd given up teaching to marry their widowed father, resuming her vocation after he died. After Juna married at age seventeen, Zenobia and their mother moved to St. Louis. Her sister eventually attended university and became a teacher herself, choosing to remain unmarried.

Juna never regretted marrying Craig. He'd been the love of her life. It was just . . . whenever she was around Zenobia, she was attuned to her sister's easy worldliness; her ability to face life with enthusiasm and confidence. Juna made tiny circles with her feet in the cooling water, knowing that while Zennie was born with these innate qualities, she was not. Where she tended to mull and worry over things, Zennie charged ahead. Was it divine providence that put the school catalogue in her path? Would developing her speaking skills lead to more confidence and, perhaps, inclusion in the family business?

Turning back to the catalogue, she studied the address and the accompanying information about transportation. The school was located in the Stevens' Art Gallery Building on Adams Street, convenient to both the train station and the cable car line. That could work well. Henry could go directly to the fair with Zenobia, and they could meet up later in the day at the Missouri Building or other location. She had a moment of worry over changing her hours at the state building, but reasoned that Mrs. Fletcher would understand.

Juna held the catalogue to her chest. Signing up for the class felt both terrifying and deliciously risky. Would Seymour agree to a change of plans? It would require staying a few extra days in Chicago.

After replacing the catalogue in her bag, she dried off her feet and massaged them with a salve made with peppermint and other herbs. It was a recipe she'd perfected over the years. After finishing her ablutions, she turned in. As she listened to the rhythmic drone of insects beyond the open window, she tried to imagine herself in a classroom with other women. Independent women who knew their own minds and didn't need to ask permission from their male relations. To be fair, Seymour was generally unconcerned with her comings and goings, but this decision would affect him as well.

The grandfather clock in the downstairs parlor chimed *ten* as she pondered her dilemma. She could always attend the first week of class before contacting Seymour. If she decided not to continue, he'd be none the wiser. If the class turned out to be extraordinary, she'd request to stay an extra week. "Extraordinary," she whispered into the darkness. She thought of

Craig, who'd found joy in riding his high wheel along the Mississippi. It gave him happiness and a verve for life, and she'd cheered him on. If she could go back in time, would she discourage him from doing something that gave him such pleasure? Would she?

No, she decided. She wouldn't. Being in this vibrant city with its vibrant fair infused her with new perspective. Each day had been exceptional. Whatever anyone could say about the fair—huge, spectacular, utopian—for her, it was a vision of possibility; a place where one's wildest dreams could take firm root and grow. And if one didn't have a dream to begin with, why, certainly one could be inspired enough to figure it out. To that end, shouldn't she allow herself the opportunity?

She stretched her tired limbs and pulled the sheet up to her shoulders. This new way of thinking both thrilled and scared her. Could she do it? Should she? Three-quarters of a mile away, the Ferris Wheel revolved with its late-night passengers. Turning, turning, like the questions rolling around her brain.

Chapter Seven

One day. Henry had *one* day to experience the thrill of having his own camera. As he rounded the back of the Horticulture Building, he patted his pocket, which held twelve dollars for the rental and permit. Some fairgoers brought their own cameras, but they still had to pay for a two-dollar permit. He'd heard all the usual complaints of 'Highway robbery!' or 'That's four rides on the big wheel!' As far as he was concerned, it was a dream come true and worth every penny.

He found the Kodak office and went inside. Cameras, neatly lined up on shelves behind the counter, looked like small, rectangular black boxes. A chemical smell emanated from a back room where he assumed they loaded the cameras with film. The clerk was finishing with a customer. "Be sure and keep this permit handy," he told the man as he stamped and signed it. "The guards will check. And remember, tripods are not permitted on the grounds."

"I'm familiar with the rules *and* the photographic inspectors," the man said, sounding aggrieved. "The Exposition's got quite a monopoly going."

The clerk made a noncommittal noise as the man left. He turned and gave Henry a pleasant smile. "Are you here to rent a camera?"

"Yessir."

"Splendid." The man selected a camera. "This is a Kodak model number two. Have you used one before? No? It's simple, really. Pull this string to open the shutter. See the viewfinder on the top? Frame your subject, hold the camera as still as you can, and press this button on the side."

Henry held the camera and pantomimed pushing the button. "Like this?"

"Exactly right." The man pointed to a small key on top. "This advances the film. The number shows in the little window here." He copied the camera's identification number onto the permit and asked for Henry's name and Chicago address where the photographs would be sent. "You'll have fun with it. How long will you be visiting?"

"Three weeks," Henry said, pulling the camera's long strap over his head.

"Splendid. Are you planning to rent often?"

Henry felt his face heat up as he put his money on the counter. "No, sir. Just today."

The man regarded him a moment. "All right, then. This one has a spool of film with one hundred and fifty exposures. Expect to have plenty that are under- or over-exposed. It takes some practice." He handed him a sheet of paper. "You'll find this helpful. It has tips and suggestions for what to photograph, and the best light and time of day for the subject. That sort of thing."

"Thanks," Henry said as he scanned the sheet.

The man tapped the counter with his pencil. "One hundred and fifty seems like a lot, but you'll be surprised how quickly you'll go through them. Choose your subjects thoughtfully, take care with the light, and you should end up with plenty of decent photos. Enjoy your day."

Wooded Island provided plenty of subject matter for photographs. Henry crouched down and snapped one of Phoenix Hall while doing his best to ignore two girls giggling and whispering a few yards away. They'd been following him around for a half hour, each with a camera of her own. Every time he turned in their direction, a Kodak seemed to be pointed at him.

"What a beautiful rose," the girl with long braids exclaimed. Never mind that the bush was six feet to his left.

The taller one wearing a sailor hat gushed over a tree, ten feet to his right. "Just look at those interesting leaves." *Snap. Snap.*

"Go away," he muttered, irritated at this invasion of his privacy. He walked farther up the path for another view of Phoenix Hall. The temple-like structure was comprised of a large central room and two side rooms, connected by covered walkways. A sprinkling of visitors lingered on the building's wide porches. Henry wanted to look inside, but time was short. He'd just snapped another photo when he heard a fresh outbreak of giggling.

"Kodak fiends," said an unfamiliar voice.

He turned to see a boy of seventeen or eighteen wearing a light blue uniform and pushing an empty rolling chair. He was taller than Henry, with dark hair and a hint of a mustache—the kind of handsome looks that girls noticed.

"They've been terrorizing us chair boys all week," the boy said. He spoke with an eastern European accent. "They must have enough of me to fill a souvenir book."

Henry grimaced. "They've made a good start on a second one." They turned to look at the girls, who shrieked and ran away, laughing—in search of another victim, no doubt. He fell into step with the boy. "You work here, don't you?"

"Yes, I shuttle tired women, old men, and lazy bones all day long." The boy gave him a sidelong glance. "Beats shoveling horse dung off the city streets."

Henry raised his eyebrows, then laughed when he realized it was a joke.

The boy grinned at him. "I like to meet all kinds of people. How long have you been here?"

"Four days. My mother and I are up from Missouri. We'll be here three weeks in all."

"Don't kill yourself trying to see everything at once."

"That's what everyone keeps saying," Henry said. They chatted easily as they walked along. The boy explained that he'd worked as a chair roller since the Exposition opened. When they neared the bridge that crossed the lagoon at the northeast corner of the island, a portly woman waved her umbrella at them. "Yoo-hoo! Are you for hire?" *Hire* sounded like *hi-ah*.

"Yes, ma'am!" The boy turned to Henry and stuck out his hand for a quick handshake. "I'm Nikola." His hand was muscular and calloused.

"Henry."

"My home base is just up there," Nikola said, tipping his head in the general direction of the California Building. "Maybe I'll see you around." He sped over and helped the woman into the chair, then checked his watch and recorded the time on a card. "Where to, madam?"

The lady pointed her umbrella toward the Court of Honor, and they were off. Her voice carried. "Take me to the Administration Building, please. Then I'm meeting a friend at the Clam Bake for lunch . . ."

Henry laughed to himself. His new friend was about to walk miles and miles. He looked around to choose his next subject and was just framing the Horticultural Building in his viewfinder when a child ran behind him, crying in a hiccuping, breathless sort of way. Startled, he turned and recognized the little girl, Hazel, from the boat ride. He scanned the area for her parents, but she appeared to be alone. Was she lost? When she reached the Japanese exhibit and ran inside, Henry relaxed.

As he reframed the Horticultural Building, his thoughts returned to the little girl. Her parents didn't seem like the sort to allow their child to go off alone. Should he check on her? He hesitated, not wanting to lose the morning light. Soon the sun would be straight overhead. He returned to his picture, but unease continued to tug at him. "Well, dang," he muttered, and strode off with the camera bumping against his stomach.

A quick glance around the airy central room of Phoenix Hall revealed delicately painted walls, ceilings, and screens. A set of elaborately carved panels near the ceiling featured colorful phoenixes and flowers. At the center of the room, a man in a black tunic and trousers kneeled on a raised platform, pointing out various items to the assembled visitors. Henry was intrigued, but didn't linger. He'd come back another time with Mother. She'd be fascinated.

He scanned the group but saw no sign of Hazel or her parents. Turning toward the door that led to the room on the right, he realized Hazel was sitting behind him on a cushion at a low table. He'd rushed right past her when he charged in. She sat with an older girl dressed in a pink kimono. With a jolt, Henry realized it was the same girl he'd seen at the light show. Hazel was no longer crying. In fact, she appeared mesmerized by the girl, who folded a piece of red paper while speaking softly in her own language.

She worked quickly, with delicate fingers creasing the edges. Henry noticed her kimono had pale white flowers embroidered on it. He guessed she was about his age.

Finished, she smiled and offered Hazel a paper bird. "Origami. For a pretty girl," she said in a voice that flowed like water.

"Thank you," Hazel said, clearly delighted as she peered at the bird in her hand. "Can you make another one, please?"

As the girl reached for a piece of paper, she looked up and saw Henry standing there. "Sister?" she asked.

He shook his head, feeling foolish. "No, but I'll find her parents. Hazel, I'm Henry, from the boat," he said, moving closer. "Stay right there, okay?"

Hazel's lip trembled at the mention of her parents. "Okay," she said with a waver in her voice.

He hurried outside, wondering what to do next. How in the world could he find anyone in this huge place? A breeze stirred the trees and flowers as he tried to decide which direction to go first. The sound of quick footsteps on the crunchy path caught his attention. A Columbian guard came striding up, looking from side to side. "Excuse me," Henry said, intercepting him. "Are you looking for a lost girl?"

"Hazel. You've seen her?" the guard asked.

"She's in Phoenix Hall. She's fine."

The guard squeezed Henry's shoulder. "Good lad. I'll fetch her parents. They aren't far. Can you stay here and make sure she doesn't leave?"

"I, um—" Henry glanced at the sky. "Of course," he said.

"Good lad." The guard jogged away. Henry paced back and forth in the shade of a small tree, keeping an eye on the entrance to Phoenix Hall as visitors came and went. He couldn't believe his luck. The Japanese girl worked at the exhibit!

Fifteen minutes later, the guard returned with Hazel's parents. Her father was a few paces ahead, but the mother was keeping up admirably well as they rushed past him and up the stairs. Henry hesitated to follow, not wanting to intrude. At the same time, he wanted to see this through, and—he admitted to himself—it was an excuse to see the girl again.

The reunion scene was apparently more of a draw than the artifacts, as Henry had to maneuver his way through a crowd of sighing, rustling women. Even the tour guide was straining to see over the hats and feathers. The guard stood off to one side, towering above most of them. Hazel was barely visible, enveloped by her parents, who'd sunk to the floor beside her cushion. The Japanese girl stood a short distance away beside a large vase. The parents, still catching their breath, were too focused on their daughter to take notice.

"Why did you run away, sweetie?" her mother asked.

Hazel was staring at the paper bird in her hands. Seven others lay in a row on the table. Her lip trembled. "They were teasing me," she said in a whiny voice.

"The other children?"

Hazel nodded. "They think I have funny hair."

Henry heard a woman whisper, "Isn't she adorable?"

The girl's father smiled and winked up at the crowd. "Well, now," he said, stroking his daughter's hair. "Not everyone has such pretty locks, do they?"

"No-o." Hazel said, drawing out the word.

Her father leaned in and kissed her forehead. "Shall we go buy an ice cream?"

"Yes!" Her sudden enthusiasm delighted the crowd, who began talking all at once.

"That'll fix anything."

"I want ice cream, too."

"All's well that ends well, when ice cream is involved."

The parents, now happy and relaxed, seemed comfortable with the attention, smiling and joking with the crowd as they left the building. Several of the women reached out to touch Hazel's curls and comment on what a lovely child she was.

Henry glanced back at the Japanese girl, forgotten in the excitement. He tried to catch her eye, but she slipped quietly through a sliding screen and disappeared.

"Dang," he whispered. As he turned to leave, something inexplicable made him return and pick up one of the paper birds. He carefully flattened it and put it in his pocket. Not wanting to be greedy, he left the rest for other tourists. He found the guard waiting for him at the door.

"Thank you for your help today, young man. You did a good thing."

Henry shook his offered hand. "I recognized her from a boat ride earlier this week. I'm glad we found her."

The man looked thoughtful as they exited the building. "We don't normally have escapees from the Children's Building. I don't know how she got past the women in charge. They were beside themselves when they realized she was gone. One minute she was playing in the gymnasium and the next she wasn't. I better get back and reassure them."

As Henry left the island and headed toward a food vendor, he thought about the other girl. The fact that nobody had thanked *her* niggled at him. He didn't blame the parents—they wouldn't have noticed a band of monkeys swinging from the rafters. All the same, he felt that someone should express appreciation for entertaining Hazel.

Perhaps it should be him.

Perhaps he'd even learn her name.

"Conceivable," he said, and walked faster, whistling a happy tune.

"Henry should be here by now," Juna said, checking her watch for the third time in five minutes. She and Zenobia stood in the shade of the Chocolate-Menier Pavilion, positioned near the back corner of the Administration Building. The relentless afternoon sun slanted over the train terminal just west of them. Soupy air caused sweat to trickle down her temples and form on her upper lip, making her irritable.

"You're going to wear out the hinge," Zenobia said, and jiggled a small waxed-paper sack in front of her. "Have another bon-bon before they melt."

"But he's over ten minutes late," Juna said. "He promised to be prompt."

"You'll find that promptness is a rather loose concept here."

"So I've heard." She twisted one way and then the other, scanning the crowds of people coming and going between the terminal and the Administration Building. Had it been a mistake to let him roam the grounds on his own? "Where is he?"

Zenobia rattled the sack again. "Stop frowning, dear. You'll get wrinkles."

Juna gave her an exasperated look. "It's a mother's prerogative to frown. Especially when her son's gone missing."

Zenobia huffed. "He's not missing, Juney. He's a few minutes late."

"Fifteen now," Juna said, snapping her watch shut. "I knew this was a mistake."

"Oh, Juney, it wasn't —"

"Sorry I'm late!" Henry was suddenly in front of them, hands on his knees, panting and red-faced from running. He'd come straight through the chocolate pavilion. "I was on the other side of the plaza . . . when I realized what time it was . . . and I had to hoof it over to the photography office and . . . turn in the camera." He took several breaths. "Of course there was a line."

"We're glad you're here," Zenobia said, giving Juna a warning glance. "Did you take lots of pictures?"

"One hundred and fifty . . . I hope they turn out all right. I was trying to be careful about the light. I snapped all the major buildings . . . and a bunch of statues and flowers and stuff."

Juna, who'd been ready to scold her son, swallowed her words. Clearly, he'd tried to meet them on time. "We want to hear all about your day," she said in an over-bright voice. "Would you like to pick out some chocolate candy before we leave?"

"Yeah!"

"We'll get you a glass of water, too, and—" She glanced around. "I'll rent a chair for you since you're so—"

"I can walk just fine, Mama."

As they followed Henry inside, Zenobia raised an eyebrow at her. Juna held up a hand. "Don't say it," she murmured. She sighed to herself. Why couldn't she be more easy-going, like Zennie, when it came to Henry?

Well. She knew the answer to that.

As they left the fairgrounds, Henry relayed the story of little Hazel.

"Her poor parents," Juna said, horrified. "They must have been inconsolable when they found out she was missing." After worrying about Henry earlier, she could only imagine the wild emotion they would have experienced.

"You did a good thing, Henry," Zenobia said. "You're a hero to that girl's parents. I've never heard of such a thing happening at the Children's Building."

"I met one of the chair rollers today," Henry said. "His name is Nikola. Nice fella."

"I like that name," Juna said. "What nationality is he?"

"Not sure."

"Serbian, I expect," Zenobia said. "Like Nikola Tesla, the electricity wiz."

Henry snapped his fingers. "Of course!"

They arrived at Mrs. Wilson's and took a moment to shake white dust off their hems and shoes. Hattie opened the door and waved them in. "Come in, come in, everyone. We'll be eating in an hour." Juna felt a ripple of anticipation, for she had important news to share.

After the supper dishes were cleared away, she smoothed her skirt with sweaty hands and said, "I have an announcement to make."

Mrs. Wilson, sitting at the head of the table, smiled at her. "Please tell us, dear."

Juna took a deep breath and began. "As you know, I volunteer at the Missouri Building. Yesterday a woman—a very confident and engaging woman named Mrs. Rhodehaver—dropped off a pamphlet about a school here in Chicago, the Columbia School of Oratory. I—I have decided to enroll in their summer session."

While Mrs. Wilson gave her an encouraging nod, Henry and Zenobia's expressions ran closer to incredulity. "Why do you need to take a class?" Henry asked.

Juna had woken up with the birds that morning, shakily confident that signing up for the class was a good idea. Pushing on, she said, "One is never too old for learning. My hope is to gain new skills that I can put to use in some way." She refrained from mentioning the family business.

Zenobia, now recovered, jumped in. "It's a grand idea, Juney. Good for you. And what are we here for, if not to learn?"

"I agree," Mrs. Wilson said. "I'm not familiar with the school, but I have heard of Mrs. Rhodehaver. If she's enthusiastic about it, you can be sure it's a quality establishment." She took a sip of tea, looking thoughtful. "Though

I can't imagine why she felt the need to complete a course. She's always been outspoken."

"That's very kind of you," Juna said. "Of course, it all boils down to whether we can stay in Chicago for an extra week."

Henry's eyes lit up. "Will Grandpa let us?"

"If the classes go well the first week, I'll write to him and ask his blessing. Be prepared, though. He may insist we return, as planned."

Zenobia speared her with a look. "If you feel strongly about it, stand your ground."

"We are here on his good graces," Juna said, a shade louder. "I'll try my best to be convincing. In the meantime, let's keep this between us, please."

Mrs. Wilson looked between the sisters. "When will you sign up?"

"First thing on Monday morning. The session begins Tuesday." Juna rubbed her knees, avoiding Zenobia's gaze. "I should have gone this morning, but was wavering around about it."

"You can catch the cable line right down on 55th Street and ride all the way up to Adams." This was heartening news. Getting to her destination easily was half the battle.

"Will you be going to the fair tomorrow?" Mrs. Wilson asked.

Juna shook her head. "I need a day to wash the dust out of our clothing and prepare for the week ahead. And—" She gently tapped the table as Henry began to protest. "You have post cards to send to your grandfather, remember?"

Zenobia nudged Henry with her elbow. "Be enthusiastic about your experience here. That'll convince him more than anything."

Juna exchanged a smile with her sister. Zennie tended to have strong opinions about things, but she was nearly always right.

CHAPTER EIGHT

The Stevens' Art Building was tall and narrow, squeezed in between a hotel and a store on Adams Street, a half block in from busy Michigan Avenue. Juna craned her neck and looked up at the six-story building, appreciating the pleasing architecture. Each floor had a set of three windows framed in a variety of arches. She was sure it was pleasant and bright inside, but her feet seemed to be stuck to the sidewalk. Where had her courage gone? Evaporated with the morning dew, apparently. Or, more likely, driven off by the noisy chaos of the Chicago streets. Now that she was here, self-doubt had taken over, shrinking any confidence she'd drummed up over the scheme. In her imagination, she could feel the weight of Seymour's disapproval. "This was a silly idea," she said to Henry. "What was I thinking?"

"You were thinking it was a good idea this morning," he said, giving her a look.

"I was deluding myself. Let's go. We don't want to be late for your meeting with Mr. Peterson."

"We have plenty of time," he said, and stepped closer to look at four paintings displayed in the front window. A young man with a short beard and brightly patterned coat exited the building. Three young women wearing stylish hats followed him, chatting easily as they walked away.

Juna felt completely out of her element. "What if we just look around? Zennie tells me there are some wonderful stores nearby, and the new Art Institute where all those congresses are being held is right over there, and—"

"Good morning. May I assist you?" A neatly dressed woman with apple cheeks approached them. Her eyes were bright and interested.

Juna hesitated. "Thank you, but we were just—"

"Are you with the school?" Henry asked, holding her elbow in a firm grip. "My mother is here to sign up."

"Why, yes," the woman said. "I'm one of the principals, Mrs. Ida Morey Riley. We're normally closed on Mondays, but I'm opening today for this very reason. We often get a few last-minute students."

They introduced themselves, and Henry held the door open, looking pleased with himself. Juna raised an eyebrow at her son and received a grin in return. They followed Ida into a large foyer decorated with modern furniture and paintings. A side table held a vase of flowers. There was a pleasant odor of paint, varnish, ink, and plaster, and she could hear indistinct voices from behind closed doors. A burst of laughter emanated from one of the upper floors.

Ida led them toward a staircase. "There's an elevator, of course, but we encourage our students to take the stairs."

"Are they mainly young people?" Juna asked over their echoey footsteps.

"Most students are in their twenties," Ida said, "but we attract middle-aged students as well. In fact, our summer session has several men and women who are on an extended visit to Chicago."

"As are we," Juna said, pleased to know she'd be in good company.

They entered a landing on the second floor. "Our classrooms face the front of the building," Ida said. "The first door on the left is for regular classes. The next is used for physical culture, and our office is the third door. There are studios on the other floors. It's a lively place." She glanced at Juna. "Are you visiting the fair with your husband?"

Juna shook her head. "Henry and I are staying with my sister's friend. I'm a widow these past six years."

Ida met her eyes. "I was a young widow myself."

"I'm sorry to hear it," Juna said. A look of understanding passed between them. Ida was only a few years older than she was.

"It's interesting where life blows us, isn't it?" Ida said. "One minute, I'm a wife in Ohio, and the next, I have a degree from Emerson and a teaching job."

"That must have taken a great deal of courage," Juna said.

Ida showed them into the office, which had a desk and sitting area on one side, and full bookshelves on the other. "Courage and *encouragement*. Please have a seat and I'll get the proper forms."

Henry wandered over to the bookshelves. Juna looked out the window at the hazy sky and realized her apprehension had mostly melted away. Perhaps life was blowing *her* in a certain direction, as well. She pulled her wallet from her handbag. "And here we are," she said.

Ida returned her smile. "And here we are."

Two hours later, Henry and Peterson stood just inside the main entrance of the Manufactures Building, shaking water off their hats and jackets from a sudden cloudburst. Raindrops pounded the glass roof, adding an echoey roar to the place. Henry stared into the giant hall and whistled in admiration. Fancy pavilions lined a wide avenue that ran the length of the building. Small booths were just as numerous. Stairways led to galleries on either side and a tall clock tower bisected the center of the building. "There must be five thousand exhibits in here!" he said.

"Ten thousand, more like. This floor alone comprises nearly thirty-two acres. The galleries add another forty-five acres of floor space." Peterson patted Henry's shoulder. "It's a lot to take in. Don't worry, we'll come back several times, and you can visit on your own or with your family. We'll begin with an innovation in manufactured foods."

Henry groaned. "What foods?" They'd already seen plenty in Agriculture.

He was rewarded with a stern look. "It never hurts to think about other manufacturing possibilities. Open your mind to new ideas. Follow me, I want to show you something." Peterson led Henry to an exhibit by the Wrigley Company. "They have a fruit-flavored gum," he said. "Isn't that an interesting idea?"

"I guess so," Henry said with a shrug. He was feeling prickly after the 'Open your mind to new ideas' comment. Of course he was open to new ideas! Mostly. A fruity gum sounded awful, but he wasn't about to say it to Peterson.

A girl wearing spectacles handed them each a rectangle of thin gum. JUICY FRUIT was printed on the wrapper in red letters. "Try it," Peterson said.

Henry was conscious of the girl watching him unwrap it. The gum was soft in his fingers. He squeezed the sides together and stuffed it into his mouth. A burst of flavor surprised him. Fruity, yes, but tasty. "Nawt bahd," he said.

Peterson laughed. "See? Someone had an innovative idea. This whole fair is packed with innovative ideas," he said as they moved on. "Look there." He pointed at an elevator cage rising with its load of passengers—some visibly nervous. "Ideas all around us."

Henry thought about the vinegar factory and couldn't think past the basics of cider, barrels, and fermentation. Was it really necessary to expand on a good product? Did Grandpa have this in mind when he took Peterson up on his offer to be a mentor? *Nah,* he decided. Grandpa was particular about his vinegar production. Henry quietly snorted and whispered, "*Persnickety.*" He'd discovered that word in his thesaurus and wrote "Grandpa" beside it in the margin.

Peterson guided him around the nearest exhibit and redirected his attention across the hall. "And what about that?"

Henry drew in a breath at the sight of a colossal telescope towering high above the exhibits. Mounted on a tall base, it reached up toward the ceiling. "Whoa. Let's go there!" he said, and rushed toward it with Peterson on his heels.

They stood at the base, looking up. A spiral staircase led up to a platform that gave access to wheels and other instruments used for positioning and calibration. "The Yerkes Telescope," Peterson said. "This is just the casing, but it will eventually hold a forty-inch lens. Can you imagine how far one could see into the heavens with a lens that big?"

"It's *stupendous,*" Henry said. "The base alone is taller than a house." The tubular housing for the lens stretched up at an angle high above them.

As he craned his neck to look at it, his mentor said, "It's sixty-four feet long. Isn't that something?"

"Monstrous," Henry agreed. "I wish we could climb those stairs and get a closer look."

"That would be splendid, but I expect that privilege is saved for persons of note and leading scientists." Peterson checked his watch. "We best move along."

Henry noted that a vantage point from the gallery would give him a closer look. Another time, then. He reluctantly followed Peterson to the next thing, and the next and the next. The morning became a blur of furniture, stoves, clocks, leather goods, glassware, jewelry, fur clothing, umbrellas, rubber goods, and toys. He'd never seen so many iceboxes, cutlery, plumbing materials, or the staggering amount of ceramics, textiles, and lamps, both electric and gas.

At some point, Peterson's voice merely dipped in and out of Henry's jam-packed brain: "And here we have a marvelous example of linen and vegetable fibers . . . The clock tower, by the way, is one hundred-twenty feet high . . . Your mother would enjoy seeing that model home, don't you think? . . . We'll save the German exhibit for another time, but look at the workmanship of those iron gates . . . Those Lyon & Healy harps are world class. Do you suppose your mother would enjoy the daily concert in their pavilion?"

Henry couldn't take any more. "I reckon she would," he said. "It's stopped raining. Can we please ride an elevator to the promenade?"

Peterson smiled. "We *may*, indeed. But first, lunch." Henry agreed it was an excellent plan.

An hour later, they stood on the west side of the observation deck that encircled the roof of the Manufactures Building. "Best view of the whole place," Peterson said as they looked out over the grounds.

Henry leaned against the railing, taking it all in. They were even with the top of the golden dome of the Administration Building, and could look down on the roofs of the other Great Buildings. Flags snapped and waved in the breeze. "There's the Ferris Wheel," he said, pointing northwest. "This is amazing!" Far below, on Wooded Island, tiny figures strolled among the gardens. He hadn't had a chance to return to Phoenix Hall. Was the girl inside folding paper birds?

As they made their way around the circumference of the roof, he and Peterson chatted easily. For once, his mentor wasn't cramming facts and figures into his brain. "How'd you meet Grandpa?" Henry asked as they looked out at the lake.

Peterson considered the question for a moment. "I'm a man of opportunity," he said. "I saw your excellent product on a trip through Missouri and, after some inquiries, discovered a good man who'd risen above hard circumstances. I took a chance and introduced myself to your grandfather, who took a chance on *me*." He puffed up a little. "Four Chicago merchants were willing to sell your vinegar. We continued to expand, and here we are."

Before Henry could question him further, shouting erupted. On alert, he said, "What's that about?" They rushed back to the other side and saw a thick column of black smoke spreading over the far edge of the fairgrounds.

"Dear god," Peterson said, then called out, "Does anyone know where that is?"

A Columbian guard on roof duty said, "Best I can tell, it's the Cold Storage Building. You can just see the smokestack on the roof."

Far below, men ran in the direction of the fire. Even ladies hurried along. On the roof, people rushed toward the elevator despite pleas from the guard to remain orderly. "Let's go see it!" Henry said, turning to follow.

Peterson grabbed his arm. "No, Henry. That crowd is going to be joined by thousands more. We'd only be in the way."

"Oh, c'mon," Henry said, straining to get loose. "We can stay back."

Peterson was immovable. "What we are going to do is to go directly to the Missouri Building and collect your mother so you can go home."

"Go home? I'm not a baby!"

"No, you aren't. But it will be best to leave soon, as there will no doubt be a large exodus within the hour."

Dang. His one chance to see a conflagration and Peterson was ruining it. "Fine," he snapped, and yanked his arm away. They rode a crowded elevator to the main floor. Like smoke, word of the fire spread throughout the building. It propelled the curious outside. Most were heading for the main entrance closest to the grand plaza. Peterson insisted on leaving through the north entrance and riding the intramural railway to the platform nearest the state buildings. Henry stormed along in silent cooperation as excited visitors rushed toward the blackening sky.

As they waited for the train, Peterson put his hand on Henry's shoulder. "Son, you are going to have plenty of opportunities in your life to experience tragedies firsthand. Some of those people went to help, and many were drawn by the promise of a horrific spectacle."

Henry stared at the platform. In the excitement of the moment, he hadn't thought any further than wanting to see a big blaze. It hadn't occurred to him that people might die. His anger melted into a pool of wretchedness. What if people were dying right now? "I would've helped," he mumbled, eyes stinging.

Peterson gave his shoulder a squeeze. "That's the young man who is making his grandfather proud."

"Oh, dear," Juna said through her fingers. "How horrible." She slid her hand to the base of her throat and looked from Peterson—who'd just given her the news—to Henry, who was more subdued than she would expect under the circumstances. Well, it *was* a lot for a boy to take in.

"I recommend you leave as soon as you finish your duties here," Peterson said.

"I can leave now," she said. "Henry, please ask Mrs. Cable to show you where my things are stored." As he hurried off, she turned back to Peterson. "Is he all right? He seems upset about the fire."

"Upset with me, primarily. He wanted to see the fire up close, but I chose to keep him out of harm's way." Peterson shrugged. "I don't blame him for being angry. It's a boy's natural inclination to go where the excitement is."

"Thank you," she said, impressed with his common sense. Henry was in good hands. They both were.

Peterson held her gaze for a long moment. "Sometimes, what we long for most, directly opposes what we must do."

She nodded. "I have found that to be true."

Peterson escorted them as far as the gate, then apologized for not walking them out. "There's a man I need to see at the Administration Building," he said, jerking a thumb in that direction. "Henry, I'll see you the day after tomorrow."

They'd just finished supper when Zenobia arrived at Mrs. Wilson's. "Seventeen firemen and workers died today," she said, collapsing onto a chair next to Juna.

Mrs. Wilson gasped with the rest of them. "How did it happen?" she asked.

"The firemen were putting out a small fire in the smokestack when a rogue blaze started under the roof. Most of the men were trapped. A few jumped to their deaths before the whole thing collapsed." Zenobia pressed a hand to her forehead. "I'm glad you weren't there to witness it. I wish I hadn't."

Juna put an arm around her sister. "Oh, Zennie, I'm so sorry." Across the table, Henry stared at his plate.

Zenobia drew in a breath. "I heard a guard say it was a badly designed building. Something about airspace around the smokestack. It was a fire waiting to happen."

"Would you like something to eat, dear?" Mrs. Wilson asked in a gentle voice.

"I want nothing more than to wash up and go to bed, thank you." Zenobia squeezed Juna's hand. "Good luck with your first class tomorrow. Henry, what are your plans?"

Henry looked up. "Do some exploring, I reckon. I'm on my own."

"Good. Let's walk in together."

After she left, Hattie peeked into the dining room and whispered, "I'll take up a pot of tea, just in case."

No one felt like playing card games or singing around the piano that night. Juna lay in bed listening to the silvery night sounds and thinking about how quickly life could change. Somewhere in Chicago, a mother wept over the loss of her only son. And a wife, devastated by the death of her husband, stared into the black night while questioning God, cursing fate—and blaming herself for encouraging her husband to work at the fair in the first place. That feeling, that *shroud* of guilty remorse, would last for years. The weight of it would press against her every single second of every single day.

A tear slid down Juna's cheek as she spun under the weight of her own shroud.

Chapter Nine

July 12, 1893—The St. Louis Daily
NOTES FROM THE FAIR:

Art Appreciation. (Or not.)

While wandering the halls of the Art Palace, I observed a woman and her husband looking at a painting by Frenchman, Jules Breton. It is an exceptional work called "Song of the Lark," in which a young girl is paused mid-step in a field, listening. She holds a small reaping knife at her side. The light of early morning is captured beautifully, and one can practically hear the birdsong with her. This painting is part of a collection loaned from Chicago's own Mrs. Henry Field.

The wife said, "I don't understand this one. Is she going to kill the bird?"

"Of course not," said the husband. "She's listening to its song."

"Well," said she, "I wouldn't pay ten dollars for this one."

"You wouldn't pay ten dollars for a Renoir, Mabel. Art is completely lost on you." And off they went. I found the nearest bench and put my head in my hands.

—Zenobia A. Thom,
Special Correspondent

Clang-clang-clang! Clang!

By the time the cable car reached the busy downtown, it had slowed from a brisk fourteen-miles per hour to a slow crawl, stopping frequently to let passengers on and off. Pedestrians crisscrossed Wabash Avenue, darting between carriages, in front of horses, delivery wagons, and other oncoming cars. A woman carrying a baby rushed past—skirts billowing—mere inches away. The grip man cursed indignantly when a red-haired paper boy stopped in front of the car, laughing as he jumped away at the last second.

Juna clutched her handbag in breathless amazement as she twisted one way and another on the narrow bench. The conductor rode on a wide step and was trying to catch her eye. He'd apparently interpreted her friendly greeting when she boarded as an invitation. She ignored him, shifting her gaze to the sidewalks. People walked so quickly here! Men in suits with newspapers tucked under their arms. Construction workers carrying lunch pails as they headed to whatever new building was going up.

Young women wearing sensible outfits hurried to jobs in department stores. Older women in fashionable hats walked with purpose to their destinations. Porters and elevator operators in smart uniforms, weary factory workers, and tourists with maps strode along at a more sedate pace. A one-legged man with crutches leaned against a wall and held out a cup to passersby. His scruffy dog rested its head on the man's boot. Juna's throat tightened at the sight, and she wondered if he was a veteran like her father-in-law.

"Adams Street, ma'am," the conductor said as the car slowed to a stop.

Juna allowed him to help her step down. "Thank you, kindly," she said, relinquishing a smile before making a terrified dash to the sidewalk. The Columbia School of Oratory was just down the street. As she entered the building, excitement vied with nerves. Her feet lagged as she climbed the stairs behind some other women who seemed to be acquainted. *I'm a fish out of water,* she thought.

She reached the classroom on the second floor and took a moment to get her bearings. It was a bright room filled with tables that sat two students each. Chairs faced the front, with the windows at the back. She estimated there were about twenty-five students in the class, mostly women. Half seemed to be in their twenties and the rest were in their thirties, forties, and even fifties. Three men appeared to be with their wives.

She entered the room and chose an empty chair at the nearest table, where a woman about her age was arranging her pencils and notebook *just so* with strong-looking hands. She was attractive, with bold eyebrows and beautiful skin. Her lips curved into a lovely smile when Juna sat down. "I feel I should have long braids and a lunch bucket."

Juna's stomach unclenched a bit. "I'm glad I'm not the only one. I was tempted to buy ribbons." They shared a laugh and Juna introduced herself.

"Nancy Collins," the woman said, giving Juna a firm handshake. They didn't have time to chat further. An angular, dark-haired woman and Ida Morey Riley entered the room, smiling as they finished their conversation. The students fell silent, followed by a rustling of skirts and scraping of chairs as they oriented themselves to the front of the room.

The dark-haired woman spoke first. "Good morning, and welcome to the Columbia School of Oratory," she said in the warm, clipped voice of a New Englander. "I'm Miss Mary Blood and this is Mrs. Ida Morey Riley. We are the principals of the school and will lead classes in elocution, physical culture, and related topics." She scanned the classroom. "The daily classes will be taught by us or one of our associate teachers. We will begin with elementary methods of elocution and voice culture, followed by physical culture, because elocution begins with good posture and health."

Juna marveled at this woman who spoke so confidently and precisely. If she could attain even a fraction of her talent, she'd be happy.

Mary Blood continued. "The last section will include the practice of techniques, along with examples of dramatic reading. We are also delighted to offer guest lectures by esteemed colleagues throughout our three-week session. For those of you whom are teachers, you will have separate classes in Public School Reading."

She became animated as she began to walk slowly back and forth in front of them. "What a fortuitous season in which you've chosen to join us. When faced with something as wondrous as the Columbian Exposition, how can we deny the potential to unlock our voices, to be healthy and fit, and to speak with confidence and authority? We're never too old to improve ourselves."

She gestured gracefully. "In our jobs, in our lives, in our dealings with others, how can we best communicate? How can we best teach, or read poetry to loved ones, or speak passionately about the plight of impoverished children or conditions of the factory worker? We need to speak clearly, eloquently." Her eyebrows lifted. "Eloquent elocution. Shall that be our motto?"

Juna found herself caught up in the excitement. Any misgivings she had about taking the class evaporated. She was meant to be here. "Yes!" she replied, in unison with the other students.

Mary Blood smiled. "Good. Let us remember our motto with every lesson, every exercise, as we work our way toward our goal." She closed her eyes for a few moments, inhaling and exhaling through her nose. Her hands were clasped loosely, elbows slightly bent. When she resumed speaking, her voice was soft, but powerful. "'All that I know of a certain star, is it can throw like the angled spar. Now a dart of red, now a dart of blue 'til my friends have said that they would fain see, too, my star that dartles the red and blue. Then it stops like a bird; like a flower, hangs furled: They must solace themselves with the Saturn above it. What matter to me if their star is a world? Mine has opened its soul to me; therefore I love it.'"

The class sighed as one, spellbound. Juna was sure she'd never heard a better rendition of Robert Browning's poem, "My Star."

Mary Blood gave them a gracious nod. "I hope you will find your star here," she said, and swept out of the room. It was an effective exit.

Ida stepped forward, equally self-possessed, but softer in expression. "At its most basic, elocution is the art of managing the voice, countenance, and gesture in speaking. When we master the expression of thought, sentiment, or emotion that is intended, it is the most pleasing and effective to our audiences."

She listed seven qualifications necessary to achieve success, such as 'Control of voice' and 'Entering into the spirit of the piece.' Juna's pencil scraped furiously as she scribbled them into her notebook. The final point was, 'Have a good grasp of elementary sounds.'

"And that is where we shall begin," Ida said. She walked over to a large chart of vowels and picked up a pointer. Some students—the teachers, most likely—chuckled. Ida smiled at them. "Please bear with me for reviewing the most basic sounds. They are the cornerstone of language." She touched her pointer to the chart. "We will begin with single open vowel sounds, or monothongs. "E" as in me, eve, thee, and free; "A" as in ale, may, pay . . ."

Juna grinned at Nancy. Basic or not, familiar or not, she was having the time of her life.

Henry nudged a piece of charred wood with his boot, feeling the keen regret of a missed chance. According to Zennie, the Cold Storage Building had refrigerated food for the fair and even boasted an ice skating rink on the second floor. Judging by the lumpy, blackened ground, it had been a large building. He strolled along the perimeter, passing other curious visitors who wore grim expressions and spoke in hushed voices.

Since arriving at the fair, he'd become even more aware of the vast opportunities that life had to offer. Everywhere he looked, there was a beckoning door, exhibit, band, or building. *See me. Come here. Eat this. See that. Listen.* So many choices! Compared with this exciting place, his life back home felt heavy with expectations. Not that he was against taking over the factory someday—his grandfather and father had accomplished a great deal and he was proud of his legacy. It was just so much sooner than if Papa was still alive. By the time Henry finished school, Grandpa would be that much older and ready to pass the reins to him.

He kicked a blackened chunk out of his way. In his darker moments, he felt angry with Papa for leaving him in this position. Traveling, exploring, and taking photographs of exotic places was *his* dream, not running a business at a young age. Papa should be the one taking over the factory. And he should be *here* at the Exposition, with *him*. Henry slapped his thighs in frustration and strode off toward the main grounds. He knew his internal ranting was pointless. Grandpa and Mother were counting on him to do the right thing, which, of course, he would.

Above him, the elevated train glided to a stop at the Terminal Building. He had two hours to look around before meeting Mother and Zennie for lunch. If the fair was to be the extent of his worldly explorations, he needed to make the most of it. 'Keep track of what you see. We'll discuss the highlights,' Peterson had instructed. Henry snorted. It was his mentor's way of keeping track of him for Grandpa, but he didn't care. Time alone was time well spent.

As he walked toward the Court of Honor, he wondered how Mother was faring at her first class. Now that he was used to the idea, it occurred to him that perhaps she'd like some other choices, too. Anger at his father gave way to shame that he hadn't been awake to wish Mother good luck and walk her to the cable stop. Grandpa's voice roared in his head: *Take care of your mother.* Henry vowed to do better.

Since he was relatively close to the south side of the park, he decided to visit the Anthropology Building behind Agriculture. He'd been eager to see it after reading reports about the natural displays. Every issue of *Scientific American* featured an article or two about Ward's Natural Science exhibit. He quickened his pace, trading regret for anticipation.

Two totems, at least twenty feet high, flanked the doors to the Anthropology Building. Fierce-looking faces—human and animal—were carved into the tapered poles. The base of one had a human-like face with enormous eyes. The other had an eagle head. Henry touched his finger to the tip of its massive, curved beak. He liked that one best. Upon entering the building, he immediately felt pulled in ten directions. Everywhere he looked were exhibits that interested him: ancient artifacts, skulls, minerals and rocks, photographs of South American ruins. He took a deep breath and started at the nearest one.

When he reached Ward's Natural Science Exhibit in the upstairs gallery, he yelled in delight. Giant models of an octopus and a squid hung from the ceiling. A woolly mammoth with tusks as big as a man stood underneath. Handsome wooden cabinets contained the most lifelike examples of taxidermy that he'd ever seen: a roaring lion that looked like it would gladly eat him for a snack; a fierce-looking lioness and her cub; a sea lion whose girth was at least six feet around. There were smaller animals, too, such as a passenger pigeon and a squirrel. Tamer displays included small birds used in women's clothing, fossils from around the world, and skeletons of small mammals.

Excitement pulsed through Henry's body. He'd been fascinated by natural history and science as long as he could remember. Controversial views on evolution had gotten him into trouble with Grandpa a few times, such as the day he brandished a tadpole at him. "Look here," he said. "See its legs sprouting out? It's turning into a frog. It's *evolving*." The last word was shouted in frustration at his grandfather's ongoing refusal to listen to scientific reason. His (admittedly inaccurate) proclamation resulted in going to bed without supper. Grandpa blamed it on impertinence. Mother blamed herself for encouraging him to be curious. Henry blamed it on Charles Darwin and shoved his father's old copy of *On the Origin of Species* back on the bookshelf in his mother's room.

Awakened at first light by a growly stomach, he'd found the book just inside his bedroom door. Tucked inside was a piece of paper with a rude drawing of a tadpole—with legs—and a note in his mother's handwriting that said, 'Your grandfather may Evolve in his Ideas someday.' Henry decided that if Mother believed in him, he wouldn't give up his dream of scientific exploration just yet.

As he studied a fossil of a prehistoric plant discovered in France, he overheard two grey-haired men talking nearby. The first man, considerably taller than his friend, had a deep, gravelly voice. "This is most impressive. What's the latest news?"

"I'm planning the trip now," the second man said. He sounded more refined.

"Are you? What are you collecting this time?"

"All the usual, but hoping for samples of meteorites. They fascinate me to no end."

As they moved away, the first man said, "I know some investors who are interested in science. I'll introduce you."

Henry stared after them, dry-mouthed. Surely the second man was Henry Ward, the proprietor of this exhibit. And he was planning an expedition! Henry's head whirred with possibilities that had nothing at all to do with Louisiana, the factory, or a son's duty to his family. His feet moved of their own accord toward the men. "Excuse me, Mr. Ward?" His face grew hot when the men turned and looked at him, but he plowed on. "I couldn't help overhearing that you're planning an expedition."

The shorter man smiled. "That's right."

Henry stood as tall as he could. "I'd like to apply, please."

"What's your name, son?"

"Henry, sir. Henry Franklin Lewis."

The taller man, who was hatless and had long, neatly combed hair, elbowed his friend. "He's got a good name, Ward."

Mr. Ward raised a wiry eyebrow. "How old are you, young man?"

"Fourteen," Henry said, quickly adding, "I'd help you collect things and take photographs."

The taller man hooked his thumbs into his vest, looking amused as he listened to the exchange. Ward pulled at his beard. "Those are certainly helpful qualities, but as a rule, I don't employ boys under the age of twenty." He held up his hand as Henry slumped in disappointment. "Here's what you need to do. Finish your schooling and continue to hone your skills. Do you read scientific magazines?"

"Yes, sir. I subscribe to *Scientific American*," Henry said, feeling compelled to add, "With my own money," to show that he was a serious and hard worker.

"Keep up the good work, son. Enjoy the Exposition and visit us often. You won't find a better exhibit of natural history."

"Thank you, sir. I will." Henry shook hands with Ward and his friend, who reminded Henry of the pictures of "Buffalo Bill" Cody that he'd seen pasted here and there outside the grounds. No doubt there were men who liked to achieve the same look as the famous cowboy.

As the men walked away, Ward said, "Reminds me of me at that age."

Henry grinned after them, vibrating with the energy of a chance meeting—in a place where even far-fetched dreams felt possible.

"Tay-tee-ta-toe-too. May-me-ma-moe-moo. Lay-lee-la-loe-loo." Juna felt silly, even if the entire class was practicing the exercise. Some students tripped over the syllables, but she was managing reasonably well as they stood behind their chairs 'for maximum lung expansion.'

Ida, who was leading the exercise, said, "Very good. An awakened tongue is an eloquent tongue." There was a spatter of giggling at that. She propped up a new chart with two popular tongue-twisters. "Now that we have loosened tongues—" She paused for more laughter, "let's see what they make of these. All together now, slowly: 'Peter Piper picked a peck of pickled peppers.'" As one, the class repeated it.

"Good. A little faster this time."

They repeated the phrase over and over until the entire class could recite it successfully.

The next class section was Physical Culture with Mary Blood. She pulled a corset from behind the desk and held it up. "According to Dr. Emerson, the corset is an inquisitorial instrument of torture."

"Isn't it?" Nancy said. Juna laughed with the rest of the class, all women. The students who were teachers, including all the men, were in another classroom.

Mary Blood smiled. "He insists that true beauty arises naturally from physical culture, and that we women would rather court death with tight-lacing than look less than our best." She laid the corset on the desk. "While I hold Dr. Emerson's teaching in the highest regard, I believe that the best course of action—besides burning our corsets, of course—is to commit ourselves to a well-fitted one that is comfortably laced." She gazed around the room. "There is nothing beautiful or healthy about a compressed waist. We must be able to expand our ribcages adequately for our vital organs to be at their proper elevation."

Juna, who agreed completely with Miss Blood, noticed a few of the younger students squirming in their seats.

Their teacher continued. "Repeat after me. Physical Culture is a healthy culture."

"Physical culture is a healthy culture!"

"A deep breath is a healthy breath."

"A deep breath is a healthy breath!"

Mary Blood gave a nod of satisfaction. "As I said this morning, a foundation of effective expression is good posture and a healthy body." She lifted her hand. "Please rise and give yourselves some elbow room."

Chairs scraping and a certain amount of giggling commenced. When everyone was standing behind her chair, she said, "Some systems teach that shoulders should be thrust back in order to lift the chest and expand the rib cage. As our own system is based on the Emerson school of thought, we take a different approach. On the count of three, lift up on the balls of your feet while holding your arms in front of you at a forty-five-degree angle. Hold your head high. One, two, three."

The floor creaked as they all rose up on their toes. Juna tottered a little and had to try again.

"Now, back to the floor and let your arms hang at your sides. See how your head is high, your chest lifted and your shoulders square without being thrown back? This is proper posture, which allows your vital organs to be lifted into their ideal position. Do you feel it?"

Juna joined her classmates in an affirmative response. She'd always strived for correct posture, but this was a more confident stance. The exercise worked perfectly.

Mary Blood winked. "Tomorrow, please dress a bit looser. For logistical reasons, we will only perform the gentler exercises. The more vigorous ones, which I encourage you to practice at home, will be taught through charts, lectures, and—" She gestured toward a female mannequin in the corner. "Miss Martha."

"Shall I bring her a hat?" Nancy asked, and hilarity ensued.

"A pearl necklace would be divine," offered a young woman at the back of the room.

"A little rouge wouldn't be amiss," called out another.

"What? And make her a tart?" said an older woman in pretend-astonishment.

Juna found her courage to speak out and said, "She's a New Woman, of course."

"Of course she is," Mary Blood said, drawing the group's focus back to her. "Feel free to make her your mascot. Just don't put a corset on her. Now, let's begin with these arm movements . . ."

The final section of the day was taught by both women. "Consider this the culmination of skills you learn each day," Ida said. "We begin with methodology and apply it to literary interpretation. As we progress through the course, everyone will have a chance to practice." She gazed around the room. "As you go about your days, be on the alert for a poem, a snippet of a speech, a hymn that moves you—anything that would be effective as a short presentation piece. Please bring them next Tuesday. Your final exam, so to speak, will be a speech of your own."

The thought of standing in front of the class and making a speech made Juna's stomach lurch. She glanced at the other students. Judging by their worried expressions, she was in good company. *This is why I am here,* she reminded herself, and conjured up an image of her sister effortlessly holding forth in front of an audience.

Mary Blood's eyes twinkled as she said, "We stand on experience to assure you that by week three you will find the confidence that may be hiding today."

Ida picked up a book and stepped forward. "We'll begin with a selection by Sarah Josepha Hale on the value of books." She stilled, took a few slow breaths, and gazed around the room. Her focus was so sharp that everyone was riveted. She began:

"'We never speak our deepest feelings
Our holiest hopes have no revealings,
Save in the gleams that light the face,
Or fancies that the pen may trace.
And hence to books the heart must turn
When with unspoken thoughts we yearn,
And gather from the silent page
The just reproof, the counsel sage,
The consolation sound and true
That soothes and heals the wounded heart.'"

Juna filled her lungs deeply, realizing she'd barely breathed through-out the recitation. These accomplished women gave her hope that she, too, could cultivate some skill in public speaking—a skill she could put to good use back home.

As Juna and Nancy were leaving the classroom for the day, Ida handed Nancy a small envelope. "Will you please give this to Mrs. Rhodehaver? We gladly accept her kind offer to provide refreshments for the end-of-session party."

"She'll be delighted," Nancy said. "Aunt Ruthie loves nothing more than being in charge of dessert."

"Your aunt is Mrs. Rhodehaver?" Juna asked as they walked toward the stairs.

"The one and only. I'm living with her for the summer. My home is in Cincinnati, but I have a studio on the top floor of this building."

"Do you paint?"

"A little. I'm primarily a sculptor."

"How intriguing! May I see your work sometime?"

"Of course," Nancy said, looking pleased. "I'm working on a model for a larger piece. It should be ready for viewing in the next week or two."

"I look forward to it," Juna said as they parted ways at the stairs. A few minutes later, she settled into a seat on a cable car and reflected on her first day of class. She'd enjoyed her lessons and the teachers very much, made an interesting new friend, and navigated the cable car system by herself. A rush of buoyancy kept a smile on her face as the car passed shops, carriages, and men and women hurrying about their business: "cogs" in the greater workings of the city. It occurred to her that Chicago might be grimy around the edges, but, by golly, it was *alive*.

———◦———

Suppertime was a much happier affair tonight. Henry, who'd had a satisfy-ing day on his own, told Mother, Zennie, and Mrs. Wilson about his visit to the Anthropology Building. He described meeting Mr. Ward, but left out the details of their conversation.

"Ah, you met the man himself. I'm impressed," Zenobia said.

Mother told them about her teachers and showed Henry her notes. He learned some terrific new words, like *monothong*: a word which has the same sound from beginning to the end, such as "teeth"; and *diphthong*: a word with vowels that begin with one sound and ends with another, such as "oil."

"We also learned about subvocals, like *nasals*: home, bring, sting. And *liquids*: hill, all, rise, roar. My favorite was *explodents*: pipe, cap, rot, kick."

"Ticket!" Zenobia said with a flourish.

Henry slapped the table. "Pop!"

Even Mrs. Wilson got in on the fun. "Cup!" she said, hoisting her teacup and sloshing the contents.

"Stop!" Hattie cried as she rushed in, and they howled with laughter.

Mother wiped her eyes. "You all get a passing grade," she said, emphasizing the "p," which got them going again. After supper, she demonstrated the posture exercise in the parlor. They all had to try it, of course. Henry felt silly and turned it into a pirouette, singing, "La-la-la, la-la-la," and skipped around the room, arms aloft, causing Mrs. Wilson's potted ferns to jiggle precariously on their stands.

They'd turned in as soon as it was dark. Henry lay with his hands under his head, reliving his conversation with Mr. Ward. He planned to return to the natural history exhibit as often as he could. If he could make a favorable impression on the man, maybe he'd change his mind about hiring him. 'Why, young Henry,' Ward would say. 'You've impressed me greatly. How old did you say you were? Fourteen? Well, by gum, write to me when you're fifteen.'

Henry gave up a sigh. He was being plain silly. The only job waiting for him was back in Louisiana. "The town, not the state," he muttered, and flopped onto his stomach. He was scheduled to meet Peterson at the Transportation Building the next morning. *Joy.* The man could talk the ears off a corn stalk. Despite knowing that Peterson meant well during the fire yesterday, it still nettled Henry that he hadn't been allowed to see the fire up close. It wasn't like he was an eight-year-old in short pants.

He whispered *"monothong, diphthong,"* until he fell asleep.

CHAPTER TEN

Henry was staring into the dome of the Administration Building the next morning when Peterson appeared, fairly rippling with satisfaction. "Sorry to keep you waiting," he said. "I had a meeting with two of the commissioners. Remember what I said about being ready when opportunities present themselves?"

"Yes, sir," Henry said. "What's the opportunity?"

Peterson laughed and gave Henry's shoulder a couple of taps as they headed toward the west door. "If lesson number one is: *Be ready when opportunities present themselves*, lesson number two is: *Don't show your cards too soon.*"

Henry was tempted to say, *Then why did you mention it?* Instead, he muttered, "Yessir," and did a mental eye-roll. They walked toward the Transportation Building, which looked completely different from the other Great Buildings. Painted in earthy red tones, it had an impressive arched entrance with a golden door. They spent an hour looking around the first floor, which had examples of every kind of conveyance—from rustic carts and African canoes to fancy carriages and steam engines. Visitors could ride elevators to a cupola which, according to Peterson, had a popular cafe with an excellent view of the grounds.

What excited Henry the most were the bicycle exhibits in the upstairs gallery. Hundreds of sleek, beautiful bicycles were displayed in rows or suspended on high shelves. There were bicycles-built-for-two, old-fashioned high wheels, and interesting prototypes. An exhibit from England featured mechanized mannequins pedaling above the display on the newer 'safety' bicycles.

"Whoa," he said, turning in a circle. "This is sensational."

Peterson grinned. "I knew you'd like it. Wander around while I visit the facilities." He checked his pocket watch. "When I come back, you can show me your favorites."

"Sounds good," Henry said, hoping there was a long line in the men's toilet room. He wandered around, trailing his fingers over slim leather saddles, squeezing the handbrakes, and ringing the bells attached to some of the handlebars. Fancier models came with carbide lights on the front.

The exhibits were a magnet for other boys and their fathers. As he watched them inspect the wheels together, he felt a sharp, wistful pang. He heard a boy tell his father, "If I had a wheel like this, I'd trick it out with a bell." Henry liked that idea. He imagined speeding through the streets of Louisiana on his own tricked-out wheel, and even taking part in bicycle races along the river. Maybe he could ride to St. Louis and visit Zennie. Wouldn't that be something? He snorted, imagining *that* conversation with Grandpa.

"I'm going for a century ride, Grandpa!"

"Why in the Sam Hill would you want to do that? Riding one hundred miles on that contraption won't help you learn the family business. Sounds like an adventurous folly to me . . ."

The discussion would end abruptly with the familiar zinger that always came right before Henry was sent away to do some menial chore: *"Are you trying to get yourself killed like your father?"*

A salesman startled him from his reverie. "You like these wheels, son? Here's a list of models. All are available at our store here in the city. Chicago boulevards are a mighty fine place to ride." Henry tucked the brochure into his satchel despite knowing that Grandpa and Mother would never allow it. Riding his friends' bikes on the sly was the best he could hope for, but he could dream, couldn't he?

He forced himself to inspect the high wheels, for his father's sake. With air jiggling in his cheeks, he touched the front wheel that was as high as his chest. It wasn't a racing high wheel, as it had a brake. High wheels were still popular with a certain set of riders. Two nattily dressed college boys came along to admire an expensive new model. "I'm going to ask Father for this one," one boy said. "Anyone can ride a safety."

"*Anyone* can get killed on a high wheel," Henry told the pompous cocka-lorum, and marched off to the other side of the exhibit, ignoring the choice words being flung after him. His neck felt hot, and he took deep breaths to calm himself. It had been a stupid thing to say. He'd give anything for the chance to ride a bicycle of any kind with Papa.

His time alone passed quickly. Before he knew it, Peterson was back beside him, doing his level best to sound like a bicycle expert. Henry didn't care. He was having a good time and there were no manufactured foods involved. Presently, his mentor checked his watch. "We have just enough time to get over to the beach," he said, looking mysterious.

Henry raised his eyebrows. "What's over there?"

Peterson tipped his head in the direction of the lake. "The Viking Ship is arriving today."

Juna had just greeted Nancy, who'd plopped into her chair and whispered, "My train was delayed," when Ida Morey Riley entered the classroom and faced the students straight on. Placing fingertips on her generous middle, she took a deep breath and in a deliberate, controlled tone sang, "HA—HA—HA—HA—HA—HA—HA." Her eyes crinkled at the resulting laugh-ter, and it occurred to Juna that Ida truly loved her vocation.

"Today we begin with vocal control," Ida said. "Please stand behind your chairs." After the scraping of chairs and quick whispers of conversa-tion had quieted, she said, "As we've discussed, the basis of fine elocution is proper breathing and proper posture. Before we begin, take a moment to achieve perfect posture."

After practicing in the privacy of her bedroom, Juna now performed it smoothly. Ida led them in the HA-HA exercise (as she put it) then approached the chart which had phrases written on it. Certain words were underlined for emphasis. She placed her pointer on the first phrase and read, "'If fortune, with a smiling *face*/Strew roses on your *way*/When shall we stoop to pick them up?/*To-day*, my friend, *to-day*.'"

"We will practice this several times," Ida said. "Think about what you are saying and what the subject requires. With each repetition, speak with gradually increased force, and with each repetition enlarge the opening of the mouth and throat. Let each word become fully developed. Be natural in tone and manner."

"'If fortune with a smiling *face*/Strew roses on your *way* . . .'" Juna was glad she was part of a class and not singled out. By the fourth time, she was finding it challenging to be natural with her mouth sagging open. She dared not look at Nancy for fear of getting the giggles. "'When shall we stoop to pick them up? '*Today*, my friend, *today*.'"

"Well done," Ida said. "This time, enlarge the cavity of your mouth when uttering the open vowels. She pointed at a phrase further down the chart. Let's try this one. "'Mid pleasures or pain, in weal or in *woe*/'Tis a law of our being, we reap as we *sow*.'"

They continued through several more phrases. In the short break between elocution and physical culture, Nancy leaned over and said, "You're doing much better than I am, Juna. Have you studied elocution before?"

This surprised Juna. "Why no," she said. "Maybe I'm just good at flapping my lips."

Nancy found this hilarious and was still coughing into her handkerchief when Mary Blood walked in. Juna hadn't had this much fun since she and Zennie were girls.

The section on physical culture was similar to the day before: part lecture, part active involvement. At the end, their teacher said, "As a point of interest, Miss Collins is organizing a bicycle ride on a boulevard north of Washington Park on Monday week. Please see her for the details."

"What if we don't have a wheel here?" a woman from Wisconsin asked.

"I belong to a bicycle club," Nancy said. "The members have agreed to lend wheels to whomever needs one."

"May we wear bloomers?" another student asked.

"Recommended," Nancy said to applause. "Or at the very least, a split skirt, though the wheels are fitted with a cage if you have neither."

As they gathered their things at the end of that day's session, Nancy touched Juna's wrist. "You'll come on the ride, won't you? It's a lovely tour."

Reluctant to admit the truth, Juna shook her head. "I won't be going, but thank you." At Nancy's look of disappointment, she added, "Maybe some other time."

As she rode the cable car toward Jackson Park, Juna admonished herself. They'd be on paved boulevards, not muddy roads. And they'd be riding the new safety bicycles as opposed to the old high wheels. She pressed her fingertips to her forehead and closed her eyes. Who was she kidding? All the reasoning in the world wouldn't change her mind. Fear of riding a wheel—any wheel—had latched onto her psyche and wouldn't let go.

———◇———

Lake Michigan slapped the pavers at Henry's feet. At the sight of a dark spot on the horizon, he pointed and said, "Here it comes!"

Peterson shaded his eyes. "Right quickly, too, despite the wind blowing at them."

They stood among a large crowd gathered up and down the paved beach near the Manufactures Building. A few women perched on stools. It was a hot day and Henry had wasted no time stuffing his jacket into his satchel. A straw hat blew past him into the water, and he reached in and fished it out. The owner, a thin man with a camera around his neck, shook the moisture off and shoved it back on his head. "Thanks." He nodded toward the boat, now clearly visible in the distance. "A group of Harvard chaps joined the Norwegian crew when it arrived in New York. Can you imagine?"

Henry could imagine. Crewing a replica of the only known Viking ship must be thrilling. Peterson had filled him in during lunch, explaining that the original boat was found buried in a farmer's field. "Look how low it sits in the water," Henry said. "I bet they fished right off the side on their way over from Norway."

"I expect they did," the man said. His eyes slid past Henry and he smiled. "Come to record the action, Miss Thom?"

Henry turned to see Zenobia, notebook and pencil in hand, looking rather magnificent as her skirts billowed in the breeze. She squeezed his shoulder. "I see you've met my nephew," she told the man, whose ears had gone red.

"I'm Ned," he said, shaking Henry's hand. "I work for the *Daily* with your aunt."

"He's one of our photographers." Zenobia turned her attention to Peterson. "You get high marks for bringing Henry to see the boat."

Peterson returned Zenobia's smile. "Our young man would never forgive me if he missed out."

Henry noticed that Ned—who looked scrawny next to the robust Peterson—was giving Peterson a calculating look, as if sizing up the competition. This could prove entertaining, especially as Zennie showed no interest in either man.

The boat was now close enough that they could see a red- and white-striped sail. "Better get to work," Ned said, hoisting his camera and disappearing into the crowd. Zenobia said goodbye and followed suit.

Minutes passed, and the boat drew closer. The front of the ship featured a high, carved dragon head and equally impressive tail on the back. Round, colorfully painted shields were mounted along the sides. Passengers on the ship included several dignitaries in top hats. "There's Mayor Harrison," Peterson said, pointing out a white-haired gentleman waving with both arms. He was clearly enjoying being part of the spectacle.

They moved slowly north along the beachfront, following the boat's progress as the crew skillfully maneuvered it toward a small pier straight out from the Government Building. It would anchor there for the duration of the fair. Once the boat was secured, another cheer went up. Henry was sure that he had cheered more in the last week than at any other time in his life. He moved away from Peterson and wandered through the crowd. He spotted Ned snapping photographs of the dignitaries as they left the boat and mingled with the onlookers. Zenobia moved through the crowd, no doubt gathering material by listening in on conversations and comments. For a tall woman who drew the eye, she could be practically invisible when she put her mind to it. "*Unobtrusive,*" he whispered to himself.

Someone tapped his back and said, "Hello, my friend."

Henry turned to see the chair roller he'd met on Wooded Island. "Nikola," Henry said, grinning. "How've ya been? Where's your chair?"

"Back there," Nikola said, tipping his head toward the Peristyle. "I offered a woman a place to sit while I look at the ship."

"Decent of you," Henry said, and was about to ask him what he thought of the boat when Peterson strode up. Henry made introductions.

"I've seen you around," Peterson said. "Where do you hail from originally?"

Nikola straightened. "Serbia, sir."

"Ah," Peterson said, looking thoughtful. "I thought as much. Do you attend the university?"

"No, sir, but I'd like to."

"Very good. I hear the new university down the road is excellent."

"That is exactly where I'd like to go. I'm saving up."

"In that case, we will rent your chair if we have need of one."

"Thank you, sir." Nikola grinned at Henry. "Back to work. See you around."

"See ya." Henry watched his friend hurry back toward his rolling chair.

Peterson checked his watch. He snapped it shut and shoved it back in his vest pocket. "I need to get back to the city. I've spoken with your aunt, and she will take charge from here." He offered his hand for a quick handshake. "Please give Mrs. Lewis my regards, and I'll see you the day after tomorrow."

"Thank you, sir," Henry said. "Today was fun."

Peterson smiled and clapped him on the shoulder. "I'm glad. We'll meet at my office first and look at contracts."

Not as entertaining as looking at new wheels, but Henry knew it was an aspect of the business he needed to be familiar with. "Sounds good," he said.

Zenobia appeared a few minutes after his mentor left. "I've gotten all I need here. Are you ready to go?"

A moment later, Ned stepped up. "May I escort you back to headquarters, Miss Thom?"

Zenobia's merry laugh rang out. "Headquarters, indeed. Thank you, Ned, but I have a fine companion to whom I've promised an ice cream."

This was news to Henry, but he was happy to play along. Ned tagged along until they reached a concession. "Thanks again for rescuing my hat, Henry." He touched the damp brim and marched off toward the Administration Building.

They stepped up to the counter and ordered their ice creams, which were served in edible cones.

"Mmm. This is just the thing on a hot day," Zenobia said after taking a bite.

"Sure is," Henry said, licking a drip from the tip of the cone. The ice cream was melting fast. As they walked across the grand plaza, Henry wondered if Ned was sweet on Zennie. Not that it mattered. As Grandpa liked to say, Zennie was a 'dedicated spinster.'

Chapter Eleven

July 12, 1893—The St. Louis Daily
NOTES FROM THE FAIR:

A Bold Presence

At last! Women have a bold presence at a world's fair. One visit to the Woman's Building will convince any skeptic of woman's ability to enter and advance nearly every field. Paintings, sculpture, scientific contributions, medical innovations, original manuscripts, and handicrafts are just a few of the offerings from our sisters across the globe. Overseen by Mrs. Bertha Honoré Palmer and her capable board of Lady Managers, this edifice shines with the ingenuity of women.

It wasn't easy. Oh, no. There were mountains that had to be climbed, scaled, and conquered along the way. Every critical eye was sizing up the progress. Despite delays, bad press, and a mutiny or two within the ranks, this building—designed by Miss Sophia Hayden—was one of the first to be finished and decorated.

Come visit. Explore the many exhibits and beautifully furnished rooms. Listen to a lecture on one of many interesting subjects. Enjoy the airy porches and colorful plantings. Seek refreshment in the charming rooftop cafe. Then look toward the lake—that limitless backdrop—and ponder the infinite possibilities of womankind.

—Zenobia A. Thom,
Special Correspondent

Henry had the afternoon to himself after helping Hattie with chores. When he announced his plans to walk over to the fairgrounds, she insisted on escorting him, brooking no argument at his protests. "And what would your good mother say if ye got lost between here and there?" she said, shoving a hairpin into her hat. As she left him at the gate, she thanked him for his help, adding, "There'll be peach pie with supper tonight."

Hoping to see the Japanese girl again, Henry headed straight to Wooded Island where he found a crowd of visitors gathered in a large semi-circle outside of Phoenix Hall. Others enjoyed a higher vantage point from the porch. Looking around, Henry noticed the skinny photographer he'd met on the beach the day before and eased up beside him. "Hello, Ned. What's going on here?"

Ned gave him a grin of recognition. "Henry! Ever hear of Jodo?"

Henry shook his head. "What's that?"

"It's a defense system using long sticks."

"Sticks?" Henry laughed, remembering childhood games that involved chasing his friends through the woods with pretend swords.

Ned bobbed his head. "Sounds silly, but you'll be surprised at the effectiveness of a mere stick in the hands of an expert."

The crowd applauded as two Japanese men emerged from the Hall and strode to the center of the circle. They wore deeply pleated black trousers that swirled impressively around their feet. Henry recognized the shorter of the two as the tour guide he'd seen inside the Hall. The man carried a sturdy stick that was about four feet long. His partner wore a long, wooden sword.

Ned leaned toward Henry, while keeping his eyes on the men. "Peasants who weren't allowed to carry swords invented the form." He aimed his camera and snapped a photograph. "Enjoy the show," he said, and left to shoot from a different angle. Henry watched him, longing for a camera of his own.

After the men positioned themselves about ten feet apart, the tour guide stepped forward and swept a steady gaze across the spectators, effectively silencing them. He spoke in a confident, controlled voice that carried without the need to shout. "We will demonstrate Jodo, meaning, the Way of the

Jo," he said, and held the stick aloft for all to see. "This is called Jo. For use against the sword."

He stepped back, and the two men faced each other and bowed. The other man unsheathed his "sword." Henry was fully intrigued as he watched the men approach each other slowly, one sword raised and one stick held at the ready. At the last moment, the tour guide swung his stick up, blocking the sword as he yelled, *"Ei!"*

The crowd cheered its approval as the men backed up and prepared for another strike. This time, the swordsman approached quickly, holding the sword straight out at his opponent. Lightning fast, the tour guide knocked the sword tip downward and in one motion reversed the stick and thrust upward, stopping abruptly near his opponent's forehead. In the next move, the sword was knocked to the side, and the stick jerked to a stop in the middle of the swordsman's chest.

Henry gasped at the near-injuries and cheered with the crowd at the completion of each exercise. It was like watching a graceful dance that held the possibility of terrible violence. The men continued their demonstration, punctuating their strikes and lunges with yells of *"Ei!"* and *"Hoh!"* The swordsman brandished and attacked, knocking the stick to one side. The tour guide deftly turned and defended with a sharp *crack* as his stick deflected the sword. With each exercise, the stick swung up, down, out, or around, stopping short of the other man's chest, arm, wrist, or head.

"Stupendous," Henry whispered to himself, mentally sorting through old canes, crutches, and walking sticks tucked away back home. He couldn't wait to tell his friends about this! Remembering his original mission, he glanced toward Phoenix Hall where other onlookers were standing, and sucked in air at the sight of a sky-blue kimono. The Japanese girl stood watching the demonstration from a shady corner. Henry garnered his courage. This was his chance.

He gave up his spot and casually made his way to the porch, passing behind the spectators and silently willing the girl not to run away. He wiped sweaty hands on his trousers as he approached her, appreciating the way her small hands rested lightly on the railing. Her sleeves were pushed back, revealing slender wrists. Her expression was one of affection as she watched the men. Henry reckoned one of them was her father or uncle. Relieved that the noise of the spectators would keep his words private, he cleared his throat and said, "Excuse me, miss."

When she looked up, startled, he smiled and said, "Thank you for helping the little girl last week. Hazel." Her eyebrows raised in puzzlement, and Henry decided she either didn't hear him or didn't understand English well enough. He shuffled his feet as his face heated up. What an idiot he was! With thousands of visitors coming through, it was impossible that she'd remember him.

The crowd broke into applause as the men completed their demonstration and bowed to the audience. Feeling his chance slipping away, he tried once more. "My name is Henry." She gave him a polite smile and turned back toward the men. While the swordsman was answering a question, the tour guide looked their way and his gaze lingered on Henry a moment, sharpening slightly. After seeing the man's skill with the Jo, Henry felt a jiggle in his gut. *Uh-oh*, he thought, and took a step back from the girl. *Papa.*

"Papa" and the girl seemed to exchange a silent communication before a journalist holding a notebook and a pencil diverted his attention. Ned hovered in the background, taking pictures. The girl immediately turned to leave and, without looking at Henry, said in a quiet, clear voice, "Tomoko." With that, she hurried away and disappeared through a sliding door.

It was with great effort that Henry controlled his expression as he left the porch and began walking south toward the grand plaza. The golden dome of the Administration Building shone brightly in the distance. "Tomoko," he whispered. "Tomoko." He liked the way his mouth shaped the syllables, with the slight emphasis in the middle. "To-mo-ko." He allowed himself a wide grin. Now that they knew each other's names, he reckoned they could be friendly. He reckoned they could have a proper conversation and get to know each other.

He smiled at the sky, which reminded him of the color of Tomoko's kimono. He smiled at a massive, white cloud that was the color of her curious socks that flashed as she'd taken short, quick steps in her native sandals. And he smiled at a bed of bright yellow flowers, the color of the broad sash wrapped around the girl's middle. "Tomoko," he whispered once again, convinced these were the colors of happiness.

———◦———

"Oh, me." The latest visitor to the women's parlor sank into the chair with a groan and lifted her feet to the ottoman.

"Long day?" Juna asked, reaching for the pitcher of lemonade.

The woman spoke with a British accent. "I've walked ten miles, at least, trying to see everything. If only I could fly."

Juna handed her a lemonade, noting that her well-made shoes looked reasonably comfortable. "If only I had a dollar for every time I heard that sentiment," she said with a laugh. "I've found that soaking my feet in hot water with vinegar and herbs is a good tonic at the end of the day."

"Got any?" the woman asked. "I'd gladly pay a nickel this very minute."

It was as if a gong rang in Juna's head. *'Got any? I'd gladly pay a nickel.'* She stilled. Was the woman serious? There'd been no accompanying laugh with that pronouncement. "Would you, truly?" she asked.

The woman raised her glass. "Indeed, I would, my dear. After a soak and some rest, I'd be up for a few more hours of tramping around this vast place."

"Wouldn't it be terribly inconvenient to remove your shoes and stockings?" Juna asked.

The woman gave a small snort. "No more inconvenient than sore feet."

Juna felt a new energy coursing through her. Could she help women feel better by using her knowledge of vinegar and herbs? She thought about it for the next hour and a half as she continued to serve refreshments. She counted the number of women who seemed to be suffering to some degree, as opposed to the number who just needed to rest awhile. At least one in ten.

An idea began zipping around her brain. What if—? This was followed by doubt. Was it too far-fetched an idea? Was it even worth pursuing? Her mind whirred with arguments and counterarguments:

It's an outlandish idea!

You never know until you try.

Women won't want to trouble themselves with removing their shoes and stockings!

They would if they were motivated by sore feet, like the British woman.

Where would I even offer it? Certainly not in the parlor.

Just ask Mrs. Fletcher, you ninny!

By the time she'd finished her duties, she'd worked herself into such a conflicted state that she left the Missouri Building and headed to the best place she could think of for contemplating on her inspiration.

Twenty minutes later, she stepped into the Woman's Building. A spacious rotunda rose past second story galleries to an ornately decorated skylight. Bright, diffused light illuminated statuary, paintings, and many long cases displaying a variety of objects made by women. A fountain in the middle of the room contributed to the peaceful atmosphere.

Taking the stairs to the second floor, Juna paused to admire a cabinet filled with exquisitely dressed dolls from France. Upstairs, she peeked into an auditorium where a woman explorer was giving a lively lecture about her travels. She passed a beautifully decorated library where elegant furniture was artfully placed about the room.

At length, Juna found herself on a small balcony that looked out toward the Midway. By that point, she was convinced that her idea was ridiculous and doomed to fail. She chuckled to herself, relieved that she'd narrowly missed being humiliated. No awkward explanations would need to be made to Mrs. Fletcher. No sympathetic murmuring from her family. She smoothed her hands on the top of the balustrade and smiled, nearly gleeful in her relief. Nearly. A tiny part of her was stamping her foot and saying—

"It's quite a scene, isn't it?"

Juna turned to agree with the newcomer and was startled to see a lovely, fashionably dressed woman smiling at her. "It certainly is," she blurted, recognizing Bertha Honoré Palmer from her picture in the newspapers.

"I find it a good place to think about progress," Bertha said, nodding toward the distant Ferris Wheel. "How can one look at that spectacle of technology and not think great thoughts?"

It was as if the woman had read her mind. Barring the 'great thoughts' part, anyway. "That's what I've been doing," Juna said, compelled to venture farther. "I have an idea, you see—an outrageous one, really—and I'm trying to decide whether to act on it." A quick laugh escaped her. "I admit I've mostly cast it on the refuse pile."

Alert, intelligent eyes focused on her. "Do you? What kind of idea, if I may ask?"

Juna was reluctant to divulge the actual details, so she kept to generalities. "It's something that would benefit women here at the fair, and quite possibly my family's business."

"I see. And you are hesitant to pursue it, because—?" Bertha trailed off, raising delicate eyebrows.

Juna felt her face growing warm. Her excuses would surely sound feeble to this accomplished woman. "I suppose I'm lacking in confidence up to a point and wildly inspired up to another. I've seen and met so many women since arriving in Chicago that, on one hand, I feel part of a growing voice. And on the other, I question my own abilities as a woman in a world of men." *Gad, I'm babbling on*, she thought.

"Here's what I think," Bertha said. "Women have intelligent faculties equal to that of men, and it is by putting our forward-thinking ideas into the world that we will be considered worthy. I've found many a male visitor to this building wearing a face full of surprise and admiration."

"I believe it," Juna said. "But it's a vicarious balance, isn't it? We grasp at independence while trying to stay on the good side of our protectors."

Bertha nodded. "I believe that man and woman have a natural relationship of working together. In the best scenario, we stand side by side, each a compliment to the best qualities of the other. This is the natural state of affairs, but sadly, one that tends to be conveniently overlooked by many, including our own sex. Our goal here is to shine a light on woman's natural gifts and talents, giving humanity a vision of what women can be and accomplish."

She lay a pale, slender hand on Juna's arm. "And so, my dear, I encourage—no, I entreat you, to go forth with confidence in your scheme. For how else can you keep up with the rising tide of ambition than to act?"

Juna was awestruck. No wonder Bertha Palmer had been chosen to lead the Lady Managers. She had the ability to compel women to action. With mounting excitement and a new sureness of calling, Juna said, "All right, then. I'll do it."

Bertha's eyes shone with enthusiasm. "Good luck, my dear. Move forth with determination and inspiration. And if you need reassurance, return to this spot and remember our conversation."

"I will." Juna's voice was abruptly thick with emotion. "Thank you, Mrs. Palmer." As she watched the woman return to her domain, she was filled with determination to ride this feeling of passionate optimism. It was now or never.

She marched back to the state building and found Mrs. Fletcher in the rotunda refreshing a large vase of flowers. Taking a deep breath, Juna said, "I have an idea that would benefit women and the state building."

Eyebrows went up. "Do you now?"

"Each day I see women whose feet are sore from walking miles and miles."

"Yes?" Mrs. Fletcher said. This was nothing new.

Juna pressed on. "I've thought of a way to not only give relief to their poor feet, but to attract more visitors to our building." She detailed her idea, then waited. Mrs. Fletcher stared at her with an incredulous expression that made Juna want to turn and run away. What had she been thinking?

"You're proposing we offer a foot spa? Here?" There was a hint of amusement in the woman's voice.

Juna nodded. "I'd provide the vinegar, of course, a Missouri product. We'd need a supply of herbs to make the foot tonic, as well as basins and towels." Speaking her idea aloud made it sound preposterous. She took a breath. "And a small room with a few chairs."

"Hm. That's quite an idea." Mrs. Fletcher picked up a basket of discarded flowers. Juna's stomach was churning. She was on the verge of saying, *Never mind, it's a silly idea,* when Mrs. Fletcher asked, "How many chairs would you need?"

Juna thought fast. "Perhaps eight?" That seemed like a reasonable number.

"When do you propose we offer it?"

She'd thought about that already. "Between four and six o'clock. Women will have had a full day of walking, and it also fits into my normal time here. I'd simply add more days to my schedule in order to oversee it."

"What about the smell?"

Juna laughed. "As compared to what?" This got a chuckle from Mrs. Fletcher. There were plenty of smells far worse than a little vinegar. "Good ventilation will be important, and the breeze off the lake will be pleasant for the ladies." She thought for a moment. "We could decorate the room with vases of pretty flowers."

"All right," Mrs. Fletcher said. "I'm equally intrigued and skeptical. Let me think on it tonight and discuss it with the other managing staff. I'll give you my answer tomorrow."

At least she hadn't dismissed it outright. Juna touched the older woman's arm. "Thank you."

Juna left the building and walked rapidly down the avenue, propelled by excitement. In the far distance, the Ferris Wheel was a dark outline against the vivid sky of early evening. She'd never had such a daring idea. A foot spa, here at the world's fair? A laugh burst out of her, causing two women to look at her in amusement. "I've had an outrageous idea," she said, and kept going.

"Good for you," one woman called.

"*Bonne chance!*" said the other.

Vinegar had been good to her. It was a common household item, but marrying into a family with an endless supply of it gave her ample time to experiment. The uses were many: a generous splash in a bucket of water made an excellent solution for cleaning everything from the kitchen sink to wood floors to scraped knees. Vinegar added a delicate flavor to stews, soups, greens, and salads. Her pantry had rows of bottles filled with herb-infused vinegars. Seymour maintained that a spoonful added to his morning glass of water was 'Good for what ails you.' She steeped pungent herbs in it to make tonics, added it to soaks for sore muscles, and encouraged Henry to wipe a little diluted vinegar on his face to prevent spots.

Henry. How would she have gotten through his illness without vinegar? She'd applied rags soaked in tonics to cool and ease his rashes and soothe his raw throat. She'd held cups of tea with honey and vinegar to his lips, murmuring, "This will help you feel better," while silently praying, *Let him live.*

And he had lived. Not every child was as lucky. Five children ranging from ages one to fifteen had succumbed to scarlet fever last winter. They were buried in the hillside cemetery on the edge of town. She passed their mothers on the street and offered kind words and a gentle touch, much the same as she'd received after Craig died. That was the nice thing about Louisiana: neighbors cared for each other.

When she first married Craig, it took time to grow accustomed to the pungent smell that permeated his clothing. 'It's the smell of money,' he'd say, kissing her. 'Would you rather I was a fisherman?' And she'd say, 'Of course not. I'll take fermented apples any day. They smell like love.'

She thought about the proposed foot spa. Would vinegar, in this case, smell like a sigh of relief? She sincerely hoped so.

———◇———

My dear Seymour,

What a time we've had! The Fair is thrilling beyond belief. There are so many unusual things to see in the Great Buildings and the Midway. I trust you received our "post card." Henry thought you would enjoy seeing a rendering of the Agriculture Building. He is in his element! Despite my concerns over his health, he is gaining in strength from all the walking to be done here. He is getting on well with Mr. Peterson, whom has been helpful to both of us in his recommendations.

I have a bit of News, a Request, and a Plea for your blessing. In the interest of bettering myself, I have enrolled in the summer session at the Columbia School of Oratory. The principals, Miss Mary Blood and Mrs. Ida Morey Riley, are well-respected in the community and are skilled teachers. I am pleased with the curriculum and encouraged that I will gain confidence in speech and car-riage. If you suspect I envy my sister's natural abilities, you are right. She and Henry have encouraged me in this plan, and Mrs. Wilson has good things to say about the school.

I waited to write until I'd finished the first few days. I would dearly love to continue and complete the course on July 29. Will you please give me your blessing? We are living as frugally as possible, and, of course, saving money through Mrs. Wilson's kind hospitality.

Henry, naturally, is thrilled to be here. He explores on his own when he is not with Mr. Peterson. Zenobia assures me (daily) that it is safe for a boy his age as long as he remains on the grounds or the short route to/from Mrs. Wilson's. I know he is a capable young man, but as a mother, I feel entitled to a certain amount of worry. (My sister teases me about this.)

In other news, I am enjoying helping Mrs. Fletcher at the Missouri Building. It is so interesting to meet people of all types, from high society to the humble factory worker to visitors from other countries.

Please consider joining us for a few days. You would, no doubt, find the Fair as fascinating and instructive as we do. It is a grand thing to see our vinegar displayed so nicely in the A.B.

Lovingly,
Juna

Chapter Twelve

"There's something here you will enjoy," Peterson said as he and Henry approached the Government Building the next morning. They'd come from Peterson's office, where they'd discussed business contracts. "It will appeal to your love of nature."

Henry glanced toward Wooded Island, where Phoenix Hall sat directly across the lagoon. "Sounds good," he said, distracted by thoughts of Tomoko. Was she inside creating paper birds with her lovely hands? As soon as they entered the building, he was immediately riveted by an enormous tree trunk in the middle of the great rotunda. "*Whoa,*" he said, walking faster. "How did they do that?"

Peterson kept pace with him. "I knew you'd be thrilled. It's a two-thousand-year-old sequoia. Two fourteen-foot sections have been hollowed out, and one two-foot section serves as the floor between them."

"*Whoa,*" Henry repeated. "It must be twenty feet across."

"Twenty-three, according to that sign over there. The best part is inside." Peterson gestured to a row of benches facing out from the base of the tree. "Go on in. I'll wait for you out here."

Henry didn't hesitate. He hurried through an opening into in a large, hollowed-out room. Electric bulbs provided dim light. He breathed in the earthy wood smell and pressed his fingers into the tiny dips and ridges made by the carvers who'd scraped and smoothed the inside. The tree was big enough to be a house!

A circular staircase led to the chamber above. He took the steps slowly, imagining great forests in California where these giant trees grew. He promised himself he'd visit them one day. His thoughts turned to Papa, who'd shared his interests in nature and science. He would have loved this. Henry paused, turning to look back down the stairs. Should he invite Peterson to join him? *Nah,* he decided, and resumed climbing. He was lucky to have the tree to himself for a few minutes.

Stepping into the upper room, he walked the perimeter an arm's length out, trailing his fingertips lightly along the wall. He tipped his head back to look at the "roof" high above him and laughed in delight that he was actually *inside* a tree.

Natural light shone in from a narrow crack, drawing him to it. Pressing his cheek to the wood, he looked out across the rotunda, where visitors strolled along looking at exhibits. He was surprised to see Peterson across the room, talking to a man. They were too far away for Henry to see any details other than a dark suit and the edge of a bowler hat, as a display case partially obscured the stranger. Judging by Peterson's posture and impatient gesturing, he seemed to be annoyed. *What that's all about?* Henry wondered. He squinted to get a better view, but the men moved out of sight.

The sound of tromping feet and excited voices announced children coming up the stairs. Three little girls tumbled into the room and began a game of chase. "Wait for me!" the youngest one squealed as she scampered behind her sisters.

Henry headed back down, determined to visit again another day. By the time he exited the tree, Peterson was back in place. "Well?" his mentor said with a grin. "What did you think of the Big Tree?"

"It was terrific," Henry said. "I wouldn't mind living in it." He paused a beat, then asked, "Who was that man you were talking to?"

Peterson shrugged. "Nobody. Just a lost tourist asking for directions. It's my sworn duty to help wandering souls," he said, pressing his hand to his chest.

Henry didn't completely buy the explanation. If Peterson was so keen to help out lost tourists, why had he been acting annoyed?

"There's lots more to see here," his mentor said. "Let's start over there." The tourist forgotten, they looked at a fine collection of rifles; an impressive Indian exhibit that featured realistic-looking mannequins in beaded costumes; an amusing post office exhibit that featured "lost" items, such as snakes, numerous pistols and daggers, china dolls, chewing tobacco, and even a stuffed alligator.

The Smithsonian Institution provided an outstanding collection of stuffed birds, and they spent a good bit of time in the War Department, which had extensive displays of the newest cannons. Peterson was well-versed in this area. "See that big one there?" he asked, pointing to a rifled cannon at least thirty feet long. "It can fire a mortar ten feet in length. The range is seven miles."

Henry whistled as Peterson pointed to an even larger one.

"That one has a range of ten miles. Can you imagine? Costs the government one thousand dollars each time it's fired."

The time passed quickly. "That's enough for one day," Peterson said when Henry's attention started to lag. "I can see you need nourishment, and I need to get back to my office."

Henry was always ready to eat, especially when his mentor paid for it. "Yeah," he said. "War makes a guy hungry."

"True enough," Peterson said. "Am I leaving you with your mother or aunt today?"

"My mother. She said to meet her at the Missouri Building."

Peterson smiled. "Very good. Let's find you a sandwich and we'll be on our way."

———◇———

Juna hurried along the avenue of state buildings, singing, "Tay-tee-ta-toe-too," under her breath. It was an apt accompaniment for the butterflies swooping around her stomach. Today, Mrs. Fletcher would give her an answer about the foot spa. She'd been distracted during class that morning, causing Nancy to elbow her a couple times and murmur, "Come back to us."

Whether her idea would be accepted loomed over her. She couldn't say why it felt so important, it just did. Being here at the fair with all its ideas and innovations filled her in a way she'd never felt before. It differed from the milestones of graduating from school, or getting married, or even having a baby. Dreaming up an idea—a business born of her own imagination—felt satisfying to her core. The most surprising thing was that she'd be using a skill she already had. Could finding a way to be more useful really be that simple?

She passed a few other fairgoers who looked tired and hot. The state buildings with large porches were filled with folks resting or having refreshments, and the water booths were doing a brisk business. Juna was glad when she reached the Missouri Building. A glass of cold lemonade or tea would be welcome.

Annie Cable met her at the parlor door. "Mrs. Fletcher would like you to join her upstairs when you're ready. She's in the lecture hall." Juna rushed upstairs and found Mrs. Fletcher adjusting a lectern. A small table nearby held a bowl of fragrant strawberries and blackberries.

The woman waved her in. "Let's sit over here," she said, moving toward the front row of chairs. She pulled one out at an angle and they sat down. "Goodness, dear. You look like you've been sent to the school marm."

That was exactly how Juna felt. "I've been a bundle of nerves since yesterday," she said, wishing she'd taken time to drink some water. Sweaty and dry-mouthed was not the way she'd intended to present herself today.

Mrs. Fletcher smiled. "I must say, your idea took me by surprise. But the more I thought about it—and in discussing it with a few others—I've concluded that it's worth a try. There's a storage room near the kitchen that we can clear out. It has a window and plenty of space for at least ten chairs, though we could squeeze in a few more, if necessary."

Juna pressed her hand to the base of her throat, hardly believing her good fortune. "Thank you so much. That sounds perfect." They spent some time working out the particulars and set the start date for the following Tuesday. "I'll make a batch of tonic the day before, so we'll just need to warm it up," she said.

"The state house will pay for the vinegar, of course. Have you given any thought to advertising?" Mrs. Fletcher asked.

Juna retrieved a piece of paper from her handbag. "I have, in fact." She'd stayed up late the night before working on the wording. "If you approve, could we have it printed up and displayed in the rotunda?"

Mrs. Fletcher looked it over. "Very good. I will see to the printing and display."

"I have to ask," Juna said. "What if there are no takers?"

"A fair question. We will try it for the time you are here. If it's a success, we'll appoint someone else to oversee it. Otherwise, we'll quietly withdraw."

That sounded reasonable. "I'm grateful for the chance to try it," Juna said.

Mrs. Fletcher raised an eyebrow. "I admit I have endured a certain amount of ribbing from the other staff."

"I'll do everything I can to make it a success," Juna said in apology. Ideas zipped around her brain as she descended the stairs. She had a spa to plan! She was so wrapped up in thought that it startled her to see Henry and Peterson standing near the fountain. In her excitement over the spa, she gave them a big smile as she approached. "Hello there."

Peterson returned her smile full force. "You look like the cat that just ate the canary."

She laughed, thinking that Ida Morey Riley could use that sentence as an exercise. "Well, I do have some good news," she said, then faltered a little, remembering too late that Peterson was a direct line to Seymour. She took a breath. There was nothing for it. "I have just received permission to open a special spa for ladies with sore feet."

Peterson and Henry stared at her in confusion, clearly waiting for more information. Flustered now, her words came out in a rush. "We'll make a tonic here, in the kitchen, and ladies can come and soak their feet in it. Upstairs."

Henry burst out laughing. Peterson looked like he was trying not to.

Feeling utterly foolish, Juna turned and fled from the building. Outside, she was practically running down the avenue in the direction of the lake. People were staring. Her elation over the spa came crashing down in a second. All it took was someone laughing at her idea to make her question it.

"Mama, wait. Slow down. I'm sorry!"

"Mrs. Lewis, please stop."

Henry and Peterson jogged along beside her. Either of them could easily grab her arm and stop her, but they only kept even, apologizing and pleading with her. While this was satisfying on a certain level, she was forced to stop and catch her breath. In lieu of words and oxygen, she glared at them, panting; silently daring them to call her idea stupid.

After a minute, Peterson squeezed Henry's shoulder as if to say, *I'll be the sacrificial lamb. Pay close attention.* He took a tentative step toward her. "Please forgive us," he said. "You have a fine idea. We were merely caught off guard. Would you care to tell us more about it?"

She looked away from his earnest, handsome face and noticed that Henry had assumed a wide-eyed, interested expression. It was true that she'd told them in a rush and had left out some key points. Deciding she'd punished them enough, she relented. "All right, but I need to sit down," she said. "And I'm terribly thirsty."

"Ah," Peterson said. "I know just the place. It's not far."

Her son gave the man a look. "Don't you need to get back to the city?"

"It can wait," Peterson said, giving *him* a look.

Juna pretended not to notice. "Lead on," she said.

One minute Peterson was hot to get back to the city, and the next thing Henry knew, they were sipping jasmine tea in the Japanese teahouse. Not that he minded being there. He kept a sharp eye out for Tomoko, in case she helped there, too. The teahouse was on the northeast side of the lagoon, perched on the shore near the Fisheries Building. It featured an exotic little garden that Mother remarked on.

Peterson listened attentively as she shared details about her foot spa. What's more, he was enthusiastic about it—which was fine, of course, but the gleam in his eye was new. "It'll be a boon for Lewis Vinegar, especially with the medal to recommend it," his mentor said. "I'm sure Seymour will be all for it, don't you, Henry?"

Before he could answer, Mother shook her head in alarm. "No, don't tell him yet. I want to give it a week and see how it goes. If it flops, I'm swearing you to secrecy. If it's a success, I want to tell him myself. Promise me."

Peterson held up a hand, clearly glad to be in on her secret. "I swear on this teapot not to say a word. Henry?"

"I won't say anything," he grumbled. It irked him that his mentor didn't give him the benefit of the doubt. He supposed it all was part of trying to be gallant. He wondered if Peterson expected him to take notes, and nearly snorted tea out of his nose. At least Mother looked happy again.

"The first thing I need to do is get my hands on a supply of our vinegar," she said, making lists in her notebook. "And fresh herbs. I already have an address for an apothecary."

"I can supply the vinegar easily," Peterson said. "When and where would you like it?"

While he and Mother discussed plans, Henry slumped back in his chair and peered out over the lagoon toward Phoenix Hall. He almost suggested they walk over, but didn't want to encourage Peterson to stick around any longer than necessary.

At last, Mother said it was time to leave. "I have the day off from the state building and need to go home and study," she said as they left the teahouse.

Peterson's waxed eyebrows shot up. "Study?"

Suddenly flustered, Mother flapped a hand dismissively. "I'm taking an oratory class. For fun."

"How interesting," Peterson said. "What does your father-in-law think about it?"

"I've written to him," she said, sounding defiant.

Henry felt he should say something in support. "She's learned the proper position," he offered.

Peterson's lips twitched. "Has she now?"

"To elevate my organs," Mother said in a rush. "For speaking!" Her cheeks went pink as she charged ahead. Peterson followed, coughing into his hand.

Henry trailed along in puzzlement, convinced that he was missing something.

Right arm up. Right arm down. Right arm up. Right arm down. Left arm up. Left arm down. Left arm up. Left arm down. Bend from the waist—hands on hips—and circle to the left. Circle back to the right. Juna did the exercises as fluidly as possible in her roomy nightgown. It was her new bedtime routine. Between all the walking at the fair, her nightly stretches, and the gentle exercises during Mary Blood's class, she was feeling more fit and limber than she had in years. She ended with the posture exercise, pushing away the memory of getting bumfuzzled in front of Peterson earlier that day. *Up—arms out—and so.*

"Click, clack, goes the train on the track," she said, speaking as distinctly as possible. She repeated the phrase, a bit stronger. "Click, *clack*, goes the *train* on the *track*." Now she applied some excitement to it. "Click, *clack*, goes the *train* on the *track!*" They'd learned about articulation that day. "Articulation," she said. "Ar-TIC-ulation. Artic-u-LATION. Articulation!" She ended with a flourish, sweeping her arm toward the ceiling. In the next room, Zenobia applauded.

Juna gave the wall a couple taps as a "thank you," and sat down at her dressing table. A stack of books sat next to the lamp. She'd perused Mrs. Wilson's bookshelves for a suitable presentation piece and was trying to narrow down her selections. The thought of speaking in front of class was slightly less frightening than before, but at least she'd be in good company. And her teachers were ever so kind in their instruction.

Seymour would receive her letter soon. Would he allow her to continue with the class? Or would he insist that she and Henry return home, as planned? She touched her fingertips to the top book and spread her hand flat. The thought of withdrawing from the school sobered her. Should she have admitted that she hoped to help their business with her newfound skills? If he didn't approve of that idea, how would he react to the news of her opening a foot spa? Peterson seemed keen on the idea. He might put in a word to Seymour if she asked, but it rankled her that she'd have to rely on a man to convince her father-in-law.

She stared at her reflection in the mirror. It seemed ludicrous that she—a quiet, thirty-three-year-old widow—was not only taking a class, but opening a foot spa, of all things, in a state building, of all places. What if no one came? What if her idea failed spectacularly? She thought of Bertha Palmer and her board of women who worked tirelessly to achieve their goals, despite the challenges. How many people had dismissed their efforts? No doubt those same detractors who were now enthusiastically crowing about the merits of the Woman's Building.

Juna sat up straight, realizing that those women had to fight every step of the way. And that's exactly what she would have to do. In class that morning, Ida gave them tips on practicing articulation. "Try whispering the words," she said, then had the class whisper several selections together. Once they got past the giggles, it proved a worthy exercise. Juna now leaned forward and whispered to her mirrored self, "My dreams are my future. They are worth fighting for." The blazing passion in her reflected eyes was enough to make her believe she could accomplish anything.

CHAPTER THIRTEEN

July 15, 1893—The St. Louis Daily
NOTES FROM THE FAIR:

Finding Whimsey

Today I went looking for whimsey. There are a multitude of examples throughout the Fair, but here is a sprinkling of my "finds" in the northeastern part of the grounds.

A fine example of delightful imagination is the Fisheries Building, where every column, pediment, and balustrade is decorated with fanciful creatures of the shallow and deep. Inside the central rotunda, there is a charming fountain filled with many kinds of golden fish.

Moving north past the international buildings and just east of the Art Palace, I happened upon a curious sculpture. It is different in form and character than most of the sculptures here: A plump cupid whispering in the ear of a large female sphinx. I wonder what he is telling her? I would like to know. Whatever his secret, this half woman, half lioness, looks pleased.

Not far away is the charming Norway Building, with its many peaked gables and lovely carvings that jut out all around the roof: fire-breathing dragons that would have graced a Viking ship.

My final stop was the French Building, which commands one of the loveliest locations at the fair. Close to the shore, its two pavilions are joined at the back by a semi-circular colonnade. This forms a shady court filled with plants and an artistically designed fountain. The visitor may sit here, listening to the water splash while gazing out at the sparkling lake. Whimsical, indeed.

—Zenobia A. Thom,
Special Correspondent

Kilauea was erupting. Lava spewed all around them, boiling up from the earth's depths amid thunder, smoke, and flashing lights. The audience shouted out in alarm, as they seemed to turn in place, deep inside the caldera. Although Henry knew it was only the alchemy of science, art, and technology—and a painted canvas that rotated around the perimeter of the room—his pounding heart thought otherwise. He tore his gaze away and glanced at Mother and Zenobia on either side of him. Mother's mouth was open as she stared, transfixed, at the scene. Zenobia, who'd seen it before, had bright eyes and a satisfied expression. After the show was over, they stepped out into the heat of the Midway, with cries of 'That was sensational!' echoing around them.

"I feel as if I've traveled to Hawaii," Mother said. "Wasn't it wonderful, Henry?"

"Yes'm. It was the next best thing to being in a volcano." He turned to admire the octagonal building, with its giant statue of the goddess Pele above the entrance. Large letters on the building proclaimed, HAWAII KILAUEA, Greatest Volcano on Earth in ACTION, 9 Miles Around, 1000 Ft. Deep.

Zenobia fanned herself. "I knew you'd love it. I feel like I'm in a volcano out here. Who's ready for a cold drink?"

As they walked toward a refreshments booth near the Ferris Wheel, the women opened umbrellas to shade themselves from the mid-afternoon sun. Henry plucked at his damp shirt and decided he'd give anything to be barefoot and wearing short pants on this swelteringly humid day. Sweat dripped down the sides of his face. Despite the heat, there was still a good crowd of men, women, and children about, looking equally wilted under their umbrellas or broad-brimmed hats. Any bit of shade was sought out and occupied, and concessions that sold cold drinks had long lines of customers.

He envied some of the foreign fellows who strode around without shoes or slippers. On second thought, he wouldn't want to step on something disgusting. With this many people around, one never knew what was being thrown down or spit out. Zenobia suggested earlier that they spend the hottest part of the day in the Manufactures Building, which enjoyed the cooler breezes off the lake, but he and Mother were determined to visit the Midway. They bought glasses of orange cider and stood in the booth's shade. Nearby, the Ice Railway promised a cool, fun ride. "Let's go there next," he suggested.

Mother and Zennie answered as one. "Good idea."

A group of Nubian men and boys in white tunics and trousers trotted by brandishing swords and shields. Their hair was carefully oiled, with the sides and back hanging to their shoulders, and a large pouf on the top of their heads. The man with the biggest pouf called out, "Visit the Street of Cairo! Come see the show!" The crowds clapped and cheered, entertained by the spectacle. A good many fell in step behind the group of performers as they moved toward the entrance gate across the street.

Henry finished his drink in a big gulp. It was delicious. He filed 'flavored cider' away for a "someday idea" to prove to Peterson and Grandpa that he wasn't beyond innovation. While waiting for the women to finish their own, he scanned the street for interesting people passing by. He saw Turks in baggy pants and tall hats; a Chinaman with a long braid; and two women in oriental garb, perhaps dancers. It was then that he noticed a man standing outside a concession a short distance away, fanning himself with a folded newspaper. This in itself wasn't unusual. There were plenty of men standing around in shady spots. The difference was that the other men weren't looking directly at *him*.

Something about the man seemed familiar—the angle of his head or his long mustache, but Henry couldn't place him. Had he seen him at an exhibit or a restaurant? There were plenty of people who visited the fair multiple times. It wasn't impossible that he'd crossed paths with the same persons more than once. As he stared back, he realized it was the cab driver who had picked them up at the train station. Kramer. Henry raised a hand in greeting just as the man turned and disappeared into a passing crowd. Henry gave a mental shrug. Kramer was no doubt trying to place *him* as well.

"My, that was fun," Mother exclaimed as they once again stepped out onto the Midway. They'd ridden twice in one of four "coasters" that were strung together, relishing the cool air rushing past them as they sped down and around the icy track.

"Sure was," he agreed. "I want to come back and do it again."

"Goodness, I'm sore from laughing," Zenobia said, rubbing at her sides.

Mountainous clouds gave them temporary respite from the sun as they wandered slowly up the Midway. As they passed between the Ferris Wheel and the Moorish Palace with its blue dome, a hawker yelled, "Come one, come all! See one thousand wonders! Be astounded and amazed!"

They passed the Turkish Village on one side and the German Village on the other. Further on was the Javanese and South Sea Settlement, which featured an actual village. When the women needed to stop at a comfort station, Henry waited outside. In this central position, Henry became aware of a melding of music and exotic rhythms behind the exhibit walls, beckoning him to *Come! Look! Listen!* In one direction, he heard syncopated drum-like beats. In another, odd singsongy voices and percussive bell-like sounds. In still another, a German band played a traditional march.

He tapped his fingers against his leg, attempting to remember the patterns. He wished his instrument-playing friends could hear this. It would be fun to incorporate some of these exotic sounds into their music. He grinned at the thought of using a tambour on "Oh! Susannah."

"Henry! *Zdravo.*" Nikola was suddenly there, grinning at him. He pushed an empty chair and looked as hot as Henry felt. "Are you lost?"

"Lost in the music of the Midway," Henry said. "Isn't it something?"

"It is. Do you play an instrument?"

"Mandolin and a little piano," Henry said. "My friends and I like to play music together. How about you?"

"Violin," Nikola said, and studied him a moment. "Did you bring your mandolin to Chicago?"

"Yeah."

"There's going to be a music party on Monday night after closing. Want to come?"

"Would I!" Henry said, then made a face. "If I can get permission, anyway. Where should I go?"

Nikola named an intersection near one of the north gates. "Meet me at eleven o'clock. I'll wait for fifteen minutes. I hope you can come," he called over his shoulder as he sped off.

Henry was certain the only way his mother would allow him to be here after closing would be with a chaperone. He didn't want to involve Peterson in this, but his mentor might be the best chance he'd have. He chewed his lip, thinking of other alternatives. Zennie might go with him, but he doubted she'd want to stay up late after a long day. Mother would enjoy it, but she had an early start, too. Besides, what if only men attended?

This gave him an idea. It would be an easy thing to sneak out after everyone was asleep. He'd stay an hour or so, then hurry back home. No one would be the wiser. A twinge of guilt pushed against his middle, but he forced it away. He was fourteen, after all. And he'd be playing music, not committing a crime. What was the worst that could happen? A broken string? His burst of laughter drew an amused glance from a Columbian guard.

Chapter Fourteen

TELEGRAMS

7-17-93, 8:00 a.m.

TO: Seymour Lewis

All is well. Henry is well-mannered and curious.

Mrs. Lewis is attentive to my recommendations.

=A. Peterson

———◦———

7-17-93, 9:10 a.m.

TO: Archibald Peterson

Well done. Henry's mother has signed up for a class.

What do you know about the Columbia School of Oratory?

=S. Lewis

———◦———

7-17-93, 2:15 p.m.

TO: Seymour Lewis

The school is respected. I recommend allowing Mrs. Lewis to proceed.

=A. Peterson

——◇——

"Nancy said she'd meet us in her studio," Juna said as she led Zenobia to the top floor of the Steven's Art Building. Her friend had extended the invitation after class on Saturday, and Juna asked if she could bring her sister. Nancy readily agreed.

"There *is* an elevator, Juney," Zenobia said.

"'Climbing stairs is good for our blood's circulation and our health,'" Juna said, quoting Mary Blood.

"Is fainting from exhaustion a good thing as well?"

Juna laughed. Neither of them were suffering in the least, though the temperature was rising slightly with each floor. "With all your hoofing around the fair, I'm sure you could run up these stairs if you wished."

"That may be true, but I'm not averse to using technology."

The smell of paint, varnish, and clay grew stronger as they ascended the last flight of stairs. According to Nancy, several artists had studios on the top floor where the light was best. "There," Juna said when they reached the top. "Number Twelve."

They knocked, and after a moment, Nancy Collins opened the door. She wore a loose tunic with matching pantaloons, Persian slippers, and a floppy hat on her head. "Welcome to my kingdom," she said, flourishing an arm.

"You look straight from the Midway," Juna said, and introduced her sister.

Zenobia looked utterly charmed. "You must introduce me to your tailor," she said with a wide smile.

Nancy led them into her bright studio, where a large table held various cloth-covered lumps. An easel and some canvases leaned against one wall next to shelving that held a variety of small pieces, mostly models of the human body. At the other end of the room, a table and three mismatched wooden chairs were pushed against the wall. A large square of oriental fabric hung on the wall over a faded burgundy-colored sofa, and a Japanese screen was angled against one corner. In Nancy's work area, a long canvas apron hung on a nail.

Juna was fascinated by this bohemian space where her friend had freedom of personal and artistic expression. Ever the journalist, Zenobia asked, "May we see what you are working on?"

Nancy pulled the covering off the first piece to reveal a sleeping nymph covered in leaves and flowers. The face was only roughed in with a hint of a nose and mouth. "Keep in mind it's a work in progress," she said. "This is a study for a commission. My aunt has a friend whose husband owns a hotel in Wisconsin. The finished piece will be displayed in the lobby."

"It's wonderful," Juna said. Zenobia echoed her assessment.

Nancy's brow furrowed as she tipped her head. "I've had trouble finding the right model for the face, but I'm mostly satisfied with it."

"As you should be," Zenobia said. "Surely you have a piece at the fair?"

"I do, in fact," Nancy said as she replaced the sheet. "A statue of the goddess Pomona. It was supposed to be prominent to the fruit tree display in the Horticultural Building, but the powers that be tucked Pomona into an obscure corner."

"No."

Nancy shrugged. "It's still a man's world. I had a small model of it here, but my aunt liked it so much that she begged me for it."

"My sister and I will hunt for Lady Pomona and drag her into the open," Zenobia declared.

Nancy grinned at her. "I'd like to see that. It weighs a couple hundred pounds."

Zenobia planted her hands on her waist. "Women must be strong to be seen and heard."

"I see we have much in common. Shall we sit down and have refreshments? Aunt Ruthie sent cookies, and I have tea made."

Juna sank onto the sofa, feeling happy—and a tiny bit envious—at her sister's quick rapport with Nancy. Zennie had more in common with Nancy than she did, but why shouldn't she? Both lived in cities, while Juna was a small town gal. The conversation turned to women's rights and voting and politics—none of which Juna had firm opinions on, though she was intrigued to hear that women in New Zealand would soon have the right to vote. Beyond that, politics were lost on her.

She found herself gazing out the window past the tops of buildings to the horizon where lake met sky. What would it be like to live in Chicago? To have a place of her own? Back home, she was more independent than most women, but she still relied on her father-in-law for a home and income. When her husband died, control of their money had been placed in Seymour's hands. He was kind and generous, of course, but she'd never given him a reason not to be. She realized Zenobia was waiting for a reply to a question. "I'm sorry, could you please repeat that? I was off and away."

"Nancy suggested we visit the Art Palace together. She's quite knowledgeable about the paintings and sculpture."

"That would be lovely," Juna said. "May Henry come too?"

"Of course," Nancy said. They made plans to meet after class on Wednesday.

"I enjoyed meeting Nancy," Zenobia said as they left the building. "I was tempted to ask if she'd allow me to interview her for the newspaper, but decided I'd rather value her as a friend than as a professional contact."

Juna linked her arm with Zennie's. The love she had for her sister eclipsed her earlier feeling of envy. "I'm glad," she said. "It's good to have friends."

"Agreed," Zenobia said. "Now, where is this apothecary of yours?"

TELEGRAMS

7-17-93, 2:30 p.m.

TO: Juna Lewis

Received your letter yesterday. You have my blessing to continue the class.

You are fine as you are, of course.

=Seymour

7-17-93, 5:11 p.m.
TO: Seymour Lewis, 5:11 pm
You are a dear. Thank you!
=Juna

Henry spent the day at Mrs. Wilson's. He looked over her bookshelves, poked around her backyard, and even weeded the small vegetable garden. He unearthed a glass bead near the corn that he washed and put in his room. After lunch, he accompanied Hattie to buy meat and other supplies. In the late afternoon, he sipped tea with Mrs. Wilson and heard all about her last trip to Europe in '83.

The highlight of the afternoon was when his package of Kodak photographs arrived with the post. He rushed upstairs and spread them out on his bed. Many were under- or over-exposed, but there were plenty of good ones: the Horticultural Building with a rose in the foreground; Manufactures with a boat going by; a long view of the Peristyle, and several of the Administration Building. There were a number of good ones taken on Wooded Island. Flowers, which his mother would like, and some artistic angles of Phoenix Hall. Most had at least a couple of people in the frame, slightly blurry as they were walking in or out. The final one had a figure peeking around the corner of the farthest wing. He held the photo close to his face and was astonished to see that not only was the figure in focus, it was the Japanese girl. Her expression was unguarded; one of amused interest.

"Tomoko," he whispered. What thrilled him more than anything was that she was looking right at him. *Him.* And he'd taken this photograph at least a half hour before Hazel ran past. Tomoko noticed him playing the photographer, just like he'd noticed her watching the illumination. This realization made him ridiculously happy. And now he could look at her anytime he wanted.

When his mother and aunt arrived home, he was in the parlor practicing his mandolin. His stomach churned with a mixture of excitement and trepidation as the music party that night drew closer.

"What a day," Mother said as she dropped into a wingback chair.

Zenobia collapsed into another. "Agreed. I may need some of your foot tonic, Juney."

Henry put the mandolin back in its case. "Where did you go?"

"After visiting Miss Collins, we went searching for the apothecary so your mother could acquire bottles of lotion and herbs. Her interpretation of the address led us on a wild goose chase. Two cable car rides, many blocks of walking, and a helpful porter later, we finally found it."

Mother raised her head from the back of the chair. "How was I to know it was a European "one" and not a "seven," I ask you?"

Zenobia's fingers lifted from the arm of the chair. "Touché. We then lugged the lotion and herbs all the way to the fair—"

"We took the train."

"From whence we lugged the lotion and herbs to the Missouri Building and upstairs to the kitchen—"

"A man carried the load upstairs for us."

"Where Juney made a batch of tonic."

"True enough," Mother said.

Henry couldn't help laughing. "You should've brought me along to be your mule."

"What, and deprive me of a good story?" Zennie said.

Mother suddenly sat up. "I have wonderful news, Henry. There was a telegram waiting for me at the Missouri Building. Your grandfather approved my oratorical pursuits, which means we can stay an extra week."

"That's sensational! There are lots of places I haven't seen yet." He'd also have more opportunities to see Tomoko, but kept that to himself.

"I'm delighted you'll be staying longer," Zenobia said. "Now, tell us what you've been doing today, Henry."

He shrugged. "Not much. I helped with weeding and went to the butcher and dry goods store with Miss Hattie."

"You're a good boy, Henry. I know Mrs. Wilson and Hattie appreciated your help."

Henry was sure his self-conscious grin had guilt written all over it. "I'm going to wash up for supper now." He hurried out, needing to escape the trusting, loving expressions his aunt and mother were aiming at him. If they knew what he was planning, they'd be aiming shock and disappointment at him, instead. He splashed water on his face and reconsidered if the music party was worth it. Then he reminded himself of his commitment to have an experience of a lifetime while at the fair. *Be a man,* he thought. *Be a man!*

After drying his face and hands, he checked his pocket watch and closed it with a decisive *snap.* Four hours to go.

The last thing Henry heard his mother say as they all said goodnight was how she was going to sleep like the dead. "Same here," Zenobia said, yawning into her hand. "I'll see you on the river Styx. Goodnight, Henry."

"G'night." He couldn't resist adding, "If you hear any angels tiptoeing around, ignore them and go back to sleep." Soft laughter preceded doors closing across the hall.

The grandfather clock in the parlor chimed half-past nine. Henry removed his shoes and placed them by the door. He planned to leave by ten forty, as the intersection where he was to meet Nikola was a fifteen-minute walk from Mrs. Wilson's. He lay back and laced his fingers behind his head. A music party! Who would be there? What would they play? Would he be able to keep up?

A wisp of guilt nudged his stomach, but he reasoned it away. If he didn't take some chances now, when would he? Besides, his pals back home would be impressed with his daring, and envious of his experience. This gratifying thought made him smile into the darkness.

He woke up an hour and fifteen minutes later with his hands completely numb. Panicked, he fumbled around for his shoes with painfully prickling hands and crept downstairs. By the time he located his mandolin in the parlor, tiptoed out the back door and put on his shoes, he only had five minutes to get to the meeting spot. Nearly fifteen minutes later, he arrived at the intersection, winded and worried that he was too late. He twisted back and forth while catching his breath, but didn't see his friend. *Dang.* Had he run like a thief in the night past dark houses and barking dogs for nothing?

The street ran parallel to the Midway. It was lively with people just leaving the grounds, men and women out on the town, and a few shifty-looking characters easing through the crowds. Fancy carriages, one-horse hansoms, and two-horse hacks crisscrossed in front of him on the street. A train rumbled past a couple of blocks away. Over in the fairgrounds, some of the domes and the Ferris Wheel were still illuminated. Henry took it all in, feeling energized. He stood tall, trying to look sophisticated instead of a fourteen-year-old who was supposed to be asleep in bed.

"Good evening, young man. Waitin' for someone?" A pretty woman wearing a ruffly dress in a vivid shade of pink stood a few feet away. She tilted her head and caught the corner of her bottom lip with her teeth while waiting for him to answer.

"Uh, yes'm," Henry mumbled. He squeezed the handle of his mandolin case and shifted from foot to foot. Where the heck was Nikola? Had he already been here and given up on him?

The woman looked him over. "If your friend doesn't show, I'd love nothing more than to have you play me a tune. I simply love music, and I can tell by those long fingers that you have a way with an instrument." She purred the last word.

Face flaming at her suggestive tone, Henry ignored her and scanned the street. He noticed two men hanging back, watching them. With a jolt of terror, it occurred to him that they were working in tandem with the woman. Was she was trying to lure him into a dark corner so they could rob him, or worse? He edged closer to the lamppost. About to make a run for it, he yelped when someone slapped his shoulder. "There you are," Nikola said. "Sorry I'm late." He wore regular clothes and held a violin case.

Henry sucked in a breath to slow his pounding heart. *"Dang.* I'm glad you're here." He glanced at the woman, who bumped the air with her lips and sauntered off in the direction of her two cohorts.

Nikola grinned. "Get propositioned, did you?"

"Yeah, and nearly murdered. I fell asleep or I would've been here earlier. I thought I'd missed you."

"Does your mother know?"

Henry gave a quick shake of his head. "No. I snuck out."

"I promise not to keep you out too late. C'mon."

"Aren't we going to the Midway?" Henry asked, matching his friend's stride.

"No, but it's not far."

Henry's stomach gave a lurch. Not only was he here without permission, he wasn't even going to be at the fairgrounds. Going to a pre-approved location had taken the edge off his guilty conscience, but now it returned full force. He gripped his mandolin case and hid his discomfort under a give-a-care expression.

Fortunately, their destination was only a few blocks away at a saloon called McClellan's. Lively music was emanating from the upstairs windows, and punctuated by voices, hand claps, and laughter. "What if they don't let me in?" Henry said in a low voice.

"Act like you belong," Nikola said. "You're tall and it's dark. Follow me." He led the way inside, where the dim, crowded room was thick with pungent cigar smoke and boisterous conversation. Some customers sat at a large, handsomely carved bar. They were reflected in a wide mirror on the wall behind the barkeeps. There was a constant clink of glasses, and the music got louder as they approached a staircase at the back.

Upstairs, they entered a spacious room with a circle of musicians in the middle and tables and chairs around the perimeter. Men and woman occupied these as they nodded, tapped their toes, or clapped along to the music. But it was the players themselves who riveted Henry's attention. It was as if a giant hand had plucked musicians out of each Midway show: two or three Irish fiddlers, a Turk with a tambour, a stout Islander with a guitar; a tall African with a drum; a German with a trumpet, and another islander with a gourd covered in strands of shells.

There was a tiny Mexican woman with a guitar, and assorted Americans and Europeans with banjos, mandolins, flutes, and cellos. Off to the side, a black man played the piano with a curious jolty rhythm. Men and women alike wore western clothes, with unique touches such as a bright scarf, vest, or unusual hat. As one song ended, someone would shout out the title of another and take the lead. The others either knew it or followed along the best they could, resulting in friendly musical chaos.

Henry grinned at Nikola. "This is terrific!" His friend led the way to a pair of empty chairs and Henry self-consciously pulled out his mandolin. He'd tuned it earlier, but with this many musicians and instruments, being in tune was a lost cause. Happily, he found he could strum along on most of the songs and play a little fancier on the tunes he knew. Nikola played well, only squeaking a little. For fun, Henry yelled out, "Oh! Susannah," which resulted in an exotic, enthusiastic rendering complete with tambour, rattle, and some kind of bell-like percussive instrument.

After an hour, he and Nik packed up their instruments and waved their goodbyes. "Come again, lads," a red-haired fiddler called after them.

"This was the best night of my life," Henry said as they emerged into the pleasant Chicago night. There were still revelers walking about and carriages with fine horses clip-clopping by.

"I'm glad," Nikola said. "I'll be dreaming of music tonight."

They parted ways at Henry's street. "See ya around," he said, and sped off, frequently looking over his shoulder in case any shady characters were following. When he got back to Mrs. Wilson's, he tiptoed upstairs and hung his clothes near the window to air out. He lay awake for a long time with the rhythms of the evening pulsing through him. What a night! He couldn't wait to do it again.

Chapter Fifteen

Today was a big day. Juna woke up before dawn, with thoughts of her class presentation and the foot spa launch zooming around her brain. She took extra care with her toilet, wearing one of her nicer dresses. Now, after a long morning of nervous anticipation, she wiped sweaty hands on her skirt while listening to one of the younger students read a Psalm. Juna could see the Bible trembling in the girl's hands as she rushed through the selection, making the sweet verses sound rather melodramatic. She inhaled and exhaled slowly through her nose to calm her own pounding heart. She was next.

"A good effort," Ida said as the girl hurried back to her chair. "Continue to practice it, speaking slowly."

Mary Blood added, "Drawing out the vowels will help with pacing, as well." She looked at Juna. "Mrs. Lewis, your turn, please."

Juna took her position at the front of the room, aware of many pairs of eyes on her. Holding her hands loosely in front of her, she took a moment to breathe and feel the floor under her feet—a calming technique she'd learned from Miss Blood. She'd practiced and practiced her piece over the past few days, whispering it, reciting it forcefully, softly, and crisply to discover the right balance of emphasis and speed. "I'd like to recite a selection by Holmes on perseverance," she said, much too fast. Forcing herself to slow down, she began.

"'Stick to your aim: the mongrel's hold will slip,
But only crowbars loose the bull-dog's grip;
Small as he looks, the jaw that never yields
Drags down the bellowing monarch of the fields.'"

She glanced around to see her classmates and teachers smiling their approval.

"Nicely done," Ida said. "My only suggestion would be to slow down the words 'drags down' to heighten the emphasis." Mary Blood nodded in agreement.

Juna returned to her seat, feeling elated. Her hands tingled with energy. She'd done it!

Nancy, who'd been the first to recite—and despite her modesty, was a natural at it—gave her arm a quick squeeze. "You were terrific," she whispered.

"Thanks," Juna whispered back. "One hurdle down and one to go."

Henry arrived early enough at the fair to cut through Wooded Island, hoping to see Tomoko. He yawned as he approached Phoenix Hall, but the lingering excitement over the jam session gave rhythm to his steps. He jogged up the stairs and took a quick look inside, but there was no sign of her. Disappointed, he wandered back outside. The Hall had an interesting garden around it, with shrubs and small trees that look deformed on purpose.

Small boulders were artfully placed near the path. As he neared the end of the building, he heard a girl singing in Japanese. He followed the sound a short distance and peered around a large flowering shrub.

Tomoko, wearing her pink kimono, was perched on a boulder a few feet away. It was a private spot near the water, mostly hidden from view by a tangle of shrubs and small trees. As she sang in a sweet, clear voice, she "flew" one of her folded birds. Henry didn't want to intrude, but was so charmed by the scene that his feet refused to move. When the song ended on a soft high note, the girl gazed out at the lagoon to watch an electric launch glide past.

Henry was torn. Should he announce himself? This might be his only chance to speak with her alone. He took a tentative step forward, which made the gravel crunch and the girl jump up in alarm. Her expression relaxed when she recognized him. Relieved he hadn't scared her off, Henry raised his hand and said, "Good morning, Miss Tomoko," as friendly as he could sound. He hoped he was pronouncing her name correctly. He'd been practicing.

She bowed slightly. "Hello, Henry-san."

He liked the way her accent softened his name. Even better were the dimples that deepened with her smile before she turned and hurried back toward Phoenix Hall. He understood. It wouldn't do to have her father find her alone with a strange boy. He pushed past the shrub and stood beside the boulder. It came to his knee, and the top was flat enough to make a good seat. He tested it out, then decided he'd better go. He'd hate it if she was forbidden to sit there because of him.

He thought of the paper bird that sat on a shelf in his room at Mrs. Wilson's house. What if he left something of *his* for Tomoko to find? He felt in his pockets and found a lemon drop wrapped in waxed paper. Satisfied that it wouldn't rain that day, he carefully placed it in a small groove on the rock.

As he headed toward the Mines and Mining Building, where he was to meet Peterson, he found himself whistling. He'd check the rock later if he had a chance.

———◇———

Juna stopped at the information desk when she arrived at the Missouri Building. "Has anyone registered for the foot spa?" she asked.

The attendant shook his head. "Not yet, though I have heard a number of comments."

Juna found this heartening. "There must be interest, then."

The man fidgeted with his pencil. "*Interest* may be a strong word, ma'am, but it certainly has brightened the day for our visitors." He gave her an encouraging smile.

"Oh." She wasn't sure how to take that. "I suppose it could take a few days to catch on."

He twitched his head sideways. "Mm-hm."

She thanked him and went to find Annie. "What have you heard?" she asked, drawing the older woman aside.

Annie glanced toward a handful of women relaxing in the parlor. "The idea of it seems to be intriguing, albeit amusing. Give it time, dear. It's only the first day."

Juna went upstairs to heat the foot soak and have it ready. The spa room looked inviting, with comfortable chairs and vases of pink carnations and purple phlox. New curtains in a floral print framed the window. Each chair had a basin beside it, waiting to be used. A table held a neat stack of towels, several shoe hooks, and the bottles of lotion. Nearby, a small box for the nickel fee sat beside an unopened bottle of Lewis Vinegar. Juna smiled. Mrs. Fletcher surely thought of that special touch. This was the Missouri Building, after all.

The only thing missing was customers.

Returning to the parlor, she spotted a woman sitting with her feet propped up. She took a deep breath and approached her with a smile. "Consider treating your sore feet to our new foot spa, madam."

"A foot spa?" the woman said with a shrill laugh. "That's the silliest thing I ever heard."

"Oh, well, I—" Juna stammered, grasping for a way to respond. She noticed they'd caught the attention of three young women sitting at a table.

Annie appeared beside her. "That's what I thought, too, until I tried it," she said.

"And did it help?" the woman asked.

"Oh, yes," Annie replied. "It's got special properties."

"What are these properties?"

Annie leaned forward a little, as if sharing a secret. "I can tell you that it's a special blend of cider vinegar and herbs created by our own Mrs. Lewis. I have a bunion which makes standing for several hours difficult. After trying the soak, I walked from here to the Administration Building with almost no pain."

"My." The woman looked interested, yet skeptical.

Juna tried not to wring her hands. Annie had never mentioned a bunion, and here she was making her sound like a snake-oil salesman. Her soak was good, but certainly not miraculous.

The woman dragged her feet off the ottoman and stood up. "It's still the silliest idea I've ever heard," she said with another piercing laugh. "Good luck." With that, she picked up her things and trudged out of the room. The young women at the table grinned at each other, obviously amused by the whole spectacle. Juna felt a sinking sensation as she watched the woman leave. If this was the general reaction, the spa was doomed.

Annie looked stricken. "I'm sorry, Juna," she whispered. "I was only trying to help."

"I appreciate that," Juna whispered back, wondering why she'd pursued this ridiculous idea in the first place. "Just please don't embellish it so much."

Annie's brow furrowed. "What do you mean?"

"About the bunion and all. I don't want to give folks false hope."

"But it's true."

"It is? When did you try it?"

"Last night. My bunion was killing me after being on my feet all day."

This stunned Juna. "I do apologize, Annie. It helped that much?"

"Yes, and I really did walk to the—"

"Excuse me," one of the young women called. "We'd like to register, please."

Juna was so surprised, she could only say, "Pardon me?"

The woman gave her a bright smile. "The foot spa. May we try it? We've been walking for hours and hours and have decided it sounds sensational."

"Why, yes," Juna said. "I will meet you upstairs in a few minutes." This pronouncement delighted the women, who sprang up and began collecting parcels and lunch baskets. Juna gave Annie's hand a quick squeeze. "Thank you."

Fifteen minutes later, all three women were sitting with their eyes closed and skirts pulled to their knees as they soaked their feet in a steaming basin.

"Ooh, this is lovely."

"Heavenly."

"Mmmm."

Juna sat just outside the partially closed door, ready to give assistance, if needed, and to make sure no other visitors—men in particular—wandered past the *Guests of the Spa Only Between 4:00 p.m. - 6 p.m.* notice further down the hallway. She'd made sure the soak was warm, but not overly so due to the hot day. A breeze off the lake kept the room comfortable and circulated the pleasant fragrance of lavender, mint, and other herbs intertwined with the sweet-sharp smell of Lewis Vinegar. *Spa-like,* she thought, although she had no direct experience with an actual spa. All in all, she thought three guests on the first day was encouraging.

Mrs. Fletcher had stopped by a few minutes earlier and heard the effusive and ongoing exclamations. "Congratulations," she said in a soft voice. "They seem very enthusiastic about the experience."

"Hopefully, they will spread the word," Juna said. She knew they needed to draw at least fifteen women per day to make it worthwhile. When the twenty-minute session was over, the women set to the task of drying their feet and putting stockings and shoes back on. Juna carried the basins to the kitchen. By the time she'd returned the three basins, clean and dry, to the spa room, the women were dressed and dropping nickels into the box.

"My feet have never felt better," the one with the bright smile said. "I have to tell my mother about this." The other two concurred, naming a friend or sister they'd like to bring.

Juna knew that enthusiastic talk was just that, but welcome, nonetheless. "Thank you," she said. "I look forward to meeting them."

She took a few minutes to straighten the room, then allowed herself a little happy dance. Her idea worked! She crossed to the window and looked out at the nearby buildings and the avenue that ran between the Missouri Building and the Art Palace. There were more people out and about now that the sun was lower in the sky. A partial view of the lake revealed numerous boats in the distance.

There was a soft rap on the door. "Hi, Mama."

"Henry," she said, turning around and crossing the room. She kissed him on the cheek and smoothed a windblown curl behind his ear. "How was your day with Mr. Peterson?"

"Eventful," he said. "We started at Mining, then spent some time back at the Transportation Building looking at wheels. He's very knowledgeable about them, but I think it's all for show as he only recently took up riding. He knows a little about most everything," he added in amusement.

"I suppose that's why your grandfather likes doing business with him," Juna said. "He's good at what he does. When will you see him again?"

"Soon. He's waiting downstairs for us."

"He is?" Juna touched her hair. She hadn't looked in a mirror for hours. "I'm nearly finished here. Please tell him I'll be down shortly."

"All right," Henry said. He took a few steps and turned. "How was your spa opening?"

"Better than I expected," she said. "We had three guests."

"That's good news," he said, and zipped off toward the stairs.

A quick visit to the toilet room confirmed that, aside from a few loose strands, her hair was in pretty good shape. She collected her things and went downstairs, where she found Henry and Mr. Peterson by the fountain. "Good evening," she said. "I hear you've been encouraging my son's new passion."

Peterson feigned an abashed expression. "I felt he needed relief from rocks, minerals, and noise." He nudged Henry with his elbow. "Shall I put in a word with Mr. Lewis to buy you a wheel?"

"No!" Juna and Henry spoke in unison.

Peterson looked between them. "No?"

"He thinks they're a waste of time," Henry said.

Juna knew that wasn't quite true, so she just shrugged and gave a vague nod.

Peterson seemed to sense an underlying issue and moved smoothly to a new topic. "May I treat you and Henry to supper at the Cafe de la Marine? Their fish is excellent and the view off the veranda is pleasant."

This was so unexpected that Juna found herself stammering. "Oh! That is very kind of you. Perhaps another evening. It's been a long day and I want to get home, have a light supper, and relax with a book."

"I understand," he said. "I promise to give you adequate warning next time." He winked at Henry. "I trust you're learning from my mistakes?"

"Yessir," Henry said, smirking a little. Juna nearly rolled her eyes at the pair of them.

Peterson laughed. "Enough said about that. May I at least escort you to the gate?"

Juna couldn't think of a good excuse why he shouldn't. "Certainly," she said. "Though I fear we're keeping you from your supper."

"My appetite will keep a little longer," he said. As they walked down the avenue toward the nearest gate, he asked Juna about the spa opening and congratulated her on a successful first day. The sun was bright in her eyes, making it nearly impossible to see the Ferris Wheel in the distance. The rumble of carriages and wagons on the nearby street carried over the fence. Classical music emanated from one of the other state buildings, and the elevated train passed a few hundred yards away, making the ground vibrate.

After they exited the gate, Peterson said, "I want to propose a different activity for Thursday. I'd like to treat you both to a ride on the Captive Balloon."

"Let's do it," Henry said in excitement. "You'll go, won't you, Mama?"

The thought of going up in the balloon frightened her, but with all Peterson was doing for them, it only seemed right to accept his invitation. "I suppose so," she said, followed by a happy yell from Henry and a broad smile from Peterson. She felt her cheeks go warm. It had been a long time since a man had looked at her like that. She had to admit it felt nice, even if their relationship was strictly platonic.

CHAPTER SIXTEEN

July 19, 1893—The St. Louis Daily
NOTES FROM THE FAIR:

The Fair Betwixt Midnight and Dawn

I had a most remarkable experience last night. A group of journalists were invited to stay at the Fair until the wee hours, long after the crowds had departed, and the electricity turned off. Oh! What a different place it was, with the only illumination provided by a scattering of stars and the shy moon as it danced between wisps of clouds in the dark sky.

We stood spellbound on the Peristyle, with the restless lake behind us and the moon-kissed basin before us. The silent, sleeping palaces offered the promise of daylight-inspired grandeur, but for a time we were quietly enthralled by the Dream City dreaming.

—Zenobia A. Thom,
Special Correspondent

When class began on Wednesday morning, Ida introduced a neatly dressed man of average height. "I am pleased to welcome our guest lecturer, Professor Hiram Stone," she said. "He joins us today from the University of Chicago and will lecture on the finer points of elocution and presentation."

Professor Stone appeared to be in his mid-thirties, though closely-trimmed sideburns and mustache gave him a boyish appearance. Short, reddish-brown hair was slightly messy, as if he frequently ran his fingers through it. His looks were more intriguing than handsome, Juna decided, as he acknowledged the class with a friendly smile. "Thank you, Mrs. Riley," he said. "I'm happy to be back at your fine school."

Juna found the professor's voice resonant and exceedingly pleasing to the ear. There was a familiar quality about it, but she couldn't say why. When he turned to ask Ida a question about the placement of a chart, Nancy leaned over and whispered, "I could listen to Hiram read the train schedule." When Juna's eyebrows shot up, Nancy explained, "We're old friends."

The professor waited for Ida to sit down, then turned abruptly to the class—his manner urgent, his voice loud. "A horse! A horse! My kingdom for a horse." After a startled silence, the students laughed. "Today we will talk about stress," he said, eyes crinkling at their—obviously—intended response. "Stress relates to the way in which force of voice is applied to that which we are speaking, be it single sounds, words, or sentences. There are several kinds of stress: *Radical,* which is explosive, as I just demonstrated; *Medium,* which has more of a swell and decline; *Thorough,* when force is equal throughout; *Vanishing* occurs when the swell ends explosively; and *Tremor,* which requires a vibratory, tremulous tone." At once, his demeanor changed, and he assumed a soft, mournful voice.

"'And, oh! To see the briny tears fast hurrying down her cheek,
As she offered up the prayer, in thought; she was afraid to speak,
Lest she might waken one she loved far better than her life,
For she had all a mother's heart, had that poor collier's wife.
With hands uplifted, see, she kneels beside the sufferer's bed,
And prays that He would spare her boy, and take herself instead.'"

His delivery was so polished, so skillfully presented, that Juna found her hand pressed to the base of her throat. Judging by the awed silence in the classroom, she wasn't the only one affected.

"That was, of course, a portion of "Little Jim," by Edward Farmer," Professor Stone said. "With practice, stress will be one of the most effective tools to strengthen and develop flexibility and intonations of the voice." He turned to the chart. "Let's begin by reciting these examples of Intermittent stress."

Juna joined her classmates as they rose and performed the posture exercise.

The professor, caught off guard, said, "As many times as I've been here, that never fails to impress me."

Juna found the professor to be an excellent teacher with an even manner and a good sense of humor. In the brief break before their section on Physical Culture, he came over to greet Nancy, who clasped both his hands. "You were magnificent, Professor," she said in a voice such as one would use with a close friend.

Juna, who'd gathered her notebook and was waiting for Nancy, nodded in agreement. Her friend touched her arm and introduced her to the professor.

"I'm pleased to make your acquaintance, Mrs. Lewis," Professor Stone said. "It is apparent that you enjoy the class."

"I'm giving it my best effort," she said, noting that he was only a few inches taller than her. "Sitting beside Nancy makes it especially fun."

"Of that, I have no doubt," he said, giving his friend a fond look before moving on to chat with other students. Nancy grinned at Juna, managing to look both pleased and mysterious.

Good for them, Juna thought. "I'm looking forward to our visit to the Art Palace today," she said as they moved to the other classroom. "Henry took a little convincing—I set Zennie loose on him—but I'm sure he'll enjoy it more than he expects."

"I imagine he'd rather poke amongst the guns or Indian exhibits than view art with three old women," Nancy said.

"More likely old bones and photographs."

"He sounds like a charming boy."

Juna nodded. "He's a good son."

———◦———

It was nearly time for Henry to meet his mother, aunt, and their friend Nancy Collins at the Art Palace, but he made a quick detour through Wooded Island so he could check the rock. He hadn't had a chance yesterday and was eager to see if Tomoko had found the piece of candy. Pretending to look at the gardens, he made his way past the building to the tangle of brush near the water's edge. He didn't expect her to be sitting there, but the possibility made his heart beat a little faster.

The candy was gone. In its place was a tiny paper bird, which he picked up and held in his open hand. It was half the size of the other bird. How in the world did she do it? He liked the idea that she'd made it just for him. He patted his pockets, but had no more candy. Coins or tickets didn't seem appropriate. Looking around for inspiration, he found a pretty pebble nearby. It was tiny like the bird and had some pink color to it. Girls liked pink, and it reminded him of her robes. It would have to do. He warmed it in his hand a few moments before placing it in the small groove on the rock. Hopefully, she wouldn't brush it away without thinking.

The sound of approaching voices launched him into action. He jumped over a low shrub and made a beeline for the shore, trying not to trample the garden. Hands on hips, he made a show of looking at the boats on the lagoon and the Great Buildings that filled the view on the opposite shore. He glanced back toward Phoenix Hall, where two gardeners were pruning spent blossoms off the shrubs. They seemed relaxed and uninterested in him, visiting as they worked.

Henry made his way back to the main path, giving the gardeners a wide berth. As he passed the Hall, he made a quick decision to go in and see if Tomoko was inside. If she was alone, maybe he could thank her for the bird.

He entered behind two women and followed their lead by taking a pamphlet from a smiling attendant. The women joined a group listening to the same tour guide he'd seen before. Happily, Tomoko was at her table making birds for three children and their parents. Henry hung back and pretended to study the carved phoenix panels near the ceiling. According to the pamphlet, they were called *ramma*. He checked his watch, silently entreating Tomoko to hurry and finish the birds. He only had about ten minutes to get to the Art Palace.

"Thank you, miss," the children said as they stood up.

Henry waited until the family left, then quickly walked over and dropped down on a cushion. "Thank you for the bird, Miss Tomoko," he said in a quiet voice. "It's very nice."

Her cheeks dimpled. "Thank you for the candy," she whispered, and picked up a new sheet of paper to fold.

Henry knew it was for show in case someone was observing them. The shortness of time pressed upon him. Why-oh-why did he agree to go to the Art Palace today? His words came out in a rush. "I have to go, but I'll come again soon."

Her finger slid along the edge of a fold. She glanced over at the tour group before meeting his eyes. Her dimples deepened. "*Sayonara*, Henry-san."

He grinned and stood up. "Bye, Miss Tomoko," he said, and sauntered out, doing his best to look casual despite his heart thumping along. Fueled by elation, he jogged all the way to the Art Palace, stopping only four times to catch his breath.

He found the ladies and met Miss Collins, who was taller than Mother and almost as pretty. She wore a billowy jacket embroidered with colorful birds, stuffed her gloves into her handbag as soon as they entered the building, and seemed to wear a constant expression of private amusement. Knowledgeable about both art and the exhibits in the Art Palace, she wasted no time in hustling them to what she considered 'the most compelling and thought-inspiring' pieces. With her manly hands and give-a-care attitude, she was the most exotic and relaxed woman Henry had ever met. He liked her very much.

Since coming to the Exposition, Henry had developed a keen appreciation for art—sculpture in particular, as there were naked breasts at every turn. Smooth, sculpted, and often on statues over ten feet tall. Huge, fascinating breasts full of allegorical importance! He could get an eye-full just by pretending to study an architectural feature or *bas-relief* on the nearest building. The paintings in the Art Palace were a different matter, however, especially when viewed in mixed company.

Zenobia considered herself to be a progressive, modern woman, and believed that the human form was 'A beautiful and appropriate subject for sculpture and art. Ergo, nothing to be ashamed about.' Miss Collins heartily joined her in this view, as they were engaged in a lively conversation, which included teasing Mother who, while open-minded about such things, tended to say *'My!'* when faced with daring subject matter.

They were currently in the French section of the Art Palace, and clearly the French had nothing to be ashamed about, either. Henry hung back, wishing his friends were there to snicker with him over thinly draped goddesses and frolicking nymphs. As it was, he was too self-conscious to do more than give each painting a quick glance for fear of looking too interested in the female body. He smiled to himself—there was plenty to glance at.

As they entered the rotunda that featured a sculpture garden, the women stopped and waited for him to catch up. "Henry," Zenobia said. "Miss Collins has invited us to join her bicycle tour next Monday. Would you like to go? She'll appropriate wheels for all of us if need be."

Breasts were forgotten. "Would I!" he said. "Will you go too, Mother?" he asked, already knowing the answer.

She shook her head. "I will decline this time. I—I need to study."

Miss Collins raised straight, thick eyebrows. "You do? Come with us, Juna. It'll be fun."

"Thank you, Nancy," Mother said, resolute. "Perhaps another time."

"Are you sure?" Zenobia asked in a gentle voice.

"Mm-hm." Mother's smile seemed forced. "Let's go look at the American exhibit, shall we? A visitor at the state building recommended a painting by John Vanderpoel called "Blessed Are They That Mourn.""

Miss Collins graciously dropped the subject. "I'm familiar with that one," she said as they resumed walking. "I met the artist at a party a few weeks ago. Nice man. Short, handsome, and of fine character. He has five paintings here ..."

Henry exchanged a glance with Zenobia. They both knew that getting Mother on a bicycle would take a miracle.

Henry and Nikola sat on the Peristyle the next day eating sausage rolls and watching an array of boats out on the water. They'd seen each other near a food booth and Henry suggested they have lunch together.

Nikola wiped his mouth with the back of his hand. "Do you want to come to another music party at McClellan's next Monday?"

"Heck, yes," Henry said, confident he could sneak out again, attend the party, and be back in bed with no one the wiser. Besides, it would be the last one he could go to, as they'd be leaving a week later. He wasn't about to miss it.

"Good. We'll meet at the same corner. Maybe carry a big stick this time," he added with a grin.

Henry gave his friend a playful pop on the head. "Ha-ha."

They watched the big whaleback dock alongside the pier. It felt like ages since he and Mother arrived on it the first day. So much had happened in two weeks! He never would have guessed he'd be sitting here eating lunch with a Serbian chair roller, leaving gifts on a rock for a Japanese girl, and seeing so many interesting and unusual things.

"Boats give me a bad feeling," Nikola said.

"How come?" Henry asked.

"Terrible experience," Nik said. "My mother and baby sister died on the crossing to America."

Henry turned to his friend, dropping his hand with the sausage roll to his knee. "I'm sorry," he said. "That must've been dreadful."

Nik crumpled the paper wrapper from his lunch into a ball. "Yeah," he said. "It was."

"How old were you?" Henry asked. Having lost a parent at a young age, he felt qualified to ask.

"Eight or nine, maybe."

Henry nodded. "I can relate. I lost my father six years ago. Do you have other family?"

Nik gave him a sympathetic look. "Sorry to hear that. I still have my father and older sister, Jasna. She's married."

"What does your father do?" Henry asked before stuffing the last bite of sausage roll into his mouth.

"He worked as a bricklayer when we first came to Chicago, but he has bad eyes and went blind two years ago. Now he teaches Shakespeare at a settlement house in the nineteenth ward. He was a teacher back in Serbia."

Henry wanted to ask more about Mr. Petrovich and the settlement house, but Nikola slapped his knees and stood up. "Time to work, my friend."

"And time to meet my mother and Peterson the Knowledgeable," Henry said, stuffing his own wrapper into his pocket. "We're going up in the balloon today." He tried to sound nonchalant, though he was excited. He reckoned his friend had not ridden it.

They set out across the Court of Honor. Nikola set a good pace despite pushing a chair. "Your Peterson reminds me of the ship's captain," he said. "Big voice. Much bluster."

The force of his friend's words surprised Henry. "He does?"

"Yeah. Except the captain was a wicked man."

"He was?"

"Yeah. He threw sick people overboard."

Henry jerked his head toward Nikola as the implications sank in. "You don't mean—"

"Yeah. I do."

This was such a horrifying piece of information that Henry was at loss for words. "My god, Nik," was all he could manage.

"It was a long time ago," his friend said, "but I still dream about it sometimes." He looked away and cleared his throat.

They continued walking in silence as they began passing the Manufactures Building, where a steady stream of visitors came and went. Out on the basin, electric launches and gondolas glided through the sunlit water. At length, Henry said, "I was young when my father died in a high wheel race, but I still have flashes of memory about it at odd moments. Two racers helped bring him back to town. I remember him stretched out on a table and my mother mopping blood off his head. Grandpa was there, but I don't remember much other than him demanding explanations. I sat in the corner of the room crying my eyes out."

Nikola spoke in a kind voice. "Time makes it better, doesn't it?"

"Yeah, mostly," Henry said, realizing that this was the first time in years he'd talked about that day. Somehow, sharing the story with Nik made him feel lighter, as if a weight he didn't realize he'd been carrying had been lifted. Perhaps it was the same for his friend.

Their mutual reverie was interrupted when a man with an old woman on his arm waved at Nikola. "Are you for hire?" he called.

"Yes, sir!" Nik turned to Henry, his usual bravado back in evidence. "Thanks for lunch. Don't forget the party. I'll wait for you like last time."

"See ya then," Henry said as he veered away. "And lunch is on you next time."

"*Ti si budala.*" Nikola was grinning, so Henry reckoned it was a friendly insult.

As he continued toward the Administration Building where he was to meet his mother and Peterson, his thoughts turned to Tomoko. Had she found the pebble he'd left the day before? He'd spent the morning with his aunt and hadn't had a chance to check.

He spotted Mother and Peterson standing near the fountain. She appeared to be listening intently as he pointed out something or another. It could be anything from a sculpture to a bird. Whatever the subject, his mentor was sure to have an expert opinion about it. Henry walked faster, feeling the need to rescue Mother from Peterson's lecture.

"Here you are," she said, smiling as he approached them. "Did you have lunch?"

"Yes'm."

"Something to drink?"

"Yes'm."

"Ready to ride the balloon?"

"Yes, ma'am!"

Peterson swept an arm in the direction of the Terminal Building. "Let's take the train up to the Midway."

Henry liked that idea. He was ready to sit down and rest. What he didn't like was how Peterson touched Mother's elbow and smiled at her as he spoke.

Juna shaded her eyes and looked nervously at the Captive Balloon. Her courage had begun to waver somewhere between the Terminal Building and the Midway.

"C'mon, Mama," Henry pleaded. "It'll be fine."

"It's perfectly safe," Peterson assured her. "See the machine that controls the rope? It slowly lets it out, then slowly pulls it back down. I've been up several times, and it's a thrill."

Music from a phonograph played a popular song. The tables at the concession's cafe were filled with people, some of whom watched them with obvious amusement. She imagined that nervous Nellies like herself provided additional entertainment.

She chewed her bottom lip and reconsidered. The balloon went straight up, after all. And the thick rope looked secure enough. Remembering the excitement of riding the Ferris Wheel, and the fact that Henry was practically vibrating out of his skin, she said, "All right. I'll do it." Her son gave a happy yell, making the onlookers laugh. A few clapped.

Peterson grinned. "You won't regret it."

The balloon's captain waved them into the large basket. "And you," he said to two German men, making it a party of six. Juna held on tight to the edge of the basket, hoping her gloves hid her trembling hands. Henry and Peterson took positions on either side of her, like guardians. Feeling hemmed in by Peterson's *presence*, she edged closer to her son. Above them, the balloon quivered like an alive thing, eager for the sky.

After a few words of introduction, light-hearted warnings about keeping all body parts inside the basket, and general reassurances about the safety of the balloon, the captain signaled the man at the rope machine, and they began their ascent. The folks on the ground cheered and waved. Juna joined the others in waving back, excitement and laughter nudging her nervousness to one side.

Up, up, up, they went, with the Midway gently falling away under them. Up, up, past the rooftops. Moments later, they were even with the top of the Ferris Wheel. They waved at the passengers in the cars. Now they were higher. Up, up, up. The Midway stretched out beneath them, joining with the fairgrounds, domes, and waterways which gleamed in the mid-afternoon sun.

"Smooth," Henry said, drawing the word out. "Wish I had a camera." He pointed northward. "You can see across the entire city."

Sure enough, Chicago looked like a mass of grey, black, and green, with streets and parks, tiny people, and horses. Long trains trailed smoke. It was easy to see why the Exposition was called the White City, and Chicago, the Grey City, with the dirtier air hovering over the city proper. Lake Michigan resembled an inland sea, stretching toward the horizon. A jumble of sounds rose from the cities beneath them, intruding on the otherwise peaceful atmosphere.

One of the Germans made a remark, causing his friend to snort with laughter. Peterson leaned in and whispered, "He said, 'I hope no one is feeling suicidal today.'"

"Indeed," Juna said. Henry snickered on the other side of her. She turned her attention back to the fairgrounds. "Oh, look! Do you see the windmills way over there? And the Manufactures Building is still enormous, even at this height."

A seagull circled far below them. Henry moved away to look from the other side of the basket. The breeze at this altitude was brisk, pulling at Juna's hat. She reached up to tighten her ribbons and tottered slightly. Peterson steadied her with a large, warm hand to her back. "Thank you, Mr. Peterson," she said, grabbing the railing again.

He smiled at her, clearly pleased at her enjoyment of the ride and his opportunity to be gallant. He leaned in again. "Please, call me Archie."

Oh, dear. Juna preferred a formal distance between them, but after all his kindness to her and Henry, it seemed rude not to accept this gesture of friendship. She dipped her head. "Junaluska," she said.

"As lovely a name as I've heard."

She waved off his compliment. "A pretty name for a homely apple."

"Never," he said in a voice so low that it was nearly a growl.

She reddened, aware of the lack of conversation in the basket.

"*Liebe ist in der Luft*," said the German wit, and she felt like shrinking when all the grown men laughed. The meaning was clear enough. She brushed past them to stand by Henry, who grinned when she rolled her eyes at him.

There was a small jerk as the basket reached the end of its tether. "Here we are at twelve-hundred feet," the captain announced. He pulled an American flag from its stand and waved it. They cheered and clapped, reveling in the view.

"This is the grandest thing I've ever done," Juna said, twisting to see in all directions. "To be up high with the birds and clouds. It's like being closer to heaven, don't you think?" She fell silent, thinking of Craig and his love of adventure. He wouldn't have hesitated at all to ride the balloon. Appreciation for Mr. Peterson's—Archie's—generosity seeped into the moment. She looked up at Henry, who was staring east toward Michigan. His father would be so proud of him; happy that he was having these wonderful experiences. She covered her son's hand. "I wish he could see us now."

Henry looked at her with a gentle gaze, so like his father's. He turned his hand, enclosing her own with his long fingers. "Maybe he can."

A tug on the basket indicated the rope was drawing them back to earth. She touched the apple charm at her throat. "I wish we could stay up here longer."

"Me too," Henry said, leaning against her for a couple of heartbeats.

After disembarking, they had a snack of cold apple cider and popcorn before heading back toward the main grounds. Henry ran ahead to watch a parade of animals outside Hagenbeck's Arena while Juna and Archie followed at a more leisurely pace.

"Henry tells me he's joining a bicycle ride next Monday," Archie said. "Are you going as well?"

Juna groaned inwardly. The subject was bound to come up, eventually. "No," she said. "I'm looking forward to a free morning. I don't ride."

He smiled down at her. "I'll teach you how, if you'll allow me."

"You ride?" she asked, hoping to divert his attention. He had the ability to hold forth on many subjects.

"I do," he said. "My mates talked me into buying a wheel recently. It's last year's model from Century but performs nicely. What do you say? We could meet at Washington Park. It's not far and has a lot of open space."

Juna was feeling squirmy and determined to change the subject. "I don't believe so, but thank you."

"Oh, come now," he said, with the enthusiasm of a man on a mission. "It's a modern form of exercise for women, and highly enjoyable."

"I don't have a wheel."

"I can easily borrow one from a friend whose wife is abroad."

"I couldn't."

"You can."

"I'm clumsy."

"You aren't!"

He seemed determined to wear her down. "I don't have the right attire," she said, grasping at excuses. Men generally shied away from talk of fashion.

"Oh, ho!" he said. "Easily remedied. Wear a lighter-weight dress and shorten the skirt a couple inches."

"You are quite the expert in women's fashions," she said with a nervous laugh.

"Why on earth are you so against it?" he said, a touch exasperated. "It's fun."

Juna sighed. There was no way around it. "Bicycles frighten me because I have a bad association with them," she said.

Archie held her elbow, immediately contrite. They stood still, parting the eastward-walking fairgoers like rocks in a stream. "My dear, Junaluska,

I apologize for being a bear about it. Would you care to tell me why? You'll find my ear to be sympathetic."

"My husband died in a high wheel accident," she said, realizing that Seymour had not shared that bit of family history with him. "And since then—" She trailed off and finished with a shrug.

Archie's forehead furrowed as he lightly touched her arm. "How dreadful for you," he said. "For all of you."

She nodded. "It's been a long time now, but, as you can see, I'm still affected."

"I understand," he said as they resumed walking. "I lost my mother at a young age. There's a certain soap she used that smelled of lilacs. Now and then, in a store or on the train, I get a whiff of it and have to pretend I have something in my eye."

"Thank you for telling me," she said, glancing up and meeting his gaze. "I'm glad you have memories of her. My mother died a few months after I was born. I suppose the silver lining was a loving step-mother and a sister."

"Yes, indeed."

"Sadly, my father died just before my marriage."

"How fortunate you had someone to comfort you," Archie said in a kind voice.

"It was another silver lining, though I didn't realize it at the time," Juna said with a small laugh. "That's the challenge, isn't it? Remembering to open our eyes and look."

He smiled down at her. "Opening our eyes is always the challenge."

By the time they caught up with Henry in front of Hagenbeck's Arena, Archie was back to his usual, gregarious self. As they watched the parade of exotic animals, he said, "Look at that elephant, Henry. Did you ever fancy a ride on one?"

"Of course. I'm game for anything with altitude," Henry said, making Juna laugh. Her son had his father's zest for life. She swiped at her eyes. It sure was dusty on the Midway.

CHAPTER EIGHTEEN

July 21, 1893—The St. Louis Daily
NOTES FROM THE FAIR:

A Surprise in Choral Hall

The oddest thing happened yesterday as I was passing Choral Hall. Expecting the usual choir or soloist, imagine my surprise when I heard the sound of yodeling drifting from the open windows. I couldn't pass this up, naturally, so in I went. It seems that a member of a visiting choir from Austria had gotten separated from his compatriots and was sending out vocal versions of smoke signals. I begged him to continue, and he graced me with the dearest little song in which his voice jumped and cracked in the most splendid way. Soon thereafter, his friends—delighted with his ingenuity—rushed in and led him away to the nearest chocolate seller.

———————————

One, two, three. One, two, three. This was the timing of the loveliest waltz I've ever heard. An adept orchestra entertained my friends and I last night as we dined in the German Village. Pork chops and sauerkraut tasted even more divine under the stars, with the Ferris Wheel lit up and turning, and the crowds enjoying a perfect summer evening. We raised a glass of Riesling and toasted the food, the restaurant, the music, the White City, and each other.

—Zenobia A. Thom,
Special Correspondent

After a morning of poking around the Anthropology Building, Henry headed up to Phoenix Hall. The grounds were damp from an earlier shower, and now the hot sun made the air extra steamy. Here and there, workmen tended the grass and flower beds. Visitors strolled along the pathways or lingered in the shadier spots. Gardeners attended the rose beds on the south part of the island, but the Japanese gardens were deserted. Good. He headed straight for the rock, full of questions. Had Tomoko seen the pebble and recognized it as a gift? And if so, would there be a new gift for him?

The rock was empty, but Henry's burst of excitement was short-lived when he found the pebble at its base. Luckily, he'd come prepared. He reached into his pocket and pulled out a clever thread-holder he'd found at a souvenir shop on the Midway. Fashioned from smooth wood, it was in the shape of a bowling pin smaller than his pinky. An etching of the Art Palace decorated the outside, and it pulled apart to reveal a tiny double spool of brown and white thread. It seemed like the kind of thing a girl could use. Henry was proud of his purchase. "Tomoko," he whispered and placed the thread-holder in the groove on the rock. Beside it, he left the pretty glass bead he'd uncovered in Mrs. Wilson's garden.

Out on the lagoon, an electric launch passed by the island. It would be fun to ride a boat with Tomoko. He imagined helping her in and sitting beside her. "See that dome?" he'd say, pointing at the Illinois Building. "My aunt Zenobia calls it 'ostentatious.'" Then they'd laugh at the sound of the big word. She wouldn't know what it meant, of course, but would understand that he was trying to be funny.

"May I help you?"

Henry jumped. He'd been so lost in thought he hadn't heard the man come up behind him. He turned to see the tour guide—the man who was possibly Tomoko's father.

"I—I'm just looking around," Henry stammered, trying to appear friendly and unsuspicious. "You have a nice garden." He edged in front of the rock, worried the man had seen him putting the gifts there.

The tour guide managed to smile and look stern at the same time. "Please stay on the path." He spoke carefully, like he'd had lots of practice dealing with inconsiderate fairgoers.

"Yes, sir," Henry said. "I'm sorry." After hoofing it back to the main path, he considered coming back later and checking inside Phoenix Hall, but discarded the idea as too risky. He wasn't sure if the man would recognize him out of thousands of visitors, but one never knew—especially now that they'd spoken. With some chagrin, Henry realized he'd have to space out his visits. "*Dang,*" he muttered.

On a whim, he took a smaller path into a garden with trellised vines and other flowers. He recognized zinnias, as there were millions of them around the fair. A man was kneeling in front of a plant that had large clusters of purple flowers, his hat dangling from one hand. It was John Thorpe, the floriculturist. Henry started to greet him, then hesitated. The man looked so reverent that he didn't want to disturb him. As Henry turned away, the man spoke.

"Madam phlox is a queen in the garden. We must offer her proper respect." He stood and brushed the moisture off his knees. "Young Henry, as I recall?"

"Yes, sir. Sorry to interrupt you."

Thorpe smiled and looked around him. "This is my church. The flowers are my angels. I'm always ready to meet a friend here." He closed his eyes and breathed deeply through his nose. "Have you ever smelled such sweet air?"

Henry agreed to a point. "I guess it depends which way the wind is blowing."

Thorpe smiled. "You're an astute young man." His clear blue eyes sharpened. "Have you been taking photographs?"

"I did once. I want to again."

"Good. Good. You should certainly do that." Thorpe looked over at a large white flower, then shook his head and grinned at Henry. "There is humor in nature, if one chooses to listen."

Henry had no idea what the man was talking about, but played along. "Mm-hm?"

"I once had the task of rejuvenating an old Damask rose that hadn't bloomed well for years," the man said. "I pruned and fertilized with little result. One day—in desperation, mind you—I threw down my nippers and yelled, 'Madam rose, what is it you require to become a blooming show-off once again?' I listened carefully, and the thought entered my mind to turn around. I did, and do you know what I saw?"

This was clearly Henry's prompt. "What?" he asked, drawn in.

"A maple tree," Thorpe said with a look of astonishment. "And I burst out laughing." Which he did, for effect or from memory, Henry wasn't sure, but he joined in out of sheer amusement.

"So, was the tree funny?" he asked.

"Oh no," Thorpe said, dragging his sleeve across his eyes. "I'd received the message loud and clear that Madam rose needed more sunlight. It was an obvious solution that my young mind had somehow overlooked. That's when I learned to listen and pay attention to nature. The answers usually present themselves."

Henry thought about that after he said goodbye and returned to the main path. He listened hard, but all he heard were snippets of conversations, the sound of people walking, and a hundred other noises around him. He slapped his thigh in frustration. Nature wasn't helping him in the least. How in the world could he have a friendly conversation with the girl? There must be an obvious solution, like Thorpe turning around and seeing the maple tree.

Cutting across the plaza, he headed for the fountain, where he leaned against the balustrade. Water cascaded into the basin where, further out, boats and gondolas glided with their passengers. It was a pleasing scene. He blew out a breath, taking in the wide view. There was so much to distract the eye, it was hard to know where to look first. And just like that, an idea sailed into his brain and dropped anchor. He laughed and said, "Eureka."

———◦———

In the spa room, ten women of all ages were in ecstasy. The window was wide open to let fresh air mix with the steaming fragrance of vinegar and herbs. It was day four, and each of the twenty-minute sessions had been filled to capacity.

"Good heavens," Annie Cable murmured to Juna, who sat just outside the door. "Folks'll think we're running a pleasure house in here with all that feminine moaning."

Juna whispered, "I've gone through four batches today. Word is spreading." Women were flocking to the spa, armed with their own towels, shoe hooks, and a few pennies to throw in the basket. Privately, she was thrilled. Not only was it gratifying to help these women, she'd gotten three inquires today about where to acquire more of the foot soak. When a visitor from Georgia suggested that she 'sell the stuff,' an idea began to circle around her brain. *Could* she sell it? The thought made her giddy.

"We have plenty of vinegar, but our supply of fresh herbs is dwindling," Annie said. "Shall I order more? The ladies have been generous in their donations."

"Oh yes, thank you," Juna said. "I'll make a list."

"Mrs. Lewis?" It was a woman from the information desk. "You have visitors downstairs."

A stately older man about Seymour's age stood beside the young woman with the lovely smile who'd been one of her first customers. Her smile was in full evidence as she said, "Mrs. Lewis, I'm Sarah Tompkins and this is my father, William Tompkins. He's a shoemaker in the Leather Building."

"To what do I owe the pleasure?" Juna asked.

Sarah deferred to her father, who said, "My daughter has been telling me about the success of your spa. I wonder if we might help each other?" He pulled a shoe hook from his pocket and handed it to her. "Would you consider giving these hooks to your customers as a complimentary gift?" Tompkins Fine Shoes was stamped on the handle. "A gift to reward customers and a little free advertising for our booth at the Leather Building."

"I see," Juna said, studying the little hook used for shoes that buttoned. "I would have to check with our manager first. We try to focus on Missouri products here."

Sarah giggled and her father said, "Look again. We're a Missouri company."

Sure enough, a tiny St. Clair, Missouri, was stamped at the base of the handle.

"Well then, I'll speak with Mrs. Fletcher," Juna said. "Thank you. I'm grateful to Sarah and her friends for helping spread the word about the spa." Father and daughter rewarded her with two dazzling smiles.

When she left for the day and met Zenobia and Henry outside, she held up the shoe hook. "Look at this," she said. "Our little spa is attracting attention."

As they walked toward Mrs. Wilson's sharing details of their day, Henry said, "I have an idea. Let's visit Phoenix Hall tomorrow morning. It's full of old artifacts. You'll love the decorations, Mama, and you could write an article about it, Aunt Zennie. What d'ya say?"

"I'd say that's a fine idea," Juna said. "I've been eager to see it."

Zenobia tapped her chin. "Yes," she said after a long moment. "That will work with my schedule. It's a very interesting place; one I've been meaning to feature."

Henry beamed at them. "Terrific!"

Juna smiled at her son's enthusiasm. She didn't realize he had such an interest in Japanese art, but that was the wonderful thing about the fair. Each day brought new discoveries and surprises. Something that you didn't even know existed on a Tuesday could be your new passion by Wednesday.

Chapter Nineteen

The sun was high by the time Henry, his mother, and aunt crossed the bridge to Wooded Island. "What a nice day," Mother said. "I've already counted five launches and three gondolas."

Henry adjusted the strap of his satchel. It took great effort to slow his pace and hide his glee over his brilliant scheme. What better strategy than to act the tourist with his mother and aunt in tow? He now had a perfectly legitimate reason to be at Phoenix Hall. He could poke around the place and—with luck and ingenuity—finagle a visit with the girl. *Ingenious,* he whispered to himself.

His one worry was that Tomoko wouldn't be there. What if she was helping in a different exhibit today? He hoped beyond hope that she would be sitting at her little table making paper birds. If not, his plan would be for nothing. It would be just his luck if "Papa" chose this day to take his daughter to visit some other part of the Exposition, or visit some tourist attraction in the city.

By the time they arrived at Phoenix Hall, Henry's heart was thumping merrily along to a rhythmic *Will she be there? Will she be there? Will she be there?* He led the women inside where, with a furtive glance, saw Tomoko at her table. A trio of children bounced on the cushions as they watched her in fascination. Henry relaxed. She was here! So far, his plan was working. A female attendant welcomed them and offered them pamphlets. Henry declined, saying, "I've already got one, thanks."

"What a lovely room," Mother said, taking in the decorated walls and ceiling. "Look at all the phoenixes."

Zenobia looked up from her pamphlet. "This is the Central Hall, or the Tokugawa Room. It's a replica of a room in an old castle in Tokyo."

"The artwork was done by teachers and students at the Tokyo Fine Art School," Henry said. He pointed up at the carved phoenix panels. "See those ventilation panels up there? Those are my favorite. They're called *ramma*." He was enjoying playing the tour guide, as he'd carefully studied the pamphlet. "That raised area is the *Jodan-no-ma,* a sitting room for a prince." He stole a glance at Tomoko, wondering if she'd noticed him. She didn't look up, but her dimples and self-conscious smile told him otherwise. He purposely steered his mother and aunt into the short walkway that led to one of the smaller rooms. "If we go through here, you'll see a food preparation area called a *Ko-no-ma.*" He noticed that the tour guide, whom he thought of as "Papa," was not in evidence today. Good. Things were progressing smoothly.

"I'm impressed with your knowledge of the place, Henry," Mother said a few minutes later as they crossed the main room toward the passage leading to the *Shosai.* "Oh, look! There's a girl creating *origami.*"

"You know about that?" he asked.

Mother gave him a sidelong glance. "I wasn't born in the Dark Ages, son."

They found the entrance to the *Shosai* blocked by a group of visitors. "Tell us about that table, please," a woman asked someone who was hidden from view.

A familiar voice replied. "That is a lacquer table. See the beautiful design? It holds instruments for writing: ink stone, stationery for writing poems, and paperweight."

Dang, Henry thought. "Papa," was here after all, but at least he was busy. As he answered other questions posed by the group, Mother and Zenobia edged in closer so they could see the room. Henry took the opportunity to return to the central room. Knowing Mother and Zenobia, they'd have plenty of questions to ask the man. Now was his chance.

He positioned himself near the phoenix panels, angling himself so he could see Tomoko. After a few minutes, the children received their birds and left with their parents, leaving Tomoko alone at her table. With sudden inspiration, Henry caught her eye and tipped his head before strolling to the *Ko-no-ma*. He stood by a velvet rope partition and pretended to look at the tea sets, bowls, and other items.

A woman was taking photographs of the room with a small Kodak, and two men speaking a foreign language gestured toward a large bonsai at the back of the room. The woman said something to them in the same language.

"It's nice, isn't it?" Henry ventured. They all smiled and, clearly not understanding him, resumed their own conversations.

And suddenly Tomoko was there, gliding in to stand a few feet from him. "Hello, Henry-san."

He grinned back at her, noticing her eyes had a sparkly quality about them. "Hello, Miss Tomoko," he said. She slid a finger under the fabric at her neck and pulled out a white thread from which hung the glass bead. No words were necessary. Her dimples deepening said all that needed to be said. He felt his cheeks heating up as he continued to grin stupidly. More visitors wandered in, and she hid the bead away. His hope of a regular conversation was dashed by the loud and emphatic comments of a large family.

"Look at those fan paintings, Maggie."

"Did you see those teapots? How lovely."

"What's that funny-looking tree over there?"

"I'm hungry, mama."

"I know, dear. We'll go to the cafe as soon as we're done here."

"You said that ages ago!"

The family crowded around and between them, and when Henry stepped back to give them room, he saw Tomoko hurrying back to the central room. *Dang*, he thought, and followed her back inside. She lowered herself gracefully onto the cushion, then glanced up and made a face. "Oh, well," was the same in any language. He shrugged and responded in kind. It was then that he noticed the attendant staring at him. Uh, oh. He quickly moved closer to the *ramma* and made a show of studying the phoenixes with their flowing tails.

"Henry," Mother called as she and Zenobia re-entered the room, accompanied—to Henry's dismay—by "Papa." She waved him over. "Come meet

Professor Shuga. This is my son, Henry," she said, making introductions. "The Professor is responsible for some of the artwork here."

"We've been lucky to have a private tour," Zenobia put in.

The professor gave a quick bow, giving Henry that unreadable expression that was both friendly and stern. "Your son is a frequent visitor," he said.

"Oh, that doesn't surprise me at all," Mother said. "He so enjoys anything exotic."

"I—I like the phoenixes," Henry stammered, silently pleading with Mother to be quiet. "The *ramma*, especially," he added, hoping the professor would be impressed. Out of the corner of his eye, he could see Tomoko watching them with equal amounts of amusement and alarm.

Mother was getting carried away. "Back home, Henry loves nothing more than climbing a tall tree and pretending he's out on the high seas. Or at least on a boat chugging down the Mississippi."

Henry cut his eyes toward Zenobia, silently entreating her to change the subject and save him from further embarrassment. She got *most* of the message.

"Professor, is that your daughter over there?" she asked, gesturing toward Tomoko.

His expression softened. "Yes, she helps me here and demonstrates origami."

"She's lovely. May I speak with her?"

Mother was immediately on board with the idea. "How wonderful. I'd love to see her perform her origami."

Professor Shuga swept a hand toward his daughter. "Of course."

This new development mortified Henry, who hung back as "Papa" made introductions. He avoided eye contact with Tomoko, certain that he'd give himself away.

Zenobia took the lead. She plopped onto a cushion and picked up a bird from the table. "May I watch how you make these?"

Tomoko nodded and said, "Yes," in a soft voice. Her cheeks were pinker than usual.

Mother sat down and patted the cushion next to her. "Want to watch, Henry?"

"Uh, sure," he mumbled, dropping onto the seat and practically collapsing it to the floor. He wished he could disappear. What a disaster! What had seemed like a good idea had only made him conspicuous, and now "Papa" knew his name. Henry kept his eyes on Tomoko's hands as she went through the motions of creasing and folding the paper. He wondered if anyone else noticed that her fingers were trembling.

A large group tromped in and the professor bowed to Mother and Zenobia. "Enjoy your visit," he said, then leaned down and murmured to Tomoko. Her expression tightened as she gave a quick reply. Whatever it was, she didn't seem happy about it. As her father went to greet the tourists, Henry squirmed on his cushion. Professor Shuga knew exactly what he was up to. Dang. Dang. Dang.

As soon as Tomoko finished her demonstration, she stood up, bowed to the women, and left the hall in the company of her father.

"That was so interesting," Mother said as they left a few minutes later. "Though you might have said a few words to that sweet girl, Henry. I'm sure she doesn't bite."

It was pointless to argue. "Yes'm," Henry sighed, hoisting the strap of his satchel over his head and silently berating himself. How could he have been so stupid? In his arrogance, he'd given himself away. It would be practically impossible to see Tomoko at Phoenix Hall now that her father—and the attendant—would be on the lookout for him.

"Henry, how would you like to visit Machinery Hall after lunch?" Zenobia asked. "I have a surprise for you."

"Sure," he said. "What is it?"

"Something with altitude, and that's all I'm saying. Can you come, too, Juney?"

Mother shook her head. "Too noisy for me, I'm afraid. I was planning to lose myself in the Art Palace for two or three hours this afternoon before my shift at the state building."

Anticipation perked Henry right up. The nice thing about the Exposition was that there was always another distraction.

Chapter Twenty

The walls of the Art Palace were verily crammed with paintings. Smaller works snugged up to larger ones, ceiling to floor. Juna liked to stroll through the quiet, echoey wings surrounded by the ambient whispering of other visitors.

"What do you suppose that one means?"

"Oh! I surely saw that one at the Louvre."

"I wish Auntie Barbara could see it."

"Let's sit on that bench over there and study that big one, shall we?"

She found it a good place to let her mind wander while absorbing the art. As there were too many pieces to give each equal attention, she let her eyes drift here and there, alighting on a particular work or detail: a beautifully rendered face; a landscape that pulled her right in; an interesting composition of flowers or fruit.

Crowds tended to gather at works that were especially compelling, shocking, or sentimental. In the American exhibit, "Breaking Home Ties" by Thomas Hovenden was one of the most popular, showing a young man bidding his family goodbye. It was a familiar scene to many: that of a boy leaving home to seek his fortune. A brave, yet reluctant boy is quietly listening to his mother as she embraces him and gives earnest last-minute instructions. (*Please write when you get to Chicago—or Lincoln—or Sacramento. Do you have your money safely tucked away? Your extra sweater?*)

Two forlorn sisters are on opposite sides of the room. One is looking at the dog— equally forlorn as it gazes at his boy—and the other, near the door, is holding back tears. Gosh, they're gonna miss him. Granny, a veteran of loss, quietly sits at the large table. She memorizes the curly brown hair and gently sloping nose of her grandson. (*Goodness, how he's grown. Such a handsome young man. Will I live long enough to see him again?*) His uncle stands at the door waiting to drive the wagon to the train station. The father, walking away from the viewer, stalwartly carries his son's suitcase toward the door. (*"Kiss your mother goodbye, son. Train leaves in one hour."*)

Juna had visited this painting many times, always aware of women and men alike dabbing their eyes—in empathy with the boy who was putting on a brave face, and with the family who would miss him. Perhaps they anticipated their own child leaving home one day. She pressed her lips together as the usual wave of emotion washed over her. It was easy to imagine the mother's anguish. She would surely feel the same if she was in a similar position.

The mother in the painting wears a resigned expression. How many nights had she paced the floor of her cozy farmhouse, while coming to terms with the situation? Was it a matter of keeping the farm? Was her dear son leaving to find a job so he could send money back to his family? It was a grim reality in many places, especially in these troubled times. Juna could only imagine how she'd feel if Henry set off to seek his fortune, not knowing where he was or if he was safe. The mother in the painting had surely grappled with that unspoken point. It was there in the set of her mouth and her hands on the boy's shoulders.

Eyes welling, Juna turned to leave and collided with a man who *ooffed* and caught her arms to steady them both. "Whoa there, are you all right?" he said.

Juna instantly recognized the man and the voice. "Professor Stone! Do forgive me," she said, horrified that her brimming tears had leapt their boundaries. She took a small step back and swiped at her face. "I'm afraid you've caught me at a vulnerable moment."

"Looks like Hovenden's done it again," he said, laughing a little as he scooped his hat off the floor. "Judging by the amount of white cloth flashing here, I'd say you are in good company."

"I am, at that."

"You're Nancy's friend from class, aren't you? Mrs. Lewis, the enthusiastic note-taker."

"The one and only," Juna confirmed, impressed that he remembered her name. "Though my note-taking skills normally exceed my clumsiness."

"And my teaching skills normally exceed my abilities to be a wall," he said, grinning back at her.

Needing to make way for other visitors, they moved across the gallery to a lonelier group of paintings. "Did you come to see anything in particular?" she asked.

He reached into his coat and pulled out a pocket diary. "No, I'm exploring and taking notes. I find it helpful to bring my students to the Art Palace. One carefully chosen painting can inspire young minds even better than a long-winded lecture."

Juna nodded, thinking of the Hovenden. "I've found that to be true. Though your lectures are anything but boring."

By unspoken agreement, they strolled on through the galleries, pausing now and then to comment on paintings they liked. The professor seemed to be well-versed in art, though not in a high-brow or condescending way. She found his manner relaxed and interested—nice qualities for a teacher, and a good match for Nancy Collins, she thought with approval.

"Where are you off to now?" Professor Stone asked when they were in sight of an exit.

Juna checked her watch pin. "I have an hour twenty before I'm needed at the Missouri Building. I'm mostly letting my feet wander of their own accord."

"And I have plenty of time before meeting Nancy and Mrs. Rhodehaver for supper," he said. "May I order you a coffee at my favorite outdoor cafe? It's not far, and the coffee is complimentary."

She only hesitated a moment. Professor Stone was a perfect gentleman, and it appeared, safely attached to Nancy. Why shouldn't she go? "I'd like that," she said, enjoying this new experience of unhindered freedom.

<hr>

The Brazilian Coffee Pavilion consisted of a low platform tucked among a grove of trees. Men and women chatted at bistro tables, giving the place a pleasant, noisy ambience. The professor led Juna to an unoccupied table and held out a chair for her. She sat down and inhaled the rich aroma that suffused the area. "I could just sit here and breathe all day," she said.

"Many people do." The professor shrugged out of his jacket and hung it on the back of his chair. "I like to bring a book to read or post cards to write. Before I know it, two hours have passed and I'm getting significant looks from the establishment."

A handsome young man in white linen took their order and soon returned with two steaming cups. Juna lifted hers up with both hands. "This smells heavenly."

"Just wait 'til you try it," the professor said, adding a dollop of cream. "The only problem is that all other coffee will forever taste second rate."

Juna took a careful sip. "Oh my goodness, it's a revelation. Strong, but smooth on the tongue. If there's one thing I'll miss, it will be the food and drink here. I'm a regular customer at the Ceylon Tea House."

Stone laughed. "I've been chased out of there, as well."

"You must write a lot of post cards."

"Yes, I have family and friends who cannot travel this summer, and some that need convincing."

"Let me guess. Are they from New York?" she teased. Many there were still smarting from their state being passed over for Chicago, and visitors from that state often arrived with preconceived ideas and a condescending attitude. Happily, after experiencing the grandeur of the fair, the visitors almost always revised their opinion.

Professor Stone gave her an amused nod. "You're a perceptive woman, Mrs. Lewis."

"I've been encouraging my father-in-law to visit, but he claims he's too old to leave Louisiana. Though, personally," she said with a smile, "I think he's convinced that his factory will burst into a raging conflagration if he leaves town."

"Louisiana? Are you near New Orleans?"

"It's a river town in Missouri. About seventy miles north of St. Louis."

"You must get that question a lot," he said.

"It's an easy assumption. We like to say that the river connects us, so it's not too far of a stretch."

"Tell me about this factory."

She rested her cup on the table, pleased that he'd asked. "My father-in-law and my late husband began Lewis Vinegar in the mid-seventies. With all the apple orchards in the area, including my father's, it was a good business. They became prosperous enough to move to a larger building near the river the year our son Henry was born. They'd been there eight years when my husband died."

Professor Stone's gaze was steady. "I'm sorry to hear it," he said. "Was he taken ill?"

She shook her head. It was the usual question. "He died during a bicycle race when he plunged head-first off his high wheel."

The professor sagged against the back of his chair. "Terrible. Now I understand your hesitation to ride. Does Nancy know? I'll have her back off trying to convince you."

Juna found his display of protection endearing. "It's all right. A wise friend says it's time to meet my fears. I agree with him, in principle, but—" She trailed off and shrugged a shoulder. "He's standing ready to teach me if I ever find my courage."

"You'll manage when you're ready. I assure you that the new safety bicycles are a world away from the old high wheels. Those took a certain amount of daring."

"Craig was certainly daring," she said. "He 'caught the bug' after watching a race in '86, and bought an older model from a businessman in town. He practiced every spare moment for the century race the following year. I admit I was his biggest supporter. Our son, of course, was thrilled by it all."

The professor's attentiveness made it easy to talk freely. It had been a long time since she'd revisited that dreadful day with another person. Taking a deep breath, she continued. "It was rainy the night before the race, and the road was muddy and slippery. He must've hit a pothole or a rock and plunged down an embankment. As you know, those old racing wheels had no brakes. Two racers found him and brought him back to town. He'd hit a tree head-on."

The professor winced. "I'm sorry," he said. "Truly."

His kindness touched her in a way that made it impossible to reply in words. A quick nod was all she could manage. The waiter refilled their cups, and they sat quietly for a few minutes, lost in their own thoughts while letting the specter of her husband's death dissipate. A breeze off the lake shimmered through the surrounding trees, making patches of sunlight dance across their table.

At length, Professor Stone said, "I understand your sorrow. I lost my wife five years ago to a wasting sickness."

"Oh!" Juna pressed her hand to her chest. "I'm very sorry to hear it."

"Her death ultimately brought me to Chicago. I needed to escape my melancholy, and the university needed an oratory professor."

Juna held his gaze for a long moment. "We never escape it entirely, do we?"

His smile was gentle. "No, indeed. We simply try our best to outrun it."

"What was her name?"

"Sandra, but everyone called her Bootsie."

Juna raised her cup. "Well, then. To the memories of Bootsie and Craig."

"To Bootsie and Craig," he said, tapping her cup with his own. In that moment, they shared a bond of mutual empathy. For how else could one understand the unique pain of losing a beloved, except to have experienced it?

When they left the coffee pavilion, their conversation slipped into the realm of oratory classes, Stone's work at the university, and their mutual high regard for Nancy Collins.

"How did you meet Nancy?" Juna asked.

"Nancy and I have known each other since our college days," he said. "She helped me find my feet when I moved to Chicago. Mrs. Rhodehaver is like a mother to me. I can't imagine life without either of them."

"Please give Nancy and Mrs. Rhodehaver my best," Juna said as they parted ways at the Missouri Building. She was sincerely happy that her friend and the professor had found each other. "Thank you, Professor Stone. I had a lovely afternoon."

"As did I," he said in his splendid voice. It continued to resonate within her as she entered the building with a light step and a lighter heart.

Later, after cleaning up the spa room, Juna stared out the window while fingering the apple charm at her throat. In every direction she saw people walking, children skipping ahead of their parents, trees moving in the wind, boats out on the lake, a carriage taking a visiting dignitary to an event or meeting, flags snapping in the wind. This relentless movement was mirrored by a restlessness in her body. She recognized it as a longing to be part of something larger than herself.

She thought of Archie's offer to teach her to ride, and of the professor's kind reassurances. This train of thought led to a terrifying question. Pressing both hands to her neck, she took slow, deep breaths as blood pulsed beneath her fingers. What would it be like to share in Henry and Zenobia's eager anticipation for Monday's excursion? Was it time to make peace with the instrument of her husband's death?

The faint fragrance of vinegar and herbs lingered from another successful spa day. They'd even turned a few ladies away, sending them off with a shoe hook and a promise that they'd be first on the list tomorrow. She turned slowly, taking in the pleasant room. What would Craig think if he could see her? Would he cheer her on as she had cheered him on? Would he speak words of encouragement in the face of her doubts? Would he be proud of her, even if her idea failed?

A sigh escaped her lips. *Yes,* she thought. He would. If he had lived and been the very last racer to cross the finish line, she would have treated him as a winner. In private, she would have kissed him and proclaimed him 'the prince of adventurous follies,' and they would have giggled into their pillows. It took courage to open the spa. Certainly she could find the courage to master a bicycle.

That evening during supper, she summoned up the nerve to say, "I have another announcement to make."

Zenobia looked up from cutting her roasted chicken. "What now?"

Henry, who had a mouthful of potatoes, slowed his chewing. Mrs. Wilson set down her teacup with a soft *clink* and regarded Juna with curious eyes. "Tell us, dear."

Juna hesitated, knowing that once she made her pronouncement, there'd be no going back. She squeezed and released handfuls of her skirt, then plunged ahead. "I've decided to face my fears square on and learn to ride the bicycle."

The outburst of cheering brought Hattie racing in from the kitchen. "I heard what you said, Mrs. Lewis. Don't ye be entertaining any ideas of wearin' bloomers."

"Well, that's no fun," Zenobia said, winking at Juna.

Having given voice to her decision—and heartened by the response—it surprised Juna to find that her fear was tamped down a few degrees.

"How are you going to learn?" Henry asked. "You don't have a wheel."

"Mr. Peterson has kindly offered to borrow a wheel and teach me. I'll send a note for you to give him in the morning." Her son's expression altered slightly, as if he didn't approve of the arrangement, but as he was still grinning, she concluded it was only her imagination.

"I have a split skirt you may use," Zenobia said. "You'll need to hem it up a few inches, but it should fit fine."

"That's generous of you," Juna said. "What will you wear on Monday?"

Zennie gave her an impish grin. "I have new favorites."

"What's a split skirt?" Henry asked.

"One step closer to trousers and three steps more suitable to bicycle riding than a regular skirt," Zennie explained.

Juna smiled at the puzzled look on her son's face. Despite her lingering worries, she found she was anticipating her riding lesson.

Chapter Twenty-One

Dear Archie,

After considerable thought, I have garnered my courage and will take you up on your kind offer to teach me the wheel. I don't know if I can master it quickly enough to join the ride on Monday, but I'm willing to try.

Thank you for encouraging me in this regard. It is time I took a chance at falling. I realize from experience that one can make the choice to get up again.

Yours sincerely,
Juna

My dear Junaluska,

It would be my utmost pleasure. Please have Henry escort you to Washington Park at 7:00 o'clock tonight.

Your humble servant,
Archie P.

Washington Park was lovely in the light of early evening. Lawns and flower gardens swept up to a large conservatory. Families and friends strolled or bicycled on wide lanes that cut through the park. Couples walked arm-in-arm along wooded pathways. Children chased balls and each other in spacious meadows.

Juna stood with Archie at the edge of such a meadow. It gently sloped to a small lake. According to Archie, a flock of sheep clipped the grass down, though it was currently crunchy-brown from the July heat. It was not the state of the grass, however, that was occupying Juna's attention, but the substantial bicycle standing a few feet away. She'd balked at her first sight of it, and stood rooted to the ground as Henry inspected it with enthusiasm. He tested the bell, squeezed the brake, and ran his fingers over the sleek frame. "It's swell," he said, grinning at her. "See, Mama? There's a carbide light on the front for riding at night, and it has a shield to keep your dress from getting tangled in the tire."

"Goodness me," she said, and caught her lip between her teeth, wondering if this was such a good idea after all.

"It's an 1890 New Era," Archie said. "Made by a Chicago-based company known for its high-quality wheels. It certainly has all the bells and whistles. It's heavy, but should serve your mother well on the boulevards."

Henry lifted the bicycle off the stand. "May I ride it?"

"By all means."

As Juna watched her son speed off across the meadow, Archie said, "Henry informed me, in no uncertain terms, that he would need to approve any wheel that I provided for you."

Juna pressed a hand to her throat. Henry was watching out for her. Of course he was. "He doesn't want to lose me, too," she said. "I hadn't thought past my own fears. Am I being unkind? Perhaps I should abandon this idea all together." She half-hoped that Archie would agree.

Peterson briefly pressed his hand to her back and gave her a gentle smile. "It's an important step for you both, don't you think?"

"I suppose it is," she said, noting that Peterson was finding more ways to touch and comfort her. "He seemed to like the idea when I announced it."

"As a young man, the idea naturally excited him, and as your son, he naturally wants you to remain safe." He held her gaze. "As do I, of course."

Juna felt her cheeks warm up as she stepped away. Henry had reached the far side of the meadow and was heading back toward them. While she regarded her relationship with Archie, *the mentor*, as purely platonic, today she was very much aware of Archie, *the man*. He wore no jacket or vest and had rolled up the sleeves of his shirt to reveal muscular forearms. As a woman, she couldn't deny her attraction.

Henry slowed to a stop, dismounted, and propped the bicycle back on its stand. "It handles easily, Mama. Are you ready to learn?"

Juna hesitated as apprehension came roaring back. Before she could respond, Peterson said, "I have a method in mind for teaching your mother." He gestured toward the bicycle. "If I may?"

Henry nodded and stepped back. "Sure."

Peterson addressed Juna. "Remember, you're the human animal here. You are superior to a machine, even if the machine requires respect. Approach the wheel with determination, not timidity. Show it you mean business."

Juna took a deep breath. "All right." She marched over and gripped the wide handlebars. "How's this?" In a corner of her brain that wasn't trembling, she appreciated how nicely her hands fit on the cork handles.

"Well done," Archie said. "Relax your hands slightly. Blood flow is a desirable thing."

Laughing despite herself, she relaxed her hands. With her left thumb, she flipped the lever for the little bell mounted on the handlebar. *Brrring. Brrring.* With her right hand, she squeezed a thin lever mounted under the handlebar, causing a spoon brake to depress on the front tire. She released the handles and stepped back. "Now what?"

"First thing, get to know the bicycle. It's quite different from the old high wheels, which you may be more familiar with."

Juna exchanged a quick look with Henry. It was only an offhand statement—and was, in fact, true—but the subject still touched a nerve. Archie patted the leather seat. "You should be comfortable on this saddle, as it has a spring underneath." Juna's eye was drawn to a slit in the middle of the seat, clearly designed to accommodate her anatomy. She stifled a nervous giggle.

Archie pointed toward the pedals. "See that chain? As you pedal, the chain turns and makes the wheels turn. It's an ingenious invention." Juna wasn't entirely ignorant about the workings of a safety bicycle, but could tell that Archie was enjoying his role as teacher. In fact, she found his confident instruction reassuring. He lifted the bicycle off its stand. "Try walking the wheel in a big circle."

Taking a deep breath, she grabbed the handles once again and pushed forward. She felt awkward and slightly off-balance while trying to keep enough distance to avoid catching her skirt on the spinning pedal. Archie walked on the other side, and Henry hovered just beyond. "It's heavy, but does move easily," she said once she got the hang of it.

"Very good. Now try out the brake."

She obeyed, and the bicycle glided to a stop.

"Remember to give yourself time to slow down," Archie warned. "You have to think ahead."

Henry chimed in. "The faster you are going, the longer it will take to stop."

Juna had to admit this part was rather thrilling. After she completed the circle and came back to their starting point, he touched the back of her hand. "Are you ready to practice mounting the wheel?"

Juna nodded, determined to muster up her courage. "I believe so."

Henry was there in a flash. "I'll help hold the wheel steady," he said, grabbing the front of the handlebars.

"Thank you, Henry," Archie said, with a hint of annoyance in his tone. He held onto the back of the bicycle. "First, step through and make sure your skirt is even on both sides. Ah, a split skirt. Very good. Now put your foot on the lower pedal and lift onto the seat." After a few false starts, she gained the saddle and found that her feet reached the pedals comfortably. This pleased Archie. "The seat is at the correct height," he said. "Now, take a moment to accustom yourself with how it feels."

"I feel very high up," she said, holding onto the handles and looking at the ground. "And a little frightened."

"You can do it," Henry said.

"We'll go slowly," Peterson assured her. "I want you to step back down and practicing mounting and dismounting fifty times before you attempt to ride. It needs to be second nature."

Relieved that this task required no forward movement, Juna stepped back to the ground and remounted. "One . . . two . . . three . . ." Henry counted along with her. By the time she reached fifty, she was performing the maneuver smoothly.

"Excellent," Archie said as she stepped back to the ground. "Now the real fun begins. This time, push off with the higher pedal. Don't worry, Henry and I will hold on and walk beside you. The trick to staying upright is to keep pedaling."

Now that the big moment was here, Juna's fear came rushing back, knocking away her tenuous shred of confidence. Visions of Craig and his damaged high wheel spun through her mind's eye. With a dry mouth, she cried, "I can't do it. It's too big for me. I'll fall!"

Archie spoke in a soothing tone. "You can do it, Junaluska. I won't let you fall, I promise."

"You can do it, Mama. I'm right here," Henry said, stepping closer.

Juna brushed at her eyes, feeling foolish. "Are you sure?"

"Yes'm," Henry assured her.

"Cross my heart," Archie said.

"All right, then." She took a deep breath, gripped the handle, and pushed off, with Archie keeping a firm hold on the frame as she slowly moved forward. Henry walked inches away, his hand hovering near the handlebars. The bicycle wobbled, causing Juna to panic and squeeze the brake. After five more false starts and plenty of encouragement from Archie and Henry, she pedaled a little harder. To her amazement, the wheel stayed upright.

"Keep pedaling," Archie said as he jogged beside her. Halfway across the field, he panted, "You're doing great. I'm going to let go now. Don't stop pedaling!"

"Go, Mama, go!" Henry called after her as she quickly outpaced them.

As she flew across the field, her insecurity turned into a shaky sense of confidence. She was up! She was moving faster than she'd ever done under her own steam—and it both thrilled and frightened her. Had Craig felt this exhilarating sense of freedom as he sped along the roads near their town? He had, surely. Memories circled around her: Craig returning from a ride, sweaty and happy as he rubbed a towel over his face; Henry sitting on the high wheel with his bare feet dangling far above the pedals. Those were happy times she hadn't thought of in years. Happy times that were eventually cut short in a devastating way—but happy, nonetheless.

Executing a wide, cautious turn near the lake, she headed back as Archie and Henry cheered her on. Drawing near, she looked up and gave them a big smile. Intent on celebrating her accomplishment, she didn't see the large stick in the grass until she was nearly on top of it. Panicking, she jerked the handlebars sharply, throwing the bicycle off-balance. She hit the ground hard, with the breath knocked out of her as she landed in a tangled heap.

"Mama!" Henry and Archie were there in an instant, pulling the heavy bicycle off her as she gasped for air. Henry dropped to his knees beside her, rubbing her shoulders and arms helplessly. "Are you hurt? Can you speak?"

Archie knelt on her other side. "Give her a minute, son."

The feeling of suffocation passed, and she began to breathe normally again. With a groan, she pushed herself up into a sitting position, testing her legs and rubbing at her shoulder. "I'll have some bruises, but otherwise, I think I'm fine." Henry's face crumpled, and she pulled him to her. "I'm all right," she whispered. "I'm all right. I'm all right."

Chapter Twenty-Two

July 24, 1893—The St. Louis Daily
NOTES FROM THE FAIR:

Way Up in Machinery Hall

On Saturday, I toured Machinery Hall from "on high." There is a clever traveling crane used to move machinery from one end of the building to the other. This platform also moves tourists for a noisy, grand view of the many wondrous machines below. My young companion, who adores heights, compared it with the thrill of climbing to the highest branches of a mighty tree. For those of you less inclined to risk life and limb, I urge you to try this safer alternative.

What a day at the races! No horses, mind you. Canoes were the steeds, manned by men of all sorts: Europeans, Indians, South Sea Islanders, and our "own" boys, to name a few, paddling under the hot sun on the Grand Basin. Whiter arms in rolled-up sleeves, browner arms and bare backs, oiled. It was a spectacle of good health, a vision of God's own creations. We cheered them on, happy for any of them to win. It was a close finish between the Europeans and the Islanders, who won by mere inches.

—Zenobia A. Thom,
Special Correspondent

Today was the day. Juna woke up early to stretch her sore muscles and apply herbal salve to her bruises. Despite protests from Henry and Archie, she'd insisted on getting "back on the horse." By twilight, they pronounced her ready for today's tour. Archie escorted them back to Mrs. Wilson's, pushing the borrowed wheel for Juna after a friend of his dropped off another wheel—a Century—for a delighted Henry.

She held out the sides of her split skirt, which was like wide trousers. Hanging down, it was hard to tell the difference from a regular skirt, aside from the sensation of fabric brushing the insides of her legs. Regardless, it felt daring to wear a garment so unlike any of her other clothes. As she secured her straw hat, the door opened and Zenobia pranced in. Juna stared at her, aghast. "What in the world are you wearing?"

Her sister did a couple spins and kicks, arms aloft, to show off her outfit of burgundy-colored bloomers and matching jacket, paired with boots and gators. "It's the latest in bicycle fashion and allows unencumbered freedom of movement." She gave Juna a sly grin. "You should try it."

"Oh no," Juna said. "I'm not that brave. I'll stick with my split skirt."

"As you wish," Zenobia said. "It's an odd feeling at first, but I quickly became accustomed to the idea. All it took was one ride to win me over entirely. Pedaling without having to worry about all that fabric is pure heaven and imminently safer."

"Hm." Juna was privately intrigued, but refused to admit it. "Has Mrs. Wilson seen your costume?"

"She was horrified, as expected, but warmed to the idea when she heard that Mrs. Rhodehaver wears them as well."

"Shocking."

"Oh, yes. Nancy badgered her aunt into trying them. Now she's an enthusiastic proponent."

Juna laughed. "Nancy is the consummate bohemian. You seem quite taken with her."

"She's loads of fun. None of my friends in St. Louis are nearly as daring, so I'll have to pack my bloomers away there. It will be good to get back to teaching, but I will certainly miss the excitement of Chicago," she added wistfully.

"At least it's an easy train ride if you care to visit."

"True enough." Zennie turned toward the door, then whirled around and gave Juna a careful hug. "I'm proud of you, Juney. I realize what a big step this is for you. And Henry."

"Thank you, Zennie. Let's just hope it's not an—"

"'Adventurous folly'?" Zenobia said with a grin. It was Seymour's favorite phrase that could either be a tease or a criticism. She kissed Juna on the cheek. "I'll finish my toilet and meet you downstairs."

Juna turned back to the mirror to look at her modest outfit of split skirt and white shirtwaist, wishing for the millionth time that she had her sister's *joie du vivre*. At least her straw hat had a bright green ribbon, and her gloves were a buttery yellow. She wasn't entirely dull. She took a deep breath and exhaled slowly. The high emotion and headiness of the previous evening had subsided, giving way to nervous excitement. She planted her fists on her waist. "I can do this," she told her reflection in a firm voice, then whispered, "I have to."

They met the others at Drexel Park, a small area adjacent to the north end of Washington Park. A tall monument and fountain dominated the space. Juna was surprised to see Professor Stone there with Nancy, then realized it made perfect sense. It occurred to her that she should have invited Archie to join them. She hoped her lack of courtesy hadn't offended him.

"Juna, you're here!" Nancy said as they rode up. She held a smart-looking wheel that featured a front basket, and wore an outfit similar to Zennie's, with the addition of a matching cap. "What changed your mind?"

"A miracle of eleventh-hour courage and a patient teacher. Though, I may need some hand-holding on the busier parts of the boulevard."

"I'll ride behind you and practice my skills in projecting." Nancy introduced them to Professor Stone, who wore a pair of knickerbockers, the same as Henry.

"Welcome, all," he said. "I'm glad to see another fellow in the group." Henry seemed equally pleased. The professor turned to Juna. "It's nice to see you again, Mrs. Lewis."

"I can hardly believe I'm here," she said, ignoring Zenobia's raised eyebrow. She'd explain the situation later. "Your words of encouragement helped me over the proverbial fence."

His grin mirrored her own. "I'm pleased to hear it."

While they waited for any late-comers, Nancy explained the route. "We'll take Drexel north to Oakwood and come back south on Grand, ending up in Washington Park. Go single file or in two's, depending on the traffic. Be careful of carriages, do nothing to spook the horses, and watch out for scorchers."

Zenobia cut in to explain. "Scorchers are men who fancy themselves professional cyclists and speed along without courtesy or regard for human or animal."

Juna gripped her handlebars a little tighter. "I'll be careful," she said, and gave Henry a reassuring smile.

Nancy continued her instructions. "If you want to pass the rider in front of you, state your intention loudly and clearly. This should be no problem for the oratory students," she said, getting a laugh. "We'll let the men go first, as they tend to go faster. Professor Stone will lead the way. I'll take the last position so we don't lose anyone. If you need to stop, say, 'Rest break,' loudly and the message will be passed up the line. Any questions?" She paused a moment to scan the group. "No? Well, then. It appears no one else will be joining us. Time to line up."

Juna's heart was thumping along as she took the next-to-last position behind Zenobia. They set off and rode north on Drexel Avenue, a spacious boulevard bordered by rows of narrow stone houses on the east, and a wide strip of trees and paths on the west. Beyond it was another boulevard, Grand Avenue, bordered by similar homes on the opposite side.

The avenues were moderately busy this time of the morning, with carriages, delivery wagons, and hansoms being the primary traffic. Juna found the close proximity of horse's hooves and the jarring chaos of wheels on the pavement frightening at first, but the professor kept them close to the right-hand side of the street. His pace was moderate enough that Juna had time to enjoy the scenery and reflect on how incredible it was that she was riding a bicycle at all, much less *on a street in Chicago.*

Plenty of people were about, walking on the sidewalks and paths. The sound of hammering carried over from a nearby street. It was a lively neighborhood and a primary route for folks going to the fair. What would Seymour say if he could see her now? Would he be glad for her, or shake his head and pronounce it 'an adventurous folly'? Would he worry that his grandson was as enamored by wheels as his own son had been?

Ahead of her, Zenobia was pedaling comfortably in her bloomers. What a different kind of silhouette she made. Aside from her hat and hair, it was hard to tell she was a woman. Now and then she'd glance back, ostensibly to make sure Juna was still there. At the front of the line, Henry and the professor visited as they rode. How nice for Henry, she thought. A boy needed men in his life. While Mr. Peterson had been generous with his time, the professor was a quieter sort—a welcome change of pace for her son. She was glad they were getting on well. Behind her, Nancy began singing the song, "Daisy Bell," and Juna hummed along.

It seemed like no time at all until they were turning left onto Oakland for a short distance, then south on Grand. As they came in sight of Washington Park, Juna heard Nancy cry out. A second later, a man sped past, mere inches from her own bicycle, causing her to shriek and put a death-grip on her brake, nearly causing a collision with Nancy.

Up ahead, Professor Stone yelled, "Warn us next time!" then motioned for the group to pull off to the side. "Everyone all right?" His gaze lingered on Juna, and she nodded shakily, glad to have her feet back on *terra firma*.

Zenobia gave an indignant huff. "I'd like to give that man what-for. No courtesy at all."

Henry looked after the rider, long gone. "I wonder what he was riding? He was fast!"

They all laughed, breaking the tension. Professor Stone said, "Good lad. Is everyone ready to resume?"

The remainder of the tour was pleasant, with no further mishaps. As they were all hot and thirsty, they rode directly to a public water fountain in the park. Gliding to a stop beside Zenobia, Juna felt a burst of relief and satisfaction. She'd done it! "What an exciting ride," she said.

"Indeed, it was," Zennie said. "I'm proud of you, Juney. I had every faith in your abilities."

Henry bounded over and steadied her wheel while she dismounted. "Good job, Mama," he said, giving her a tight hug. "I knew you could do it."

Professor Stone dropped his hat beside his wheel and joined them. "Well done, Mrs. Lewis. You kept up admirably for your first time on the boulevards."

Juna's heart was full. "Thank you," she said, beaming at the group.

Nancy spread a blanket on the ground next to a flower border. "Let's celebrate Juna's accomplishment with a cookie."

"I can vouch for them," the professor said as they settled on the ground. "Mrs. Rhodehaver's baking skills are exceeded only by her vibrant personality."

Juna couldn't remember having a more pleasant morning. She discovered that Nancy and Professor Stone became good chums while attending college in Ohio. In fact, it was Nancy who'd recommended him to Mary Blood and Ida Riley. "When Aunt Ruthie mentioned the school was looking for guest professors for the summer session, I told her that Hiram was the man for the job," Nancy explained. "I knew that once they heard him speak, they'd hire him on the spot."

Professor Stone shook his head and spoke in an exaggerated tremolo—not in the least like his own voice. "To teach or not to teach? That was the question."

"Ah, a natural actor," Zenobia said, clapping. "Have you considered the stage?"

"They talked me into trying out for a few productions at the university," he said, giving Nancy an affectionate look. "But I suffer from stage fright and—"

"Nonsense," Nancy said. "He was sensational as Hamlet."

"Did you take to the stage as well?" Zenobia asked. Juna recognized the journalistic light in her eyes.

Nancy waved a hand. "No, no. I was—"

"She was part of the true arty crowd," the professor said. "Sculptors, painters, and other sorts of mavericks with colorful clothing and avant-garde hairstyles." That his own hair was sticking up in damp spikes added to the hilarity.

"Weren't actors considered arty?" Juna asked.

He shrugged. "I found I had a different calling. Teaching has been a most rewarding experience."

"Hear, hear," Zenobia said, raising her cookie in toast. "I feel the same way. As much as I love writing and reporting, teaching is the most gratifying part of my life."

The professor turned to Henry. "And what do you, as a student, find most gratifying? What are your interests? Besides bicycles, of course."

Henry thought for a moment. "Photography. And science. Learning about faraway places." He grinned. "I like a lot of things."

Professor Stone nodded in approval. "It's healthy to have many interests. Do you like to read?"

"I subscribe to *Scientific American* and *Youth's Companion,*" Henry said.

"Ah, yes. Outstanding publications."

"Did you learn the American Pledge?" Zenobia asked.

Nancy raised her eyebrows. "What's that?"

"A pledge that school children learned as part of the national celebration leading up to the dedication of the fair. It was first published in *Youth's Companion.*"

Henry nodded. "Yes'm. We practiced for days, then performed it for the parents on Dedication Day last October."

"Would you care to recite it?"

"No, I don't think—" Henry began, but was interrupted by everyone, Juna included, begging him to do it.

"There's even a flag over there," Zenobia said, pointing at a flagpole in a nearby flower bed.

They all looked at Henry expectantly. He slapped his knees in surrender and heaved himself up. Juna and the others followed suit. It was with considerable effort that she didn't smile at his put-upon expression.

Henry faced the flag and held his right hand to his forehead in a salute. "I pledge allegiance to my flag," he began, then gracefully extended his hand from his forehead, palm upward, toward the flag. "And the republic for which it stands: one nation indivisible, with liberty and justice for all." He dropped his hand to his side, and they all clapped and cheered.

"Nicely done, Henry," the professor said. "Thank you."

"It was utterly captivating to hear the children reciting it together," Juna said as they settled back on the blanket. "The little ones, especially, were so earnest."

"As they were at our school in St. Louis," Zenobia said. "Did you follow with "My Country 'Tis of Thee?""

"Oh, yes."

"Don't start singing, please!" Henry said. "You've embarrassed me enough."

Nancy reached over and patted his foot. "You're a good egg, Henry."

Juna caught her son's eye and winked at him. His mouth twisted into a smile as he dropped his gaze and grabbed another cookie.

"By the way," Nancy said, "There's going to be a Wheelman's Parade at the fairgrounds the second weekend in August. It should be quite an event. My women's club has been invited to ride along. Come join us if you're able."

"Count me in," Zenobia said. "I'll still be here."

Juna and Henry exchanged a look of regret. "What fun that would be," she said, "but we'll be back in Louisiana by then."

"The town, not the state," Henry said around a mouthful of cookie.

As they said their goodbyes, Professor Stone rolled his wheel closer to Juna's. "You survived your first tour. Congratulations," he said. "I enjoyed meeting Zenobia and Henry. Your son is a credit to you."

"It's been an astonishing day," she said, glad her cheeks were already flushed from the heat. "If you'd told me a week ago that I'd be doing this, I wouldn't have believed you."

"It is in times of personal striving that we surprise ourselves the most," he said. "By the way, I will be leading a general tour of the grounds a week from Wednesday. It's a shame you're leaving. Nancy is planning to attend."

"You're walking the *entire* grounds?"

"I didn't explain adequately," he said with a laugh. "I've reserved an electric launch for a tour by water."

She stared at him a moment as an unfocused memory floated into her mind's eye and sharpened into a clear picture: a man, at the front of a boat, on the day they arrived at the fair. His melodious voice rising and falling as he pointed out the sights to the passengers. "That sounds wonderful," she said. "I'm sorry to miss it."

He touched the brim of his cap. "At any rate, I'll see you and Nancy this Saturday at the end-of-session party."

As they rode back to Mrs. Wilson's, Juna pedaled with the energy that one can only get from sheer happiness. She couldn't wait to tell Archie about her adventure. She owed this victory to his prodding, yes, but even more to his passionate belief that she could succeed. She'd have her chance tomorrow. When they'd parted ways the evening before, Archie invited her to tour the Illinois Building with him and Henry in the afternoon.

The streets of the neighborhood were quiet, aside from a few dogs who barked at them and the distant WHACK-whack, WHACK-whack of construction. Juna waved at two children playing with a ball in their front yard, and a woman with a baby carriage resting in the shade of a tree. In every regard, it had been a milestone day.

Chapter Twenty-Three

Beneath the excitement and thrill of the day's ride, Henry's anticipation of the music party tumbled between his brain and his middle. Should he go? Was it worth the risk? Was he too tired? An afternoon nap on the porch swing rendered the last question moot. And that evening, everyone went to bed by nine o'clock. "Nothing like fresh air and exercise to send one quickly and deeply into dreamland," Mrs. Wilson told her sleepy guests after two games of Old Maid.

"If I meet any insomniacs, I'll recommend they take up the bicycle," Zenobia said, yawning into her hand.

Determined to stay awake this time, Henry kept a lamp on and looked over his photographs. He studied Tomoko through a magnifying glass while devising an elaborate fantasy. In his imagination, he held her hand as they walked around the Wooded Island. He'd impress her by naming all the flowers—an equally outrageous fantasy—and then he'd buy her an ice cream. Or a chocolate. Then they'd wander over to the Midway and ride the Ferris Wheel. 'What a handsome pair,' people would exclaim.

At ten-thirty, full of happy thoughts, Henry slipped downstairs and retrieved his mandolin from the parlor. As he tiptoed out of the house he heard the distant rumble of thunder, but dismissed it as being too far away to be a problem. When he arrived at the meeting place, Nikola was waiting for him, violin case in hand. They grinned at each other by way of greeting, and began moving along with the late-night crowds.

Henry felt a new sense of boldness tonight as he walked beside the older boy. Grandpa was always telling him to be a man. Well, by gum, he was doing just that. Nothing bad, nothing daring, just two friends on their way to a gathering of musicians. "Think the same players will be there this time?" he asked.

Nikola shrugged. "Mostly. Others come and go. Or they bring a friend. The group has doubled in the last month." Without warning, he pulled up short and grabbed Henry's arm to stop him.

"What the—" The words stuck in Henry's throat as Peterson stepped into their path. He was not smiling.

"What a surprise. Does your mother know you're here?" he asked in a deadly calm voice.

Henry's newfound boldness pooled around his feet—the same general area where his stomach had dropped. He shook his head.

Nikola said, "It's my fault, sir. I invited him."

Peterson stared at him. "We've met, haven't we?"

"Nikola Petrovich. I work at the fair."

"Ah. The chair roller."

"Yes, sir."

"You may go. I will see Henry home."

"Oh, c'mon—" Henry began.

Peterson cut him off with a look. "I'm sure you'll find plenty to amuse yourselves with at the fair. During the daytime."

"Yes, sir," Nikola said in a quiet voice. "Henry, I'll see you around." He gave Peterson a measured look, then turned and hurried away.

Peterson jerked his head in the opposite direction. "Let's go."

It was a long walk home, with the man lecturing him in low tones about the dangers of the city, betraying his trust, his mother's trust, his aunt's trust, his grandfather's trust, yak-yak-yak-yak-yak. Aside from an occasionally mumbled, "Yessir," Henry kept his mouth shut and his eyes on the sidewalk in front of him. When they got to the corner closest to Mrs. Wilson's house, Peterson said, "I'll wait until you're back in the yard. This conversation is not over. In the meantime, I'm going to think long and hard about reporting this incident to your mother and grandfather."

Henry knew he'd be on the next train home if that happened. "Please don't tell them. I won't do it again, I swear."

Peterson's face was barely visible on the dark street. "We'll continue this conversation tomorrow. Now, get home and to bed."

When Henry got to the corner of the house, he looked back to see a dark shape turn and disappear into the night. At midnight, he was still wide-awake, curled tightly under his sheet. Beyond his worry that Peterson would tell his mother or grandfather, and frustration that his fun evening had been ruined, it embarrassed him that Nikola had seen him treated like a child. Of all the nights Peterson had to attend a concert or some Midway show, why did it have to be this one? Of all the gates he could have exited, why did it have to be the gate they were passing?

A sharp clap of thunder preceded a cloudburst. Henry got up and lowered the window most of the way. He flopped onto his stomach and hung his arms off the narrow bed, listening to the staccato rhythm of the rain as it pattered against the glass. He blew out a heavy breath. *I'm an idiot,* he thought. *Why did I sneak out in the first place?*

Outside, insects gradually resumed their night songs. Rain-cooled air tickled over his bare shoulders. Praying he wouldn't have to pack his bags the next day, he resolved to throw himself on Peterson's mercy. Yawning deeply, Henry curled onto his side and allowed drowsy thoughts to float through his brain. *I'll promise to do anything he asks . . . I'll inventory the entire Agriculture Building . . . I'll encourage his lectures . . . I'll shine his shoes . . . I'll—*

Chapter Twenty-Four

July 25, 1893—The St. Louis Daily
NOTES FROM THE FAIR:

The Sage of Anacostia

It's always a thrill to see the "Grand Old Man." A glimpse of a dignified, white-haired silhouette is usually all I get, as he's invariably surrounded by a host of bowlers, top hats, and bonnets eager for a wise word or a worthy decree. Others merely want to shake his hand and thank him for all he's accomplished. A steady voice emanates out to the ears of his group of listeners, both black and white, detailing his passionate call-to-action in the name of the Afro-American.

As the appointed representative for the Haitian Pavilion, Frederick Douglass takes his role seriously, joining his associates in condemning the hypocrisy of the "powers that be" and the limited role of the Negro at the World's Fair. He, however, goes a step further and encourages his people to visit and enjoy the Fair; to be seen as respectable and accomplished Americans. I am happy to report that many have listened and responded.

I had the pleasure of meeting three young journalists from Atlanta University in Georgia. These young men are part of a group of fifteen students working at the Fair. They document their experiences in articles for their school newspaper, *The Atlanta University Bulletin*. When I inquired as to their experience thus far, they all expressed satisfaction—and not a little surprise—at their welcome here. One student, who occupies his days as a chair roller, said he's been treated well for the most part. "No more, no less than the white boys," he said. "Folks are grateful to get off their feet for a spell."

The university's extensive exhibit in the Manufactures Building is outstanding. As a teacher myself, I am encouraged that bright, young minds will emerge from this excellent school, uplifting all humanity. I have no doubt that Mr. Douglass would agree.

—Zenobia A. Thom,
Special Correspondent

"I've decided it would be in your best interest—and mine—to keep last night's incident to ourselves," Peterson told Henry. They were in the south part of the fairgrounds walking past the windmill exhibit.

Henry, tired and bleary-eyed, slumped in relief. Peterson had kept to business for the first hour, which had him swinging between dread at what the man might say and just wanting to get it over with. He'd barely been able to concentrate on the impressive cannons in the Krupps Building, and when questioned about yesterday's ride, had mumbled that it had been fun and left it at that.

"But here's the deal," Peterson continued. "I expect you to act responsibly and seek your mother's approval, or mine, for future activities."

It rankled Henry that one slip-up was enough to throw his integrity into question, but he also wanted to remain in his mother and grandfather's good graces. Peterson apparently felt the same, as if Henry's behavior would reflect on him.

Peterson gave him a flicker of a smile. "By the way, I would have taken you to McClellan's myself if you had asked me."

"Thank you," Henry said, thinking, *In a pig's eye.*

"Son, you need to be careful of the company you keep. It appears your Serbian chum is leading you into risky behavior."

"He's not," Henry said. "I wanted to go. *Dang,* why does everyone treat me like a child? I stay out after dark all the time back home."

Peterson shot him a look. "This is a big city, Henry, not a river town. One you shouldn't be exploring after dark, particularly with an older boy you barely know."

"Nik is my friend. He's a good guy."

"Be that as it may—and I *am* glad you've found a friend here—I expect you to remain on high moral ground." He stopped and held out his hand. "Are we in agreement?"

"Yessir." Henry shook his mentor's hand as a mix of emotions jangled through him: relief that he'd gotten off easy, regret that he'd missed his last music party, and the realization that although Peterson had the power to tell him what to do, he was clearly on his side.

Peterson checked his watch. "We have some time to spare. Shall we look at the wheels in Transportation before meeting your mother?" That was the thing with Peterson. As maddening as he could be, he always redeemed himself in the end. They set off at a brisk pace. To their right, windmills of all shapes and sizes sliced through the hot July air.

Juna met Henry and Peterson at the Illinois Building, which commanded a conspicuous position just north of Wooded Island. She was eager to tell Archie about yesterday's bicycle tour and launched right in after they greeted each other. "We had the grandest time," she said, beaming at him. "I am in your debt."

His smile was a mixture of pleasure and I-told-you-so. "Not too scary on the boulevards?"

"I admit to fearing for my life a few times, and my hands were cramped from clutching the handles, but I rode between experienced riders who encouraged me. Dear Professor Stone and Henry were our fearless leaders. It was a lovely ride, despite being an amateur."

"Is this professor one of your teachers?"

"Not a regular one," she said. "He gave a guest lecture last week, and is a particular friend of my classmate, Miss Collins."

"Very good." Peterson gestured toward the building. "Shall we?"

As they moved toward the entrance, Henry joined in the conversation. "The professor is a fun chap. He and I set the pace. Then we had cookies, and everyone made me recite the American Pledge, and . . ."

It relieved Juna to hear Henry's enthusiasm as he recounted the day. He'd seemed out of sorts at breakfast. Whatever was making him prickly, it appeared that Archie had known just the right thing to say. How glad she was that her son had this man to guide him. As they entered the building, she gave Peterson a warm smile of gratitude.

The Illinois Building featured many kinds of exhibitions. "You won't find a better display," Peterson said. "Geology, agriculture, mining, floriculture, and horticulture are all represented, as are educational institutions, examples of women's work, and many other things." He gestured toward one of the side wings. "Let's go this way first. There's something that's sure to delight you both."

He led them to a clever tableau built by the State Fish Commission, which featured a miniature lake fed by water that ran down a mossy, vine-covered hillside. They stood on a small arched bridge overlooking the pool, where a sampling of Illinois fish swam along the perimeter and around a central hub of plants. "Though lake water is used," Peterson said, "the commission devised a filtration system that keeps it clear as glass."

"How marvelous," Juna said, leaning over the railing to peer at the many varieties of fish. "You can practically count the scales. Is that a sunfish, Henry?"

"Yes'm. And there's a bass and a bluegill over there," Henry said, and sped back to the floor level for a closer look.

"Henry's in his element," Juna said. "He loves to go fishing with his friends."

"I can imagine he does, living by the river. Do you fish, as well?"

"I used to, when Zenobia and I were girls. We had a grand time tramping along with our poles and buckets, each of us determined to catch the first one. Whomever caught the first fish got the prize."

"What prize was that?"

"The egg sac, if we caught a fish that had one. My stepmother would batter and fry it. It was a special treat."

"And what if there was more than one? Did you share, or was it a winner-takes-all situation?" he teased.

"Oh, we shared them, but the winner got the first one out of the pan," Juna said, enjoying the way she and Archie could share an easy laugh.

They wandered through the exhibits, with Archie pointing out interesting features and Henry darting away to inspect things that caught his eye, such as an impressive ornithological and insect exhibit. Juna was impressed with an immense "painting" of an Illinois farm made entirely of grains and grasses. "Remarkable," she said, laying a hand on Archie's arm. "From a distance, I thought it was paint."

"We're fooled by the best illusions, are we not?" he said, lightly touching her waist as they moved on.

When they reached the upper floor, Archie led her to an outdoor balcony to rest their brains. Henry stayed inside to continue his explorations.

"How's this for a view?" Archie said, sweeping one arm outward. The Wooded Island stretched out before them with the Great Buildings along the periphery. Boats glided on the lagoon. Flags waved in the warm afternoon breezes. On the strip of land in front of the building, many visitors walked, sat in a shady place, or stood in line at a food booth.

"It's spectacular," Juna said. She pointed at the golden dome nearly a mile away. "If Zenobia was standing on the roof, we could wave at each other."

"I'll see if I can arrange it," Archie said, grinning down at her.

"You've been very kind to Henry and me," she said. "It doesn't seem possible that our time here is drawing to a close. Our trip has been a dream and I'm not ready to wake up." She let out a breath. "I'm going to miss . . . everything."

Archie slid his hands back and forth on the railing. "The White City will lose some of its luster when you leave, Juna. I would be most gratified if you'd spend time with me. I have become quite fond of you, and—"

She stopped him with a hand on his arm. "Please don't say it. I'm not ready to be more than friends."

"You're a lovely woman, Juna. Do you find my company so disagreeable?"

His passionate delivery took her aback. "No, no. Of course not. It's just that I'm not ready to give my heart to anyone, you see." How could she explain that her heart still belonged to Craig?

Archie's hands moved restlessly over the railing as he looked out over the grounds. "I know you miss your husband, Juna. I won't pretend I could ever replace him, but the heart is a buoyant thing if you allow another's affection to lift you up."

She felt a twinge of guilt for disappointing him. Was she really allowing her grief to anchor her heart? Was she being selfish with this generous man?

"I'm sorry, Archie. You've been a fine friend and—" She stopped as Henry bounded up.

"There are some terrific fossils in the Paleontological Department," he said, grabbing her hand. "You have to see them."

As Henry led her inside, Juna gave Archie a look of apology. She supposed there was nothing more to be said.

As they later left the building, Archie said, "How would you like to tour the city on Thursday, Henry? There are buildings worth seeing, and an outstanding new sculpture of Lincoln on the north side."

"Sure," Henry said. "May I go, Mother?"

"That sounds like a grand idea," she said. "I hear the Auditorium Theater is something else."

Archie nodded. "It's on our itinerary. We'll spend the day exploring, then meet you at the state building. It would be my pleasure to treat you both to dinner."

Juna hesitated. Would accepting his invitation only encourage his romantic interest? Before she could answer, Henry said, "That would be swell."

"We'd be delighted," Juna said, seeing no gracious way out.

As Archie walked them to the exit, he murmured, "As friends, of course." Judging by his mischievous expression, it appeared all was forgiven.

That night, Juna knocked on her sister's bedroom door. Zennie opened it, hairbrush in hand; her hair hanging loose around her shoulders. "Come in."

"I'd like your opinion on something," Juna said.

Zennie waved her toward the bed and plopped back down on her vanity stool. "Fire away," she said, and resumed brushing her sleek, coffee-colored locks.

Juna made herself comfortable and plunged right in. "Our Mr. Peterson has expressed a particular interest in me." She gave a little shrug as if to say, *Can you believe it?*

"Has he? I'm not surprised. Do you like him?"

"Well, yes, but I don't want to encourage him. We had a frank conversation this afternoon, and he seems amiable to remaining friends."

"I see." Zennie studied her for a moment. "Do you enjoy his company?"

"He's been a gentleman and is kind to Henry. It's just that, well—this sounds silly, even to me—he fills up a room, if you know what I mean."

Zenobia nodded. "Does that bother you?"

"It's hard to explain," Juna said. "Perhaps it's that he's so different from Craig. With Craig, I felt the same size, if that makes sense. With Archie I feel small, like some precious thing that needs careful handling."

"He is quite tall and broad-shouldered," Zenobia said. "I'd think many women would appreciate being treated like a priceless vase. Not me, of course," she said, waggling her hairbrush. "I value my independence."

Juna thought about that for a moment. She'd certainly come to value her own freedom at the fair. Would stepping out with Archie change that? It just might. "I've made my decision," she said, standing up. "Now that I've had a taste of independence, I believe I'll keep it that way."

Zenobia raised an eyebrow. "There's magic at the fair that turns the most stalwart souls into hopeless romantics."

Juna swirled her hands through the air. "The widow Lewis is impervious to this magic," she said in her most dramatic voice, and swept out of the room.

Chapter Twenty-Five

July 27, 1893—The St. Louis Daily
NOTES FROM THE FAIR:

An Army of Artists

If it took an army to build the Exposition, it took another to decorate and adorn it. The art defines the Fair; enlivens it. Artists from all over the world have left their loving imprint over the grounds. I've had the privilege of meeting some of these men and women, witnessing their earnest labors in the days before the grand opening.

The bridges alone are worth a trip to the Exposition, with mighty elk, deer, moose, buffalo, jaguar, and bear ornamenting each like proud sentries. I give you Edward Kemeys and A.P. Proctor, sculptors extraordinaire.

I'm particularly impressed by the contributions of our talented youth. Who has not gazed into the soaring dome of the Administration Building and wondered at The Glorification of the Arts and Sciences mural? Or taken in the sight and sound of the Columbian Fountain? Or admired the noble angels that adorn the Woman's Building? I give you William de Leftwich Dodge, Frederick MacMonnies, and Miss Alice Rideout: three young gems among the treasure of talent at the Fair.

And there were none more dedicated than the "White Rabbits," those intrepid young women who worked long hours alongside their teacher, Lorado Taft. Look at the sparkling groups in and around the Horticulture Building and be amazed.

Such dedication! Truly, their herculean efforts are a gift to the world and to our own creative hearts.

—Zenobia A. Thom,
Special Correspondent

On Thursday morning, Henry accompanied Zenobia to the train stop at the north part of the fairgrounds. The day was overcast and humid, but the threat of rain seemed remote. "Have a good day in the city," she said. "Your mother and I are going to lose ourselves in the Shoe and Leather Building today."

Henry had an hour before meeting Peterson, so took a chance and dashed to Phoenix Hall. It had been five days since The Great Debacle—as he thought of it—and was desperate to see Tomoko. He'd left a souvenir thimble on the rock two days before, but had avoided going inside the Hall. He couldn't stay long. A quick look would have to be enough. And, with luck, her father wouldn't notice one more visitor.

He arrived, sweaty and out of breath, thrilled to see Tomoko at her table. She was making birds for three girls sitting politely on the cushions. Other visitors stood watching, and he slipped in beside them. Tomoko looked up to acknowledge them with a smile, dropping her eyes quickly upon seeing Henry. Her expression became self-conscious, and it pleased him to know that he was the cause. Glancing around, he saw Professor Shuga pointing out the phoenix panels to a group of well-dressed men. Unfortunately, he chose that moment to look in his daughter's direction, meeting Henry's gaze straight on. Henry quickly turned back, berating himself for being careless. When a woman moved closer and blocked Tomoko from view, he left the building and circled around to the rock.

The thimble was gone. In its place was a blue feather striped with black, most likely from a blue jay. He smiled to think of Tomoko picking it up with him in mind. In its place, he left a shiny button he'd found by the bandstand next to the Administration Building. He stayed a few minutes longer, etching the rock and Phoenix Hall into his memory. A few more days were all they had left. Would he get another chance to speak with her? He couldn't just disappear, never to be seen again, without some explanation.

With no time to spare, he left Wooded Island and hurried toward the rolling chair pavilion near the Woman's Building. He hadn't seen Nikola since their discovery Monday night, and he wanted to reassure him that all was well. He envied his friend's freedom to come and go as he pleased. As much as Mother had loosened the reins, he had no illusions that she would approve of late-night sessions at McClellan's.

At the pavilion, two boys sat in their chairs waiting for a hire. One had a sunburned nose and was eating a sausage roll. The other, a boy wearing spectacles, was engrossed in a book. They both looked up as Henry approached.

Henry looked from one to the other. "Say, I'm looking for Nikola. Could you give him a message for me?"

The boy with the sausage roll spoke with his mouth full. "He's gone."

"What do you mean? Pushing a customer?"

"Gone. He was sacked."

It was as if a stone had been heaved into Henry's stomach. "What happened?" he demanded. "Why would he be sacked?"

"Dunno. Someone must've complained."

"But why? He's a good guy."

The boy with the book nodded. "We stuck up for him, but the manager had his orders, apparently."

Henry stomped his foot in frustration. "Any idea where he lives?"

"Never really talked about personal stuff. Sorry."

Henry was still mulling over this revelation as he and Peterson walked toward the train station. Should he mention it? He felt the need to talk to someone about the situation. Despite his mentor's concerns about his friend, he plunged ahead. "Nikola got sacked," he said.

Peterson glanced at him in surprise. "I'm sorry to hear that. Any reason given?"

"No idea. I haven't talked to him." Henry huffed. "It stinks."

"There must have been a reason. Stealing fares or flirting with young women, maybe?" A smile played around Peterson's mouth. "It could be any number of things."

"Nik's not like that," Henry retorted. "He's honest."

"Whoa there." Peterson lifted a hand in apology. "I didn't mean to malign him. Sometimes a misunderstanding can be enough to get a worker dismissed. Would you like me to inquire?"

Henry shook his head. Nikola was a poor immigrant. No one would take his word over some socialite or businessman. "Nah," he said. "Thanks anyway."

After a few steps, Peterson said, "I'm glad you confided in me, and hope you'll regard me as a friend and supporter in the years ahead."

His declaration caught Henry off guard. "Um, thanks," he said, feeling a ripple of remorse for any unkind thoughts he'd had about the man.

As they neared the train stop, they passed a man leaning against a building reading a newspaper. Henry recognized Kramer, the cab driver, with his drooping mustache and hooded eyelids that reminded Henry of crocodile eyes. Perhaps he was taking a break from his cab duties. He turned to mention it to Peterson, but his mentor chose that moment to point out a popular restaurant. When Henry looked back, the man was gone.

The train platform was wide but crowded. A short distance away, a small steam engine approached, pulling a line of cars painted green. A woman who was trying to manage several parcels dropped one of them onto the platform. Peterson stepped over to help her, and Henry turned back to watch the train. As the engine got closer, he was aware of more people surrounding him. He edged this way and that to avoid elbows. When the train was a half block away, Henry felt a hand in the middle of his back. In the next instant, the tracks rushed toward him. He hit the metal rails with a jolt of pain that shot through his arms and legs. People yelled as the train screeched toward him, mere feet away. In a blink, someone dragged him off the tracks. The train slid by an instant later and slowed to a stop.

Henry lay on the platform, breathing hard. Peterson gripped his shoulders. "My god, Henry," he said in a shaky voice. "Are you all right?"

"Yeah, I think so," Henry said, moving his legs a little. "Nothing's broken." He scanned the circle of faces looking down at him, but he only saw horrified and concerned expressions. Doors to the train opened, and the platform was abruptly a river of trousers and dresses flowing around them as passengers disembarked and mixed with those waiting to load. Henry closed his eyes and listened to Peterson's tense reassurances.

"He's all right . . . The boy took a tumble . . . No, a doctor won't be necessary, thank you."

Footsteps pounded up as the platform cleared. "What happened?" a man yelled. Henry cracked his eyes open. It was the conductor.

"The boy lost his balance and fell onto the tracks," Peterson said.

"I'm okay." Henry winced as he sat up. He was tempted to correct Peterson, but was already questioning himself. Had he really been pushed?

"You'll have some fine bruises to show for it," the conductor said as he walked away. "Stay farther back next time."

Peterson was stricken. "I had no business having you stand so close to the edge. Forgive me."

"Not your fault. Gonna be sore, is all," Henry said. A few feet away, the train heaved itself forward. Curious passengers stared at them as they passed.

Peterson gave him a ghost of a smile. "Your mother will know what to do—right after she kills me."

"You saved my life. You'll be the hero."

"I doubt she'll take that view. C'mon, I'll see you home in a cab. You need rest. I'll get word to your mother and aunt."

Henry groaned as Peterson helped him to his feet. He took one shaky step forward, then another. By the time he'd been delivered into Mrs. Wilson's care, he was so stiff he could barely navigate the front steps. Horrified, she'd immediately called for Hattie to prepare a bath with Epsom salt.

As he soaked in the warm water and studied his darkening bruises, he replayed the events of his near death over and over: The crowded platform. The hand pressed to his back. The shove that sent him hurtling toward the tracks. Emotion overtook him, and he covered his face with a washrag to muffle the sound. What if he'd been killed? What would Mother do without him? He was supposed to take care of her. It was his duty. He couldn't do something stupid and get himself killed. It was pure foolishness to dream of exploring and collecting with Henry Ward. What if the ship sank? What if he contracted a disease? He thought of his father dying and leaving her alone. He couldn't do the same thing. He'd promised.

A week after his father's funeral, Grandpa had found him sitting in the oak tree behind the house. It was his favorite spot to watch the Mississippi far below. He could even look across to Illinois. That side was lower, making the view of the horizon go on and on. He spent hours there, alone or with his friends, pretending they were steamboat captains and crew.

"Come down, son."

He wiped his eyes and climbed down. Grandpa didn't like it when Henry cried, so he did it in secret.

"Sit with me." Grandpa led him to a bench. He was big and strong, despite his hurt arm. His hand had been amputated during the war. *Am-pu-tated.* Henry had rehearsed that word since he was a tyke. It was an awful word, but he liked how the syllables felt in his mouth when he said them. He liked words.

Grandpa seemed a little smaller and weaker today. Perhaps he cried in secret, too, but when he spoke his voice was as strong and sure as ever. "Son, you're the man of the house now."

Henry bumped the ground with his bare toes. "Aren't you?"

"Yes, but now that your father is gone, you need to help take care of your mother. Women need taking care of, you know. They need us men to protect them. Don't forget that. When you are older, you'll take your father's place at the factory." He nudged Henry with his elbow. "And someday, you'll take mine. Understand?"

"Because that will help Mama?"

"Yes."

Henry squirmed. It was a lot to take in. The words seemed to press down on him. He wanted to be taken care of, not the other way around. But he knew he'd do it because Grandpa asked him to do it. Henry loved his mama. Of course he'd protect her. "I'll try," he said in a small voice.

Grandpa hooked his elbow around him. "By hook or by crook?" he asked.

Henry smiled at their old joke. "Yessir."

"Good boy."

Henry splashed his face with the cooling water. Today's events made him realize he needed to toe the line and put his dreams on a shelf. Grandpa was right. He needed to act like a man now. He also realized that he needed to keep his suspicions about the accident to himself, or they'd be on the next train home. Peterson would feel obligated to tell Mother. Or worse,

Grandpa. In a big city like Chicago, there were bound to be bad people who were mean for the fun of it. He'd simply been in the wrong place at the wrong time. He was sure of it.

He reached for the towel. Better to keep the truth—and his dreams—to himself.

Chapter Twenty-Six

The Shoe and Leather Building stood in the south part of the park between the Forestry Building and the Krupp's Gun exhibit, right on the lake shore. The intramural railway took the sisters practically to the doorstep. "Now, that's what I call service," Juna said as she and Zenobia descended the stairs to ground level. They walked toward their destination, enjoying the breeze off the lake.

"I've only been here once," Zenobia said as they approached the entrance. "It has a lot of interesting displays, but not so many as to make one's head explode."

"That's a relief," Juna said. "My head threatens to explode daily. *Mmm,* don't you love the smell of leather?" she asked as they pushed through the doors. The building was a long rectangle, with case upon handsome case filling the lower floor. A stuffed moose and other leather-producing animals stood watch around the room like sentries.

"I do love it," Zenobia said. "There is every type of product made from every type of leather here. Shoes, bags, belts, you name it."

"What's up there?" Juna asked, pointing to the gallery where the whirring sounds of machinery mixed with footsteps and conversation. It was a noisy, but not unpleasant accompaniment.

"Shoe-making equipment," Zenobia said. "It's very interesting, but you'll be disappointed to know there are no cobbler's elves. I've looked."

Juna planted fists on her waist. "What? We might as well leave now."

Zennie laughed. "Yes. But first I want you to see an exhibit of shoes worn throughout the ages. You'll find it makes up for the lack of elves."

"If you insist," Juna said, linking her arm with Zennie's. "Lead on."

Her sister's recommendation proved fascinating. There was everything from sensible Roman sandals—"I wouldn't mind a pair of those in summer"—to not-so-sensible high-heeled creations from seventeenth-century France. "Why, those are for men."

She stared, astonished, at a pair of Chinese slippers designed for binding the feet. "Gosh."

"Indeed," Zenobia murmured.

They moved on.

Other cases held examples of modern-day wear by companies around the world. They stopped to moon over a gorgeous display: walking shoes in the softest leather, fancy slippers to be worn with a ball gown, sturdier men's shoes that were very handsome. "Oh, to be a Palmer, Vanderbilt, or First Lady," Zenobia said. "It looks like 'Tompkins Fine Shoes' is the manufacturer."

"Oh! I've met Mr. Tompkins," Juna said. "His daughter is a regular at the spa, and we hand out their shoe hooks to customers." She looked around. "I wonder if he's around here somewhere. I'd like to say hello."

Zenobia nodded toward the gallery. "Let's look up there."

On the way to the stairs, they gawked at an enormous elephant hide that purportedly weighed five hundred pounds. Upstairs, Sarah Tompkins greeted them in a spacious booth where shelves of more casual shoes were on display. "Mrs. Lewis, how nice to see you." She sat at a desk, taking orders. "Look who's here, Daddy," she called to Mr. Tompkins, who was chatting with one of the other shoemakers.

He excused himself and came right over. "Welcome, welcome."

Juna introduced Zenobia and proceeded to gush. "You have the most beautiful shoes," she said. "Congratulations."

Father and daughter beamed at them. "Thank you for noticing," Mr. Tompkins said. "We stand by our quality."

"Don't you mean, 'You stand *on* your quality?'" Zenobia asked.

Sarah clapped her hands. "Our new motto: 'We stand *on* our quality.' That deserves a shoe hook and a coupon," she said, grabbing the items off her desk.

Mr. Tompkins leaned in. "I must say, Mrs. Lewis, that we've seen increased sales because of your spa. It's been a good partnership, indeed."

Juna smiled. "I'm so glad to hear it."

"As long as you're here, ladies, may I show you our World's Fair Specials? They are a good value, and we'll certainly apply the spa discount," he added with a wink.

"How can I refuse?" Zenobia said with a laugh. "Too bad the *Daily* won't consider new shoes a reasonable working expense. I walk so many miles here, I've worn out one pair already."

"And how about you, Mrs. Lewis?"

"Perhaps another day, but thank you." She didn't want to spend the money.

He persisted charmingly. "May I suggest we at least measure your feet and keep your information on file for a future purchase?"

"C'mon, Juney," Zenobia urged. "What's the harm?"

"Oh, all right," she said, shooting an exasperated look at her sister, who was making a feeble effort to control her victorious expression. They followed Sarah to a row of chairs where she carefully measured their feet. Zenobia took advantage of the coupon and splurged on two pairs of walking shoes.

"Visit us again," Mr. Tompkins called as they said their goodbyes.

"What a lovely father and daughter," Zenobia said as they approached the stairs. "And, good gracious, I'd like to meet their dentist."

They took the elevated railway back to the Terminal, and walked to the Administration Building so Zenobia could drop off her shoes. When they reached the journalism office, a thin man wearing a straw hat approached them. "You have a message, Miss Thom," he said, handing her a piece of paper. He touched his brim to Juna and continued on his way.

"Thank you, Ned," Zenobia called after him. She unfolded the note and drew in a breath. "It's from Peterson. Henry is hurt. He's okay, but banged up."

Juna's stomach swooped. "We have to go," she cried, already rushing for the stairs.

It was well after midnight, and Juna was wide awake and pacing. She'd known. Deep down she'd known that coming to Chicago was a bad idea. 'Calm down, Juna,' everyone kept saying. 'It was an accident. Henry's all right.'

Yes, accidents happen! she wanted to scream. She knew all about accidents. They started innocently enough with an intriguing idea. Bicycle racing, for instance. They should leave. Tomorrow. She'd skip her final two days of class and take Henry back to Louisiana, where the dangers seemed more manageable and familiar, like the deadly undertow of the Mississippi. Or wild animals, or—

There was a soft knock on her door. Zenobia, most likely, determined to reason with her. She yanked open the door, saying, "Go away, Zen—" Her indignant words melted at the sight of Mrs. Wilson in her robe and slippers. A thin, white braid trailed over her shoulder. It mirrored Juna's own blonde one. "I'm sorry, Mrs. Wilson. I thought it was—"

"I know," the older woman said. She gestured toward the room with her cane. "May I come in, dear?"

Juna backed up and opened the door wider. "Of course, though I'm dreadful company at the moment."

"I'm aware of it, my dear. Your room is above mine. I concluded that offering a listening ear would be a greater kindness than ignoring your anguish."

"Forgive me," Juna said after closing the door. "I pace when I'm addled. Please, do sit down." Mrs. Wilson sat in the room's only chair and gestured to the bed. Juna plopped down on the edge. They spoke in low voices.

"I'm a river town girl, myself," Mrs. Wilson said. "Years of living by the Mississippi taught me that there is more going on under the surface than one realizes." She reached over and patted Juna's hand. "Tell me, child. What is churning under the surface?"

Juna's chin trembled. "I keep thinking about the day my husband died. I encouraged him to take up the wheel and enter the race. And today, Henry almost died after I encouraged him to go on an excursion to the city with

Mr. Peterson." She took in a stuttering breath. "I almost lost him to illness this past winter. I can't lose him, too. I just can't."

Mrs. Wilson gave her a kind smile. "I understand. But if guilt is a deadly undertow that lurks in the background of our minds, fear is what keeps us rooted to the riverbank. Life is made for risk-taking, my dear. What if we never left our safe riverbank? What if we never explored further than our immediate surroundings? What would be the point of living? We find joy in life by embracing it, not by flinging it away."

Juna dabbed her eyes with her sleeve. "That's true. It's selfish of me to expect Henry not to take risks or have adventures. He's like his father in that way."

The old woman was silent for a few moments. "When I was a little girl, I found a butterfly struggling to emerge from its cocoon. Convinced that it was going to expire in its efforts, I helped it come out. Do you know what happened? It limped around for a few hours, then died. In trying to help, I inadvertently doomed it." She reached over and took Juna's hand. "We need to follow our natural instincts, my dear. Henry is a fine young man with an adventurous heart. He'll be all right. You're a wonderful role model, after all. Look at everything you've embraced since coming to Chicago."

It's true, Juna thought. She *had* embraced new things for herself: classes at the oratory school, the foot spa, even bicycle riding. "You're right," she said. "I will encourage Henry even more. It's unreasonable to sit someone at a feast and not expect them to eat it. And he would be so disappointed if we left five days early."

Mrs. Wilson smiled. "That's the spirit."

When Juna was settled enough to go to bed, her thoughts turned to Archie. Tonight, he was her hero for saving Henry. Beyond that, he was respected by Seymour and liked by her son, which counted for a great deal. Perhaps it was time to give him a chance, even if her time in Chicago was ending soon. Though, she had to admit it was a relief knowing their departure the following week would likely be the end of it.

She slid her hands down her torso. She wasn't so young anymore, but still cut a good figure. Tomorrow she'd ask Nancy to go dress shopping with her after class. *Risk taking,* she decided, required courage and a new frock.

Chapter Twenty-Seven

"Mrs. Fletcher is in a right tizzy," Annie Cable whispered to Juna when she arrived at the Missouri Building the next day.

"What's going on?" Juna wearily stowed her hat and handbag in a cupboard. Mrs. Fletcher was often bustling around, but not usually in a 'tizzy'.

"The final lecturer for the fruit production series canceled for next Friday, and now Mrs. Fletcher is scrambling to find a replacement. It's hard to enlist someone on short notice, you see."

"What a shame," Juna said. "Surely there's someone here who could fill in?" She checked her watch. "I best get upstairs and heat the foot soak."

Annie's expression turned wistful. "The spa has been a grand success. It won't be the same without you, dear. Must you leave so soon?"

"I'll have been here the better part of a month," Juna said, giving her a quick hug. "Believe me, I wish I could stay longer. I'm going to miss it here." She lowered her voice. "Would you like to hear a secret?"

Annie's grey eyebrows shot up. "Certainly."

"I'm going to ask my father-in-law to produce my foot tonic."

"Wonderful," Annie said, clapping her hands together. "I'd love a supply for my bunions."

Juna shushed her with a smile. "Please keep that to yourself. He may refuse and that will be that. Anyway, you'll have the recipe once you're in charge."

Each of the twenty-minute sessions were full again that day and the ladies were generous with their donations. When Juna took the cash box to Mrs. Fletcher's tiny office near the auditorium, the woman waved her in.

"Sit down, please." Mrs. Fletcher took a moment to blot the ink on a letter she'd been writing, then leaned back in her chair with a sigh. "What a day. I've been dashing off notes to busy men with better things to do than whip up a lecture in a week."

"I'm confident you'll find someone suitable," Juna said, setting the cash box on the desk. "Here are today's earnings. I'll make sure to leave you with a good supply of vinegar. Herbs will need to be replenished in a week or so."

The woman gave her a warm look. "What a blessing you've been. Three months ago, if you'd have told me that Missouri would end up hosting a foot spa, I'd never have believed it. Your bold idea is bringing more visitors to the building and earning a little extra money, to boot."

Juna smiled. "I wouldn't have believed it, either."

"You can be very proud of yourself, dear. I have observed a marked change in your countenance. You not only speak with more confidence, you have a contentedness about you that was missing before."

"I have Mary Blood and Ida Riley to thank, then. And Mrs. Rhodehaver, of course. If she hadn't dropped off those catalogues, I wouldn't have signed up for the class in the first place."

"And look at all you've accomplished here. Goodness! So many women have benefitted from your excellent foot soak."

"I'm a little amazed myself," Juna said, giving a modest shrug. "Who would have known?"

Mrs. Fletcher leaned forward and rested her arms on the desk. Her expression was noticeably brighter. "I'm always impressed by women who are experts in their field, aren't you?"

"Oh yes," Juna said, warming to the subject. "I've found my teachers so very inspiring, and I've heard some fine speeches at the Woman's Building. I've met many outstanding women during my stay in Chicago."

Mrs. Fletcher gave an enthusiastic nod. "Yes, indeed. What a gift it is to have a place where these women can share their knowledge with others."

"Absolutely."

"And what a blessing it is for the rest of us to be on the receiving end of that knowledge."

"Oh yes," Juna said. "My own horizons have expanded considerably."

"I know the feeling," Mrs. Fletcher said. "It's almost a duty for a woman with particular expertise to share it with others. We're all in this together, don't you agree?"

"Completely," Juna said. "What if my teachers had chosen a different track? And I'm grateful to you for letting me try out my outrageous idea."

Mrs. Fletcher pinned her with a triumphant look. "Exactly. Which is why *you,* dear Juna, should give the lecture next Friday. "Uses of Apple Cider Vinegar" should do nicely as a topic. It's time to put your knowledge and speaking skills to good use, don't you think?"

Juna stared at the woman. "But, I'm leaving on Monday," she said in a weak, breathy voice which Mary Blood would find appalling.

Mrs. Fletcher fluttered a hand. "I'm not unreasonable, dear. I'll give you two days to work out the arrangements and give me an answer."

Juna rose from her chair, feeling muddled. What had just happened?

"I have every faith in you," Mrs. Fletcher called after her.

Downstairs, Juna collected her things from the parlor, noticing that Annie was studiously pouring lemonade and chatting with visitors. Had she given Mrs. Fletcher the idea?

She emerged into the bright July evening to find Henry and Archie waiting. Archie tipped his head, appraising her. "You look discombobulated," he said. Beside him, Henry mouthed the word, *discombobulated.*

"I am, at that," she said. "I've been invited—summoned, really—to give a lecture on the uses of apple cider vinegar. Next Friday."

Peterson gave a bark of surprise. "What marvelous news!"

"It is?"

"Of course. It will be good advertising for Lewis Vinegar, and—" He smiled broadly. "You and Henry get to stay another week."

Henry jumped on board immediately. "Yes! Do it, Mama."

She pressed her hand to her forehead. Why did everyone except her think it was a grand idea? She put forth her best argument. "Seymour will want us home. We've already stayed longer than originally planned. I wouldn't dream of—"

Peterson waved off her excuses. "I'll telegraph him tonight. He'll be all for it."

"No, no," she said, quickly. "*If* I decide to give the lecture, I will contact him."

Henry grasped her shoulders. He was practically glowing. "You. Can. Do. It," he said, emphasizing each word with a little shake. He was, no doubt, motivated by the prospect of staying another week, but she appreciated the sentiment.

She patted his hands. "Thank you, Henry." She looked into their expectant faces and heaved a great breath. "I'll sleep on it, all right?"

Peterson beamed. "A prudent idea when making a big decision."

As they walked toward the exit, Juna quietly assessed Henry's physical state. Despite pleas by all the females in the Wilson household, Henry insisted on keeping his session with his mentor that day. Thankfully, Archie kept it short, meeting during Juna's time at the state building, which gave Henry most of the day to rest. "Henry had his fill of maps today in Manufactures," he said.

"They were interesting," Henry said, "but after the twenty or thirtieth, the details ran together. Vermont looked like Switzerland and South Carolina looked like Timbuktu."

After exiting the grounds, Henry stopped to look in a souvenir stall. "He's having a wonderful experience here," Juna told Archie as they waited. "Thank you."

"He's a good lad. We get on all right." Archie cleared his throat and smoothed his mustache before turning to her. "Might I ask you a question, Junaluska?"

"Certainly."

"There is to be a performance of Handel's *Messiah* tomorrow evening at Music Hall. Would you like to join me? We'll call it a celebration of completing your course."

"A concert sounds very nice," she said. "Is Henry invited?"

"I asked him, but he says he has plans with his aunt." His eyes shone with amusement.

"I see." Juna's stomach was clenching—from hunger or nerves, she wasn't sure. And what mysterious plans did Henry and Zenobia have? She thought of her emotional change-of-heart last night, but was feeling less confident now that the opportunity had arrived. Faced with making yet another big decision, she plunged in. "I will be happy to attend," she said, silently blessing Nancy for shopping with her earlier that day.

The force of his happiness was almost palatable. "Excellent. As friends, of course," he added.

She laughed. "Of course."

Henry returned and held up a small wooden box with the Ferris Wheel and *1893 World's Columbian Exposition* painted on the lid. "For my souvenirs and stuff," he said.

They said goodbye to Peterson and began walking back to Mrs. Wilson's. "So, what are your and Zenobia's plans for tomorrow night?" she asked.

"She's taking me on the Ferris Wheel for a nighttime ride."

"Lovely. Is Zennie aware of this scheme?"

Henry grinned at her. "Not yet." He proceeded to whistle "Daisy Bell" the rest of the way home. She noted he had a bounce in his step despite his recent injuries. Perhaps an evening at the fair was just the thing they all needed to put yesterday's terrible episode behind them.

As she got ready for bed that night, Juna found herself humming the same tune. While conflicted about whether to give the lecture, she had to admit that staying in Chicago for another week was an attractive prospect. Mrs. Wilson and Zenobia had been delighted to hear about Mrs. Fletcher's "offer."

"Of course you may stay another week, my dear," Mrs. Wilson said. "To think of it! A world's fair lecturer staying under my roof."

"You *are* going to say yes, aren't you?" Zenobia said. "You'll be sensational, and I'm sure we can convince Seymour."

"Mr. Peterson seems to think he'll be all for it."

"I'm sure he will."

"I've something else to report," Juna said, feeling a little overwhelmed. "I've agreed to hear a concert with him."

"Enjoy it, my dear," Mrs. Wilson said. "I've been a widow over twenty years. Even at my age it's nice to have a man's attention."

Zennie had been more to the point. "Good for you, Juney. You deserve to have a little fun after six years of being alone."

"I have had fun and I haven't been alone."

"You know what I mean. You're long overdue. Besides, it's a concert, not a proposal of marriage."

"I'm nervous," Juna said. "Isn't that silly?"

Zenobia tapped her lips, thinking. "I have an idea. What if Henry and I meet you two after the fireworks? Apparently, I'm treating him to an evening on the Midway," she said with a wink. "We can walk home together, and it might save you from any awkwardness when you say 'goodnight.'"

Mrs. Wilson had actually giggled. "*Awkwardness* can be mighty pleasant." This pronouncement made Juna blush and Zenobia hoot with laughter.

Juna ran her fingers over her new dresses hanging on hooks in her wardrobe. They were the prettiest things she'd ever owned: a grey-green summer dress with lace trim and ruffles on the skirt; a blue-flowered print with a scooped neck; and a dusky pink skirt and matching jacket. She'd splurged on a new hat and ribbons to match each dress, and lightweight gloves in a soft grey. Nancy had exclaimed, 'Oh Juna, you're a picture,' with each new outfit. She'd topped off her purchases with a sturdy yellow parasol.

She gave up a happy sigh, relieved to have nice things to wear for her last class, the lecture—if she decided to give it, and potential evenings out on the town. She drooped a little at the sight of her old pair of shoes, but new ones would have to wait. In the meantime, she'd shine up her old reliables.

Henry lay in bed and whispered into the dark. "Marvelous! Sensational! Grand! A miracle! Astonishing! Fabulous! Wondrous! Please, please, please, please, *please* agree to do the lecture, Mama." Thoughts of Tomoko filled his mind. Staying an extra week would give him more opportunities to see her. Maybe they'd even have a proper conversation. He could also visit his favorite exhibits and keep an eye out for Nikola.

The promise of an evening on the Midway added to his giddiness. When Peterson invited him to the concert, Henry knew it was just a ploy to convince Mother to go. He owed Peterson for saving his life, so he used Zennie as a convenient excuse to bow out. Thank goodness she'd gone along with his scheme. If he was honest with himself, he was happy for Mother. She deserved to have fun, even if Peterson was the one providing it. At least the man couldn't talk her ears off during the concert.

Henry's mind wandered as he listened to the nighttime rhythms of peepers and crickets. *What if?* What if Mother allowed Peterson to court her? He yawned deeply as he considered the ramifications. While it was a long stretch to view Peterson as a potential stepfather, it was a shorter stretch to see the advantages for himself. He yawned again as visions of south sea islands, rocky coasts, and exotic cities gently drew him toward sleep.

Chapter Twenty-Eight

"You've been an outstanding group of students," Mary Blood told the class in her final remarks.

Juna wasn't the only one to release an audible sigh. She was sad the three-week session was over. They'd each recited one last piece, and her teachers had encouraged them to go out into the world and let their voices be heard. Some of their guest lecturers were on hand. Professor Stone had applauded enthusiastically when both she and Nancy received their certificates.

Refreshments, organized by Mrs. Rhodehaver, were served in the other classroom, where Miss Martha, the mannequin, was decorated for the occasion in a fancy hat and feather boa. Juna walked over to pay her respects to their mascot and tip the hat into a jauntier angle.

"You're looking lovely today, Mrs. Lewis."

She turned to see Professor Stone holding two dessert plates. She *was* feeling rather pretty in her new print dress. Before she could thank him, he handed her a plate with a chocolate dessert. "The Exposition is all well and good, but you haven't lived until you've tried this confection from the Palmer House hotel. It's called a 'brownie.'"

She studied the dessert that was denser and flatter than chocolate cake, with walnut pieces baked on top. "This looks delicious," she said, and took a bite. Her eyes closed of their own accord as a surprising fruity tang was followed by the crunch of nuts and rich gooey-ness of chocolate. She chewed slowly to savor the divine combination of flavors. "Oh, my gosh," she murmured. "This is heavenly."

Professor Stone gave her a bright *I knew you'd love it* look. "Mrs. Rhodehaver tells me it has an apricot glaze," he said, and tucked into his own brownie. They spent the next few minutes in culinary ecstasy. When Juna reluctantly finished her last bite, the professor took her empty plate. "Nancy tells me you've been conscripted into service at the Missouri Building," he said.

Juna gave a little shrug. "I'm still deciding if I'm up to giving a lecture *and* up to approaching my father-in-law about staying longer."

"You know the subject, certainly."

"Well, yes," she said. "But a week isn't much time to prepare adequately."

"In that case, would it help to have someone listen to your speech and give recommendations?"

"Good idea," she said. "I suppose my sister or Nancy could listen to my—"

He smiled and held up his hand. "In the interest of friendship, I'm offering my services as listener and teacher."

"Oh! That is very kind of you," she said. The monumental task of giving a speech suddenly seemed less daunting. She couldn't ask for a better person to give her an opinion.

"Consider your first obstacle overcome," he said. "I will speak to Miss Blood and Mrs. Riley about using a classroom, as they'll be between sessions. Perhaps Wednesday? In the meantime, I suggest you contact your father-in-law, posthaste." He winked and left to visit with the other students.

Juna turned back to Miss Martha. "It seems I've decided to give a lecture," she said. "Whether it actually happens will be in the hands of Seymour Lewis."

———◦———

Mrs. Wilson's backyard was filled with the crescendo and decrescendo of cicadas. Henry stretched and felt his bones pop. He'd been sitting too long in one position on the back porch swing while reading *Scientific American*. Dropping the magazine onto the floor, he stared out at a shrub with pink flowers. He'd overdone it yesterday and was tired. Now that his initial euphoria about staying longer had subsided, his thoughts turned to Nikola. Where was he now? What would his blind father do without his son's income?

He gave the floor a push to get the swing moving and lay down with his legs draped over the armrest. Nik was smart. He'd find something else to do. It was just that the thought of not seeing his friend again left him with an empty feeling. He wished he could tell him how he nearly got killed. 'Course, Nik would probably slap him on the back and call him a *'budala,'* whatever that meant.

The back-and-forth motion of the swing lulled him to sleep. He woke up briefly when Lovey jumped up and curled on his chest, offering a comforting blanket of sound.

"Henry?" Hattie's voice startled him awake as she called him from the back door. Lovey jumped off and made herself comfortable on the cushion of a wicker chair. The sun was further west, slanting in through the maple trees in the backyard.

"Yes'm?" he asked, pushing himself up into a sitting position. He scrubbed his face and hair to wake up.

"You have a delivery, dear. A box. I've put it on the dining room table."

He jumped up and hurried inside to find a medium-sized box tied with string. It had his name and Mrs. Wilson's address on it, but no other identifying information.

Henry pulled off the string. "Did the delivery man say anything?"

"Just that it was for Henry Lewis, and to treat it gently."

He opened the flaps and quickly pulled out wads of newspaper. "Oh, my gosh. It's a Kodak!" He carefully lifted the camera out of the box and looked at it from all sides. "It's a Model Two, like the one I rented at the fair." He placed the strap over his head, enjoying the weight of it hanging from his neck. He couldn't stop grinning. "I wonder who sent it?"

"That's a dear gift," Hattie said, and rummaged inside the box. "Here's an envelope."

Inside was a piece of stationery wrapped around some bills. Henry read the note, barely able to breathe.

Dear Henry,

You have impressed me with your cooperation and curiosity. I trust you will make good use of this during the remainder of your time here. I've enclosed money for a permit to get you started.

Your faithful servant—

"Archibald Peterson," Henry said. "Do you reckon he's feeling guilty that I fell on the tracks?"

"Guilty for saving ye?" Hattie said, raising an eyebrow. "I'd think not. More'n likely, he's impressed with what a fine young man ye are."

Henry pointed the camera at Hattie and pretended to take her photograph. "I can't believe it," he said, feeling a niggle of guilt at his frequent unkind thoughts about the man. "My own camera! From Peterson, no less. I'll have the chance to thank him tonight."

Hattie stuffed the newspaper back into the box. "This calls for a celebratory plate of cookies."

———◎———

TELEGRAMS

7-29-93, 2:00 p.m.

TO: Seymour Lewis

I have exciting news and another plea. Mrs. Fletcher has invited me to fill in for an indisposed lecturer at the Missouri Building next Friday, August 4, which would require us to remain another week. May I have your blessing? I will be speaking about vinegar. Mrs. Wilson is agreeable to an extension at her home.

=Juna

———◎———

7-29-93, 3:12 p.m.

TO: A. Peterson

What do you know about Henry's mother giving a lecture?

=S. Lewis

———◎———

7-29-93, 4:08 p.m.

TO: S. Lewis

I recommend it as a good punch for Lewis Vinegar. Mrs. Lewis is up to the task.

You may count on my continued guidance to her and Henry.

=A. Peterson

———◎———

7-29-93, 5:50 p.m.

TO: A. Peterson

Very well. Thank you for your fine efforts.

=S. Lewis

———◎———

7-29-93, 6:00 p.m.

TO: Juna Lewis

You have my blessings, of course. Good luck!

Tell Henry he'll owe me another post card or two.

=Seymour

———◎———

7-29-93, 6:22 p.m.

TO: Seymour Lewis

Thank you! I will set Henry to the task.

Are you using your salve?

=Juna

Chapter Twenty-Nine

Music Hall was situated at the north end of the Peristyle; a sister building to the Casino on the south end. Inside the elegant auditorium, Juna followed Archie up to the columned balcony, which swept a semi-circle some twenty feet above the main floor. They chose seats straight out from the stage, which Archie assured her were just as satisfactory. "The acoustics are quite good," he said. "See how the stage walls form a hemicycle? It projects the sound."

Juna peered down at the large stage with its high, arching roof. Empty risers stood waiting for the choir. On the main floor, members of the Exposition orchestra sat on a platform and tuned their instruments. Long notes were matched and adjusted, lifting to the skylight high above them. This mixed with a hum of conversation from the audience scattered throughout the expanse of seats.

Archie leaned closer. "The director there is Theodore Thomas, also in charge of music for the fair," he said. The mustachioed man was currently pointing his baton toward the first chair violinist, who was playing the tuning note.

"What a grand space," Juna said as she smoothed her new pink dress; feeling rather grand herself. Archie, who'd been generous in his compliments when he picked her up in a cab at Mrs. Wilson's, was dressed in evening clothes and looked every bit the handsome man about town. Upon entering the Hall, they'd drawn appreciative glances from other concertgoers which, she had to admit, was an unexpected thrill.

Archie's eyes softened as he smiled at her. "Chicago's own Apollo Musical Club boasts five hundred voices. You'll never hear a more professional-sounding chorus."

"I can hardly wait." Juna had heard portions of Handel's *Messiah* over the years, but never on this large a scale. She scanned her program, which gave the names of the five soloists on the front. The inside featured the lyrics for each section.

The orchestra fell silent at a signal from Thomas, and a ripple of excitement spread throughout the auditorium. "Here they come," Juna said, leaning forward and joining the spontaneous applause as the men and women of the chorus filed out through doors leading onto the stage. The women wore light-colored dresses while the men wore suits of black. They filled the risers in an orderly fashion. So many! At last, the principal soloists took their places in the front. The choral director, a slender man with a trim mustache and beard, paused beside the podium.

"William Tomlins," Archie murmured.

The man bowed to the audience and turned to exchange a smile and nod with Thomas before stepping onto the podium. With a *tap-tap-tap* of a baton, the program began.

The opening instrumental section was uplifting and bright, filling Juna with breathless anticipation at the promise of magnificent things to come. Notes rose and fell and swooped around her in lovely, round tones. In the next movement, a tenor soloist stepped forward and his fine voice soared up to the ceiling as he skillfully navigated the challenging score. When the chorus burst in, singing, *"And the glory of the Lord shall be revealed,"* Juna was unprepared for the sheer majesty of sound that five hundred voices could produce. It filled and expanded her, pressing against her ribs, and catching in her breath. Beside her, Archie listened with rapt attention.

A bass soloist took over for two movements. His voice was deep, with a pleasing rustic quality. His performance featured an exciting interplay between voice and orchestra. Once again, the chorus! Music and voices slid up and down the scale in a brilliant waterfall.

Juna pressed a hand to her throat as a long-forgotten memory swirled to the surface. Craig—how could she have forgotten this?—had performed selections from the *Messiah* with their church choir the first Christmas after they were married. In the days leading up to the concert, she'd hear him humming the choruses as he did chores or worked in the garden. He'd abruptly break into song, making her laugh and applaud. His was an unstudied voice, but he gave it a good effort and enjoyed it.

She could feel his presence here, in the music and in the gladness of her heart. For once, she was free of the sadness that often accompanied memories of Craig. This realization felt as momentous as the music surrounding her. Retrieving a handkerchief from her purse, she dabbed the moisture from her eyelashes.

"Beautiful, isn't it?" Archie whispered in her ear. She could only nod in reply as she brought her attention back to the present.

Now it was the alto's turn. She sang in a strong, clear voice that made Juna shiver. The concert continued with its moving solos and thrilling choruses. From time to time, Juna and Archie would share a smile, in silent agreement that they were both having a delightful experience. When the soprano soloist sang the gentle aria, *"He shall feed his flock like a shepherd,"* Juna noticed Archie brushing away a tear. Her own throat tightened at the beauty of the melody.

And when five hundred voices sang, *"Hallelujah! Hallelujah!"* in a gloriously exuberant blaze of sound, the audience rose to their feet, as one. Juna's shoulders shook as tears flowed unrestricted down her cheeks. Music and voices sparkled around her, expanding her own joy until she was fairly bursting with it.

"Hallelujah! For ever and ever. Hallelujah! Hallelujah!"

At the end of the concert, when the final brilliant notes dissipated high above them, she and Archie joined in the enthusiastic ovation and shouts of "Bravo!" As they mopped their faces with damp handkerchiefs, Archie said, "Handel was a genius, wasn't he?" Considering her current state of buoyant emotion, Juna couldn't agree more.

They left the Hall and walked along the Peristyle, where electric lights, high above in the ceiling, filled the space with a soft glow. Thick columns on either side stood like tall sentries guarding their passage. Out on the grand plaza, people gathered for the fireworks show. Pleasure boats drifted on the lake, where cheery voices carried over the water. Gondolas and electric launches dotted the Basin. "It always feels festive here, doesn't it?" Juna said. "It's like a party that never stops."

Archie laughed. "Indeed, it does. Shall we attempt to find a bench, or watch from here?"

"I doubt there's a bench to be had at this point," she said. "I don't mind standing after sitting for so long."

At the other end of the Basin, a brass band began playing a rousing number as the sky exploded in showers of jewels and ribbons of colorful lights. Juna joined in the *oohs* and *ahhs* coming from every direction, aware of a burst of happiness that reflected the gloriousness above them. In that moment, all was right with the world. She tucked her hand into Archie's elbow and leaned into him, just a little. He covered her hand with his own, sliding his fingers gently over the fabric of her gloves. She felt more than heard the rumbling sigh of his own contentment.

Chapter Thirty

The view from the top of the Ferris Wheel was incredible. Lights from the Midway stretched out toward the fair proper, dotted with its own lights that outlined buildings and domes and lit the promenades where evening visitors strolled. To the southeast, fireworks exploded in plumes and starbursts against the inky blackness of the lake, eliciting delighted reactions from the other passengers. To the north, sparser lights were sprinkled throughout the city.

Henry stood at the front of the car. "*Smooth,*" he whispered past the lump in his throat. He wished the ride would stop there for an hour, allowing him to look and look and look. He wondered where Tomoko was right then. Was she somewhere out there watching the show, or asleep in bed dreaming of her far-away home?

It had been a fun evening. Zennie treated him to supper in A Street in Cairo, where they ate lamb stew and sipped mint tea on an outdoor veranda. A band of drummers, dancing girls, and even a camel parading past provided entertainment. A group of veiled women made a high-pitched trilling sound, which Zennie explained was their way of cheering. Afterwards, they'd visited the Hagenbeck Arena, where they viewed lions, bears, ponies, monkeys, a baby elephant, and many other animals in the menagerie. It was interesting, but he'd been glad to return outside and breathe the fresh air.

Music drifted up from far below. Henry felt the rhythm of drums, the rippling swell of a gong, the squeak of a violin playing an odd-sounding melody. He closed his eyes, taking it all in, this spirit of the Midway.

It whispered over his skin, pressed into his ears and hands and heart. He opened his eyes and exhaled.

Beside him, Zenobia said, "Did you ever think you'd see such a sight?"

He mutely shook his head, feeling like he was in a science fiction novel; that once he left the fair and went back to Missouri, the images and memories would recede to a shelf where they would slowly fade under the accumulated dust of time. The thought made him melancholy. "I never want to leave," he said.

Zenobia put her arm around him. "I know," she said in a subdued voice. "I know."

It was past midnight when Juna sat by the window of her bedroom, legs pulled up under her nightgown. Outside, peepers and crickets stroked the darkness with their silvery songs. As she contemplated on the events of the evening, she found herself bemused by her softening feelings toward Archie. Was she under the influence of the 'fair's magic,' as Zennie had put it, or was she truly falling for the man? Alone with the quiet, it was hard to tell. Yes, he was jovial and kind. And yes, he was a man of ambition. And yet . . .

And yet.

If she was honest with herself, her feelings for Archie were, at first, colored by a sense of obligation. They'd both danced around the fact that he wanted to be more than friends, but once she'd drawn her boundaries, she found it easy to be with him. He'd been perfectly respectful. But now, by her own doing, her boundaries were getting thinner and thinner.

Oh, what a good time she had tonight. The music . . . the fireworks. Afterwards, they'd met Henry and Zenobia, who'd had a full evening on the Midway. As they walked toward the exit, Henry chattered away about the nighttime view from the Ferris Wheel, and thanked Archie profusely for his wonderful new camera. Archie insisted on flagging down a cab and accompanying them home. Before Juna climbed the front steps after her sister and son, he'd taken her hands and gazed into her eyes. "Thank you for a delightful evening, Junaluska," he said, and gently kissed each hand, lingering just long enough for her to feel his warm breath.

She'd been wearing a silly smile when she entered the house.

Henry was already upstairs, but Zennie lingered in the foyer. "So much for being a stalwart soul," she murmured, sending them both into a fit of barely suppressed giggles.

Juna hugged her knees tightly and sighed. How could it be her last week here? How had so much happened in this brief span of time? The spa was a great success; she had new companions in Nancy, Professor Stone, and Archie; she'd discovered new confidence in herself; and she and Henry were having a lifetime's worth of experiences.

It occurred to her that, in all she'd gained, something had been lost. The wedge of grief so firmly lodged in her chest for six years was now replaced by a sense of peace. She still loved and missed Craig, but now those feelings were surrounded by the light of love and the sweetest of memories. With poignant joy, she raised the tiny apple charm and kissed it. "Thank you," she whispered, and the shroud of guilt that she'd worn for so long gently slipped off her shoulders.

Chapter Thirty-One

The sun was still low in the sky on Monday morning when Henry, Mrs. Wilson, Mother, and Zenobia loaded into a cab and headed to the train station. Henry sat with his mother on one side facing Zenobia and Mrs. Wilson. A picnic basket sat at their feet. Mrs. Wilson had suggested they go on a picnic in a town called Glen Ellyn. "It has a small, picturesque lake," she'd said. "And won't it be nice to escape the city for a few hours?"

The women visited, but he wasn't paying attention. Still sleepy, and lulled by the steady clopping of horse's hooves, he leaned back and looked out at houses and yards in the neighborhood. Once they'd turned onto a busier street, he watched store owners washing windows or sweeping sidewalks. As they turned another corner, he saw a street sweeper pulling his cart. The shovel lay on top of a steaming pile. Henry smiled to himself, glad to be the one in the cab. He watched the boy stop and grab his shovel to scoop up another manure plop. As he turned to sling the load into his cart, golden light from the rising sun illuminated his face. Henry sat up, stunned. Nikola!

He peered closely at him as they passed, just to make sure, then slumped back in his seat. As glad as he was to see his friend, surprise gave way to anger. Why hadn't Nik tried to find him if he was so close? Was he afraid Henry would despise him? *Dang*, most of his friends were sons of farmers or shop owners. They weren't afraid to get their hands dirty, and neither was he. Squeezing his eyes shut, he tried to make sense of the situation. His funny, intelligent friend was shoveling dung. Were he and his father managing? Did they have enough to eat?

"You're being awfully quiet," Zenobia remarked later as they found seats on the train.

"Just sleepy," he said.

The train left the city and passed into a more open landscape with fields and farms. Mother alternated between staring dreamily out the window and writing in her notebook. Zenobia and Mrs. Wilson chatted about the scenery. After several stops at small towns, they arrived in Glen Ellyn. Henry carried the basket to the small lake where a few other picnickers were enjoying the day. Mother and Zenobia spread out a large blanket in a shady spot near the water, but Mrs. Wilson sat on a portable camp stool. "My old bones have their limits," she said. "Who's ready for a ham sandwich?"

Being in new surroundings helped take Henry's mind off Nikola. After lunch, he hiked around the lake looking for frogs and bugs while the women played a card game on top of the picnic basket. When he found a gold-colored pebble sticking out of the mud, he cleaned it off and added it to the growing collection in his pockets: a twig with smooth bark; an empty snail shell; and a small stone in the shape of smooth grey rectangle. It reminded him of the paper that Tomoko folded so precisely. He looked forward to placing these items on their rock over the next week. He picked up a flat rock and skipped it over the water. It bumped three times and sank. His time in Chicago was nearly at an end, and it saddened him to know he'd never see her again. He thought of her pretty face and delicate hands. At least he had her picture, even if he needed a magnifying glass to see it.

The grasses and plants brushed his legs as he trudged toward a wooded spot. Sitting under a large oak tree, he spread out his treasures. "Tomoko," he said, absentmindedly, as he rearranged the order. "Exemplary, impossibility, culture-ality (he wasn't sure it was a word, but it sounded good), conventionality, sexuality." He snickered and looked around. "Lips, hips, nips, toes. Eyes, teeth, ears, nose." The rough bark of the tree pressed into his back as he slumped against it. Was he ever gonna miss that girl.

His thoughts returned once more to her tiny photograph. If only he had a larger image of her. *"Huh,"* he said, as an idea popped into his head. Could he arrange for her to be sitting on their rock when he *just happened* to be on the island taking photographs? He laughed out loud, feeling his spirits lift. It could work.

"Henry?"

Mother and Zenobia were close by, calling his name. He stuffed the items back into his pockets and got to his feet, surprisingly reluctant to return to the city. Being out here in the woods reminded him of home. Despite not wanting to leave Chicago, he missed his friends. And Grandpa.

When his mother and aunt were close to the tree, he sprang out at them—an act that resulted in two very satisfying screams, followed by being chased all the way back to the picnic area.

CHAPTER THIRTY-TWO

August 1, 1893—The St. Louis Daily
NOTES FROM THE FAIR:

The Glory of Germania

One of the most striking exhibits in the Manufactures Building is in the German Pavilion. After the visitor passes through an imposing and ornate wrought-iron fence, she is presented with an equally grand display. The massive Porcelain Porch features the central masterpiece, The Glory of Germania. Composed of over 1,000 hand-painted tiles, it measures over 18 feet in height and 14 feet in width.

Central to the painting is the noble Germania herself, set against the spires of the Dome of Cologne. She is surrounded by beautiful muses of art and poetry, scientists, craftsmen, and men of thought. In the lower half, Father Rhein laughs with a pair of merry dwarves and a voluptuous maiden. It is a spectacle worth seeing!

—Zenobia A. Thom,
Special Correspondent

—◦—

The next day, Henry went straight to Phoenix Hall. He got lucky and followed a batch of schoolchildren and their parents into the building. Being
older and taller, he hoped to look like a big brother tagging along. Once
inside, his hopes plummeted at the sight of an empty table. It occurred to
him that Tomoko might be taking a break to sit on the rock. He rushed out
the door and plowed straight into Professor Shuga. "Sorry, sir," Henry said,
steadying him.

The man's expression hardened. "You come here many times."

A rush of heat lit Henry's face. "I, uh, I like it here."

"I see you looking at my daughter."

"S-sorry," he stammered. "I don't mean any disrespect."

"Best to stay away," the man said in a low voice. "You have plenty of fair
to see." He gave a hint of a bow, his eyes never leaving Henry's.

The conversation was over. It was tempting to argue, but Henry thought
better of it. "Yessir," he muttered, and clamored down the steps. *Dang*, he
thought, as he stomped down the path. Lots of people looked at his daughter. She was pretty, wasn't she? Everyone seemed to adore her. The women
fawned over her hair and clothes. Had her father warned off other boys, as
well? He gave a low growl, not liking that idea at all. Maybe she was promised to a boy back home. He liked that idea even less, but at least the imaginary boy was back in Japan.

The long walk to the Agriculture Building softened the edge of his
disappointment. He stopped to rest his sore legs and watch a canoe race
between four Indian teams. Spectators lined the edge of the basin, cheering
them on. He had no claim on Tomoko, but why couldn't they be friendly?
This was a meeting of cultures, after all. He was merely getting in the spirit
of the Exposition. Soon enough, he'd be heading home and that would be
that. The thought tugged at his heart. At least they had their secret rock.

The enthusiastic crowd cheered for the winning team. Henry checked
his watch, wishing he could skip his meeting with Peterson. He'd rather walk
around by himself today, but the man insisted on continuing his mentoring

during Henry's 'bonus week,' as he put it. Resigning himself to the inevitable, he shoved his watch into his pocket and trudged toward the entrance.

An hour later, Peterson turned to him and said, "You have a sullen quality today. Is something bothering you?"

Henry wasn't about to tell him the truth. "Sort of," he said, "but I'd rather not talk about it."

"Very well. If you need a sympathetic ear, and all that."

"Thanks. I'll be all right."

When they paused to look at the metal-encased Mammoth Cheese, Peterson said, "I remember being your age very well, Henry. The world could seem like that big cheese hanging over your head. In my case, it was a mother dying of tuberculosis. As for my father, let's just say his grief caused him to be extra harsh."

"I'm sorry to hear it," Henry said, feeling a rush of compassion for his mentor. Losing a father was bad enough, but a mother? That must have been awful. Tuberculosis was a dreadful disease. Everyone knew someone who had died from it. He couldn't imagine life without his own mother. Suddenly, his own worries seemed petty by comparison. "Where did you grow up?" he asked as they moved on. As much as his mentor talked, he hadn't shared many specifics about his past.

"Ohio," Peterson said. "My father and his brother ran a dry goods store in New Bremen. When he died a few years later, my uncle and I kept it going for ten years until it burned down. At that point, I moved to Chicago."

"And your uncle? Is he still living?" Henry asked.

Peterson didn't answer right away. "Unfortunately, he died in the fire," he said. "In one cruel stroke of fate, I lost my uncle and the business I was meant to inherit."

There was an edge to his mentor's voice, so Henry didn't pursue that line of questioning. Peterson was obviously bitter about losing the business. Maybe his uncle was drunk and tipped over a lamp. Back home, Grandpa constantly reminded Henry about the dangers of fire. Many businesses burned down because of carelessness.

Peterson gave Henry a sad smile. "It's hard to lose family, isn't it? I miss my mother to this very day."

"Yessir," Henry said. "Sometimes I miss Papa so much I'm sure my ribs will crack."

"I know the feeling well," Peterson said. "C'mon, son. Let's find a cafe. Nothing lifts a melancholy spirit like a cup of hot chocolate."

When they left the Agricultural Building for the day, Peterson asked, "Does your mother have any favorite spots on the Midway? She's agreed to accompany me there tonight."

Despite the obvious advantages, the thought of Mother and Peterson together still made Henry squirm. "She likes a lot of it," he said. "The kababs and the Ferris Wheel, the music at German Village, and—" He paused as it occurred to him that Peterson was trying to impress Mother. He thought back to previous visits. What had she commented on? "Last week she admired the earrings at the Libbey Glass Company," he said.

Peterson grinned like he'd just won fifty dollars. "Thank you, Henry. That is an excellent suggestion."

After a delicious meal at the Vienna Cafe, Juna and Archie strolled eastward along the Midway. The evening air was pleasant, and the streetlights were already glowing. Despite the hour, the Midway was as festive as ever. "I enjoy people-watching as much as anything here," Juna said. "It's an international parade, isn't it?"

"Yes, indeed," Archie said. "It's the world come together in a mile-long strip of road. Shall we have a look in the Libbey Building up ahead?"

She'd recently visited, but it was a fascinating place worth seeing again. "Why not?" she said.

The glassblowing demonstrations were closed for the day, but the souvenir shop was doing a lively business. Displays of jewelry, figures, vases, and many other objects made from glass sparkled under electric lights. Juna stopped to admire a delicate pair of drop earrings that featured oblong balls of glass streaked with blue. She'd noticed them before, but chose to save her money. "Such skill," she said.

Archie leaned down to take a closer look. "Do you like them?"

Without thought, she answered, "I love them."

"Well, then." He beckoned to the woman behind the counter. "We'll take those, please," he said, pulling his wallet from inside his jacket.

"A lovely choice," the woman said, retrieving the earrings.

"Archie, I didn't intend for you to—" Juna began in an undertone. She stopped when she saw the pleasure this was giving him. And truth be told, she was delighted. Why pretend otherwise? When he finished the transaction, she said, "What a lovely surprise. Thank you, Archie."

His eyes twinkled as he presented his gift to her. The earrings were tiny in his large hand. "Would you like to put them on?"

"Of course, but I'll need a mirror."

The saleswoman pointed to the end of the counter. "There's one just there."

It was a popular spot, with several women vying for position. "We'll have to wait our turn," Juna said.

"I have an idea," Archie said. "Follow me." He led her to a less busy spot at the side of the room. "I can help you, if you like."

"All right," she said after a moment's hesitation. She reached up and pulled her own earrings off and tucked them into her purse. "I'm ready." She tilted her left ear up, thinking she'd have a great laugh about this later with Zenobia.

Archie angled her toward the light and leaned in, looking for the tiny hole. She nearly stopped breathing when he put his fingertip behind her earlobe. The action felt excruciatingly intimate. "Here goes," he said. It took two attempts, but he managed to gently poke the wire through. He straightened up and made a show of wiping his brow. "That's a first."

Juna released a breath, disguising it as a laugh. "One more and you'll be an expert," she said, presenting her right ear. Out of the corner of her eye, she noticed the mirror was free, but was enjoying herself too much to mention it. There was something endearing about a man helping a woman with her toilet. A faded image of Craig brushing her hair popped into her mind's eye. She cleared her throat and slammed that memory shut. "It does take a certain amount of courage to be a woman," she said in an over-bright voice.

"I should think so," he said, leaning down once more. She was aware of his breath on her hair; the tang of white wine they'd had with dinner, and the sweet-smelling cigar he'd enjoyed afterwards. She bit her lip as he placed his other fingertip behind her earlobe. "There you go," he said, standing tall. "First try. Want to have a look?"

At the mirror, she turned her head from side to side. "They're lovely, Archie." She smiled at his reflection in the mirror. Their moment ended when two women stepped up to view their own purchases. Back outside, she and Archie resumed walking toward the main grounds. It felt perfectly natural to put her hand in the crook of his arm.

"When I was a small boy," he said, "I'd play at being a pirate. I wanted nothing more than a hoop in my ear and a parrot on my shoulder. My mother loved to tell the story of finding me with her sewing needle ready to jab a hole in my ear."

"Ouch! It's a good thing she saved you."

"*Saved* is a relative term," he said. "While my ear was saved, my backside was not."

Juna smiled. "When Henry was four, he climbed up an enormous oak tree behind Seymour's house. Right up to the top. He was pretending to be in a ship's crow's nest—probably looking out for pirates such as yourself. The trouble was, he couldn't get down again. My husband had to climb up and retrieve him."

Archie harrumphed. "He still has a propensity for heights, doesn't he? He always goes to the highest place in any building, be it by stair or elevator."

"He certainly does," she said, hoping it hadn't been a mistake to mention her husband. "He still climbs that old tree and gazes out at the Mississippi."

Archie covered her hand with his own. "It's good to have dreams," he said. As they walked in companionable silence, the distant dome of the Illinois Building reminded Juna of her efforts to deflect Archie's attentions.

What a difference a week made.

Chapter Thirty-Three

Henry stood at the corner where he'd seen Nikola two days before. The sidewalk and streets were damp from an early morning shower, and moisture hung in the air. It was going to be a hot, sweaty day. Twisting one way and then the other, he scanned the length of the street. Surely his friend was somewhere around here. Turning east, he walked toward the lake but only saw an older, rather hunchbacked man with a manure cart.

Retracing his steps, he went a few blocks further west toward Washington Park and spotted Nikola dashing into the street with his shovel. Henry hesitated. What if Nik didn't want to be seen doing this job? Would it embarrass him to be found out? *"Pertinacious,"* he muttered, and strode over to the cart.

Nikola came hurrying back with his shovelful, dodging a cab and a delivery wagon. He pulled up short. *"Proklet.* Henry!" His expression seemed to be equal parts shock, embarrassment, and happiness. He dumped his shovelful. "What are you doing here?"

Henry grinned. "Good to see you, too. Where the hell have you been?"

Nik told him the story in short bursts between dashes into the street. "I lost my job for no reason. One day everything was good, no problems. The next day—" He made a face and darted back into the street, continuing after he dumped his load. "Nobody would tell me anything. The manager just said he'd gotten complaints. From who? Why? *Pfft.* Nothing! So now—" He gave a short laugh and hoisted his shovel. "Instead of pushing a chair, I push horse shit."

Henry didn't laugh. He couldn't imagine his friend made much money. "I wish I could help you," he began, but Nikola shook his head.

"No," he said in a fierce voice and shoved the cart further down the street.

Henry followed. He wanted to argue, but knew it would be pointless. Nik would rather shovel dung all day than accept a handout. "Stubborn mule," he muttered as his friend rushed into the street again. When he returned, Henry said, "I have to go, but I'll find you again, okay?"

Nikola nodded. "You're a good friend, Henry." He gave him a light punch on the arm before rushing away.

Henry watched him for a few seconds, then pulled three dimes from his pocket and tossed them several feet further down the street. They scattered and bounced before coming to rest. Hopefully Nik would see them as he moved along. Henry hurried away in the opposite direction, disgusted by his friend's unfair treatment and his own inability to help.

It was a short walk back to the fairground entrance. By the time he arrived at the Photography Office to buy a permit, the sun was high, and he'd stuffed his jacket into his satchel, trading it for his camera. It felt good hanging from his neck. Official. Like he was a professional photographer. It was with this confident attitude that he marched over the bridge to Wooded Island and straight to Phoenix Hall. He'd walk right in, find Tomoko, and arrange to meet her at the rock. This determination was tempered by the fact that he'd peek inside first to see if "Papa" was around.

At first glance, it appeared that luck was on his side. Her father was not in evidence. A different man was giving a tour. Unfortunately, Tomoko was not in evidence, either. Henry sagged and blew out a breath. She was probably playing the tourist with her father. They could be anywhere. An awful thought seized him: What if she'd gone back to Japan early?

He left the building with slower footsteps than when he'd first charged up. For the heck of it, he checked their rock. Maybe she'd left a goodbye note or another gift. Let it be a gift, he thought, pushing past the shrubs. His heart leapt when he saw an object on the rock, but on closer inspection found that it was just a dry leaf. He sank down on the rock, peeled off his sweaty cap, and wiped his forehead with his sleeve. Out on the lagoon, electric launches glided by in both directions. Mother had mentioned something about a tour today, but he'd been too preoccupied with his own plans to pay attention to the details. Further out, a brown-skinned man paddled a kayak along the shoreline, dipping his long, double-sided oar into the water in a meditative rhythm. Henry took a photograph, but doubted it would turn out well.

A wave of desperation washed over him. He dreaded going back to Missouri in a week. After being here, how would any town, any life, measure up? He imagined looking out of the upstairs window at the factory, caught in a constant daydream of white palaces, lagoons, and exotic people. How long would these memories last? Would Tomoko, Nikola, and even Henry Ward eventually fade to mere apparitions, like ghosts in his brain?

He heaved himself up. He needed to take more photographs before meeting Zenobia for lunch, but was having trouble stirring up enthusiasm for much of anything. Stepping back, he photographed the rock from several angles. It would serve as a reminder, at least. Would Tomoko do the same? Would she store her secret gifts from him in a special box? He reached into his satchel and retrieved the rectangular-shaped stone he'd found by Lake Ellyn. Rubbing the smooth edge with his thumb, he found he was reluctant to part with something that reminded him of her. Suddenly desperate to help Tomoko keep *his* memory alive, he raked his brain for a way to do it that wouldn't be obvious to her relatives.

He looked over at the bridge connecting the northeast side of the island with the main grounds near the Fisheries Building. As usual, crowds of people were coming and going. They walked at varying speeds: strolling, ambling, hurrying, or stopping to take in the surrounding views. It created a cadence on the bridges and promenades, forming the unique heartbeat of the Exposition. And within that heartbeat, the spark of an idea flashed into his brain like a shooting star. It quickly took shape into a scheme, and he chuckled out loud. It could work—if Zenobia agreed to help him.

Saving the rectangular stone for his souvenir box, he rummaged through his other "finds" and chose the gold-colored pebble. He pressed it briefly to his lips and placed it in the tiny crevasse in the rock. Returning to the main path in a more hopeful state of mind, he hurried toward the Administration Building, whistling as he walked.

———◦———

The electric launch glided along, creating a breeze that felt good on Juna's face and neck. She was glad for the canopy roof, though the sun still slanted in depending on which way they turned. She shared the boat with graduates from their summer session, and Nancy sat beside her with a violet parasol across her lap. Professor Stone perched at the helm, facing the group as he relayed interesting details about the buildings.

"None of this is new to me," Nancy said in a low voice as the boat slowed to a stop in front of the Government Building. "I simply enjoy being with friends and finding inspiration in this grand place."

"I quite agree," Juna said, aware that she was concentrating more on the sound of the professor's voice than on the details he was sharing. There was something enticing about seeing a man in his element. Now that she'd studied elocution, she couldn't help but notice his techniques and the nuances of his voice.

"I was hoping Zenobia could join us today," Nancy whispered, diverting Juna's attention again.

"She wanted to come, but she needed to finish a column. She and Henry are meeting for lunch."

"Ah. I'm going to miss all of you."

"You must come visit," Juna said.

"I'd like that very much."

"Shhh." A woman turned and gave them a look.

"Sorry." Juna mimed pinching her lips together. She returned her attention to the professor, who pointed out an architectural detail of the magnificent dome. She watched him, absorbing the rise and fall of his voice more than listening to specific words. At one point, he met her eyes and held her gaze for a long moment as he rattled off the height and width of the dome, leaving her slightly breathless. She glanced at Nancy, who was trailing the tip of her parasol in the water, dreamily lost in her own thoughts.

Juna sat up straighter, determined to pay better attention to the lecture and less attention to her guilty conscience. He was Nancy's special friend, after all. And Archie seemed to be *hers,* or at least things seemed to be moving in that direction. She supposed men and women could appreciate the other sex as one appreciates fine art, with detached appreciation. *Detached appreciation.* That fit the situation perfectly, she decided. The professor was a nice friend. That was all. He'd been generous in offering to hear her speech and give suggestions. Consumed with writing it, she'd put on the finishing touches that morning. Despite being happy with the result, her stomach still fluttered at the thought of giving a speech in an auditorium.

When the boat tour was over, they disembarked at the Art Palace, where the professor added an impromptu visit. Juna and Nancy parted ways with the group in the rotunda. "I'll see you tomorrow afternoon, Mrs. Lewis," Professor Stone said as they thanked him and said goodbye.

They walked through the building to the north entrance, a quick route to the Missouri Building across the street. "I found the perfect model for the face of my sculpture," Nancy said. "She's sitting for two sessions this week."

"Marvelous," Juna said. "I look forward to seeing the finished piece."

Nancy smiled as she retied the ribbon on her hat. "I'm ready to be finished with it." She gave Juna a hug. "I'll see you Friday night. You're going to be terrific."

"I'm so glad you're coming. Having a sympathetic face in the crowd—if there is a crowd—will shore up my courage."

"Whether it's five or fifty, I'm sure everyone will love you."

"If they don't love my speech, I'll surely win them over with a slice of apple cider cake. It's my father-in-law's favorite," Juna said, smiling at the thought of the old man. She missed him.

"Aunt Zennie, would you have time to help me with a photograph?" Henry asked. They were eating their lunch on the veranda at Machinery Hall. It was an excellent location to view the Court of Honor and people walking between the Terminal Station and the Administration Building.

"Certainly," she said, and took another bite of her sandwich.

A half-hour later, they stood on the southern edge of Wooded Island, about fifteen feet from the bridge that connected the island to the grand plaza. "Here's what I want you to do," he said. "I'm going to wait on the other side until there are a decent number of people crossing over, then fall in with them. When I'm on this side of the bridge, I'm going to stop and pretend to look at the island. That's when you will snap some photos. I'll just be one tourist of many. See?"

Zenobia looked in the viewfinder and took a few steps forward. "I've used a camera like this before. Ned showed me how. I frequently have visitors asking me to take their picture with something noteworthy in the background. Whether they were successful, who knows? I'll do my best."

"Good," Henry said, thankful she had asked no questions. "Let's do it." He crossed to the other side and waited at the edge of the bridge until there were twenty or thirty people crossing toward the island. Hurrying along until he passed the apex of the bridge, he stopped and looked in Zennie's general direction. He felt silly arranging his face in an interested, scanning-the-countryside expression. After a couple of minutes, he looked directly at his aunt and grinned before jogging over to join her.

"I snapped several," she said, handing him the camera. "Would you like some closer in?"

He started to say no, then decided a few close ones would be nice to remember how he looked here. "Sure," he said, glancing around. "How about over there, with Phoenix Hall in the background?" They found a suitable spot, and after his aunt snapped a couple of Henry, they asked a man to take one of the two of them posing with their arms linked. Henry was happy to have a photo of his aunt. "I'll give you and Mother a copy," he said.

Zenobia smiled. "I'm counting on it. I'm glad you're having fun with your new camera. You certainly have an artistic eye for photographic composition." She checked her watch. "Back to work."

"Thanks, Zennie." Henry gave her a kiss on the cheek, desperately hoping there was at least one useable photo of him in the bunch. "Before you go, remember my friend Nikola? You met him the day the Viking Ship arrived."

"The chair roller? Yes, he seemed like a friendly fellow."

"He is, and that's the point," Henry said. "He got sacked for no good reason last week." Zenobia's eyebrows shot up. He had her full attention now.

"I saw him this morning. He's—he's working a menial job for not much money, and his father is blind, you see, and well, I want to find out what happened. Can you help me? You know people here."

Zenobia frowned. "I'm sorry to hear about your friend. The manager gave him no reason?"

"He said there'd been complaints. Nik demanded an explanation, but the guy wouldn't give him any. Just told him to turn in his uniform and clear out."

"That is strange," Zenobia said. She tapped her lip, thinking. "Give me a couple of days to investigate. I'll see what I can find out."

TELEGRAMS

8-2-93, 4:30 p.m.
TO: S. Lewis
I have had the pleasure of two delightful outings with Mrs. Lewis.
=A. Peterson

8-2-93, 6:15 p.m.
TO: A. Peterson
I am happy to hear it.
=S. Lewis

Chapter Thirty-Four

On Thursday, Henry found himself back in the Anthropology Building. He wandered among the displays at Ward's Natural Science exhibit while practicing interesting words under his breath. *Ammonite, Jurassic,* and *Eocene* rolled around his mouth like candy. He kept an eye out for Henry Ward, but the man didn't appear to be around.

A tall glass case held animal skeletons, including those of a tiny bat. Fascinated, he studied the delicate bones that were carefully laid out. Its wings were outstretched, with slender "fingers" forming a fan shape. He wondered what tools Ward and his people used to do such delicate work. *"Ammonite, Jurassic,"* he whispered as he gazed at more skeletons of birds, squirrels, and monkeys. *"Eocene, Ammon—"* The word caught in his throat. Tomoko and her father stood across the room looking up at the giant squid. She wore a pretty yellow dress with puffy sleeves. Professor Shuga wore a dark grey suit and carried a stout walking stick.

What struck Henry most was how relaxed they were, enjoying the fair as much as any visitor. And why shouldn't they? As they smiled and pointed at the squid, Tomoko said something that made them both laugh. They moved on to a display of fossils encased in rock, and she leaned in to take a closer look. Professor Shuga moved around the case, focusing on items of interest. He rolled his walking stick between his fingers, seemingly out of habit.

Henry tried to square this loving, indulgent father with the stern professor who'd warned him away from Phoenix Hall. He wanted to dislike the man but found he couldn't. He realized the professor was no more or less protective than other fathers, and couldn't help but feel a grudging respect for him. Henry rested his forehead against the glass case. Tomoko was lucky to *have* a father.

A man reeking of sweat and too much hair pomade stepped close and nudged Henry with his elbow. "Always somethin' interesting to see here, be it stuffed lions or heathen Chinee," he chortled. "Pretty one, there."

"Um, yeah." Henry edged away, feeling his face heat up. Was his spying that obvious? "Anyway, they're Japanese," he said.

The man grunted. "That so? Same difference, I reckon."

"I guess," Henry mumbled, deciding not to waste his time convincing the man otherwise. With one last glance at Tomoko, he left the exhibit. Outdoors, he stumped along the promenade, feeling grouchy. Because he'd been caught looking at Tomoko? he wondered. No, that didn't feel quite right. Was it the tourist's condescending attitude? Maybe. And then it hit him: Was he embarrassed that he'd been seen admiring a girl from another culture?

The truth of it shamed him.

He clenched his fists and resolved to do better next time. Next time, he wouldn't be such a coward. Next time, he'd stand tall and say, *Yes, she's a pretty girl, and she's my friend.*

It was good to be back in the Stevens' Building again. Juna climbed the stairs toward the second floor, breathing in the familiar smells of paint, varnish, and clay. She wondered if Nancy was in her studio upstairs. It would be fun to pay her a visit after meeting with Professor Stone. He'd arranged with Mary Blood and Ida to use an empty classroom for an hour. How lucky to have a friend who was also an expert orator! If she didn't wilt before his scrutiny, she'd most likely be fine for tomorrow's presentation.

It was quiet on the second floor. Juna waved at Ida as she passed the office, where her teacher sat at the desk talking with a woman, presumably a future student. Professor Stone was already in the main classroom, where he sat at the first table reading a book. He smiled and stood up when she entered the room. "Good afternoon, Mrs. Lewis," he said. "Ready to practice?"

"Ready as I'll ever be," she said, placing her satchel on the table. She pulled out her speech and took a couple steps backward. "Shall I stand here?" Her heart was galloping along, either from nerves or from taking the stairs.

He nodded. "Yes. But first, take a minute to relax. Close your eyes, feel your feet on the floor and take some slow, deep breaths."

She felt self-conscious, but did as he suggested. Widening her stance a little so she wouldn't be tippy, she breathed in through her nose and out through her mouth as she'd learned from her teachers. Focusing on her feet, she imagined her tension draining out through the floor. She was aware of the rumbling sounds of traffic, the *clang-clang* of a cable car, a train whistle to the south, and the professor's calm, steady presence as he breathed along with her. Opening her eyes just before he opened his own, they shared a charged moment of peace.

"Better?" he asked.

"Yes," she said, and took a few seconds to get into proper posture. "I'm ready."

Professor Stone sat down and assumed an interested expression. Juna looked out over the classroom and began. "My topic today is apple cider vinegar and its many applications. In Roman mythology, Pomona is the goddess of fruit trees, gardens, and orchards . . ."

As Juna recited her speech, she looked up frequently and gazed out over the classroom. She was aware of the acoustics of the room and how her voice sounded fuller. Despite this, she could hear a self-conscious quality in her voice, and attempted to incorporate the techniques she'd learned in class.

When she finished, the professor said, "Nicely done. I can tell you paid attention to your teachers."

"My furious note-taking paid off," she said, relieved she'd made it through with no major mistakes. He'd only stopped her a few times, to remind her to speak slowly or to make suggestions about phrasing and stress. "Thank you for your help, Professor. If I end up on the floor in a quivering heap, you can rest assured you did your best."

He came around and sat on the edge of the table. "I have never lost a student to hysterical prostration. Hives, perhaps," he added lightly. "Remember to pace yourself. It's easy to rush when nervous." He hesitated, then said, "I believe we're good enough friends for you to call me Hiram. May I call you Juna?"

His declaration caught her by surprise. "Of course," she said, noticing that his eyes were a lovely shade of dark blue. He gazed at her with easy affection, such as one would give an intimate friend. She turned and reached for her satchel. This apparent dissolving of student-teacher distance both alarmed and thrilled her. He was Nancy's particular friend, after all. She couldn't deny an attraction to him, but surely it was harmless. Hiram was a kind, confident teacher with a devastating voice. Who wouldn't be attracted to that? Needing to return to safer footing, she said, "Do you suppose Nancy is in her studio today? I'd like to pay her a visit."

"Yes," he said. "We arrived at the same time and she was carrying a plate of her aunt's cookies. Shall we go up together?" They took the stairs to the third floor, and Hiram gave a couple sharp raps on her door.

"One moment," Nancy called from inside, followed by the sound of a chair scraping and low voices. Juna looked at Hiram and raised her eyebrows. He responded with a shrug.

Nancy opened the door. She wore an apron over her bohemian work outfit and was wiping her hands on a towel. "Juna! Hiram! If I'd known you were coming, we wouldn't have eaten all the cookies." A familiar laugh came from inside the room.

Hiram stomped his foot. "I'm leaving."

"Oh, do come in," Nancy said, pulling him inside. "Look who's here," she said to someone.

Juna followed the couple into the studio and stopped in surprise. Zenobia sat on the old couch, feet tucked under her and looking comfortable in a similar outfit to Nancy's. Her hair hung loosely around her shoulders. "Zennie, what are you doing?" Juna said, "You look like an elven queen." She did, in fact, look quite beautiful.

Her sister tipped a cookie toward Nancy. "Modeling."

Nancy continued the explanation. "When I first met Zenobia, I realized she had the perfect features for my sculpture. I do have an eye for beauty, after all," she added with a smug look.

"Oh, yes," Juna said, remembering their conversation from the day before.

"Are you going for a mysterious countenance?" Hiram asked.

"It's hard to explain," Nancy said, shooting a quick smile at Zenobia. "Her bone structure and demeanor fit my vision for the piece."

"Spoken like a true *artiste*," he said.

Nancy curtsied and said, "The *artiste* needs to return to work."

"So does the journalist," Zenobia said, putting the back of her hand to her forehead.

"Please, carry on," Juna said, laughing. "I'll see you later, Zennie." She gave Nancy a kiss on the cheek. "I miss our classes, don't you?"

"They were fun, weren't they? I find I need to say hello to Mary and Ida once a day just to hear their voices." Nancy gave her hand a squeeze. "I'll see you at your lecture. You're going to be sensational." Zenobia and Hiram echoed her sentiment.

"Don't jinx me," Juna said, waving her hands in front of her. She and Hiram said goodbye and left the studio. "Did you know about Zenobia modeling?" she asked him as they tromped downstairs.

He shook his head. "Nancy mentioned finding a model but didn't say who. Perhaps sculptors keep their models secret, like journalists keep their sources secret."

"True enough." While surprised that Zennie hadn't at least told *her*, it made Juna happy to see her sister enjoying Nancy's company.

They rode the cable car to Jackson Park. Hiram had a curriculum meeting at the university, and Juna wanted to help Annie with the spa. He walked her to the nearest gate. As she turned to go, he stopped her with a touch to her arm. "I enjoyed our time today, Juna. Do you . . . I was wondering . . . that is, might we have dinner tonight after you finish at the state building?" The normally even-keeled professor was suddenly acting like a nervous schoolboy.

"What about Nancy?" she asked. "I thought you two were together."

Hiram shook his head and smiled. "Nancy and I are old chums, nothing more. Aunt Ruthie is like a mother to me."

Juna felt her face heating up. "Oh," she said. "You and Nancy are cousins?"

"No, no. 'Aunt' is merely a term of affection. Besides," he said. "I'm not Nancy's type."

"You aren't?"

"Nope. Not her type at all. She's a good friend who helped me through a rough time in my life. I owe her an enormous debt of gratitude."

"Oh," Juna repeated. "You were never attached?" She was having a hard time believing it.

"Never. Just close friends." He seemed to have his speech back under control. "Now, about dinner?"

She wasn't sure how to answer that. Since she'd stepped out twice with Archie, was it right to have dinner with another man? Knowing Archie's feelings for her made the situation tricky, even though Archie agreed to her terms to remain friends. She looked at Hiram's hopeful expression and asked herself, *What's the harm in having more than one male friend?* She came to an impulsive decision. "I'd love to," she said, delighting in the way his eyes lit up at her reply.

"Wonderful. I'll meet you at the state building."

As they went their separate ways, she was very much aware of her own light heart—and was determined to keep 'the magic of the fair' firmly in check. Regardless, when Henry showed up at his usual time, she'd actually blushed when explaining why she wouldn't be accompanying him back to Mrs. Wilson's.

He'd grinned and said, "I like the professor. Have a good time, Mama."

She was glad he approved.

———◇———

The Cafe de la Marine was a large, multi-story restaurant specializing in seafood. Situated near the lagoon just north of the Fisheries Building, its fanciful design featured conical and pyramidal towers of varying heights.

The irony did not escape Juna that this was the very place Archie had planned to bring her and Henry the day of the train incident. It seemed surreal that she was here instead with Professor Stone, to whom she now addressed as 'Hiram'.

They sat at a cloth-covered table on the upstairs veranda, which provided a wide vista of the fairgrounds. The hum of many conversations and occasional bursts of laughter from larger groups of patrons filled the busy restaurant. Glasses clinked, utensils scraped, and efficient waitstaff brought food out, poured wine, and whisked away empty plates and serving bowls. They'd enjoyed a delicious dinner of white fish, roasted potatoes, salad, and cheese, and now lingered over their coffee. A pleasant breeze and purply red sunset provided the finishing touches.

"What a marvelous view," Juna said for at least the third time that evening. She couldn't seem to help herself. One exclamation didn't seem adequate with the deepening twilight changing the scenery minute by minute.

"The best," Hiram said, clearly pleased by her reaction. "Do you know this is the first time I've seen this particular view? It never fails to thrill me when I see the Exposition from a new perspective."

"I agree," Juna said. "There is always one more reason to fall in love with the place, isn't there?"

"I find that to be true," he said, eyes remaining on hers as he took a sip.

She felt her cheeks warming up and gazed out toward Wooded Island, where hundreds of lights winked among the trees. "Oh, look," she said. "Isn't it magical?"

"It is, indeed."

"I've always admired the island at night," she said, "but only at a distance."

Hiram smiled. "Then by all means, let's go. It's an experience not to be missed."

By the time they left the restaurant, it was fully dark. Lamp posts lit the path as they made their way to the bridge that led to the northeast side of the island. Plenty of visitors were still about, though not as many as during the day. Juna and Hiram took their time, pausing frequently to remark on the sights around them. It occurred to Juna that time with Hiram was quieter and more reflective than her time with Archie. Time with Archie was entertaining, of course, but it was the difference between a string quartet and a brass band. One invited you to close your eyes and listen. The other compelled you to pick up your feet and march.

Out on the lagoon, a small fleet of gondolas strung with lamps added to the festive—and yes, she admitted, *romantic* atmosphere. The island beckoned them like a secret wonderland, and she didn't think twice about holding Hiram's offered hand as they strolled past night-kissed flower beds. Trees were strung with hundreds of oil lamps, as well as electric lights that provided soft illumination for the limestone path. "It's a fairyland," she said.

A party was being held at Phoenix Hall, but they kept moving, drawn to the quiet, wooded paths further in. Crossing through the middle of the island, they ended up on the west side. "I want to show you my favorite spot," Hiram said, guiding her to a garden with trellised vines and roses. He pointed to a bench. "Shall we sit?"

Juna settled onto the bench and took in the view. Across the lagoon, the giant dome of the Horticulture Building pressed against the black sky like an illuminated soap bubble. Further south, faint strains of organ music rose like a nimbus from the Choral Building. The garden felt secluded, even with the frequent sound of voices and footsteps passing by. No others sought refuge there. Perhaps they were searching out their own private corners.

Hiram broke the silence in a thoughtful, controlled tone:

"'We are the music makers,

And we are the dreamers of dreams,

Wandering by lone sea-breakers,

And sitting by desolate streams;

World-losers and world-forsakers.

"On whom the pale moon gleams:

Yet we are the movers and shakers

Of the world for ever, it seems.'"

He turned and smiled at her. "The opening of "Ode," by Arthur O'Shaughnessy."

"The 'dreamers of dreams' and 'movers and shakers,'" Juna mused. "We have an abundance of evidence here at the fair, don't we? Every inch of ground, every square foot in every building. The inventions, the art, the electricity, the flowers—" She swept her hand out. "This whole place is the result of dreaming."

"And do you think we'll wake up soon?" Hiram asked, angling his body to face hers.

"I'm not sure I want to," she said, turning toward him and resting her elbow on the back of the bench. "But in three days, I have to be wide awake on a train to Missouri."

"Ah, Missouri. I've never been there. Tell me about your home."

"Louisiana is a modest-sized river town on the Mississippi," she said. "Henry and I live with my father-in-law high on a bluff that looks out over the river and into Illinois. Rounded hills, which we call 'knobs,' surround the town. It's beautiful there." She laughed softly. "Talking about it makes me homesick."

He touched her elbow. "How would you describe the Mississippi? Give me some adjectives besides 'mighty.'"

She shifted her body to face the dome once again. How *would* she describe the great river? At times it was a swift, charging horse and, at others, a swollen, slow-moving chameleon.

"Changeable," she said. "Reflective . . . powerful . . . stunning . . . unique."

Hiram leaned closer and repeated her words back to her, uttering them gently; his rich tenor stroking her ears. "Reflective, powerful, stunning, unique."

She squeezed the edge of the bench and kept her eyes focused on the dome, not daring to look at him. It was a struggle to breathe evenly. "It's getting late, and I have a big day tomorrow," she said. "Perhaps we should—"

"Juna." He spoke her name in a voice rich as velvet. If her name was a cat, it would be purring. She slowly turned to meet his eyes—those warm, witty, beautiful eyes that were looking at her like she was the most precious thing in the world. She hadn't been a recipient of this look in six years. Even Archie's tender gazes seemed proprietary by comparison. But this—this she remembered. Her heart remembered. It was such a profound moment that, to her horror, her eyes filled with tears.

Hiram reached out and lightly cupped the back of her head. "Can't blame Hovenden this time," he murmured, and pressed his lips to hers for a long, sumptuous moment. It was as if he took as much care as when speaking words correctly. *Safe . . . serene . . . selfless . . . secure.* The kiss ended as gently as it started. "I wish I'd met you sooner," he said, trailing a finger across her cheek and wiping away a tear with a feather touch. "You've intrigued me since the day I saw you in class, looking at me with those lovely eyes and scribbling ferociously in your notebook."

Juna smiled as happiness swirled within her, sparkling and bright. "You're an excellent teacher and have a divine voice," she said. "What else could I do?"

They took their time walking back to Mrs. Wilson's, stretching out their enjoyment of being together. When they reached the front steps, he kissed her cheek and said, "Sweet dreams."

She entered the quiet, mostly dark house and leaned against the closed door. It occurred to her that she'd barely given a thought to Archie the entire evening. She released a breath and touched the apple charm at her neck. "Junaluska Lewis," she murmured, "what *have* you done?"

Chapter Thirty-Five

August 4, 1893—The St. Louis Daily
NOTES FROM THE FAIR:

An Amusing Observation

There is a cluster of benches just outside the Manufactures Building, which affords a pleasant view of the lake while resting one's tired feet. Two elderly women—sisters, perhaps—sat on the adjacent bench. It wasn't their age that caught my attention, or the sweet little bonnets perched fetchingly on their grey heads. What drew my eye and kept it there was their serious expressions as they chewed. Chewed and chewed and chewed and chewed and chewed.

There were no lunch pails or greasy sausage papers in evidence. No sandwich or apple sitting on their laps. No bag of taffy to be shared between them. Nevertheless, the level of concentration given to this task was impressive. As I gathered my courage to inquire, one of the grand dames turned to the other and said, "I just don't see the point."

The other nodded her agreement. "It's plain silly and makes my jaws hurt something awful."

"Well, we can tell Jimmy we tried it," said the first.

With that, they each produced a Wrigley's Gum paper and spit out the offending product. The mystery solved, I smiled at the old dears and quietly reached for my notebook.

—Zenobia A. Thom,
Special Correspondent

Juna yawned as she walked to the bakery a few blocks from Mrs. Wilson's house. Hattie was gone for a couple days to attend her niece's wedding in Milwaukee. She'd left plenty of provisions, but Juna insisted on contributing fresh rolls and loaves of bread to the household.

She'd had a restless night. Between her newly awakened feelings for Hiram, her complicated feelings for Archie, and nervous anticipation of her lecture, she'd tossed and turned until well after midnight. How was it possible, after all these years of evading men, that she now liked *two*? And such different specimens! They both had their good qualities: Archie was a take-charge kind of man who moved through life like a dervish. Hiram was steady and confident, a thinker and a good listener. One had the voice of Zeus. The other, the voice of an angel. Both were fun to be with, of course, and brought out the best in her.

Waiting to cross the street near the bakery, she continued her musing. If she had to choose, which man would win? Was it Archie's raw power that made her heart race? Or Hiram's earnest blue-eyed gaze that caused her breath to stutter? Not that any of this mattered. She'd be leaving in three days and that would be that.

Lost in thought, she was vaguely aware of men shouting but paid little attention. Men were always shouting about something, and there were many noises in the city: trains, carriages, hammers pounding, people talking, horses clopping and wagons rumbling past. One had to largely ignore it to avoid being overwhelmed. At a gap in traffic, she stepped into the street, ready to rush to the other side.

"*Pazi!*" someone yelled, followed by a pair of arms dragging her back to the sidewalk. Two horses pulling a delivery wagon pounded by as their driver struggled to bring them under control. Other carriages and wagons swerved away just in time.

Juna clutched her bag to her pounding heart and turned to face her rescuer. A tall boy dressed in a worn vest and rolled-up shirtsleeves stood panting. If not for the horrified look on his face, he'd be handsome. She was certain her own face wore the same expression. "You saved my life," she said in a shaky voice.

He peeled off his cap and ran his fingers through his sweat-soaked hair. "Something must have spooked the horses," he said. "That *budala* is going to kill someone if he can't control them." The boy had a European accent, but spoke English clearly.

She looked around. The street seemed to be back to normal. "May I give you some money as a thank you?" she asked, thinking he could use it.

"No madam," he said. "I have my shovel." He pointed to a small cart a short distance away.

"Oh, I see," she said, touched by his display of pride. Still, she wanted to reward him in some way. The sign hanging over the bakery across the street caught her eye. It gave her an idea. "How about some buns from the bakery?"

A smile transformed his face. "Yes, ma'am."

"Very well," she said, noting his nice manners. "I will meet you back here in about ten minutes."

The bakery smelled wonderful. Fresh loaves, buns, and other tantalizing items were displayed behind a glass counter. Trays of cookies decorated to look like the Ferris Wheel seemed to be a popular item, particularly as the real thing was visible in the distance. She included a dozen with her order. Henry would like them, too.

Back at the corner, she waved to the boy, and he hurried over. She handed him a sack filled with rolls, buns, and cookies. For all she knew, that would be the sum of his food for the day. "Thank you," she said. "I wish you well."

He placed a grubby hand over his heart and gave her an exuberant smile. He had a degree of refinement that seemed out of place for a poor boy shoveling manure. "*Hvala, draga.* You are my angel." With that, he ran back to his cart and pushed it down the street.

As Juna walked back to Mrs. Wilson's, three things occurred to her. One: Like Henry, she had been saved from certain death. Two: She didn't dare tell anyone about it for fear of worrying her family. And three: When it came to helping a less fortunate soul, personal conundrums paled in comparison.

———◦———

Henry and Zenobia sat at the dining room table eating a late breakfast. Mother had already left for the Missouri Building to make sure things were ready for her lecture. She looked awfully pretty in her new dress, and Henry'd told her so. "You're going to be stupendous," he added, and she hugged him to her and said, 'I love you, son,' looking a little teary as she said goodbye.

"I have news about your friend," Zenobia said, bringing his attention back to the present. "Remember my colleague Ned?"

"Yeah."

"He knows the man in charge of hiring and firing for the rolling chair concession. It seems Nikola was well-liked and a good worker, but apparently a friend of the manager's called in a favor."

Henry jerked upright. "What? He fired Nik because a friend wanted him to?"

"Apparently so."

"And did he say who this friend was?"

Zennie's mouth was a straight line. "He did. None other than our Mr. Peterson."

"*What?*" Henry stared at his aunt as this revelation sank in. "*Peterson?*" He jumped up and began pacing back and forth beside the table. "I can't believe it," he said. "It makes no sense." Anger at Peterson washed over any warm feelings he had for the man. Why would his mentor have his friend sacked? Because he'd invited Henry to a music party? His steps slowed as the truth of the situation sank in. "He did it because of me," he said, and dropped back onto his chair, feeling wretched. "It's my fault for—for hanging around with Nikola. Peterson thought he was a bad influence on me."

Zenobia gave him a sharp look. "Was he?"

Henry wasn't about to admit sneaking out and getting caught, so he went with an easy excuse. "I don't know. Maybe 'cause Nik's a Serbian immigrant, or something." He headed back to safer territory. "Can we get him back on? I'm leaving soon. It's not like I'll be around for him to *influence* me," he said in disgust.

"I doubt it. There's always a long line of people wanting work. I'm not sure there's anything we can do."

"It's not fair!" Henry said. "Nik is shoveling horse dung because of me. He has a blind father, you see, and—" Voice catching, he slammed a fist on the table in frustration, making the plates rattle.

His aunt sighed. "I don't blame you for being angry. I'm sure Peterson was convinced he was acting in your best interest. He takes his position as mentor seriously. How could he face Seymour—and your mother—if something happened to you?" She leaned forward and rested her arms on the table. "He did you a favor by not telling your grandfather about the train incident. As much as you'd like to rail against him, you need to remain civil and be grateful that you have him in your corner. Besides, today is a big day for your mother. We can't ruin it for her."

Henry slumped back in his chair. Zennie was right, of course. Peterson was merely doing his job in his usual big way. Still simmering, he muttered, *"Proklet,"* on Nik's behalf.

Zennie gave him a sympathetic smile. "Indeed."

They arrived at the fair nearly two hours before Mother's lecture. "I'll meet you at the state building a half hour before it starts," Zenobia said. "I have a column to turn in at the Administration Building."

This gave Henry a good excuse to wander over to the Wooded Island. It was a nice day, not as hot as it had been. Checking the rock first and finding it empty, he returned to the main path. He walked along, looking at the flower gardens while keeping an eye on Phoenix Hall. He didn't dare go in, but it was a comfort knowing that Tomoko might be inside. At the south end of the island, he passed the garden where he'd seen John Thorpe, the head floriculturist. He smiled, remembering their bizarre conversation about listening to nature.

"Hello, Henry-san."

He whipped around to see Tomoko walking on the far side of the path. She wore her pink kimono and rested a yellow parasol against her shoulder.

Remarkably, she was alone. "Hello, Miss Tomoko," he said, falling into step with her and keeping several feet between them. They pretended to ignore each other. Just two people who happened to be walking along the path at the same time, enjoying the gardens.

"Thank you for the pretty rock," she said.

He dared a quick look, and they grinned at each other before looking away. He noticed she was twirling her parasol.

"I'm glad you liked it," he said to the ground in front of him.

"I must be careful. My father is watching me more."

That explained the empty rock. "It's okay," he said. "I don't want to make trouble for you. He warned me off, you know. That's why I haven't been around for a few days." She made a derisive sound, and he reached out to brush his fingers against the soft petals of a pink rose. "Did you sneak out for a walk?"

"I told him I need to breathe fresh air and will not be long. He was talking to a woman with many questions."

Henry laughed. After a few steps, he brushed an imaginary piece of lint off his shoulder so he could look at her. It surprised him to see a pensive look on her face. "What's wrong?" he asked.

"I saw something," she said, adjusting her parasol.

"What?"

"I saw a man watching you."

"You did? When?"

"On Midway. I saw him watching you and your mother."

"That was my aunt," Henry said, wishing he'd seen *her* on the Midway. "What did the man look like?"

"American man with a hairy face."

Henry snorted. "That could be anyone. Maybe he liked looking at my aunt. She's pretty."

Tomoko shook her head. "I see him before. I don't like him. He stares with big eyes." She opened her own eyes wide to demonstrate.

There was only one person who came to mind. Henry dragged his fingers on either side of his mouth. "Does he have long whiskers?"

Tomoko nodded. "Yes."

"I know who that is," Henry said. "He's all right, just a bit dour."

A wrinkle appeared on the girl's forehead. "I think he is a bad man. Be careful."

"I will," he said. "Thanks for the warning." While touched by her display of concern, he was sure it was just a coincidence. Maybe the man had been drunk or in a foul mood or something.

They walked until they reached a fork in the path. "I must go back," Tomoko said. She gave him a sweet smile. "I am glad I saw you."

"Me too," he said, wishing he could stop time. Desperate to have a few more seconds with her, he said, "You look very pretty, by the way."

Her dimples deepened. "Thank you, Henry-san. *Sayonara.*"

"Bye, Miss Tomoko." As she made her way up the path, he admired her graceful manner and how her bright clothing and parasol matched the colors in the flower borders. Just before she rounded a bend and moved out of view, she glanced back and they shared one last smile.

As he left the island and headed toward the Missouri Building, he realized he'd forgotten to tell her he'd be leaving in three days. His burst of dismay was quickly followed by a more hopeful thought: If the photograph he planned to leave on their rock arrived in time, he'd have another reason to seek her out.

Chapter Thirty-Six

Everything was set. A table at the front of the auditorium held a bowl of apples, a bottle of Lewis Vinegar, a basket of fresh herbs, and a large tray of apple cake. A vase of pretty flowers from Archie was a last-minute addition. "You're going to be marvelous," he'd said, kissing her cheek before she went to wait in the spa room.

It was hard to imagine being marvelous with her heart pounding. She rubbed sweaty hands on her skirt and tried to visualize a calm pool of water. She breathed in through her nose and out through her mouth, as she'd learned in class.

The door opened and closed. "I thought I'd find you in here," Zenobia said.

Juna sank onto a chair. "Remind me why I'm doing this?"

Zenobia knelt and took her hands. "Because, my dear sister, you know your subject and will present it like the expert you are. As I've heard you practicing nightly, I speak with authority."

Juna laughed. "I'm terrified out of my wits, but I'm still glad you encouraged me."

Zennie stood and pulled her up. "You will be speaking to family and friends. We're all up front."

Mrs. Fletcher opened the door. "It's time, dear."

Juna went through the motions of achieving proper posture. The familiar exercise helped her feel more confident. Head held high, she said, "All right, then. I'm as ready as I'll ever be."

When she took her place at the lectern, she found it comforting to see familiar faces in the front row. Archie, tapping a restless rhythm on his knees; Henry, with his legs stretched out in front of him; Mrs. Wilson, looking regal in an elegant dress from the '80s; Zenobia, notebook and pencil ready; Nancy, wearing one of her multi-colored jackets; and Hiram, who gave Juna a special smile and wink of encouragement. Mr. Tompkins and his daughter were in the fourth row back, and there were about thirty other people scattered throughout the room. Most everyone was looking expectant and interested. Mrs. Fletcher hovered near the door, pointing out seats to latecomers.

Juna smiled at her audience and began, grateful that her skirt hid her shaky knees. "My topic today is Uses for Apple Cider Vinegar. In Roman mythology, Pomona is the goddess of fruit trees, gardens, and orchards. Her name is from the Latin, *pomum*, fruit. *Pomme* is the French word for 'apple.'" Hiram touched his ear and raised his eyebrows, signaling her to speak louder. She increased her volume and projected her voice toward the back of the room. "I have an affinity for apples," she said. "Not only was my father an apple farmer, I am named after an apple called a 'Junaluska.' My father never knew it was named for an Indian chief in North Carolina. He just thought it sounded pretty." She paused while the audience laughed. Hiram gave her a nod of approval.

More relaxed now, she continued. "When I married into a family with a small vinegar factory, I went from making apple pies and applesauce to figuring out how to use an endless supply of this pungent nectar of Pomona." She smiled. "I'm making it sound like a fine wine, or at least an excellent cider, aren't I? The fact is, vinegar is a useful product. I've made herb-soaked vinegar and used it in cooking. Vinegar mixed with water is excellent for washing floors and windows. And, of course, we use a vinegar tonic down the hall in our very own foot spa for ladies."

This statement resulted in a smattering of applause. Sarah Tompkins called out, "Hear! Hear!"

Juna described other uses for vinegar. She shared favorite recipes and made recommendations concerning health and hygiene. People came and went, but she paid little attention. It's just how things were in a building with so many things to see and do.

Before she knew it, she was at the end of her lecture, inviting the audience to try a piece of cake. "My mother-in-law was as sweet a person as one could ever meet. She called this her 'Happy cake,' because no one could eat it and remain sad. Let me know if you need an extra slice," she added with a wink. "Thank you for your kind attention."

She stepped to the side of the lectern and gave a small bow. Happiness roared through her being. She'd done it! The applause was generous, and well-wishers quickly surrounded her.

"Well done, Juney."

"That was great, Mama."

"Nicely done, Juna. Very nicely done."

"You'd make Miss Blood and Mrs. Riley very proud."

"Marvelous, Junaluska!"

"I'd like that recipe. Mrs. Tompkins would enjoy it, I'm sure."

"Well done, madam. One of the better lectures I've attended here."

"Wonderful, my dear. I knew you could do it."

The crowd thinned out as people got their slices of cake and left. Juna noticed a man at the back of the room get up and slowly make his way up the aisle. His carriage was dignified, his clothes were of good quality, if outdated. Thinning grey hair had been combed but needed a trim. He carried his hat in the crook of his left arm.

Emotion rose in her throat as he approached. The sound of conversation continued around her, but it was as if she was in a bubble of silence. When one sees someone in a place they aren't expected to be, the brain doesn't quite comprehend it. The fact that she knew this man was her logical response, but in all the years she'd known him, she'd never seen him cry. He looked at her as if he was seeing her for the first time, clearly proud of her efforts tonight. She took a step toward him as Henry shouted, 'Grandpa!' and broke the spell.

———◦———

Grandpa's arrival stirred up considerable excitement among their small group. After exchanging hugs with his family, a handshake with Peterson, and was introduced to Mrs. Wilson, Professor Stone, and Miss Collins, he was now the center of attention. Henry helped the professor pull chairs into a circle, and they were enjoying the remaining slices of cake.

"This is the best thing I've eaten in a month," Grandpa said, taking a large bite.

"Oh, now," Mother teased. "I left you with all kinds of food."

"But not 'Happy cake,'" Grandpa said, and winked at Henry.

"It seems to be working a miracle now," she said, patting the old man's arm.

Peterson chuckled at her joke. He had so much energy emanating from him that Henry was sure he'd spontaneously burst into flame. Was it because of Grandpa's surprise appearance? Henry reckoned that if he had a boss show up unannounced, he'd be on edge, too, especially if he'd been friendly with the boss's widowed daughter-in-law.

Henry smirked. Now that he knew about Peterson's involvement with Nikola getting fired—even if the old blowhard had good intentions—he didn't have much sympathy for him. Let him squirm. Henry noticed something else, too. Professor Stone watched Mother an awful lot and Miss Collins didn't seem to care. She and Zenobia were sitting together, laughing over something or other. 'Course, Peterson was watching Mother a lot, too, but all her attention was on Grandpa.

Mrs. Fletcher came in and politely asked them to move along. "We need to rearrange for an event tonight," she said.

Peterson immediately took charge. "Shall we decamp to the Cafe de la Marine for an early supper?" he asked, looking between Grandpa and Mother. "My treat."

"What a wonderful idea, Archie," Mother said. "The food is delicious and the view from the veranda is spectacular." Everyone who'd been there before concurred with enthusiasm, though Peterson raised his eyebrows at Mother's declaration.

Grandpa replaced his hat. "Thank you, Peterson," he said. "But with all the considerable work that you've done for the Lewis family, this will be *my* treat."

Peterson inclined his head graciously. "Thank you, sir."

Despite everything, Henry couldn't help but feel respect for his mentor. It was true: his family owed a lot to this man.

Chapter Thirty-Seven

"Just look at all these wheels, Grandpa." Henry swept his arm toward the displays in the gallery of the Transportation Building the next day. After looking around downstairs for an eternity—Grandpa had inspected every last model of ocean steamers, and Mother lingered at the carriage exhibits—they were finally, *finally,* to his favorite part of the building. Henry realized that bicycles were a sore subject, but Grandpa insisted on visiting the exhibits that Henry liked best.

Grandpa gave an impressed grunt. "I've never seen the like. Look at 'em all."

"Come look at these Century's," Henry said, pulling Grandpa's sleeve. "They're real whackers."

"Henry would live in this building if he could," Mother said. "And the Anthropology Building, of course."

They'd spent the better part of the day giving Grandpa a tour of the grounds. They started at Agriculture, where Grandpa brushed at his eyes upon seeing the bottle of Lewis Vinegar so proudly displayed. Then Anthropology, where Henry took them straight to Ward's Natural History Exhibit. Grandpa marveled at the collection. Afterwards, they had lunch and a rest on the veranda of the Machinery Building, where Grandpa dozed in his chair. Mother worried over him, suggesting they call it a day, but he'd insisted on seeing the Transportation Building. "I promised Henry we'd visit it today, and that's what we'll do."

After inspecting the newest models of men's and women's bicycles, Grandpa asked, "If you had a favorite, which one would you pick?"

Knowing that Grandpa was just having fun, Henry made a show of choosing one that featured a carbide light on the front and a bell on the left handlebar. Mother pretended to be delighted with a safety bicycle with a nice basket on the front. Henry was amazed: Grandpa was acting twenty years younger, and he hadn't mentioned the factory all day.

"Well then," Grandpa said, waving over one of the two salesmen. He pointed toward the chosen wheels. "We'll order one of those there, and one of those over there."

Henry looked at Mother, who was as gape-mouthed as he was. They both stared at Grandpa, who shrugged and said, "Zenobia tells me you have a parade next weekend." They pounced on him, whooping with glee.

"We're staying another week?" Mother asked, sounding incredulous.

Grandpa laughed as he hugged them back. "I've been an old fool long enough," he said, and pointed once more at Henry's favorite bicycle. "Make that two." After Henry and Mother gave another surprised outburst, he said, "I'll count on you to give me lessons when we get home."

While Grandpa made arrangements for the bicycles to be delivered to Mrs. Wilson's house, Mother put her arm around Henry's waist. "We're witnessing one more miracle of the fair," she said.

Henry couldn't agree more.

"What's that over there?" Mother nodded toward a group of easels that held small photographs mounted on display boards.

"Don't know," he said as they moved closer. "It's something new. Looks like old photos of races. See the high wheels?"

Mother leaned in close to look at one in particular. "Eighteen eighty-seven," she said. "These are from your father's race. See that banner in the background?"

He peered closely at it as an odd feeling shot through his stomach. A photograph from *that* race. From *that* day. Most were taken prior to the race, as the groups of men posing beside their high wheels were neat and clean. He swallowed. "Is Papa in one of them?"

They studied the pictures carefully, but Craig Lewis didn't seem to be in any of them. Mother touched the board with her fingertips. "Ah, well. There were a lot of racers, after all." She gave his arm a gentle squeeze, then rejoined Grandpa and the salesman.

Henry continued to scrutinize each photograph, hoping beyond hope that he'd get a glimpse of his father. If he could only see him frozen in time, alive and well before the race, then perhaps he could insert that image into his memories. He'd give anything to replace the awful one etched into his brain. A few photographs included spectators and other racers in the background, but they were mostly blurred. Then a trio of racers caught Henry's eye. The men sported handlebar mustaches and were smiling, yet retained enough toughness to look like serious competitors. "Wait a minute," he said under his breath. He stared hard at the man in the middle. He was thinner and younger, but there was something about the tilt of his head and the attitude of his body. "Pardon me," he said to the other salesman who was nearby. "Do you know who took these photos?"

The man joined him. "I took the more recent races and collected the others," he said, then tapped his finger on the first man in the picture of the trio. "That's me, in my glory days," he said with a laugh. "After that, I traded my wheel for a Kodak."

Henry pointed at the familiar-looking man. "Who is that?"

The salesman thought a moment. "Peterson. Don't recall his first name. We were on the same Chicago team for the century race in Clarksville, Missouri. He was one of our best, but he and his friend dropped out to help when . . . well, they stopped to help another racer who'd had a terrible accident." He shook his head. "Such a tragedy."

Henry took a breath and spoke calmly with an effort. "Thank you," he said, then strode over to where Grandpa and Mother were waiting. He slapped on a smile and thanked Grandpa again for the new wheel, but inside he raged with the impact of this new revelation. Good ol' Peterson, who swore he'd never touched a bicycle until recently. Peterson, who claimed his first trip to Louisiana was in 1888, a year after Papa died. Peterson, who was courting Mother and hoodwinking Grandpa. Henry shoved his hands into his pockets and clenched them. There'd been no need to ask about the third man on the team. He'd know those eyes anywhere.

As they walked back to Mrs. Wilson's house, his mind whirled. His family deserved to know the truth, but what if Peterson had a reasonable explanation? Maybe he'd simply wanted to spare them the pain of association. If so, his heart was in the right place. Henry found that he wanted this to be true.

Off to their left, faint sounds carried over from the Midway. The Ferris Wheel slowly rotated with its load of passengers. What should he do? Grandpa's favorite admonishment circled round his brain: *Be a man. Be a man.* Henry let go of a breath. All right, then. That's what he'd do. First thing Monday morning, he'd go to Peterson's office and confront him. He'd sort this out before telling anyone. If it was all a big misunderstanding, then he wouldn't impinge on their happiness. And if it wasn't? Well, he'd think of something.

Grandpa gave his shoulder a soft bump. "You're being awfully quiet, young man."

"Just tired," Henry said, feeling every bit of fourteen.

Chapter Thirty-Eight

Two days later, Henry barged into Peterson's office. "Where were you on May twenty-second, eighteen eighty-seven?"

"What's that?" Peterson asked, leaning back in his chair.

"You heard me."

"How would I remember? That was, what, six years ago? Do you remember what you were doing six years ago?"

Henry stared at him. "I do, in fact." He waited, searching Peterson's face for a sign of recognition or guilt. Was there more sweat on his forehead now? Was that an eye twitch?

Peterson shrugged. "I give up. Enlighten me. What were *you* doing when you were eight? Playing pirates with your friends?" A smile played about his mouth.

His guess would have been close to the mark on an ordinary day. "No," Henry snapped. "I watched my mother mop blood off my dead father's face. What do you think of that?"

"I think that's very sad, Henry. Your mother has told me a little of it. I can only imagine how you felt, and—"

"Stop with the horse dung, Peterson. We both know you were there. You and that cab driver. Kramer. You were both in the race that day." Henry trembled with anger. "How could you lie to us? We trusted you." He braced himself, expecting Peterson to rail against him and deny it. What he didn't expect was the man to drop his head and be silent.

An entire minute went by. Two. Henry waited, tensely shifting his weight from foot to foot. When Peterson raised his head, gone was the jovial, cocky attitude. In its place was tired remorse. "Yes," he said. "I was there. But it's not what you think. I never intended to mislead you. In fact, I was trying to protect you."

"Bull," Henry said.

Peterson gave him a sad smile. "I know. I don't blame you. Will you at least let me try to explain my side of things? Please," he said, gesturing toward a chair on Henry's side of the desk. "Give me a chance."

Henry yanked the chair over and plopped down. "Okay. I'm listening."

His mentor released a great breath. "The truth is, when I approached Seymour about a business arrangement, I was prepared to admit everything. But as we spoke, it was clear that he didn't remember me. I made the decision to wipe the slate clean. If it wasn't necessary to remind him of that terrible day, then why bring it up?" His eyes implored Henry to believe him. "I was simply a racer who lent a hand in a tragic situation. A year later, when I returned as a more successful man, I saw an opportunity to forge a mutually beneficial arrangement. And honestly, I was more than relieved not to be associated with your father's death."

"Were you planning to tell Mother?" Henry asked. "Don't you think she deserves to know, especially if . . . if . . ."

"Yes, of course I would," Peterson said emphatically. "If our relationship progresses to that point, I'd absolutely give your mother the chance to back out."

Henry pressed the point. "You couldn't tell her now?"

Peterson took a moment to answer. "That's a good question, but would you have me bring it up when she's having such a fine time at the fair? It is the truth, surely, but do you feel it would be kind?"

As much as Henry detested Peterson's betrayal, he liked even less the thought of Mother's time at the fair being marred by unpleasant revelations. "I guess not," he said.

Peterson pressed a hand to his chest. "Please forgive me, Henry. I should have come clean. I have the deepest respect for you, your mother, and your grandfather. I'd never want to hurt them. Do you see? By keeping that bit of history to myself, I'm protecting them. I'd hoped to protect you, too. I'm dreadfully sorry you found out." He tipped his head slightly to one side. "How did you find out, exactly?"

"Saw you in a photograph in Transportation," Henry said. "A salesman had a bunch from old races."

"Huh," Peterson said. "Isn't that something?"

"So, what are you going to do?" Henry said, unwilling to let the subject drop. "Are you going to 'fess up to my mother and grandfather after we go home?"

Peterson drummed his fingers on the desk and looked out the window. "What do you think I should do?" he asked, shifting his gaze back to Henry. "Is it worth upsetting your family, or shall we keep this between us, man to man?"

As Henry considered this, it occurred to him that Grandpa might very well fire Peterson once he learned the truth of the situation. Did he really want that? Especially after all the man had done for the business? "It's good to be honest," he said. "I'll think on it." He cleared his throat before plunging in another direction. "There's something else you haven't explained."

"What's that?" Peterson asked.

"The cab driver, Kramer. Where does he fit in?"

"Kramer? He's an old acquaintance. We lost touch after the race, but we see each other occasionally in passing." Peterson smoothed his mustache, thinking. "The last time we spoke was the day you arrived in Chicago. I hired him to see you safely to the whaleback, as I could trust him not to abscond with the tickets."

As explanations went, it seemed reasonable. Henry realized he wanted to believe him. He really didn't want to make Peterson a liar and a con man. But still. He thought back to the day in the Government Building when he'd observed Peterson talking to a man—supposedly a lost tourist. Had the man actually been Kramer? Not ready to let Peterson off the hook, he broached a more pressing question. "Do you have him following me?" he demanded.

Peterson blinked. "What do you mean?"

"I mean exactly that," Henry said. "Do you have him following me or not?"

Peterson let loose his trademark laugh. "Of course not. Why would you think it?"

"Because I'm convinced he has been," Henry said. "I've seen him near me on a number of occasions, and . . . and someone else has observed it."

"No-no-no. Kramer's as straight as they come," Peterson said, laughing again. "Pure coincidence. It's a small world, even at the world's fair."

Henry leaned forward and placed his hands flat on the desk. "All right, I believe you. But I want your word on something. Your identity will be our secret until you judge the time is right to tell my family. From here on out, I want you to be honest with all of us. Remember," he said, giving Peterson a wry look, "I'm going to be running the factory one day."

Peterson inclined his head. "Of course, Henry. Lewis Vinegar has a fine reputation to uphold, and I'm grateful to be involved." He stood up, signaling an end to their meeting. "It appears that we each hold a secret for the other," he said, then offered his hand. "Friends again?"

Henry pushed himself to his feet. Was his mentor giving him a subtle warning, or merely making an observation? "Yes, sir," he said, and they shook hands across the desk.

Peterson walked him to the door. "I promised your grandfather a tour of the pump house next to Machinery Hall. Shall we meet there today at three o'clock?"

"Sure," Henry said. "He'll like that."

"Good. And will your mother be joining us?" Peterson asked, looking hopeful.

"I don't think so. It's her last day at the state building. She wants to give Grandpa a tour of the place, then we'll head down to the pump house."

"In that case, may I treat your family to supper after she's done? Seeing that I didn't get the chance after her lecture," he added with a chuckle.

"I'll relay the message," Henry said, then smirked. "What will you do if Grandpa grabs the check?" He'd rather enjoy seeing *that* little showdown.

A gleam appeared in Peterson's eyes. "I'm sure I'll think of something. You'll find, Henry, that in life, as in business, sometimes you have to initiate a new plan when the circumstances change."

"Makes sense," Henry said, thinking of Tomoko. "See you later."

Juna opened the door to the foot spa and led Seymour and Henry inside. "Here it is," she said with a sweep of her arm. She shared an expectant look with her son and watched as her father-in-law took in the cheery room with its comfortable chairs, sparkling clean basins, and fresh flowers. His gaze lingered on the display bottle of Lewis Vinegar, and the neat row of shoe hooks and coupons from Tompkins Shoes. He stepped over to the window and surveyed the view before turning around, nodding as he spoke. "You've done well, my dear. I'm impressed with your arrangement."

Juna beamed at him. Relief at his reaction made her words come out in an enthusiastic rush. "I'm glad you think so. Scores of women from the world over have sat in this room, sighing with relief. Our vinegar—our *award-winning* vinegar—has not only helped many a world's fair visitor, it is helping to bring more sightseers to the state building. It's been a good partnership for Missouri *and* Lewis Vinegar."

"I agree," Seymour said. "Peterson tells me the state building ordered enough vinegar to keep the spa going through October." He cocked an eyebrow at Henry. "It appears your mother has a mind for business. Shall we make her a consultant?"

Henry's grin encompassed them both. "Yes, sir."

Juna figured Seymour was just having fun, but she took advantage of the moment. Standing tall, she pulled a sheath of papers out of her satchel. "To that end," she said, speaking in her most accomplished and confident voice, "I have a business proposal to share with you both. This seems as good a time as any." She gestured toward the chairs. "Please, have a seat." Seymour and Henry turned to each other with eyebrows raised and, seemingly lost for words, sat down.

Juna remained standing as nervous energy coursed through her body. She'd been planning this moment since her father-in-law's unexpected arrival. What better place to show the value of her idea than right here? "When we first began the foot spa," she said, "my aim was to provide a pleasant benefit for women with sore feet. We quickly achieved success, as well as interest from a shoe seller here at the fair, as you've seen. When

I began receiving enquiries for the foot tonic itself, my original idea took a new direction—a direction that could be an even greater benefit to women and to Lewis Vinegar."

She paused for effect, pleased to see Seymour and Henry listening attentively. "I propose that Lewis Vinegar expands production to include a new product." She held up a rough sketch of a bottle and label. "I give you Lewis Vinegar's Tonic for Tired Feet. I'm no great artist, but you get the idea."

"Well, well," Seymour said as he and Henry leaned forward to study the drawing. "You've put a lot of thought into this, my dear. It's an interesting idea, certainly. I will need to think on it, of course, run the numbers, etcetera."

Juna felt the beginnings of a gentle brush-off. "I've worked out some rudimentary figures," she said, handing him a sheet.

"I like the idea," Henry said, giving her a grin.

Seymour tapped the sheet a couple times with his stump. "Let me think on it, Juna. I'll confer with Henry and Peterson, and—"

"Me," Juna said in a firm voice. "You will also confer with me. It is my idea, and I want to be involved." She trembled with defiance, refusing to be dismissed. "You wouldn't deny me that, would you?"

Seymour cleared his throat and regarded her silently for a moment. "No, my dear." He stood up and smiled. "You have impressed me beyond measure. Before we talk further, I need to let your idea sit in this old head for a few days."

"Fair enough," Juna said, and kissed his cheek. "That old head needs a haircut when we return home. Maybe it will help."

Seymour guffawed. "I've missed you, my dear."

"It's time to head to our meeting with Peterson," Henry said, closing his pocket watch. "Ready, Grandpa? It's a long walk and I want to cut through Wooded Island."

On the way to the stairs, they passed Annie Cable in the hallway. "I'll be right back to help with the tonic," Juna told her.

"Take your time, dear. It's plenty early," Annie said, adding, "You have a talented daughter-in-law, Mr. Lewis. Her tonic works miracles!"

Chapter Thirty-Nine

Machinery Hall was a riot of engines whooshing, banging, clanging, and whirring. "Isn't this something?" Henry yelled. It was the only way to have a conversation in there.

"Those dynamos are remarkable," Grandpa yelled back, referring to the engines powering the fair. They'd arrived early for their meeting with Peterson, and walked through the building looking at textile machines, printing machines, book folding machines, sewing machines, and every other kind of machine man could conceive.

Henry checked his watch. "We should get over to the pump house." He knew Grandpa was eager to see it. They left the building and had a few minutes of quiet outside. "One of the pumps processes forty-thousand gallons daily," he said, thinking back to one of his mentor's lectures. "Lots of toilets to flush here." They entered the cavernous pump house and were back to speaking loudly. "Peterson'll be here soon," he said, looking around. Other than a couple of maintenance men at the far end of the building, they were alone.

Grandpa made a beeline for the nearest pump. It was a huge thing with large, curving pipes. He inspected it from all angles, clearly fascinated by how it worked. Henry didn't waste any words on explanations. Once Peterson arrived, Seymour Lewis would get an earful. *Two* earfuls, he amended with a snicker.

He enjoyed watching Grandpa crouch down to get a closer look at a moving part. For a man who was stuck in his ways, it was entertaining to see him discover new technology. The Exposition was breathing new life into the old man, and it thrilled Henry to be a part of it. How would their lives be different when they returned home? He was surprised by a flicker of anticipation at being back in Missouri with his family. Surely their lives would continue to reverberate their experience here, especially if they began producing Mother's foot tonic.

A movement to his right caught his attention. He turned to see a man standing a few feet away, staring at him. Henry stared back in disbelief, taking in the drooping mustache and those familiar grey eyes. A feeling of irritation shot through him. He was sick and tired of this man—this Kramer—following him. Regardless of Archie's opinion, this man was trouble. "What do you want?" he demanded, taking a step forward. Out of the corner of his eye, he saw that Grandpa was oblivious to the situation. Henry took another step. "What's your game? What do you want?"

That's when he saw the gun at Kramer's side. The revolver looked tiny in the man's hand, but Henry knew it was plenty deadly. Too shocked to move, his eyes were riveted on the barrel as it swung up in a smooth arc, reflecting light from the windows. When it reached a level with his chest, he knew he was done for. He was going to be killed. He was going to be killed and leave his mother bereft of a son. *No*, he thought, bracing himself. Not *this*. He was supposed to take care of her, protect her. This could not be happening.

Kramer gazed at him, his crocodile eyes expressionless above his outstretched arm. With a sudden, quick adjustment, he pointed the gun at Grandpa and fired. At the same time, a walking stick swung up and hit the man's wrist with a hard *crack*.

"*Ei!*"

The bullet missed Grandpa and ricocheted off the pump with a loud *ping*.

"*Ei!*"

Kramer screamed and dropped to his knees after a second strike knocked the gun from his hand. As the smell of sulphur bloomed around them, fresh fury unfroze Henry. He charged Kramer and forced him to the floor. "You rat," he snarled, grabbing the man's collar. The man screamed again as his broken hand and wrist flopped against the floor. Henry didn't care. He shook Kramer again and again, yelling, "What . . . do . . . you . . .

want?" He was aware of people shouting, but he paid them no mind. He raised his fist, determined to flatten the man's nose, but was seized by Professor Shuga and Grandpa. "Let me go!" he wheezed, straining against them as they pulled him up.

Grandpa gripped his shoulder. "Easy, son." Henry stilled, quivering with breathless anger. The professor tucked his walking stick under his arm as several guards arrived. Tomoko, who must have summoned them, rushed to stand beside her father. Henry felt his stomach lurch at her wide-eyed look of horror.

"What happened here?" a guard demanded.

Henry pointed a trembling finger at Kramer, who lay curled on the floor, moaning as he cradled his arm. "H-he was trying to kill us."

The guard gestured toward the gun on the floor. "That his Lemon Squeezer?"

Henry stared at it. His brain seemed to be full of molasses. That little gun . . . It nearly killed Grandpa and surely would have killed him, too. "Y-yes, sir," he said.

"You break his arm?"

"N-no, sir. That man there—" Henry became momentarily speechless as the facts lined up in his addled brain. The man he considered a barrier to Tomoko . . . the man he was sure detested him . . . the man who told him to stay away from Phoenix Hall. *He* saved them? "Professor Shuga," he said with a mix of wonder and confusion. "You saved our lives." The professor gave him a small nod of acknowledgement. The barest of smiles played around his lips.

"We'll get your story later, sir," the guard said, then gestured for his men to pull Kramer to his feet. "Was this man trying to rob you?"

Henry shook his head. "He's been following me, I'm sure of it. I don't—I don't know why."

Grandpa's grip on his shoulder tightened. "You say you've seen that man before?"

Henry nodded. His limbs felt like jelly now, and he glanced around for a bench to sit down on. Where the heck was Peterson?

"Don't worry, we'll get answers," the guard said. "Wait here." The guards moved Kramer a short distance away to question him.

"Good thing it's noisy in here," Grandpa muttered. People were starting to gather and stare.

For the first time, Henry took in the lines of worry etched deeply in his grandfather's face. "I'm glad you're all right," he said. Suddenly overcome, he clutched the old man to him. "I was so scared. I couldn't move. What if you'd been killed?"

Grandpa's arms tightened around him. "I've faced guns before, son, and it's a natural response to freeze up. How do you think I lost my hand?"

"I'm sorry," Henry choked out.

"It's all right," Grandpa said. He stood back and gave Henry's shoulder a gentle pat. "Now, it's time to brace up. I'd like to meet the man who saved us."

Henry cleared his throat and introduced Grandpa to Professor Shuga and Tomoko. "How did you know?" he asked.

Tomoko deferred to her father, who spoke in a fierce tone. "My daughter saw that man following you on the island. She told me he was a bad man. He was watching you and we were watching him."

Henry was stunned. "Thank you," he said, and bowed. It seemed like the right thing to do. Tomoko gave him a tense smile as her father bowed in return.

"Thank you, sir, and young miss, for saving us," Grandpa said with a catch in his voice. Perhaps the professor recognized a kindred spirit in Grandpa, for he clasped the old man's hand in both of his own and murmured something in his own language.

Three guards strode back over, looking grim, as the remaining guards removed the injured man from the building. Henry reckoned Kramer would have his arm set before being tossed in jail.

"Are you Henry?" the guard in charge asked.

"Yes, sir."

"Does the name Archibald Peterson mean anything to you?"

Henry sucked in a breath as the truth of the situation became clear: Kramer worked for Peterson. Of course he did. It was no coincidence that Henry had seen *him*—not some tourist—talking to Peterson in the

Government Building. And he'd been watching Henry on the Midway on at least two occasions. What's more, Henry realized with a sudden chill, Kramer was in the vicinity of the train station the day he was pushed onto the tracks. "We know Peterson," Henry said as fresh energy coursed through him. "He wants us out of the way so he can—" He stopped abruptly and grabbed Grandpa's arm. "Mama."

Grandpa, who'd drawn himself up and was looking thunderous, took charge. "I don't know what's going on, but we need to get to the Missouri Building. Fast."

The guard turned to his men. "You, stay here and interview the professor. And you, procure a launch. We'll be right behind. Run!"

Henry hesitated, knowing Grandpa wouldn't be able to keep up.

"We'll get him there, son," the guard said. "Go!"

Chapter Forty

Juna hummed happily to herself as the fragrant tonic cooled on the stove. Seymour's careful response to her business idea was no surprise, but she was encouraged that he hadn't dismissed it outright. She hoped that Henry's enthusiasm would influence his decision.

Mrs. Fletcher peeked in the door. "You have a delivery, dear," she said, looking unusually cheerful. "In the spa."

Juna placed a jar of dried lavender back on the shelf. "More herbs or vinegar?" she asked.

"Something better."

She hurried to the spa room and found four boxes embossed with Tompkins Fine Shoes sitting on the table. What in the world? She hadn't ordered any shoes. The first box revealed a beautiful pair of walking shoes with button closures and a low heel. "Oh, my," she breathed, and grabbed a shoe hook.

They fit perfectly. She walked the length of the room several times for the sheer pleasure of it. Never had she experienced so much comfort right away. Thinking the other boxes held the same shoe in alternate sizes, she opened the next one out of curiosity. "My!" she exclaimed, and lifted out a pair of slippers. They were fine enough to wear to one of Mrs. Palmer's galas. The third box revealed a pair of fur-lined winter boots, and the last offered up a curious pair of low shoes indicated for bicycle riding.

Stunned, she ran her fingers over each pair, admiring the fine craftsmanship. She'd never owned such beautiful shoes. Was there a mistake? Did

Mr. Tompkins expect her to buy all four pairs? She changed back into her own shoes and returned the first pair to its box. If no bill arrived by the end of the week, she'd give them back. *Well,* she amended, *I'll certainly buy the walking shoes.*

After stowing the boxes away, she moved around the spa room, trailing fingertips over the backs of chairs, rearranging the bottles of lotion, and neatening the shoe hooks. A faint tang of vinegar lingered in the room like a pleasant memory. She sighed as a sweet poignancy settled inside her. Next week she'd be back to cooking, cleaning and taking care of Henry and Seymour. While she loved her family, she couldn't help but wonder: How much of her newfound skills and independence would she take home? How much would she leave here in Chicago? Would Seymour agree to produce her tonic, or would her dream simply languish on the spa room floor?

A light knock on the door frame roused her. "I thought I'd find you here," Archie said as he stepped inside, tapping his hat against his leg.

"For women only," she teased, noticing he looked quite handsome in a new jacket.

"In that case," he said, "shall we go for a walk?"

She looked around. "I suppose there's time. Annie's running the show now, but I'd like to come back and help her."

"I promise not to keep you overlong," he said with a smile.

"Weren't you going to meet Seymour and Henry?" she asked, puzzled by Archie's presence.

"There was a conflict in timing that required us to alter our plans," he said.

"Oh? When did you speak with them?"

"I managed to send them a message."

"I see," she said, slowly. "They'll surely find other places to visit." After she retrieved her new parasol, they left the building and walked east toward the lake. The Art Palace, as always, had many visitors coming and going. Juna slipped her hand into the crook of Archie's arm. "I am going to miss seeing the art," she said, aware of an undertow of melancholy beginning to ebb and flow within her.

"Then you'll have to come back and visit," Archie said. "The Art Institute will be open for business after the Exposition. I offer my services as a guide."

"Are you an art expert now?" she said, smiling up at him. "One more talent to add to your considerable list of accomplishments?"

He gave her hand a squeeze and spoke passionately. "I would paint them for you if I could."

A whisper of guilt rippled through her. Archie was skilled at many kinds of discourse, but for something as refined as art, she naturally thought of Hiram. They walked in silence for a time, passing the young and old; the energetic and weary. Was anyone else wistful? Or restless, as Archie was? He was practically bursting at the seams with an abundance of energy.

When they reached the promenade near the international buildings, Archie led her to a bench. "Let's sit here, shall we?" When they were settled, he said, "Because our time together is limited, I'll get right to the point." He took a breath and looked around as if gathering his thoughts. There was a sense of preoccupation about him as he took her hands in his. "We've had a grand time here, haven't we?" He waited for her affirmation, then continued. "I've become fond of you and Henry, and I have the greatest respect for Seymour. You are a fine family."

"Thank you, Archie," she said, wondering where this was leading. "You've made our experience here most memorable."

His eyes flashed with feeling. "What I am about to say has been fully endorsed by your father-in-law and your son. I have spoken with them at length, and they have encouraged me to be bold." He gave a short laugh. "Henry took some convincing, but he's fully on board. In fact, it was his idea to change our plans today for this very reason."

Juna's breathing became shallow as she waited for whatever Archie was about to say. She was extra aware of the lines framing his eyes that deepened when he smiled, and the sharp, waxy points of his mustache and beard. She had an inkling, of course, of what was transpiring. Her stomach tightened at the possibility.

"My dear Junaluska," Archie said in a solemn, yet urgent voice. "Won't you marry me?"

Chapter Forty-One

Henry ran as fast as he could toward the nearest dock, pressing his hand against a stitch in his side. Other guards joined them as they passed between the Transportation Building, Meniere's Chocolate Pavilion, and the Mining Building. The guard in charge explained the situation in short bursts to the other guards.

Visitors turned to watch. "What's going on?" they called out. A number of boys and men ran with them, not wanting to miss a potential spectacle. Even women and girls picked up their skirts and hurried along after them.

Henry was tired and dropping behind. *Mother,* he thought with desperation. He had to get to Mother. Who knew what Peterson had in mind. Was she in danger?

"Almost there," the guard in charge said, slowing to keep pace with him. By the time they reached the dock, another fifteen to twenty guards had joined them. They piled onto the launch and the guard ordered the driver to get them to the Art Palace as fast as he could.

Henry's heart slammed against his chest as he fought to catch his breath. Before his illness, running this far would never have been a problem. On the dock, excited fairgoers were waving down other launches and passing along the news: "Whatever is going on, it's in the Art Palace!" Others began hurrying up the promenade by foot, joined by people coming out of the Horticulture Building who sensed an event taking place.

The guard sitting beside Henry groaned. "Swell. We've drawn the interest of the curious masses."

Henry wasn't paying much attention to the excitement-seekers or the chatter of the guards. He turned his attention northward. *"Faster,"* he urged, though judging by the whine of the motor, the boat was going at peak speed. He hoped the guard with Grandpa could find a free one.

Now that he had time to think, the details of the situation swooshed around his brain. Good 'ol Peterson had hoodwinked them all. Henry felt a new rush of anger—at himself, primarily—that he'd been taken in by that smooth-talking scoundrel. He should have seen it! He should have prevented it! He should have known Peterson was putting on an act. His helpful, opportunistic mentor had set his sights on taking over the factory all along. They were all pawns in his scheme.

The launch hadn't even cleared the island yet. Henry gripped the edge of the boat and swore. *"Faster."*

Chapter Forty-Two

An incredulous laugh burst out of Juna before she could stop it. She'd been expecting a declaration, but not a proposal. "Marry you?" she said, then worried that she'd offended Archie, added, "I'm flattered, of course, but you caught me off guard. Shouldn't we get to know each other better before making that kind of commitment?"

Archie gripped her hands and spoke beseechingly. "I want to share my life with you, Juna. I'd be a good father to Henry and a good son to Seymour. I've proven my loyalty to Lewis Vinegar and will do my level best to make it even more prosperous. Seymour and Henry are counting on it," he said with a low chuckle. "Seymour offered to take me on as a partner, which makes me very happy. But my dearest, I will be a thousand times happier if you consent to marry me."

As his words settled into her brain, Juna strove to make sense of the fact that Archie wanted to marry her, and Seymour and Henry were all for it. They'd even invited him to be a partner in the factory. Why hadn't they said something? Why hadn't they involved *her* in either decision?

"My dear," Archie said, frowning. "You appear vexed. Have I upset you?"

She stood and began to pace in front of the bench. "It's not that I don't appreciate the offer. I'm just surprised that this is the first inkling I've had of any of it. Since coming to Chicago, I have opened my eyes to new possibilities. I've been inspired by independent women—even married ones—who are doing things and making a difference."

Her volume increased as she gained emotional momentum. "I took a class and learned oratory skills. I pursued an outrageous idea and started a successful spa at a state building. I even found the courage to stand in front of a crowd and give a speech on vinegar, for Pete's sake. Henry was there. Seymour was there. Even you were there, Archie," she said, whirling toward him. "And now I hear that you've all met and made big plans that not only involve the factory, but include me as well. Did it not occur to any of you to ask *my* opinion about it?"

"Oh, my dear Junaluska," Archie said, spreading his large hands in contrition. "How unfeeling you must think us. There simply wasn't time. Your opinions do count, of course. I happen to know that Seymour was planning to talk to you tonight. I'm merely 'greasing the tracks,' so to speak. I'm truly sorry I upset you."

Somewhat appeased, she said, "Still, it's all very sudden, and I refuse to make a snap decision."

"Take all the time you require, my dear. And please know that I want to share in all your thoughts and ideas. I'll support you in all the best ways. We'd make a fine team, you and I."

"I don't wish to live in Chicago," she said, refusing to give in easily. "I want to remain with my family in Missouri. Henry needs me."

"I am already planning a move to your town," he said. "Seymour asked me to learn the details of vinegar-making so I can better assist Henry when the time comes. I will make business trips to Chicago as necessary." His voice gentled. "Remember, my dearest, your son is a young man with dreams of his own. What if he ultimately chooses a different path in life? And Seymour is aging. He needs help. I'm willing to step into whatever role I am called upon in order to keep Lewis Vinegar running smoothly and profitably." He reached out and took her hand. "With you by my side, we'll face the brightest days and the darkest nights together. Please say you'll have me."

Around them, the fair continued apace, with the crunch of footsteps on the promenade; mothers calling to their children, friends laughing together; the bright notes of a brass band over near the lake. Juna slid her hand from his and wrapped her arms around her middle. She looked back toward the Art Palace, thinking hard. Wasn't Archie offering what she'd wanted in the first place? Craig had listened to her ideas, and they'd shared dreams together. He'd made her feel a part of the family business. After he died, her role changed to merely that of a mother and dutiful daughter-in-law. Not that there was anything wrong with that—she loved taking care of her family. She simply felt less considered.

Was she ready to be married again?

She wasn't sure.

Did she love Archie?

She was fond of him, certainly. Not all couples could claim that.

Did he love her?

While Archie hadn't mentioned love, he'd certainly implied it. And she had to admit he'd been supportive of her taking the oratory class and starting the foot spa. It was likely he'd continue to support her newfound independence and business ideas.

But what about Hiram? she thought with a small ache. He'd made his interest clear, but it seemed impractical to expect more than a few lovely evenings together before leaving Chicago. With a tiny pang, she realized her decision would need to be pragmatic. What would be best for her and her family? Doing a mental version of 'getting into proper position,' she turned back to Archie. Her voice was strong as she said, "I'm not one to give false hope, but I must know a few things first."

Archie sat up straight like a recalcitrant schoolboy. "Fire away."

"Will you allow me to pursue avenues that interest me?" she asked.

"Of course."

"And will you allow me to have a voice regarding Henry's welfare?"

"I would encourage it," he said.

She paused, considering. "Will you include me in all business decisions?"

Two waxed eyebrows shot upward. "I'd never dream of not including you."

"And will you promise to take care of Seymour and Henry if anything happens to me?"

"Oh, dearest, need you ask?"

This was going rather well. "One last thing," she said. "Will you watch out for Zenobia and my step-mother—from afar, naturally—just in case?"

He tipped back his head and laughed. "That is a tall order, but yes, I will see them safe."

She took a deep breath and let it out in a rush. "Well, then," she said, "I promise to consider your offer."

He jumped up and hugged her to him. "You've made me the happiest man at the Exposition."

"I haven't accepted," she warned him.

"Nonetheless," he said. "I'm entitled to a bit of male preening, aren't I? The most beautiful woman at the Exposition is considering me for her mate."

She poked him in the ribs. "Now I know you're putting it on."

"Never, my dear. It's God's pure truth." Archie tucked her hand into the crook of his arm as they walked toward the avenue that led to the Missouri Building. "I want you to know that I will always watch out for you, regardless of how the winds blow," he said. "Consider me your most stalwart protector."

CHAPTER FORTY-THREE

When they neared the eastern edge of the Art Palace, a group of men in light blue uniforms burst out of the main entrance. "Those are Columbian guards," Juna said, squinting to see better. "I wonder what's happening?"

"No idea, but they're certainly in a hurry," Archie said.

Juna held her parasol higher to block the sun. "How strange. They're running toward the Missouri Building. I hope nothing bad has occurred."

Archie chuckled. "Perhaps the spa ladies got out of hand."

People began pouring out of the Art Palace and racing after the guards. "What in the world?" Juna said, walking faster and closing her parasol. "I better get back." As more and more fairgoers noticed the commotion, they began rushing along the avenue. Others pressed against porch railings, calling out, "What's happening?" At least two hundred people were now gathered in front of the Missouri Building, and there was a palpable energy in the air.

Archie was decidedly more serious. "This doesn't look good, does it?" he said.

Just then, the guards rushed back out of the Missouri Building, parting the onlookers like a rock in a river. As one, they began moving in their direction, with the crowd closing in behind them. Archie put a protective arm around Juna and pulled her to the side of the avenue. "Careful, we don't want to get trampled."

All around them, people began lining the edges of the avenue as if viewing an alarming and sensational parade. The trouble was, no one seemed to know what was happening.

"Is it a military exercise?" a woman asked aloud.

A man carrying a young boy on his shoulders replied, "Maybe it's one of them surprise drills."

Whatever it was, Juna was glad Archie was with her. She leaned into his side, happy to have his sturdy protection from the eager mob. They watched as the guards drew nearer, now visibly slowing down and scanning the faces of the crowd. By some unheard command, the guard who seemed in charge of the regiment held up his hand and the men stopped. The crowd kept coming, circling around them to get a better view.

Juna drew in a breath as the guard looked directly at *them.* Archie's arm tightened around her. "Whatever is playing out, I'm here for you," he murmured as the guards stepped over to them, spreading out and forming a barrier against the curious crowd.

The head guard, a man with sharp eyes and a serious expression, asked, "Are you Mrs. Lewis?"

Juna's heart began to pound. "Yes, I am. What has happened?"

Archie cut in. "What is this about?" he demanded. "You are frightening the lady."

The guard, who was nearly as tall as Archie, looked him in the eye. "Are you Archibald Peterson?"

"I am."

"And are you acquainted with a man by the name of Kramer?"

Archie paused a beat. "I once hired a cab driver by that name," he said. "That's all I can tell you."

Despite his smooth words, Juna could feel a change in his body, a tenseness that wasn't there before, like that of a tiger ready to spring. Beyond the line of guards, the crowd pressed in, straining to see and hear. "Who is this Kramer?" she asked the guard.

Henry stepped into view, red-faced and breathing hard. "The man who tried to kill us," he said.

"What!" Juna cried.

"Henry," Archie said, clearly shocked by this revelation. "What did you say? Someone tried to kill you?"

Henry grabbed Juna's hand and pulled her toward him. "Peterson tricked us, Mama. Kramer works for him."

She looked between her son and Archie. "What do you mean?" she asked. The situation was so surreal that she didn't know what to think.

"He ordered Kramer to kill us."

"Kill you!"

Archie shook his head. "You are mistaken, Henry. That man is obviously maligning me. Why would I want to harm you or your grandfather?"

The guard looked uncertain as he addressed Henry. "This is a serious accusation, son."

"He's a snake," Henry said in a hard voice. "Don't be fooled."

"Henry, are you sure?" Juna didn't want to believe it. How could Archie, the man who'd helped their business and given so generously of his time—the man who'd just *proposed*—how could he have malicious intent?

Archie pressed his hand to his chest. "You must believe me. I've only had the best of intentions for your family."

"What about your grandfather's offer of partnership?" Juna asked Henry. "Mr. Peterson has just informed me of it."

Her son stared at her. "Why would we do that? He's lying."

"I work for his grandfather," Archie told the guard. "He obviously has not shared all the pertinent information with this young man. And his mother is considering my proposal of marriage."

"What!" Henry shouted. He lunged at Archie, but two of the guards restrained him.

"Easy, son," the guard in charge said. "We'll get to the bottom of this."

Archie spread his hands and spoke with genuine concern. "As you can see, the boy is excitable. He apparently had a fright that muddled his usual good sense. It wasn't long ago that he suffered from a near-fatal illness. Something like that can leave lasting effects." He aimed a sad smile at Juna, as if to imply a shared sentiment.

She looked away, unsettled by this new side of Archie. And yet, taking in Henry's flushed appearance and the wild look in his eyes, she wondered if he *was* overwrought from the heat and lingering weakness.

"Listen to me," Henry shouted as he struggled against the guards. "He's an opportunistic schemer!" At that moment, a ripple of excitement ran through the watching crowd. They quickly made way for a paddy wagon drawn by two steaming horses who halted, sides heaving, fifty feet away. Seymour was the first to jump down, followed by Zenobia, who waved away his offered hand.

Three other guards burst out from where they'd been riding inside the wagon. They ignored the excited crowd, who once again tightened ranks, eagerly following the unfolding drama. Zenobia ran ahead and gave Juna a quick hug. As one, they turned to watch Seymour approach, flanked by two of the guards.

Over the years, Juna had witnessed her father-in-law bearing up in difficult situations. He'd stoically pressed on after his son's death, and then his wife's. Each day, he faced the unique hardship of managing life with only one hand. She'd also seen his tender moments: an indulgent smile for his grandson, a kind remark to a bereft neighbor, appreciation for a good meal.

But today, as Seymour Lewis strode toward them exuding an aura of power and outrage, Juna could see the soldier who'd once faced down bullets and cannon-fire. And now he was going to face down Peterson. Juna pressed a hand to her throat, feeling her pulse throbbing beneath her fingers. Seymour stopped beside Henry and, with a look, signaled the guards to release him. He turned to Peterson. "Explain yourself."

"There is nothing to explain," Peterson said, lifting his hands and sounding reasonable. "As I've tried telling the guards, I hired this Kramer fellow one time, and—"

"He's lying," Henry growled, but fell silent at a touch from his grandfather.

"Then answer me this," Seymour said in a deadly tone. "How did the man know we'd be at the pump house?"

Peterson stiffened. "It means nothing. He obviously had his own despicable agenda. I swear to you, I've been a loyal agent to you and your family. I'll not be framed by some two-bit hustler who—"

"Bring him out," Seymour ordered. At once, the guards returned to the wagon. Every eye was on the barred door as they opened it. A man with his arm in a sling awkwardly climbed out, wincing in pain as his feet touched the ground.

Juna's flash of pity was quickly overridden by the reality that he was a would-be murderer.

Zenobia leaned closer. "Peterson wanted proof. Here it is."

The guards marched the hapless man straight over. He looked familiar, and Juna finally connected Kramer's name with the dour cab driver who'd picked them up at Central Station. *Why him?* she wondered, as the murmurs of the crowd rose and fell in breathless anticipation.

"Well?" Seymour demanded.

"We are not accomplices," Archie snapped. "Get this low-life away from me."

Kramer's expression turned hostile. "'Low life,' is it now, Arch? This is how you treat your oldest friend? I've once again done your bidding, and this is how you repay me?" He spat in the dirt. "Go to hell."

"This proves nothing," Peterson said.

Kramer's mouth twisted into a pain-laced smirk. "No? Then perhaps the fine guards will be interested in what I have in my wallet. Inside pocket. They'll be wanting the scrap of paper with my instructions." Peterson glowered at him and said nothing.

The head guard found the note and handed it to Seymour, who spared a long, scathing look at Peterson. "It reads '3:00 p.m., pump house. The man and boy. You know what to do.'" He handed it back to the guard. "I recognize the handwriting. You'll want this as evidence, I expect."

Juna trembled as the full impact of Archie's betrayal washed over her. "How could you?" she cried. "How could you do this to us? *Why?*"

"You must believe me," Archie said, looking desperately from her to Seymour. "I swear to you, I did not write those instructions. Why would I have you harmed? I have a good relationship with you and Henry, with all of you." He nodded toward Kramer. "He is obviously working for someone else who forged that note. You must believe me," he repeated. "I am a good man!"

Juna gripped the handle of her parasol, an anchor in all the madness. She wanted to believe him, wanted to trust this man who bought her earrings, who appreciated art and music and wept at the beauty of the *Messiah*.

The man who helped her overcome her fear of bicycles and could make her laugh. She *wanted* to believe he was a good man.

Seymour seemed to consider Archie's words as he continued to stare, stoney-faced at him. Henry was scowling, but Juna could see that even he was questioning the facts as he knew them. Around them, the guards exchanged furtive glances.

It was Kramer's rude laugh that galvanized their attention. "Those are mighty pretty words, Arch. It's a shame I can't clap for ya. You've outdone yourself this time." He cackled again and turned to Juna. "It's nice to see you looking well, madam. The first time we met, you were in a terrible state."

"Shut it," Archie growled, but the man just smirked at him and turned back to Juna, who was aware of the quiet that had descended over the crowd. Everyone was straining to hear.

"What are you talking about?" she said. "You gave us one ride, days ago."

Kramer carried on as if he was chatting with a friend over a drink. "We met your fine husband the night before the race."

"What?" Juna could barely breathe as history rewrote itself. The race began and ended in Clarksville, ten miles south of Louisiana. Craig had gone down the day before and spent the night with a friend who lived there. She wanted to turn away from this horrible man with his smirking face, but his words riveted her to the spot.

Beside her, Zenobia whispered, "Dear God."

"Oh yes," Kramer continued. "You might believe that Peterson's plan began with that sad incident during the race. Oh, but it did not. We had the good fortune of sharing a table with Craig Lewis. Crowded restaurant, and all. He was certainly the chatty type, telling us all about the factory and his adoring wife and son. Saw an opportunity, didn't you, Arch?"

"Shut it." A low tone of warning laced Archie's words. The look of hatred on his face was transforming him into someone unrecognizable, which Juna found terrifying.

Kramer's voice became aggressive. "It was pure luck that it rained the night before the race. My old friend waited for a downhill stretch of muddy road and made his move. All it took was one good shove and—" He snapped his fingers. "Problem solved."

A great buzzing sound filled Juna's head as she grappled with this shocking information. *Archie Peterson murdered her husband, then lied and manipulated his way into their lives.* This was the man she entrusted with her son and very nearly her heart. The same man who gave his henchman the order to kill her family. As if in slowed-down time, she heard Henry yell and saw him charge Archie with wild anger, hitting and kicking him with everything he had. Heard the crowd yelling encouragement. Watched as the larger, stronger man put his hands around her son's throat and strangle him. The cheers turned to shouts of outrage as Henry pulled helplessly at Archie's grip—his eyes wide in panic, his knees buckling.

In her bubble of altered time, Juna breathed in and out, in and out, as a primal rage filled her, burning away the buzzing sound and replacing it with heightened clarity and the confidence to *act*. The guards swooped in, but she moved faster. Fueled by the power of her anger, she swung hard and smashed her parasol into Archie's face. He grunted and let go of Henry, who collapsed to the ground. Archie fell to his knees and clapped his hand to his nose. Blood streamed between his fingers. The guards closed in and dragged him further away.

Juna flung her ruined parasol to the ground and dropped to her knees beside Henry. They clung to each other, a unison of tears and ragged breathing. Seymour and Zenobia crouched beside them, rubbing their backs and murmuring, "Well done," and, "It's over now."

A short time later, they watched in grim silence as the guards led Archie and Kramer to the paddy wagon. Before they closed the door, Archie pulled a bloody handkerchief from his face and met Juna's eyes. What did she see there: Regret? Defiance? It was hard to tell. His lips moved, but she was too far away to read them. He may have said, 'Forgive me,' but she'd never know for sure.

Zenobia took charge, shepherding their sad little band back to the Missouri Building. Columbian guards escorted them down the avenue, keeping the curious at bay.

"I blame myself," Seymour said to no one in particular. Juna reached over and took the old man's hand, silently bearing the weight of her own complicity.

CHAPTER FORTY-FOUR

Hours later, long after they returned to Mrs. Wilson's house and shared their own stories of Peterson's betrayal; long after they'd rehashed the horrific details of the day and the even more horrific revelations of Craig's death; long after Seymour returned to his hotel and the rest of the household bid each other a weary goodnight, Juna lay in bed and stared numbly into the dark.

The clock in the downstairs parlor chimed *two*. Outside the open window, the sound of nighttime insects gently peeped, buzzed, or chirped in the warm, humid air. It was a never-ending song that accompanied her imagination as it took the new reality of Craig's death and supplanted old images with different ones. A wet, gravel road became a large hand, shoving outward. A pair of nameless racers now wore the sinister faces of Peterson and Kramer. *Accident* was now *murder*.

Another terrible scene imposed itself: Her sweet Henry being pushed by Kramer onto the train tracks—all so Archie could play the hero! It sickened her that she'd fallen for his ploy. That she'd nearly lost her son that day—and again today—twisted like a knife under her ribs. And dear Seymour, shot at by that awful man. What if he and Henry had been killed? Would she have blithely gone along with Archie's ever-increasing scheme, allowing him to take care of her the rest of her days? *What's wrong with me?* she thought in disgust. *Am I really that helpless?*

Her chest heaved with a new rush of emotion, and she rocked into her pillow as tears leaked from her tired, achy eyes. Her anguish rose and fell on waves of guilt and self-blame. If only she had taken Henry home after the train incident; never taken the class; never agreed to give the lecture; never encouraged Archie, then none of this would have happened. If only . . . If only . . .

MAY, 1887. CLARKSVILLE, MISSOURI

The first of the racers blasted through town for their fifth and final lap. The damp street was a mass of pumping legs and the sound of men taking great, grunting breaths as they picked up speed. Townspeople and out-of-town spectators cheered them on. Juna stood on tiptoes and fiddled with her shawl as she looked in vain for her husband. Craig had started strong, keeping up with the lead group for the first two laps, but by the third lap he was lagging well behind. It was no surprise that several racers had already dropped out from exhaustion, but where was he?

The most challenging stretch of the twenty-mile loop was a grueling climb at the beginning. Rising sharply from the edge of town, the road stretched back to the west and eventually spilled the racers onto flatter terrain. She chewed her lip, trying to imagine descending the hill at breakneck speed with only skill and luck to keep you safe. Hopefully, Craig could make up lost time. He knew the route well and had trained hard over the past weeks.

Eight-year-old Henry darted up to grab a cookie. "Do you see Papa?" he asked, eagerly watching the racers as they passed by.

"Not yet, but he's bound to be along soon," she said, and looked around for her father-in-law. She spotted him further down the street chatting with one of their vendors. She smiled to herself. As much as Seymour grumbled about Craig's 'adventurous folly,' she had no doubt he was quietly entreating his son to ride like the wind. They'd made a fun day of it, bringing chairs and a picnic lunch. A good number of townspeople from Louisiana had made the ten-mile trip to Clarksville, and she'd enjoyed visiting with neighbors and making new acquaintances while Henry dashed around with boys his age.

Despite rain during the night, the day was bright and sunny, which added to the festive mood.

Another ten riders sped past, more spread out now. She chewed her lip, trying hard to stay optimistic. Where was Craig? Even if he'd dropped out, he should be back by now. She covered her worry by sitting down and making conversation. "Can you imagine riding one hundred miles in a day, Henry?"

"Yes'm," he said. "I want to!"

"It would be like riding all the way to St. Louis to visit Aunt Zennie and Granny Thom."

"I'm going to ask Papa to take me," he said, then spotted a boy from Louisiana. "There's Kyle. See ya later."

"Have fun," she called after him, and smiled at the thought of her son pedaling furiously on his miniature high wheel trying to keep up with Craig, whose front wheel was several inches taller than Henry. That would be quite an adventure.

The street was empty now, except for the odd straggler who received shouts of encouragement on the way through town. As it would be some time before the leaders arrived to cross the finish line, people strolled off to buy refreshments while they had a chance. Juna lingered, reluctant to leave her post.

She heard a man say, "What's that wagon doing?" and jumped up to see a horse and wagon coming slowly down the road. It was accompanied by two racers who pedaled wearily alongside. One racer sped up and rode toward them. He was so sweaty and mud-splattered that his only recognizable feature was a bushy handlebar mustache. It was a popular look with many of the racers, including Craig.

"What's happened?" someone yelled.

The racer's voice was loud, but hoarse. "There's been an accident," he said. "A man is dead."

A ripple of horror-tinged excitement ran though the spectators. Juna's mouth went dry. "What's his number?" she called. The racer slowed down enough to jump off. He wobbled, and hands reached out to steady him and his wheel. He slumped in exhaustion. "Number twenty-three, ma'am."

The air rushed out of her lungs. She grabbed at her skirts and ran toward the wagon, dimly aware of others running beside and ahead of her; the shawl sliding off her shoulders; of men shouting, "Fetch Seymour;" of Henry scream-ing, "Papa!"

Fifteen agonizing minutes later, the doctor pronounced the cause of death. "Broken neck," he said, adding gently, "He would have died quickly." They were in the doctor's surgery where Craig's body lay on a table. Juna numbly dipped a rag into a bucket of water and vinegar. Cleaning her husband's ruined face gave her something to do. She'd wash the mud off his body later. Henry sat on the floor with his knees pulled up to his chest, looking miserable, and the two racers who'd accompanied the wagon stood quietly to one side. She had paid little attention to them. Aside from a slight difference in height, they might as well be twins with all the grime on their faces. Seymour turned toward them, his voice sharp with grief. "How did this happen?"

The racer who'd first reported the accident spoke in a weary, rapsy voice. "I saw it happen, sir. He was ahead of me, going a good pace. Must've hit a patch of gravel or a hole. You know how the road was with the rain and all. He flipped down the embankment and hit a tree head-on. At that speed, well, I'm sorry." The other racer gave Juna a pitying glance but stayed silent. Henry let out a sob. She rushed over and put her arms around him, resting her cheek against his head; her tears falling freely into his hair.

"We'll go now, unless there's something else we can help you with," the racer said.

Seymour shook his head, looking defeated. "There's nothing. Thank you." As he walked the men out, Juna held tightly to her son, fighting the gravity of a fiercely tipping world.

A soft rain pattered against the window, silencing the night sounds. As Juna lay exhausted, listening to the cadence of her breath, she knew two things. One, she'd never return to the fair. And two, it was time to go home.

Chapter Forty-Five

Henry sat on his bed and absentmindedly strummed a G chord on his mandolin. They'd all hung about the house that day, not doing much of anything. Even Zennie, who hardly ever missed a day at the fair, spent a good portion of the afternoon reading in the parlor. When asked, she said, "I'll write my column another day, Henry. Right now, I need to lose myself in Marie Corelli's latest novel."

They'd all slept late. Mother was the last to arrive at breakfast, puffy-eyed and sad in her washday clothes. After giving him a hug and applying salve to the bruises on his neck, she'd mostly kept to herself, doing laundry, and cleaning their rooms with furious intensity. He supposed it helped take her mind off things.

For his own part, he'd poked around the yard, taken a nap on the porch swing, flipped aimlessly through some old magazines, and tried to avoid thinking about yesterday. His throat hurt from being strangled and his voice was raw. He'd talked, yelled, and expounded enough the day before to last a lifetime. Grandpa remained absent, taking care of business matters and talking to the police. He sent word late afternoon that he was tired and would take his supper at the hotel. Before leaving last night, he'd hugged Henry and said, "You were a man today, son. I'm proud of you." Henry fell asleep clinging to those words.

Switching to a C chord, Henry finally allowed himself to examine the painful revelation that had sucker-punched his heart: *Peterson killed Papa.* Peterson killed Papa because he'd seen an opportunity. How could anyone be so cold-blooded? So greedy? He'd fooled them all. Past moments with his mentor marched, unbidden, through his brain: visiting the farming exhibits and bicycle exhibits; laughing together over something or other; Peterson holding forth on many subjects as they walked from one Great Building to another; Peterson looking puppy-eyed at Mother . . .

Henry strummed a little harder, switching back and forth between two minor chords. How could he have even considered encouraging Peterson and Mother? The idea of it made him feel sick to his stomach. How could he have wished, even a little, for that? He realized that, on some level, he'd viewed Peterson as a way to escape Louisiana. And now the man was out of their lives, which pretty much sealed the nail in the coffin for Henry. He'd never get out-of-town now. How could he even think about going off on his own? Grandpa would need his help more than ever. It was selfish to think otherwise.

These dark thoughts were quickly countered by other thoughts: Should he just talk to Grandpa and admit his true feelings? Wasn't that what a *real* man would do? Henry let go of a long breath, sure he couldn't feel more miserable if he tried.

As he played a progression of C, G, and F, his eye fell on the camera. Anger rushed through him at the sight of it. Peterson hadn't given him the Kodak out of the goodness of his heart. He'd only been manipulating him to get to Mother and the factory. Henry strummed harder. For all he'd resisted Peterson, the fact was, he'd allowed his mentor to fill a portion of his heart that longed for Papa. And Peterson had betrayed him; betrayed them all.

C-G-F-C-G-F-C-G-F-C-G-F

Henry played faster and sloppier, landing on the F chord with an ugly flourish before thrusting his instrument onto the bed. Jumping up, he grabbed the camera by the strap and charged out of his room and down the stairs. Outside, he found the largest tree in the backyard and slammed the camera against it again and again, crumpling, shattering, destroying this thing he'd loved. "I hate you!" he yelled in his raspy voice. "I hate you, I hate you!" When the camera was reduced to a black lump, he sent it flying like a sad comet into the darkest corner of the yard. In the next moment, he dropped onto the dewy grass; shoulders shaking with bittersweet release.

CHAPTER FORTY-SIX

August 10, 1893—The St. Louis Daily
NOTES FROM THE FAIR:

Visitors Brave the Heat

Father Sun has turned his full wrath upon Chicago, wilting fairgoers as they trudge from the shade of one building to another. One would think the crowds would stay away, but they still come, determined to have their day. At night, when Mother Moon ushers in the cooler air, everyone perks up, walking faster and speaking louder. I remarked on this to a woman from England, who responded, "We are night bloomers, enlivened by the falling dew and the twinkle of stars."

Indeed.

—Zenobia A. Thom,
Special Correspondent

A miniature Ferris Wheel. Two pocket guidebooks. Five bottles of exotic spices. A decorative glass with "Juna" inscribed on it. A tiny silver spoon with Bertha Palmer's profile on the handle. A miniature metal boot. A smattering of ticket stubs. Post cards and programs. A pretty necklace from Mrs. Fletcher. The Columbia School of Oratory catalogue and corresponding certificate. A Japanese fan. Two Columbian half dollars. The pair of earrings from Archie.

Juna regarded the collection of ephemera spread out on her bed, ready to be packed away for the trip home. A feeling of despair washed over her. How could one possibly distill the vast experience of the fair into a small pile of memorabilia? Each item, she realized, held a story. In years ahead, each one would spark a memory, however happy or painful it might be.

She scooped up the earrings and took a moment to admire the delicate swirls of color. Her fingers slowly closed, blocking the sight of them and the unwelcome memories of Archie that rose unbidden. In the next moment, she flung them into the wastebasket. Some memories were simply *too* painful.

Lovey, napping at one end of the bed, stretched and came over to be petted. Juna picked her up and walked over to the window to catch a breeze on this hot day. The cat's contented thrum was a balm for her battered heart. It was one of the blessings she'd clung to the past three days. Tiny blessings that drew her attention away from anger and worry, like birdsong in the cool, pre-dawn hours; roses blooming on Mrs. Wilson's back fence; the freshness of sheets drying on the clothesline; the smell of bread baking in the kitchen; the sound of her loved-ones' voices. These little things helped return her to normalcy, renewing her hope in mankind.

She scratched gently behind Lovey's ears. Perhaps she'd get a kitty of her own when they got back to Missouri. She and Henry had grown accustomed to Lovey's presence. Waking up to a cuddly, purring body in the morning was a sweet pleasure, and Henry frequently fell asleep with Lovey draped over his chest. Even Seymour had napped on the back porch yesterday with Lovey curled in the crook of his arm.

Poor Seymour. He'd taken Peterson's betrayal hard. Not that he said much about it. It was there in the lines of his face and the way he stared at nothing while rubbing his stump or puffing morosely on his pipe. While he remained stoic with Juna and Henry, it was Mrs. Wilson who successfully drew him into quiet discourse with a gentle voice and a soothing hand on his arm. It must be helping. He and Henry left after lunch, on a mission to inspect Peterson's office.

Zenobia peeked in after knocking lightly on the door. "Come down to the parlor, Juney. Nancy and Hiram are waiting. I'll arrange for refreshments."

Lovey jumped down and trotted out of the room as a wave of anticipation rushed through Juna. She considered taking time to change out of her washday clothes, but decided that Hiram and Nancy were good enough friends to understand her lack of effort. She twisted her braid into a bun and pinned it up. It would have to do.

She found her friends sitting in the parlor.

"Juna!" Nancy jumped up and enveloped her in a fierce hug. "Zenobia told us what those awful men did. And how you faced them so bravely." Her voice wavered. "I'm glad you're all right."

Hiram hugged her with a gentler intensity. In Juna's fragile state, it took an effort for her not to melt against him and sob. He held her hands after she stepped back. "What can we do to help?" he asked.

"You're already helping," Juna said in a thick voice. "I didn't realize how much I missed you both."

"We would've come sooner if we'd known," he said. The sentiment was seconded by Nancy.

"That's very dear of you," Juna said. "Though today is the first day I could have faced company." She reached out and took Nancy's hand. Hiram did the same, and they stood in a circle of solidarity. "I'm grateful you're here now."

Zenobia breezed in and set a tray on a side table. "I have refreshments. Sit, everyone. Juney, what *are* you wearing?"

Juna laughed through her tears, grateful for her sister's ability to lighten the mood. "I hope you don't mind," she said, wiping her eyes.

"You're entirely charming," Nancy assured her.

They spent a pleasant hour together, and stuck to safe topics: Nancy's progress on her sculpture; a lecture on Amazonian birds that Hiram attended; and an anecdote or two from Zenobia, who'd gone back to work the day before. Juna mostly listened, feeling no pressure to contribute anything more than polite reactions. Hiram was being very careful with her, a fact she appreciated under the circumstances. He was simply being a good friend, and she was grateful for his calm presence. By the time he and Nancy were ready to leave, Juna felt considerably lighter and brighter.

"I have an idea," Nancy said as she pulled on her gloves. "Let's attend the fireworks show Friday evening."

"Wonderful idea," Zenobia said. "Don't you agree, Juney? It will be fun, and Seymour hasn't seen a show yet."

Despite her intention to avoid the fair, Juna couldn't help but feel its constant pull. Still, she hesitated. Was it appropriate to have fun in the midst of family strife? Was she even ready to leave the house? She looked at everyone's eager expressions and decided she was being silly. *Fun* was just what they needed. "Fireworks sound terrific," she said. "We all need a distraction from . . . things."

Chapter Forty-Seven

It was strange to be back in Peterson's office. Henry kept thinking of his last visit here as he helped Grandpa look over files pertaining to Lewis Vinegar. A detective rifled through papers on the other side of the desk.

"I'll be damned," Grandpa muttered as he peered at a document. "The scoundrel forged a contract and my signature, signing him on as part owner of the factory."

"Rather obvious of him," Henry said. "Seeing that we were nearly victims of a crime. Wouldn't he be discovered?"

Grandpa dropped the document on the desk. "It would have been hard to prove if we were out of the way. Marrying your mother would have saved him a lot of trouble."

"Don't tell *her* that."

"Of course not," Grandpa said, giving him a look. "I value my remaining limbs."

The detective, a stocky man with a grey-streaked mustache, peered over the top of his spectacles. "It seems your man was profiting from the demise of the Cold Storage Building. Means nothing, of course, but I do find it compelling."

"He was always on the lookout for an opportunity," Henry said. "He boasted about it on a regular basis."

"Do you believe he was behind the fire?" Grandpa asked.

"I doubt it, but I'll give you a tidbit," the detective said, lowering his voice. "Don't breathe a word of this to anyone or it'll be my job on the line.

We checked with authorities in Peterson's hometown. His uncle owned a dry goods store there for years, and it mysteriously burned down after he put it up for sale. The uncle died in the fire. Authorities suspected Peterson was behind it for the insurance money, but nothing was proven. He and his pal Kramer moved to Chicago soon after."

"When was that?"

"Early '80s, as I recall."

"Hmm." Grandpa rubbed his chin as he considered this new information. "Enough time to establish themselves and join a cycling club."

"So, it seems."

"Peterson told me about his uncle," Henry said, remembering their recent conversation in the Agriculture Building. "He was bitter about losing the store. Makes sense now, I guess. Especially if his uncle was going to sell it out from under him. Bet Peterson had Kramer torch the place."

"Could be," the detective said. "And regardless of whether the uncle's death was intentional, Peterson kept Kramer loyal by staying silent."

"And Kramer did his bidding to keep that silence," Grandpa said.

The detective nodded. "I've no doubt that Peterson's 'canary' will soon be singing a fine tune."

"Opera, I'll wager."

After they finished, Henry and Grandpa left the office and headed toward the hotel where Grandpa had a room. They walked silently, lost in their own thoughts as they maneuvered the crowded sidewalks. Henry agonized about admitting his true feelings. Taking his father's place at the factory was his duty. He knew that. And yet, his time at the Exposition had only strengthened his dreams. With sudden clarity, he came to a decision. He waited until after they'd finished lunch and moved to a veranda where Grandpa smoked his pipe. After all the betrayals, it was time to be completely honest—with himself and with his grandfather. "I can't do it, Grandpa," he blurted out. "I don't want to spend the rest of my days running the factory. I'm sorry, but I just can't."

The old man was silent for a long moment as he puffed his pipe and looked out over the lake. "When I first lost my hand, I thought my life was ruined. How would I manage? How would I earn my keep? I had a wife and baby to support. Before the war, I'd worked as a carpenter with my two older brothers." He lifted his stump. "War took my brothers and my livelihood. Those losses were devastating. The ghost pains were a constant reminder of what I longed for but could never have again."

Henry felt a flutter of remorse, realizing he'd never asked Grandpa about his experience during the war. "I'm sorry," he began, but Grandpa cut him off.

"I found other things to do, of course. When your father was old enough, he helped me when I needed it. I relied on it. We started the factory and made big plans. Then he died and his loss was another ghost pain, here," he said, tapping his chest with his pipe. "I realize now that I forced you to replace him as a balm for my grief. I owe you an apology, son."

"It's okay," Henry said past a lump in his throat. "I was the logical one to take his place."

"Yes, and no. It would follow that you would, but the thing is, I never gave you any choice in the matter. I didn't want to lose you, too." Grandpa's voice roughened with emotion. "I've been selfish, Henry. I'll not have your dreams become ghost pains."

Guilt skewered Henry. Didn't he love his family more than his dreams? "Never mind," he choked out. "I'll stay and help you."

"I'll get by, son. I always have."

Henry stamped the floor and looked away. "Damn Peterson. I *hate* him."

Two seagulls swooped overhead. The veranda vibrated as a train passed by on the track near the water. Grandpa spoke softly. "For a long time, I hated the soldier who shot me; who'd taken my hand. I used that anger to cover up my pain, but it only made me and everyone around me miserable. Eventually, your grandmother's patience, the love of my son, and a lot of prayer helped release that anger." He stopped to puff his pipe a few times, gathering his thoughts before continuing. "When your father died, I was determined not to lose you, too. I was wrong, Henry. Finish your school-ing and follow in Darwin's footsteps, if that's what you want. You have my blessing."

Hearing those words was like the heavens parting and angels singing. Six years of expectations began slipping off Henry's shoulders like a heavy cloak. He jumped up and threw his arms around his grandfather. "I'll still help you as much as I can."

"I know you will, son," Grandpa said with a catch in his voice. "I know you will."

As they both cleared their throats and swiped at moist eyes, Grandpa said, "I suppose it's pointless to ask you to be my Chicago agent."

Before a flabbergasted Henry could think of a response, the old man gave him a playful shove. "Gotcha there," he said with a chuckle. "Though I need to find another man as soon as possible. I'll place an advertisement in the local newspapers. Cross your fingers that we find the right one." He stowed away his pipe and heaved himself up. "We best report back to your mother."

Henry picked up his satchel, relieved that Grandpa had only been kidding. "Yessir. She'll be wanting to know about Peterson's office."

"Bound to upset her," Grandpa murmured.

As they left the hotel and walked toward the cable car stop, Henry reflected on the difficult position Grandpa was in because of Peterson. Having to navigate through an array of applicants in a big city would be taxing, even with Henry's assistance. He felt the familiar old guilt nipping at the heels of his elation. How can I best help? he wondered. As they waited to cross a busy street, sudden inspiration dropped into his brain like a stone dropping into a puddle. He grabbed Grandpa's arm and grinned at him. "I have an idea."

They gathered in the parlor before supper to discuss the situation. "And so," Grandpa said in conclusion, "it appears that Archibald Peterson has a past as shady as his present."

"And a future in the klink," Henry muttered as he swiveled from side to side on the piano stool. This was the first time since *that day* that they'd discussed Peterson as a family. As expected, emotions were running high.

"A forged contract?" Zenobia cried. "That conniving, underhanded rat!"

Mother looked stricken. "How did we miss his intentions?"

"That jackanapes had his sights on us for six years," Grandpa said. "He was biding his time. I blame myself," he said, shaking his head. "I fell for his scheme and took him on."

"But I promised to consider his offer of marriage. While you and Henry were being shot at!"

Henry rubbed his knees. "I should have told you about the photograph. If I'd said something sooner, maybe—"

"I encouraged Juna to spend time with the man," Zennie said, flinging out both arms. "I'm usually an excellent judge of character."

"He said and did all the right things," Henry reminded her.

"Yes, he did," Grandpa said. "He sent me regular telegrams. I never suspected a thing." There was a long pause as they all stared at him. He gestured with his unlit pipe and quickly added, "You know, just to say things were going well."

"He made out that he'd only recently taken up the wheel," Henry said, a fact that he found especially irksome.

Zennie snorted. "He pulled that off, didn't he?"

From there, everyone started talking at once.

"Such an expert on everything."

"That smooth-talking snake."

"How did we not see it?"

"And to think he was in league with that Kramer character the whole—"

"*Enough.*" Mrs. Wilson, who'd been silent up to that point, rose from her chair and steadied herself with a pearl-handled cane. She directed a stern look at each of them. "It was a combination of errors," she said. "A man like that would have found a way around every roadblock. Con men are like that. Count your blessings that you're all alive and well rid of him." She turned to Mother and spoke in a gentler tone. "I'm sorry you're heartbroken, my dear. Be glad you didn't marry him before finding out. He obviously wanted to play the hero to a bereaved woman while claiming the factory for his own."

She faced Grandpa next. "Peterson arrived at a time when you were vulnerable and in need of help. He wasn't much older than your son, was he? How could you not respond to that?"

Grandpa cleared his throat and looked at his feet.

"And Henry," she said. "You'd grown to trust Mr. Peterson, and he was, perhaps, a father figure of sorts."

"He wasn't—" Henry began, but Mrs. Wilson cut him off with an upraised hand.

"At any rate," she said, "you'd formed a friendly relationship. Am I right?"

He shrugged, not wanting to admit it.

"It always hurts to be tricked," she said. "Now. The question is: how will you all proceed from this point? From what I've observed, you are an intelligent, resilient bunch. And you've dodged a bullet, both literally and figuratively."

"That's true," Mother said, sniffling a little. "We have. I'm relieved we're all here together."

"Good girl," Mrs. Wilson said, and gazed around the room. "Are you ready to get on with your lives?"

They nodded obediently.

The old woman smiled. "I'm glad to hear it," she said. "Tomorrow is a new day. Hattie, carve the roast!"

CHAPTER FORTY-EIGHT

Chicago's nineteenth ward was a sharp contrast to the clean and spacious loveliness of the White City. Juna, Henry, and Seymour followed Nikola up creaky stairs toward the third floor of the tenement building where he lived with his father. It was an awful place, but better kept than the one next door, where flies swarmed the rotting refuse near the fence. As they passed a grimy window on the second-floor landing, she noticed a patch of well-tended vegetables in the tiny backyard.

Normal sounds of family life drifted from behind closed doors. It was the same in any language: children playing or arguing; the tap of a spoon on a metal pot; the sharp smell of potatoes, cabbage, or sausages cooking; men talking and laughing; a baby crying; an order from a sister or mother.

If it was warm at the bottom of the stairway, it was stifling nearer the top. Juna glanced back at Seymour, who seemed to be managing fine. "Does your father walk these stairs without trouble?" she asked Nikola.

"Yes, he knows each step," Nikola said. "Neighbors come out to talk to him. Everybody loves Victor."

She smiled to herself. When she realized that Nikola was not only the boy who saved her from the runaway wagon, but was Henry's friend, to boot, she'd spontaneously hugged him when he met them at the train platform. Dressed neatly and exuding an air of charming confidence, it was hard to believe this was the boy who spent his days shoveling the streets. Of course, by now she'd heard his sad story from Henry, and Archie's part in it.

At the top of the stairs, Nikola led them to a door that had a bright piece of cloth nailed to it—presumably a decoration they'd brought from Serbia. He gave it a tap. "This is so my father doesn't walk into the wrong place," he said, and opened the door. "*Tata*, we're here."

Juna wasn't sure what she'd been expecting the flat to look like, but the sight of a clean, modestly furnished room surprised her. Half of the room held two neatly made beds. There was a curtained-off corner which she assumed held a toilet chair or chamber pot. The other half was a sitting area with four comfortable-looking chairs, a game table, and two bookshelves. One held a large volume on Shakespeare. A sturdy table with six chairs sat near a door that led to a tiny kitchen. Open windows provided adequate, if smelly, ventilation.

What was most surprising was the man at the table peeling potatoes. A mountain of a man, his shoulders and back were broad, his head large and round. A fringe of dark hair was paired with impressively bushy eyebrows. The knife and potato appeared miniature in his hands. He dropped the potato in a bowl of water, wiped the knife on a towel, and dried his hands before scooting back his chair and standing up. He towered above them. Tilting his head back slightly, his heavily accented voice was surprisingly refined. "Welcome, friends."

Nikola made introductions. "*Drago mi je*," Mr. Petrovich said, looking in their general direction.

Seymour stepped over and grasped the man's hand. "Your son has been a good friend to our Henry," he said.

"And my knight in shining armor," Juna said, smiling at Nikola. Henry gave his friend a playful jab in the ribs and handed him a sack containing foodstuffs sent by Mrs. Wilson. Nikola's expression was a mixture of appreciation and embarrassment.

Mr. Petrovich tilted his head. "So, I hear. A menial job, maybe. But lucky for you, no? Young Henry has been a good friend to my Nikice, as well." The endearment sounded like *Nikitsa*. He spoke in Serbian to his son, who took the bowl of potatoes and disappeared into the kitchen. "We'll have tea together," he said, tapping the back of his chair. "Sit down, please."

As they were enjoying cups of strong tea, Juna asked about the book. "Are you a fan of Shakespeare, Mr. Petrovich?"

"Before I came to America, I was a teacher. That was no good here, of course, so I learned to lay bricks. When I lost my sight, it forced me to reach to the past. Instead of young students, I now teach carpenters, bakers, and dock workers at the settlement house."

"How fascinating," Juna said, trying to imagine immigrants from Europe and beyond crowded together on folding chairs to learn about sonnets and plays. "Do you have a favorite?"

Mr. Petrovich's attention seemed to turn inward as he considered her question. After a few moments, his expression became somber as he began to speak. "'O, she doth teach the torches to burn bright. It seems she hangs upon the cheek of night like a rich jewel in an Ethiope's ear; Beauty too rich for use, for earth too dear. So shows a snowy dove trooping with crows, as yonder lady o'er her fellow shows. The measure done, I'll watch her place of stand, and touching hers, make blessed my rude hand. Did my heart love till now? Forswear it, sight! For I ne'er saw true beauty till this night.'"

The last word hung in silence for a few seconds before they erupted into applause. "Marvelous," Juna said, thinking she'd have to introduce him to Hiram. Perhaps there would be a place for Mr. Petrovich at the university.

"'Romeo and Juliet,' Act One," he said, looking pleased.

Henry pointed to a small brass bowl hanging by three thin chains near the door to the kitchen. "What's that?"

"Our *slava*," Nikola said. "For Saint Luke, the patron saint of our family."

"He guides us in healing the wounds of our soul," Mr. Petrovich said. He spread his massive hands. "We have plenty, no?"

Juna and Seymour murmured an agreement. Henry studied the *slava*, lost in his own thoughts. Seymour cleared his throat. "To that end, I have a proposal. I presume Henry told you what transpired recently with our Mr. Peterson?"

Nikola and his father nodded. "The grand *budala*," Nikola muttered.

"Well, then," Seymour continued. "You'll know that we are without an agent here in Chicago. I'm looking for someone I can trust who is a resourceful and hard worker. Someone who will represent the interests of

Lewis Vinegar and build our business here. My grandson has put you forth as a worthy candidate, Nikola Petrovich. Would you like to be the Chicago agent for Lewis Vinegar?"

Juna felt a little breathless as she watched a parade of emotions passing across Nikola's face. He turned to his father first. "Okay, *Tata?*" he asked, seeming to want his father's blessing.

Tears pooled in the man's sightless eyes. *"Da, Dragi,"* he said. "These are good people."

Nikola grinned and reached across the table to shake Seymour's hand. "Yes, sir!"

Mr. Petrovich extended a hand in Seymour's direction. *"Hvala,"* he said in a thick voice. "Thank you."

Henry let out a whoop and slapped Nikola on the back.

"Welcome to Lewis Vinegar," Juna said, giving the boy a broad smile as she reveled in the exuberant atmosphere and happy faces surrounding her.

Late afternoon, Henry rushed into the Anthropology Building for one last visit. With something akin to desperation, he drank in the sight of the giant paper mâché octopus and squid hanging from the ceiling; the great mammoth with its tusks as tall as a man; the whale skeleton stretching nearly sixty feet overhead; and the many cases with their wide range of treasures. He dug his notebook and pencil out of his satchel and wrote down a last few interesting words as he moved among the now-familiar exhibits: *facelina bostoniensis; arietitidae.*

He let out a breath, already feeling a sense of loss. He lingered at the cabinet containing skeletons of small mammals where he'd seen Tomoko, resting his fingertips on the glass before moving on. Rounding a cabinet containing rock samples, he was surprised to see Mr. Ward neatening up a display of fossils. "Good afternoon," Henry said, noticing that the man had added some shell-like specimens to the group.

"Why, hello. Henry, isn't it?" Ward said, straightening up. "I've been adding and rearranging a bit. Would you like to see what I've brought?"

"I sure would."

"Good. We'll start right here." Ward pointed at a large cone-like rock. "We found this fossil in a river near Paris . . ."

At the end of his private tour, Henry thanked him and said, "My family is leaving on Monday. It was awfully nice to meet you."

Ward pulled a card out of his pocket. "I've been impressed with your interest and enthusiasm for natural history," he said. "Here is my information. Finish your schooling, attend university if you can, and write to me occasionally. I like to encourage young scientists."

Henry promised he'd keep in touch and left the building with a lighter step. With one last mission to accomplish, he headed straight to the rock on Wooded Island. His packet of photographs had arrived earlier that day, and he'd been relieved to see that his experiment worked. Zenobia seemed to have natural skill with the Kodak, as many of the photos of him standing on the bridge were good ones. Some of the people were looking at the camera out of curiosity, featuring a range of expressions that were slightly blurry. Others were deep in conversation or looking down. He was almost an afterthought, standing there and gazing out at the island.

The last photograph in the bunch featured him grinning at the camera like a gump. Deciding he liked the idea of Tomoko looking at his smiling face, he included it with two of the other bridge photographs. He lay an envelope on the rock. If someone else picked it up, they'd just think a weary tourist had left it there by accident. And if Professor Shuga found it? Well, it wouldn't be so bad now, even if he wasn't wild about Henry's interest in his daughter.

Henry hadn't seen the girl or her father since the day at the pump house. Surely, they'd be wondering about him. Returning to the path, he entered Phoenix Hall to at least wave and let Tomoko know that he was okay, but her table was empty. He looked in the other rooms, but neither she nor the professor were there. It was with a heavy heart that he trudged back to Mrs. Wilson's, figuring he'd never see Tomoko again.

———◇———

As Juna performed her bedtime exercises, Zenobia tapped on the door and entered the room. "I have something for you," she said, and handed her a small bundle wrapped in fancy tissue paper.

"How mysterious," Juna said. Judging by the bulkiness, it could be a new shawl. She carefully pulled off the paper and was pleased to find soft red fabric. When she shook it out to full size, her surprise turned to shock. "Oh, no. No, no, no, no, no," she said, shaking her head emphatically.

"Oh, yes," Zennie said in a cheerily firm voice. "Oh, yes."

Juna stared at her, aghast. "I could never."

Zenobia reached out and plucked the tissue paper off the bed. "You can, dear sister, and you will," she said, and sashayed out of the room, flourishing the tissue like a dancer's veil.

Chapter Forty-Nine

My dear Mrs. Lewis,

By now you will have received your delivery from Tompkins Shoes. You have provided a bright spot of respite enjoyed by many women, including my wife and daughter, and you have generously allowed my company to advertise. As we have received many orders from visitors carrying our special coupon from the spa, the least we can do is thank you with a few pairs of your own. I trust they fit exactly as they should.

If you ever decide to bottle your excellent Foot Tonic, we would like to offer it through our catalogue, which enjoys a wide readership. My daughter is especially enthusiastic about heading up this venture, as it was her idea.

Most sincerely, your humble servant,
Frederick Tompkins

———⊙———

The fireworks were in full glory. The Grand Basin reflected the bright flashes and patterns that lit up the inky sky, bursting in time to popular tunes being played at the nearest bandstand. Juna stood with her family and friends on the balcony of the Electricity Building, a fine vantage point recommended by her sister. They were spread out along the railing: Henry, Juna, Hiram, Nancy, Zenobia, Mrs. Wilson, and Seymour.

It had been a day of revelations. First, the surprising letter from Mr. Tompkins. Juna smiled at the thought of her beautiful new pairs of shoes. Then, at supper, Zenobia announced that she would be accompanying Nancy on a tour of Italy. "I've developed a taste for travel," she said, beaming over her Beef Wellington. "Nancy wants to visit friends next summer at an artist's colony near Rome. It may lead to some good newspaper or magazine articles."

Last, Seymour convinced Mrs. Wilson to come see the fireworks. After she pleaded age and arthritis, he'd prevailed by assuring her he would appropriate a rolling chair. Henry had been happy to "drive." Juna noted that Seymour was being very solicitous. Mrs. Wilson was visibly delighted with the fireworks—and the attention.

"It's a spectacular evening, isn't it?" Hiram said, leaning closer.

"It certainly is," Juna said. "I enjoy being high above the masses." The bridges and balustrades seemed especially crowded tonight. She looked out over the basin and the Great Buildings, and sighed. "I'm going to miss every bit of this."

"I feel the same," Hiram said. "At least you'll leave on a high note after tomorrow's festivities."

Before Juna could respond, Henry touched her arm and spoke into her ear. "Do you mind if I say goodbye to a friend? I'll come right back after the show."

"All right," she said, nearly adding, *Be careful,* but thinking better of it.

Henry rewarded her with a grin. "Thanks," he said, and dashed away.

"Where were we?" she asked Hiram. He shrugged as if to say it was of no consequence, and held her gaze for a long, charged moment that brought back memories of their kiss on Wooded Island. On the other side of him, Nancy and Zenobia were laughing about something with Seymour and Mrs. Wilson.

"May I write to you?" Hiram asked. The syllables whispered over her cheek.

"I'd like that very much," she said, thinking how simple words became a thing of beauty when uttered in his splendid voice.

"I will miss you, Juna."

She slid her hand over and covered his where it rested on the railing. A colorful explosion made his skin glow briefly, and she was aware of a subtle shift within herself: an absolute awareness that her heart would be safe with him. "Come visit us, won't you?" she said. "You'd like the Mississippi."

Stupendously miraculous, Henry thought as he hurried down the stairs. Mother let him go with barely a glance. That would never have happened a month ago! 'Course, her attention was on Professor Stone, which was just fine. Henry liked him and was happy to see Mother smiling again.

He jogged out of the building and across the bridge to where he'd spotted Tomoko ten minutes into the show. Like a beacon in the night, her pink robes had reflected the light during an especially bright firework, making Henry whisper, "Eureka!"

He hung back a few minutes to catch his breath, then eased in beside her. No one around them took notice. They were too busy exclaiming over the flash and sizzle of red and blue stars. She didn't see him at first, so he nudged her with his elbow in the brief darkness.

She glanced up at him and smiled, edging nearer so their arms were nearly touching. His chest clenched. He wanted to say things to her; to make her understand that, though he was leaving soon, her memory would go with him. Taking a chance, he eased his hand over and was surprised to find her's waiting. She turned her small, smooth hand into his, entwining their fingers. Henry was sure he'd burst with happiness. With their hands hidden by her long sleeve, he knew this silent, secret act was as close to a romantic relationship as they would ever come.

The next forty minutes were among the happiest and the most exquisitely painful he'd ever experienced. It was as if each explosion in the sky was accompanied by his soul soaring and his heart breaking. He did his best to memorize each detail: how the Great Buildings reflected the light; the press of the surrounding crowd; the splash of fountains; and the sweet way that Tomoko drew in a breath and squeezed his hand after each stunning display. He longed to lock these last moments deep into his brain; to force the memories into his cells.

During the grand finale, when the very heavens seemed to be a spectacle of light and sound; when everyone was looking up in wonder, he and Tomoko only had eyes for each other. Instead of the sky, it was her eyes that reflected the sparkles and flashes.

It was over too soon. In the semi-darkness that seemed deeper and blacker after all the brilliance, they shared one last look, one last tightening of fingers before she slipped away to join her people. The crowd dispersed around him with a blending of languages discussing the impressive show. The group of Japanese slowly made their way along the Grand Basin; their bright colors merging with the shadows. Try as he might, Henry couldn't think of one word to describe this moment. He stood there, thick-throated, and listened in vain for the voice that reminded him of bright, flowing water.

CHAPTER FIFTY

August 13, 1893—The St. Louis Daily
NOTES FROM THE FAIR:

Looking Ahead

As my time at the Exposition draws to a close, I lift an imaginary pair of binoculars and gaze to the end of October. The cool, northerly breezes sweep across the grounds, sliding over darkened domes and empty promenades. The golden statue no longer presides over enthusiastic crowds, the dancing fountains, and snapping flags. Instead, it watches over lonely, still water.

The Midway is silent. No more lively Bavarian trumpets or South Sea marimbas. No more barkers or donkey rides or mysterious women with their lively castanets. The Ferris Wheel is a great, sleeping hulk.

What does such a sight do to a tender heart? I'll tell you. It is like experiencing the death of a loved one, where only the sweetest of memories rise to the fore. We've had a glimpse of utopia, a vision of a well-planned city. We've seen the best efforts of men and women, the best of technology and invention, the boldest and loveliest art, and the unequaled experience of meeting our brethren from around the world.

Bolster your heart and soul with these finest of memories and look even further into the future, for that is where the brightness lies.

—Zenobia A. Thom,
Special Correspondent

It was a beautiful summer day. The sky was the color of forget-me-nots, and the air shimmered with the roar of tires speeding around the Grand Basin. Juna rode near the front of the parade among a sizable group of women cyclists. How odd it was to feel her legs pumping up and down without the usual restraining layers of fabric. Wearing Zennie's surprise gift of soft, red bloomers felt almost obscene in a thrilling sort of way. A white shirtwaist, boater with a red ribbon, dark stockings, and the bicycling shoes from Tompkins completed the outfit. Even Hattie had grudgingly admitted the costume looked 'Daring, yet modest.'

Her thoughts flitted briefly to Henry and Hiram, who were following the women in the sizable ranks of wheelmen. They'd donned colorful socks and vests for the occasion, and added Chinese lanterns to their handlebars. It was a tame display compared to some of the more outlandishly decorated wheels featuring ten or more lanterns.

As she began the wide turn around the east end of the basin, she spotted her father-in-law and Mrs. Wilson at the front of the onlookers. Seymour swung his good arm in a circle and yelled, "Go-go-go." She grinned and gave them a quick wave as she passed by.

Things were looking up for Lewis Vinegar. Nikola was eager to begin his new position, and Seymour had surprised her this morning by declaring, 'Lewis's Tonic for Tired Feet will soon be in production. And you, my dear, will be in charge of this new department.'

She touched the tiny apple charm on her necklace. If Craig could see her now, would he approve? *Yes,* she decided, he would. Of course he would. Glancing over at the Peristyle with its majestic columns, she remembered the astonishment she'd felt when she and Henry stood there on the first day. What a different woman she'd become since then. And Henry! Craig would be so proud of their son if he could see him. Perhaps he could. This was a place of miracles, after all.

Behind her, Zenobia called out, "Don't dawdle, sister. The men are gaining on us."

Juna laughed into the wind and pedaled faster.

Acknowledgements

Oh! What a journey it's been. From the earliest days when my interest and wonder in the Columbian Exposition exploded like a firework in my writerly sky, to the publication of DREAM CITY DREAMING—the whole process has been a labor of love. Deep dives into books and online resources, visits to Chicago museums and other institutions, and research trips and "explores" with my husband were just plain fun. There were many moments of serendipity, which added a whole level of joy to the experience.

Part of the delight in writing historical fiction is taking occasional liberties with the facts to better suit the story. My depictions of certain buildings, events, weather, cameo appearances of real people associated with the fair, as well as the *Notes from the Fair* columns, are entirely from my imagination. I hope you enjoyed it.

An unexpected pleasure was making new acquaintances along the way. Steve Sheppard, collector extraordinaire, sold me my first piece of WCE memorabilia and subsequently became an engaging correspondent. Judy and Allen Koessel, kindred spirits, shared their magnificent mural study for *The Glorification of Arts and Sciences* by William DeLeftwich Dodge with us and became dear friends in the process. Thank you so much.

There were many, many helpful people and institutions along the research road. To name a few:

The Bicycle Museum of America in New Bremen, Ohio: A gold-mine for all things bicycle. Big thanks to docent, John Boeke, who took us on a behind-the-scenes tour of their deep storage areas—and introduced us to the 1890 New Era that Juna rides in the story. What a thrill it was to flip the lever on the bell and hear its *brrring, brrring.*

Many thanks to Jan Chindlund, former Dean of the Columbia College Chicago Library, who casually mentioned the college's ties with the WCE to my husband at a staff meeting. To Heidi Marshall, Head of College Archives & Special Collections who shared information and digital files with me. And to Dominic Rossetti, College Archivist, who patiently retrieved documents relating to the Columbia School of Oratory, Mary Blood, and Ida Morey Riley. Holding the catalogue for the 1893 summer session was a singular experience.

The Apollo Chorus of Chicago: My eternal gratitude to the late Robert Anderson, who put this long-standing institution on my radar; Jim May and David Braverman for their helpful assistance with the history of the organization; and the stellar members, principals, and orchestra for a riveting performance of Handel's *Messiah* at the Harris Theater on December 14, 2019.

Special thanks to Norman Hopkins and Kenneth Johnson for answering my questions about vintage guns, and to the National Vinegar Company for clearing up a few details regarding apple cider vinegar shipping and storage in the 1800s.

My thanks to Holly Mebury, librarian at the Public Library in Louisiana, Missouri. She put me in touch with Charlotte Perrine, who kindly opened the Louisiana Historical Museum for me and answered my questions. You both are wonderful ambassadors for your beautiful river town.

Thank you to fellow WCE-enthusiast, Charlie Celander, for sharing books (and a cool map) with me.

Many thanks to the helpful staff at The Chicago History Museum Archives; The Newberry Library reading room; and the Special Collections and Preservation Division of the Chicago Public Library.

We're grateful to have these fine museums to explore for WCE artifacts: The Art Institute of Chicago; The Field Museum; Museum of Science and Industry, Chicago; Dank Haus German American Cultural Center, and The Richard H. Driehaus Museum.

Much gratitude to the curators of *worldsfairchicago1893.com*, an outstanding website for all things Columbian Exposition, for putting several key events on my radar at just the right time.

A nod to the Field Museum for their outstanding "Into the Vault" exhibit (2013-2014), which showcased 200 artifacts from the WCE. I walked around with a lump in my throat, feeling the same sense of wonder that fairgoers would have experienced.

Heartfelt thanks to Dawn Triveline and Danielle Dvorak, who were aware of my project from its inception, and cheered me on. Your love, support, and feedback meant the world.

My deepest gratitude to Michael Rabiger, whose thoughtful feedback encouraged me and helped take my story to the next level. And to Nikola Vlahovich, for teaching me Serbian words and phrases. Any inaccuracies are mine.

Enormous thanks to my amazing sisters, Cathy Angell and Barbara Angell Vogl, as well as to Nancy Mattei, Bob Young, June Young, Ronna Biggs, and Cathy Johnson for your excellent input, encouragement, and enthusiasm for my story.

Love and thanks to Greg Trafidlo and Judy Larson for music, laughter, and fun. Hugs to Wendy, Jude, Tina, Vicky, Kris, Rosann, Margaret, and Margi for your friendship. And special thanks to Greg Trafidlo's Illinois realtor, Anne-Marie Vespo-Mueller, who lent me the vintage book, *Dream City*, for a day.

Much gratitude to my incredible editor, Susan Barnes, for helping me dig deeper. And to my equally incredible cover designer, Lynn Andreozzi, for your design magic.

Poignant thanks to my late mother, Dorothy Buttler Angell (1923—2014), for her unfailing love and encouragement.

Endless appreciation to my husband, Dennis Keeling, who is the best cheerleader, research assistant, feedback provider, tech support, and friend that any author could hope for. And to Lauren Keeling and Conor Keeling, my wonderfully talented children who have grown into impressive adults during the writing of this book. I love you all so much.

About the Author

CINDY ANGELL KEELING writes historical fiction. Based near Chicago, she delights in the serendipities of research, enjoys gardening, cooking, and playing clawhammer banjo for her family and a small flock of backyard chickens.

Visit cindyangellkeeling.com

Author photo: © MK Photography

* * *